DEAD POINT

LAVONNE GRIFFIN-VALADE

Severn River
PUBLISHING

Severn River Publishing
www.SevernRiverPublishing.com

ISBN: 978-1-64875-093-9 (Paperback)

For Tom, whose love, humor, wisdom, and abiding kindness have made me more loving, humorous, wise, and kind. I would not be laughing every day, let alone writing, without you.

In memory of my mother.
You paved the way.

ALSO BY LAVONNE GRIFFIN-VALADE

Maggie Blackthorne Novels

Dead Point

Murderers Creek

Never miss a new release! Sign up to receive exclusive updates from author LaVonne Griffin-Valade.

SevernRiverPublishing.com/LaVonne

PROLOGUE

The sky was platinum. I could smell the scent of trout and crawdad rising from the river. Barbed wire fencing listed toward the water's edge. Cottonwoods clambered above a grizzled orchard. I had come here with my mother, Zoey, many times as a child. In the close heat of summer we would pick chokecherries, stash our bucket of burgundy fruit, strip naked, and sit in icy water to wash away the dark stain of bitter juice.

This is your lot if you never leave, Zoey had said of the surrounding alkali ash, the fossil-carved shale, and sage ticks. This is a place to abandon before it abandons you, she had warned, one full of small-minded and weak individuals.

Yet after nearly twenty years, I had moved back to the John Day Valley, to the river, the land and sky, even the people. I could hear Zoey's deep contralto, scolding, speaking of squandered youth and lost promise, of settling. Even from the afterworld, a mother can question a daughter's choices. Such as the sidearm strapped to my thigh and the badge pinned over my heart.

I ground the heel of my boot into the sodden clay of the riverbank and crossed my arms. Breathing deeply, I let the earthy oxygen fill every cell, bone, and muscle. I removed my Stetson and stifled a pressing desire to weep. "We could forgive one another, Mama. Forgive Tate, too. And ourselves."

Hot wind whipped through a coarse stand of juniper, casting its pungent musk over burning water. Sighing in the swelter, I put on my hat and moved up the embankment back toward my police vehicle.

1

A carcass hung from the branch of a Ponderosa at the southern edge of Logan Valley. The ball-eyed head lay felled among matted grasses, its jaw cocked open, the veined tongue dangling. A mass of entrails glistened on stone-hard ground. Two men slashed knives, skinning the young doe. A thirty-aught-six rifle sat on the open tailgate of the immense flame-red pickup parked alongside, and a stout Rottweiler paraded at the verge. Late-winter dusk, a lavender haze of earth's dissipating warmth, circled round. So did the blowflies.

I lowered the binoculars. "Dumb fucks." The goddamn Nodine twins. I'd known those boys my whole life.

I moved along the forest perimeter toward them, staying within the tree line and stepping warily among rotting pinecones and windblown limbs. At fifty yards, I heard the Nodines talking, tossing scraps of gristle and fat across the forest duff. Back and forth, they shared a small bong.

Dry bramble cracked under my boots, inspiring the Rottweiler to rise and flex. Pace and howl. Bark loudly. I moved the binoculars a few inches from cover, put the makeshift slaughterhouse in my sights. Ears erect, the agitated dog stood on point, searching across the scrub grass. I gauged the animal's speed and the distance between us, should he take off in a dead run: too fast and too close.

One of the twins aimed the thirty-aught-six my direction. Zeroed in the scope. Shit. Who was the dumb fuck now? No backup plan, and my Oregon State Police vehicle sat off the highway about a mile away. I shivered against the wind, buttoned my peacoat, and checked for cell service. Nada.

"Christ." I sped briskly toward the men. Joseph, or maybe it was Dan, put down the weapon and held up a hand as if to wave howdy. His brother shouted, opened the driver's-side door, and signaled the Rottweiler to hop in.

The engine rumbled awake—a Cummins diesel by the sound of it—and the truck backed up under the carcass. The Nodines hastily lowered the half-skinned doe, which swayed heavily and slumped into the pickup bed. They stuffed the heart and liver in a muslin game bag, covered their kill with camouflage tarp, gave the canvas a rudimentary tie-down, and jumped in the cab. A well-practiced maneuver, no doubt.

The Cummins turbo revved, and the twins peeled out in a blast of diesel-charged thunder, racing straight toward me across Logan Valley's wide swath of dwindling bunchgrass, tule, and juniper. Artifact thieves regularly scavenged and pilfered arrowheads buried in the meadows and rocky grass-land. Mule deer trails sliced through, but no graded roads. Still, the high-riding Ram 3500 ripped forward like nothing, spraying mud and basalt and shards of obsidian.

I braced myself, legs held slightly apart, my left hand resting on the holstered Glock. The flame-red gargantua pulled up and idled, towering above me.

Dan, at the wheel, rolled down his window and spat a wad of chew. "Trooper Blackthorne. Need a lift?"

"Shut off the engine and step out of your vehicle." I

nodded toward the bed of the pickup. "I'm confiscating the venison and issuing a citation for unlawful taking of deer."

"I don't think so, Maggie."

I snapped open the holster and drew out my pistol, but the red truck was already roaring back toward the highway. In its outsized side-view mirror, I glimpsed a rampage of dust, my flailing hair, and the frantic riffle of Stetson brim.

I was a good shot and could've fired the weapon, blown out a tire, rendered that fancy new pickup immobile. It might have done the trick, put a halt to their getaway. Yet it was also conceivable I'd puncture the auxiliary tank, trigger a fuel explosion, and kill both men. One slaughtered deer wasn't worth risking fatal injury, not even to those sorry-assed individuals.

I holstered the Glock and sprinted back to the highway where I'd left my dented OSP Chevy Tahoe parked on the shoulder of the road. It sat unscathed. No flattened tires, no broken windows or headlights, and the one cracked taillight had been that way for a while.

But I had no clue which direction the Nodines had headed.

"Bastards," I whispered, as if half expecting them to be waiting for me to catch up.

The twins had always been wild and imperfect replicas of one another. Like my second ex-husband, they grew to be devious men and a torment. Neither ever married. Both served time for dealing meth and bouncing checks, on top of a bunch of dimwit petty shit. The Ram 3500 was a sign of sudden income—a good run in Winnemucca, an illicit deal with some badass, or worse.

· · ·

On the way back to John Day, I radioed the station hoping Hollis wasn't at home with Lillian Two Moons, his very pregnant wife.

"Evening, Sarge," Hollis said in that voice somewhere between Barry White and Johnny Cash.

"I'm out of mobile comp range. Run a plate for me." In a moment of lucidity back there, the Nodines hauling ass out of Logan Valley, I had memorized the number.

"I'm all ears, Maggie."

Senior Trooper Hollis Jones was a good cop. Smart, reliable, unflappable. Back during police academy, we'd been OSP recruits and outcasts together. His transfer to my unit last year was a boon to my sanity, even if he didn't necessarily see it as a stellar career move at the time. He appreciated my sense of humor and tolerated my cynical streak, which definitely couldn't be said of the humorless, by-the-book types typical to the organization. Plus he gave me good-natured shit for already making sergeant.

"Ram heavy-duty truck, 2017 model, registered to a Frank Sylvester in Burns," he said, coming back online.

"A couple of local poachers drove off in the thing before I could issue a citation. Twins. Daniel and Joseph Nodine. Spelled N-O-D-I-N-E. State corrections grads. See if you can pull up addresses. And notify regional dispatch. Also, call Henry Tom at Burns Paiute Police. They killed a mule deer out in Logan Valley, a good deal of which is under the tribe's jurisdiction."

"Oh, I know Henry. He's my brother-in-law."

"Lillian's brother?"

"Well, her half brother."

"God, Holly, you got any other secrets I don't know about?"

"Sure, plenty."

"You'll have to fill me in next time I'm bored. See you in twenty."

The poacher tip line call from a Mr. Anonymous had come in late in the day. Taylor, the fish and wildlife officer in our unit, usually handled those reports, but he was out on vacation, and Hollis had gone with Lillian to a doctor's appointment. We were also down one trooper due to budget cuts, so I'd listened to the recording and headed out to investigate.

Winding back down Canyon Mountain on Highway 395, I reminded myself to listen again to the tip line message. I might just recognize Mr. Anonymous's voice, although my hunch took him to be from elsewhere. A man who didn't agree with killing game out of hunting season, but a different sort of scofflaw, maybe someone digging nearby for arrowheads without an antiquities permit, or looking for a way around the federal land agreement with the Paiutes. A dude with his own moral threshold to abide by, I'd wager.

I parked in front of our police station, a squat, airless modular equipped with an evidence locker, some battered office furniture, and four late-model computers. A faded American flag guarded the entrance.

Hollis looked up from his computer. "I ran the Nodines through DMV. The only locals with that surname are Lynn Nodine here in town and Farley Nodine over in Mount Vernon."

"Their mother and their old man. Nothing on either brother in surrounding counties?"

"Nothing in the entire state. LEDS lists them as address unknown."

"What the hell?"

"They're off the ex-con reporting grid, I guess. I'll do some more sleuthing. Run them through the western states databank."

Hollis was the best there ever was at fact-checking. Any nugget buried deep inside some cyber cave, he could dig it up.

Waiting for the icons to populate on my computer, I glanced at the reminder note I'd stuck next to the screen: *baby shower March 2nd, Holly's place.* "How's Lillian feeling?"

"She's having Braxton Hicks."

"Braxton Hicks? Is that your kid's name or something?"

"No, but I'll be sure to add it to the list," Hollis cracked wise. "Not sure why they're called Braxton Hicks, but it means practice contractions. Lil's have gotten a little stronger."

"Time to get your tail home, Holly."

"I'm taking off soon. First I wanted to tell you the rest of it. Frank Sylvester also owns a long-haul trucking outfit. With the same Burns address the poachers' rig is registered at."

"Burns is your turf. You ever heard of the guy?" By habit, I stood and paced the perimeter of our huddle of desks.

"Not him or his company."

"Any wants and warrants?"

"Nope. No stolen vehicle report. Nothing." He logged off and locked his desk drawer. "I'll be at home if you need me for anything else tonight."

"Thanks. Got it under control."

"Always, Sarge." He fetched his red plaid jacket from the coat hook by the door. "Say, Maggie. Lil's feeling a little nervous about the baby coming and all. I thought you could give her a call, maybe drop by."

"I'm probably the last person in the world to give advice about that kind of thing."

"Lil just needs to talk to another woman. She doesn't have sisters. Or close pals, really. And her mama'd just say, 'Leave that Black son of a bitch and come home where you belong.'

So, I'd appreciate you reaching out, just for a conversation. No medical exam necessary, I promise."

On occasion I forgot about the bullshit Hollis and Lil had to put up with, between redneck racists and the bigotry of their own families.

"Your wife's the best, Holly. Not sure what she sees in you, but I'd be happy to talk to her."

He smiled and nodded. "Thanks, Sarge."

Lack of doula expertise aside, I could understand how Lillian might be lonely and anxious. In her place, I'd be scared to death. And I was willing to do just about anything for the two of them.

Shortly after eight o'clock, Duncan McKay cracked open the office door, his solid frame filling a good share of available space on the public side of the service counter. I hadn't seen much of the man since he quit bull riding and came off the rodeo circuit. He'd moved back to John Day six or seven months ago to run the family's combination feed store and tack shop. Also came home without that barrel racer he'd been married to. And with a busted kneecap, I'd heard.

Duncan had a serious air about him, combined with considerable shagginess around the edges. I'd also heard he was a bit on the grouchy side, but he managed a half smile, reminding me of the boy I'd known growing up.

"I need to file a police report, Maggie."

He removed his McKay Feed and Tack cap. It was probably tough being surrounded all day by the accoutrement of buckaroo life. Or he might have decided that's just how it was now. Better than winding up gored by a cranky bull, I supposed.

He quietly cleared his throat. "I had some stuff stolen from my business."

"Shouldn't you be reporting that to the locals?"

Duncan snorted derisively. "Nobody home at the sheriff's office or the town police station tonight."

I got his drift, seeing as how all the bars in town were open until at least midnight. Between the unemployed drunks and the working-stiff drunks, somebody should've been at the ready with a key to a holding tank or jail cell.

"Okay, then. I'll take your information." I opened a new report form. "When did the theft occur?"

"Not sure. Within the last week, I think." He raked an immense hand through his thick hank of sandy hair tinged with gray. I'd nearly forgotten about the brilliant copper color that had once been his calling card. Big Red McKay.

"Any sign of forced entry?"

"Not that I could tell."

"Got a tally of missing items?"

He produced a folded sheet of paper from his coat pocket, placed it on the counter. His clear green eyes looked straight into mine.

"Two forty-pound salt licks. A pair of fence cutters. Two pricey rechargeable cattle prods. Also, a carton of packaged jerky from my storeroom," he said slowly and slid the paper toward me.

The list, neatly printed in small, elegant script, detailed product specifications, brand names, and retail prices. In all, some thief made off with about a thousand dollars in merchandise. Probably less than Duncan's deductible.

"What made you suspect any goods were stolen?"

"Customer came in today to buy one of the Hot Shot DRX rechargeable cattle prods. My inventory tracking software listed four in stock. There were only two. I got a special deal from the wholesaler. No other outfit this side of the state carries this particular model. Not that it means much to most people, but they're supposedly the best. The safest."

"Might you be out more inventory?"

Duncan gave out a tired-man sigh, rolled his shoulders forward, rolled them backward, and shoved his massive hands into the front pockets of his Levi's. "I spent about three hours this evening scan-counting product, but I could have missed something, I suppose. I'll double-check and let you know, but I might not get to it until Sunday when we're closed."

I started to tell him I planned to ship his report to the sheriff and town police, so any new info should go to them, but I decided to let that go. "Any suspicious activity or people hanging around lately?"

"The shop's been busier than usual. People gearing up for lambing season, getting in repairs while they can, that kind of thing. Nobody out of place or anything strange that I noticed."

"Your nephew works for you, right?"

"Yeah. He helps part-time. On Saturdays. Sometimes during the week after school."

"And Frankie Jacoby works at the feed store too, right?"

Duncan nodded. "You know Frankie. He's not capable of theft. And he's worked for our family for a dozen years or more."

"Do you keep your storeroom locked?"

He removed his broad bull rider hands from his pockets and placed them palms down on the counter in front of me. "No, but it's right behind the cash register. I'd likely notice somebody going in there."

I contemplated asking how someone might have managed to steal from the storeroom, then. But decided to let that go, too. "Out any cash?"

"I reconcile nightly. Never been short."

I studied the permanent tan lines where his wedding band used to be and the patch on his wrist where he must have worn a watch at one time. The man had clearly spent too much time out in the weather.

I entered his contact info at the store, along with the list of stolen merchandise, on the report form and angled my computer screen toward him. "Is everything correct, and can I send it to you electronically?"

He read over the theft report and placed a McKay Feed and Tack business card on the counter. "Looks good. My email's there on the front."

I typed in the address and sent him the document. "Done."

Duncan put on his cap and directed his green eyes my way again. "I appreciate your help tonight." He shifted his gaze toward the stained ceiling tiles and slowly scratched his day-old beard along the jawline.

I found the gesture of looking up and crabbing at his chin whiskers charming. "I'll be in touch if any of the stolen merchandise turns up."

After Duncan left, I wrote the name and model number of the two missing cattle prods along with a list of the cheaper items on the blank side of his business card and slipped it into my pack. After filing his report and sending copies to the sheriff up at the courthouse in Canyon City and to the town police station a block west of my office, I vacuumed the dinky waiting area.

I scarfed down a bologna sandwich with mustard and a side of low-fat Ritz crackers and tried calling Dan and Joseph's mother and father. Lynn didn't answer, and Farley's number had been disconnected.

I secured the back door and the cranky, rusted lavatory

window for the night and bolted shut the front door. I decided to go on a late-night tavern tour—the Den, the Cave Inn, the Gold Nugget Saloon, the Rifleman Club—and look for signs of the Nodine brothers and their Ram 3500. But I suspected even those boys weren't that stupid or conspicuous.

I parked in the rear lot at the Rifleman Club, where Farley Nodine tended bar. The air, clear and brittle, held the sweet odor of dry snow. Taking in the patch of stars burning through the roaming clouds, I lingered before entering the dank, rancid-smelling tavern.

Ariel Pritchett, a woman I'd known since elementary school, slouched awkwardly toward me dressed in once-white sneakers and a baby-blue server's uniform. "Maggie. It's slow tonight. I was just gonna lock up," she said.

"Is Farley here by any chance?"

"Nah. Already left."

Ariel had always been quiet, squirrely, with the same square face and deep-set eyes as her siblings, cousins, uncles, and aunts who all lived in a complex of trailer houses up along Dog Creek. The Pritchett clan, or what remained of it.

"Have his sons come by the bar lately? Maybe this evening?"

She massaged her neck with her right hand. "Danny and Joey? Nah. They don't get along too well with Farley."

"Have you ever seen them driving a large red crew cab pickup?"

Ariel paused. "I know they still got that old green army jeep."

"Would you mind giving me a call next time they drop by?"

She stroked a grungy tabletop with her wet bar rag. "Sure, I guess. Long as I don't get too busy and forget."

"Thanks, Ariel. Nice to see you."

She would never have told me a thing, not even if the Nodine boys had been hiding in a back room three feet from where the two of us stood talking, let alone give me a call if they showed up at the bar. It didn't pay for people like Ariel to help any cop, childhood acquaintance or not.

Bone-tired, I drove to the Castle Thrift Store. I lived upstairs in the dumpy studio apartment I shared with Louie, my sixteen-year-old tabby. Before I reached the steps, Dorie Phillips, white hair cut crisp around her pocked face, waved from the window of her thrift store. Dorie had been tight friends with my mother, had taken Zoey's suicide hard. That shared hurt was the bond that would forever tie me to Dorie.

She opened the door and moved outside. "Maggie," she whispered hoarsely, the vapor of clove cigarettes drifting across the space between us. "You're home late tonight."

Dorie was definitely a lot more than a landlord to me. She rented to me for a song and dropped by at least once a week with a home-cooked meal. She was a comfort, for sure, until the talk turned to Zoey, or my choice in men, or all that cussing. Well, not so much that last thing, it being more of a character flaw than a memory of heartbreak or wretched stupidity.

"Sorry if I was too noisy just now," I told her.

"Heck, I'd welcome more noise from you. Some laughing, some singing, even some thudding around from a little hanky-pank would make me think you were finally getting back to normal."

Dorie was one of those rare Christians who see the Bible as a giant allegory meant to teach humankind that lust is the embodiment of divine joy. Or something like that.

"Maybe I can train Louie to knock over the furniture occasionally. Or yowl instead of purr."

"Har har. You're too young to be an old maid with a pet as your only companion. You've been living back in town more than two years now and never even had a date as far as I can tell."

"Let's just say, the pickins are mighty slim around here."

She patted my arm lightly. "And maybe you're just too particular."

"You didn't say that about the last husband I brought around for a visit."

"I knew that was a rebound romance. You were the one who figured it out too late. But you did figure it out." Dorie pulled her terry robe tighter and pushed her hands into its pockets.

"That's one way to put it."

"How about Zach Davis?" she suggested.

I rolled my eyes.

"Or Sean Mayhew? He's a nice guy. Smart. And not entangled. Not gay either."

"How do you know that?"

She winked. "I've got a sixth sense about these things."

"Why didn't you warn me when I brought the first husband around?"

We laughed and sat down on the bottom step of the stairs leading up to my place.

"Oh, that Morgan. He's such a sweet man. Just fooled me is all," Dorie said.

"Fooled himself for a long time, too."

She lifted her hands from the robe pockets and clasped them around mine. "I'm serious about you finding somebody to date."

It struck me as not like Dorie to leave Duncan McKay's

name off of her list of possible suitors. I might've even been open to it, but I wasn't about to let her know that. "You're going to freeze your ass off out here."

"Don't change the subject, and don't cuss so much. Cripes, I know you better than you think. You need a lover to share your hurts with, laugh with. You need a man. A good man, but a man," Dorie said, tapping her temple. "Sixth sense, remember?"

"What I need most right now is sleep." I stood, extended a hand, and helped Dorie rise from the step. "I'll give your dating suggestions some thought, but I'm not much in the mood these days."

"Uh-huh. Well, we're talking about your mental health here, Maggie. Anyway, you know where I live if you need to chat." She stepped inside the thrift store, retreating to the separate rooms in back where she took up residence.

Upstairs in my compact living space, Louie greeted me with his best cat pout. I hunted around in the kitty cabinet and found a fresh packet of Feline Greenies, which seemed to appease him. I put a frozen entrée in the microwave and opened the county library's copy of *Libbey vs. Chase*. I'd renewed the dueling-cop-duo novel twice already and still hadn't made it past page eighty. The timer finally dinged, and I drew back the steamy coverslip and nibbled away resolutely at the desiccated meal.

Close to midnight, Louie padded to his tattered cat pillow at the foot of my bed, and I climbed under the covers. Before dousing the light, I picked up the photo of my mother and father propped on the nightstand, one taken long before all the heartbreak began. In it, Tate displayed his cowpoke swagger, a long arm around Zoey's small waist. She wore the high platform sandals fashionable in the day and barely reached the height of his shoulder.

Tate had passed down to me his thick, black hair, but otherwise, I was much the image of Zoey. I placed their framed photograph back on the nightstand and shut off the lamp. At my feet, Louie's engine rattled under the luminous curtain of winter's waning moon.

2

Tate stroked the palomino's ivory mane, loaded the animal in our busted-down horse trailer, and drove past the decrepit little cemetery with its forgotten dead relatives, toppled grave markers, and overgrown patch of wild yellow roses. At the gate, he lifted a fifth of Sonny Brook to his lips, looked out across the simmering black river and the broad alfalfa plain. He tipped back the bottle, drank its golden liquid, saluted the basalt rune of Aldrich Mountain, and moved his old truck onto the highway.

I wrenched awake, leaving that old dream in the murk of sleep. I knew how it ended. Tate sold off his horse and traded in a life with Zoey and me for booze full-time. I switched on the lamp and pulled the comforter around my shoulders. From the other side of my apartment, the oven clock beamed fluorescent.

"God. Four thirty," I rasped.

Through the cracked window above the sink, I watched a juniper toss in the bitter wind while the old furnace battled to heat the apartment. I wished for more sleep, but I was wide-awake. "Might as well get your ass in to work, Blackthorne."

It was close to six when I stepped inside our trooper station. Hollis was already there, plowing through more LEDS data, searching for some clue about the Nodine twins. I was used to his tenacity, the ardent expression he wore peeling back the layers in a trove of data. A set of furrows had lined his brow years before, the payoff for all that deep digging.

"Those two are in here somewhere," he said.

"You know what they say about the early bird. Speaking of early?"

"Couldn't sleep."

"I had the same problem. Maybe it's this mud we drink all day." I poured warmed-over coffee into a heavy blue willow mug and sipped. "This shit's awful."

"Yeah, I know. I'll speak to the help about it."

I opened my computer and waited for it to roll through its near-death rattle. "How's Lil this morning?"

He stopped slapping his keyboard. "Still eight-and-a-half months pregnant. You're going to talk to her, right?"

"Right after I pay a visit to the Nodines' mother and father."

I drank my coffee, checked agency updates online, and listened to Hollis grouse at his computer—the State server's slow speed, the ignorant browser, the even dumber spellcheck feature.

"Okay, I'm leaving you to your love-hate relationship with that old Dell. I'll be back in a few hours."

Lynn Nodine had raised her rowdy boys in a sweet little place up Canyon Creek near the courthouse. As a girl, I'd wanted to live in a house like that, one surrounded by green grass, a patch of purple iris and snowball bushes, not alkali mud, cheat weed, and seven busted-down dog kennels.

The blinds were shut tight at Lynn's. "Mrs. Nodine? It's me, Maggie Blackthorne," I called out, knocked at the door.

Through the leaded glass window, I saw a light switch on at the rear of the house. After a few minutes, she moved into view. She always had been an attractive woman. That and pretty surly, demeanor-wise.

Lynn Nodine stood behind the locked door. She checked her watch. "What is it, Margaret?"

No other local had called me by that name since back before Zoey drove off Widow's Creek Bridge a quarter century ago. "I need to talk to your sons, ma'am."

She slowly slid the lock pin and opened the door a crack, leaving the chain in place. "I haven't spoken to those boys in nearly a year."

"I was hoping you might have their contact information."

"We don't stay in touch. Why do you need to see them so bad?"

"They poached a deer yesterday and took off before I could issue citations."

Lynn's piercing glare contained not one whit of subtlety. "I seem to recall a supper of fresh venison, biscuits, and gravy at your mama and daddy's house one New Year's Day. Even years ago, January was a ways from hunting season."

I remembered it exactly. Zoey and Lynn in the kitchen frying up Tate's illegal meat—the animal's prized, tender backstrap, in fact—the three of them drinking highballs and arguing politics. In the next room, the twins and I played Pig, a kid card game invented by Zoey. Later we watched a rerun of *The Dukes of Hazard* and competed for best ten-year-old belching artist. Memory might be a trickster, but it seemed for a while back then things would turn out fine for all of us.

"Like you say, ma'am, that was years ago." When I was a girl and before his liver gave out, Tate always hunted game out of season, some combination of subsistence lifestyle, renegade mindset, and poverty.

Lynn pressed an open palm to leaded glass. "You call me *ma'am* one more time, and I'll come out there and pop your smart lip."

I could see she dyed her hair that deep auburn, the trademark of her well-known temper.

"Try their cousin Jess Haney. Lived in Burns, last I knew." Nothing else to say, she shut the door, slid the lock pin in place, and ambled back to the rear of the house.

I glanced around for signs of her sons having paid a recent visit. No heavy-duty truck tracks, and the garage, listing to one side, stood wide open and empty except for Lynn's old orange VW bus.

Using mobile comp from my police vehicle, I checked DMV and LEDS for the cousin. No licensed driver in Oregon had the name Jess Haney no matter what spelling I tried. I searched the internet on my phone. Again, nada.

I phoned Hollis. "The mother says she hasn't spoken to the Nodine men in about a year. Suggested I talk to a cousin. Jess Haney. Might live in Burns, but I found no one by that name in the system. Gone into the ether like Dan and Joseph, I guess."

"Is Haney a male or female?"

"Shit. Didn't ask. I could barely get a name out of the woman."

"I'll see what I can come up with."

"I'm off to Mount Vernon to check with their old man."

As I pulled into Farley Nodine's place, a bluster of rain and snow mix kicked up. He opened the door and signaled for me to pass through into his low-lit kitchen. We sat at the massive wooden spool that once held yards of barbed wire and now served as his dining table. It was garnished with an old hubcap filled with cigarette butts. None too pleased to see me, he was still more hospitable than his ex-wife.

"Something wrong?" he asked.

Farley was a faded man, skin and hair the color of beeswax. Good thing he had to wear that long black apron at the Rifleman Club, otherwise the sheer filthiness of his clothing might have driven away even the most indiscriminating of drunks. Evidently he wasn't making much on his bartending wages, living as he did in a broken-down shed probably built for tool storage.

"I need to get in touch with your sons." My visible breath took up space in the unheated room.

Farley's head bobbed just above the tabletop. He picked through the collection of butts cradled in the hubcap until he found one with a surviving nubbin of cigarette. He lit it, sucked in the nicotine and particles of tar.

"Did you hear me?" I asked.

"I don't know where they live, let alone got a phone number. Maybe their mom?"

"No. Lynn says she hasn't talked to them for some time."

His cigarette now burned to the filter, he threw the remains back in the hubcap. "You asked Ariel, right?"

"I did." But I hadn't learned a lot. Clearly I needed to ask her again.

He shrugged. "Then I don't know what to tell you."

I handed him my card. "Call me if you hear from your boys. Top number's my cell."

Farley placed the card on the spool table. "That everything?"

"For now," I said, rising to leave.

He stared blankly, his lips dredging forth the tobacco leavings of a new cigarette butt.

"You have a good day, Farley."

On the way to Hollis and Lil's house up on Airport Road, I considered Farley and all the people I'd known like him. Despondent and defeated, blaming their dark fortunes on some underhanded twists of fate. Forever poor of spirit and means and losing hope fast. That was about the time some folks got religion, if they were ever going to.

Lillian Two Moons sat in a rocker on her front porch, bundled in a wool blanket. We shared a few traits in common, including having a bit of an attitude and a romance with the arid expanse of eastern Oregon, despite everything else that came with calling the place home.

"Lil? You're not too chilly sitting outside?"

"I get tired of being cooped up in the house."

I sat down in the other rocker. "You can see the whole valley from here. Nice. I should think about buying a house out in the country. Louie would balk at moving, though."

"Louie?"

"My old cat."

Lil smiled. "Nice to see you, Maggie. Why are you here?"

"I should have dropped by before this. For some girl talk."

"Oh, come on. Sergeant Maggie Blackthorne doesn't do girl talk. I actually count on that."

"I just thought I should stop by. See if you're doing okay. I mean, I've never given birth or raised a child, but I wanted to once. With all my heart."

She took all that in for several beats. I must've thrown her off guard revealing something personal about myself.

"Hollis sent you, right?"

"He mentioned it."

"He thinks I'm frightened about having this baby, but it's Hollis who's scared. Hell, I'd rather give birth at home, but he won't have it."

Lil was a strong woman; of that much I was certain. "You'll do fine, I just know it, and your baby will be gorgeous."

"Yes. He will."

"A boy?"

"Henry Justice. Henry after my brother, and Justice is a name Hollis likes. His lodestar, I guess you'd say."

I understood what she meant. Hollis had been handed a fairness compass at birth. "Henry Justice Two Moons Jones. Kind of hippie-dip, but I like it."

Lil giggled softly and absentmindedly massaged her belly. "We'll probably call him Hank."

I could easily have been envious of Lil and Hollis, their bond, their house on the hill, and their child on the way. But no, I'd gotten sick of pining for that life a while back.

"Is there anything I can help you with? Anything you need?" I asked.

"I know you've been sent out here to dispense some female wisdom or something."

Her remark made me laugh harder than I had in a long time. "I warned him I didn't have any advice to pass along, especially about childbirth, raising kids."

"He forgets what community I was brought up in. We're taught to be mindful that giving birth is a natural experience. And in this case, one I'm open to."

I reached across the space between us and squeezed her hand. "I can hardly wait to meet Hank. But right now, I should get back and check on his daddy."

"And will you tell him that I'm fine? Not scared. Not lonely. Not miserable."

"I'll pass that on."

She stood when I did, and we shared a brief embrace.

"Crap. Coffee. I forgot to offer you some, Maggie."

"It's okay, I've got plenty of crap coffee back at the station."

Hollis looked up from rattle-tapping his keyboard. "Jess Haney —the cousin in Burns—is a female. Bennett's her last name these days. And get this, she's licensed to drive semis."

"A female long-haul truck driver? Can you believe they'd allow such a thing?"

Hollis sighed at my sarcasm "Sergeant Brown in Burns sent an officer to her place. Nobody around, though." He pulled up the Bennett woman's DMV photo.

I considered the blurred image on his monitor. "She looks a lot like Dan and Joseph."

"Tiny thing, for a trucker. She's probably tough like you. Like Lil. Thanks for checking on her, by the way. She texted me right after you left. She's pretty smitten with you now."

"And who wouldn't be?"

"Lieutenant Jeremy T. Lake comes to mind."

An old enemy who also happened to be my supervisor. I groaned and changed the subject. "I'm patrolling south on 395 this afternoon, and the area around Seneca."

"Logan Valley? Where you spotted the Nodine brothers?"

I nodded. "And I'd like you to take 26 east to Austin Junction or so."

"State po-po will be out in force today!" Hollis said in an exaggerated drawl.

"That reminds me, when is Taylor back from vacation? I'm tired of covering his fish and wildlife route. And since you mentioned that asshole J.T. Lake, it's thanks to him the fourth trooper position was cut from our budget."

"I don't see that changing, do you? And Taylor's signed out for a few more days."

We listened to the recording of yesterday's poacher tip line report that had led me to the Nodine boys. Played it twice all the way through.

"Recognize the voice?" Hollis asked.

I shook my head. "It doesn't sound like he's from around here, does it?"

"Well, there's no country twang, if that's what you mean."

I played the recording one more time. "He sounds educated."

"The two of us are educated."

"There's a difference between being educated and being smart."

"Which are we?"

"I don't know about you, but I'm both."

"I like to think I am too."

"If you're so smart, why haven't you tracked down an address for the Nodines?"

He faked a grimace. "Maybe they're smart too, or smarter than we think."

We listened to the tip line recording once more.

"He's awfully specific about their location in Logan Valley," I said. "Milepost number and everything. I wish he'd mentioned they were a ways from the highway. I might have used a different pursuit strategy."

"It means he also would've been a ways from the highway if he witnessed the Nodines gutting that doe."

"Maybe part of the hunting party? Backed out at the end?" I put my hands up in surrender. "Christ. The whole thing has already taken up too much of our time."

"But that's not going to stop you from going back out there to take a look, is it."

. . .

Leaving town, I drove by Lynn Nodine's place hoping I might spot Dan and Joseph's flame-red pickup parked out front. But of course not. Why would those boys have chosen this day to suddenly pay their mother a visit? The statewide alert hadn't rendered even one call. I was beginning to think the twins had driven that diesel hog halfway across the country by now.

A second trip to Logan Valley could be pointless too, except for the speeding drivers I might encounter along the way and be obliged to pull over. Still, I wasn't ready to give up the chase just yet. So I headed on up Highway 395 over Canyon Mountain, passing long snowdrift pastures and turning left onto Route 16, the county road running east through Seneca, and eventually pulling north toward Highway 26 and the peaks of the Blues.

Freezing rain coated the surface, making for a greasy slog over gray mud and ice. Six miles in, I slowed at the turnout where I'd parked the day before. The Nodine twins had shot and gutted that doe close to a mile from here. But off-roading in heinous weather across Logan Valley's boggy grassland and spiky frazil in search of those men wasn't an option. Not even in my heavy-duty Tahoe.

Continuing east on Route 16, I drove along the rim of Strawberry Mountain Wilderness, through stands of larch and pine until the road narrowed to one lane and descended sharply. When the pavement ended, cut off by a mire of boulders and slurry, I turned around. It was never wise to get stuck in backcountry with no cell signal and out of radio range. Not in wintertime, anyway.

Returning to Seneca, I sensed driving around hunting for the Nodines had amounted to nothing more than a waste of time. Which didn't deter me from touring the seven-block radius of the old mill town looking for the Ram 3500 parked next to some shanty or mobile home.

After coming up empty again, I wound my way back to 395, past the old mill site, and north toward John Day. A mile or so before the junction with Izee Road, I spotted Guy Trudeau's Torino lumbering over the rise. It passed slowly on my left, going south. A slate-gray cattle truck with *Frank Sylvester Trucking, Burns, Oregon* printed in stylized cursive on the cab door followed on its tail.

"Interesting," I said, turning my Chevy slowly around, bouncing over ruts in the pavement, sliding in gravel. Jesus, how had old man Trudeau's low-slung beater driven through this mess? I flipped on my warning lights.

The semi pulled to the narrow shoulder, and I parked behind it. Moving out of my rig, I signaled for the truck driver to do the same. A woman opened the door, popped onto the icy step-up, and leapt to snow-covered ground. Batted one boot against the other, shit-kicker style.

"Driver's license, please," I said.

Except for her stark blue eyes, the woman held an uncanny resemblance to me—elfin stature, raven hair, wary countenance. She took off her retro trucker's hat, a well-used oily one with the International Harvester logo stitched on the front.

She fished in her hip pocket, brought out a battered wallet, and handed over the license. It read Jessica H. Bennett.

Up the road, Trudeau reversed his Torino and then pivoted slowly forward. Navigating between the gullies on either side, he kept repeating that move, working to turn the car around.

"You with Mr. Trudeau?"

"Yeah," she said.

"Is he driving pilot car for you or something?" Big rigs

sometimes needed that traveling on narrow highways. Advance warning for other oncoming vehicles.

"Old fart's packin' heat. Protection. For me, or rather for his load of cattle."

I glanced at the license photo once more. "You're Jess Haney, right?"

"Haney's my maiden name. I was married to a Bennett for a while."

"Cousin of Dan and Joseph Nodine?"

"Excuse me?"

"The Nodine twins. You're their cousin, correct?"

"Can you tell me why you're asking?"

I gave the woman my blankest stare, something I was good at.

"They're in trouble again, right? I figured they were when they showed up at my place with that giant four-wheel drive."

"When was that?" I asked.

Jess had a way of gazing west to discover her answers. "Couple of weeks ago or so."

"Why'd you think they might be in trouble?"

She shrugged. "Don't have real jobs or any money far as I know. And that set of wheels alone is worth a chunk of change."

"I need to see your vehicle registration, please."

She climbed back into the livestock truck, removed a folded and wrinkled document from the dashboard. She stepped down from the cab and offered it over. Hollis had already dug up the detail that Frank Sylvester was the owner of the Nodines' Ram 3500 and a trucking company, both with the same address out in Burns. The vehicle registration was further confirmation.

I spotted Guy Trudeau on the shoulder of the road. He had parked his Torino and was trudging slowly toward us.

"Is there a phone number for Mr. Sylvester?" I asked Jess.

She wiped the back of her hand across her full lips. "I don't know the man."

I flashed another blank stare, this time for real.

"He doesn't live in Burns, I mean. Owns the company, but he stays at his place out in Wagontire. His trucking business is run by another guy."

"By the name of?" I had tired of Jess Bennett's westward glances.

"Seth."

I didn't bother to stifle a deep sigh.

Jess took the hint. "Flynn. Seth Flynn."

"His contact information?"

"Do you really need all that?" It was her turn to sigh, but she managed to scroll through the contacts list on her phone. She shoved the device forward and leaned hard against the truck's sleeper compartment.

I jotted down her phone number, along with the two she had for Seth Flynn, and took note of the photo displayed on the screen: Jess holding an infant.

"Thank you," I said, handing back the phone. "Cute baby."

The withered old rancher now stood next to the semi, huddled against the weather.

"Girl, do not say another word to that officer," Trudeau huffed, used to forcing his way on people through sheer meanness and money. "She ain't nothing but a Podunk with a gun."

"Good afternoon, Mr. Trudeau," I said.

Classy as ever, he hocked one up and spat a pool into the snow-covered alkali. Speaking of Podunks with guns. For the second time in two days, I rested my left hand on my holster.

"Why've you stopped my driver?" he demanded, caught his breath, and propped himself against a front tire rim.

"Part of an ongoing investigation," I said. "I pulled the truck over to check the contents. And talk to the driver."

"Pure bull. I run a lawful business, as you well know."

I knew no such thing, actually. "Mr. Trudeau, have you seen or spoken to Dan or Joseph Nodine recently?" A question out of nowhere.

He glared at Jess Bennett. "I don't generally converse with such low life."

"Answer the question," I said.

Trudeau shifted his nasty expression back to me and shook his head slightly, which I took as a no. He hacked and spat again. "Unless you have some reason to detain my driver, we're done here."

"Ms. Bennett, show me your bill of lading." I invented my authority. And not for the first time.

"There's no bill of lading," Jess said.

"Escort me around the truck, then."

"Who the hell do you think you are?" Trudeau asked.

"Oregon State Police Sergeant Margaret Blackthorne." That's who. Motherfucker.

Jess led me to the back of the truck, told me she was delivering twenty-seven steers to the Boise stockyards. I peered through the slats, estimated there were about that many head of Black Angus huddled in the semi. Even on a cold day, the odor was formidable.

Out of Trudeau's sightline, I inquired about a phone number and address for the twins.

Jess glanced over my shoulder and lowered her voice. "They always just use burners. And they stay somewhere around Seneca's all I know."

"We *are* somewhere around Seneca. Can you be more specific?"

"Honest, I don't know where they live."

"Okay, let's get this over with," I said.

We walked the remainder of the truck perimeter and I wrote down her travel permit details, load specifications.

"How long have you worked for Frank Sylvester Trucking?"

"A couple of years."

Jess and I made our way back to the driver's side of the cab where the old man, true to his nature, waited in a state of pissed off, ornery, and agitated.

"Okay, you're free to go, Ms. Bennett, but I may contact you with more questions. You too, Mr. Trudeau."

He stood squarely in the path between the semi and my SUV. "You will regret this intrusion."

I stepped around him and got back in the Tahoe. The woman and Trudeau returned to their vehicles, and on his signal, continued to drive south. I couldn't put my finger on it, but something about the encounter with those two hung in the air. Much like the lingering stench from that truckload of Black Angus.

3

I radioed Hollis at the office. "I'm flummoxed about where the Nodine brothers are hiding out, but I did just now come across Jess Haney Bennett."

"Their cousin?"

"Yep. Hauling a load of steers. And guess who she drives for?"

"Not that outfit from Burns, Frank Sylvester Trucking?"

"Bingo. I saw the company name in shiny letters on the semi, and I just had to pull over the driver. Then it turned out to be the Bennett woman."

"What are the odds?"

"Probably has something to do with population density, or rather the lack of it. Anyway, she told me Sylvester lives out in Wagontire. Some guy called Seth Flynn actually manages the trucking business. I asked about the Nodines but didn't learn much."

"I'll see what more I can find out about Sylvester. Flynn too."

I read off the contact info I'd pried loose from Jess Bennett and clicked off. Less than twenty minutes later I was still on the road and Hollis radioed back.

"Did you find something?" I asked.

"What? Oh, not yet. Lil's in labor, so I'm going home. We'll likely head on to the hospital soon."

"How's she doing?"

"Claims she's fine. And I believe it. That woman's remarkably tolerant of pain."

"It's got to be all that practice putting up with you, Holly."

"I know, right?"

"Go take care of your wife. Take care of yourself too. And text me when the little guy gets here, if you think about it."

The landline was ringing when I unlocked the office door. Caller ID signaled *UNKNOWN*. I definitely wanted to let the call go to voicemail, but I picked up.

"Oregon State Police," I answered.

"Maggie?"

I would've recognized Joseph Nodine's nasal twang anywhere.

"Are you there?" he asked.

"Are you ready to turn yourselves in?"

"We've got something else to talk about."

"First we talk about killing that doe. Then we talk about where you got that red pickup."

"We're in trouble, Maggie. Bad trouble."

"What did you boys do now?"

"We messed up big-time. And now somebody's coming after us."

"How do you know that?" I asked.

"A guy we know warned us earlier."

"Who's coming after you?"

"We'd rather talk to you in person. Soon as possible."

"I'll wait for you here at the station."

"Nah. That won't work. Meet us at the old Seneca mill. You gotta hurry, though."

"That abandoned dump? You've been hiding out there?" I'd driven by the place less than a half hour ago, and I'd seen no sign of the twins or the Ram 3500.

"Son of a bitch!" Joseph screamed. "Damn it, no!"

I heard Dan Nodine yelling frantically in the background and their yelping Rottweiler. Then two blasts from what sounded like a shotgun. "What's going on? I'm headed there right now. Joseph? Jesus! Tell me what's going on!"

His phone clicked off. I hit redial and let it ring. I locked up, moved to my police vehicle, and continued punching redial. I switched on the emergency lights and siren and headed south on 395. There was no calling Hollis for backup. Besides, whatever mess I was charging into might be nothing more than a brawl between the Nodines and the miscreants they pissed off. Yet I sensed it wasn't just a tiff between two factions of the outlaw element. Knew in my gut it was more. Also knew I should report the call to J.T. Lake, or at a minimum, contact dispatch to request assistance from Burns. Instead, I gunned the Tahoe up Canyon Mountain.

Loose fencing surrounded the deserted mill property, shuttered now for thirty years. The single gate hung from its twisted hinge, a battered and broken birdwing. In the darkening twilight, I scanned the five acres of cracked concrete overgrown with salt grass, knapweed, and planer junk. A wigwam burner—a teepee-shaped colossus at least sixty feet tall and nearly seventy-five feet wide at the base—stood near the fence line, its metal shell rusted, decrepit but intact. An outhouse for millworkers, the only other structure remaining, had fallen to ruin. Besides an owl and a beady-eyed possum, the old industrial site was largely occupied by silence, and from where I sat in my rig, there was nothing to indicate the presence of the Nodines or their muscle-bound dog.

In my headlights, a gale-swept flurry of corn snow hurtled across the sparse plot of cement and thrashed at the wigwam burner's loose metal siding. I cut the engine and warning lights and opened the gate.

In the mill yard, I gripped my Maglite and Glock and called out for the brothers. The scent of rot and blood wafted from the maw of the wigwam burner's open access door. I entered the immense, annular space of the burner, my flashlight illuminating the domed peak of steel mesh at the top of the structure, the decaying walls, and the Nodines' Ram 3500. Cow pies littered the sooty earthen floor nearest the vehicle along with cigarette butts, gum wrappers, and an unopened can of Red Bull.

A large silver livestock trailer was parked beside the red diesel truck. One of its wheel wells had been shot-gunned. Squatting near the ground, I shifted the Maglite's yellow beam under the trailer. The twins' Rottweiler lay among the filth, gut-shot and dead.

Stifling a scream, I used the battered wheel well to pull myself erect. Something other than the dog emitted a thick, foul stench. I eyeballed the camouflage tarp draped loosely across the pickup bed.

"Fuck." Even as a whisper, my voice echoed from the charred walls of the burner.

I holstered the Glock and warily yanked back the tarp. The remains of yesterday's poached deer lay in a putrefying mess in the glare of my flashlight. I dropped the camouflage canvas and placed the back of my forearm over my mouth and nose to quell the overwhelming urge to retch.

Advancing along the interior wall of the wigwam burner, I flashed the Maglite toward the ring-shaped base of metal and sod. The Nodine twins sat on the ground in the shadow of the diesel truck and livestock trailer. Their legs extended forward, their backs slumped against the rusted edifice. Each wore cheap Wrangler jeans and a down jacket. One had on Nike cross trainers, the other wool socks and Birkenstock knock-offs.

I recognized the dour serenity of death. It had been present in the lifeless bodies of my mother and father, and in Alligator Paulus, my best friend in high school lying cold in her coffin, and in the kid who crashed down a ravine when I was still a rookie officer.

I checked each man for a pulse, knowing I'd find none. Both had been shot in the chest and torso with what appeared to be a high-powered weapon. Blood, still with sheen, seeped crosswise over their jackets and soaked into the earthen floor. Joseph's arm draped aimlessly across Dan's. A phone, presumably the one Joseph had used to call me less than forty minutes ago, lay on the ground between them.

Gaping at the carnage, a wave rolled through me—nausea, disgust, disbelief. One brother's scream surely followed the other's, a greater agony to have endured. What kind of beast kills like this? The kind who'd blow away a tiny girl-cop, alone and without cover, in a desolate and abandoned lumber mill.

I drew my weapon, activated the tactical laser, and braced my body against the sooty wall. Forcing myself to breathe, I moved outside. With my left hand, I pointed the Glock straight into the dark. Cold air clattered with movement, footsteps padded across the mill yard. The beady-eyed possum passed through the green beam of light projecting from the laser mounted on my pistol barrel.

"Mother of God." I tucked the butt of the Maglite in one armpit and pulled up the night vision binoculars that hung from my neck. I rotated slowly in an awkward circle, perusing the property and desert beyond. Through the optics, I detected only the arc of storm clouds pressing in, lit by a mass of hot stars.

I holstered the Glock, stashed the binoculars, and walked back to my vehicle. Those men, the tow-headed boys of my childhood, what had they done to deserve this? I trembled and held in check a rage of tears.

I reported the murders to regional dispatch and waited for instructions, the Tahoe's heater cranked to high. At six forty-five, a Detective Alan Bach with the State homicide unit out of Bend radioed that he was en route.

His voice crackled across the airwaves. "I'm on my way to pick up Dr. Ray Gattis, the medical examiner. We should be there by twenty-one thirty or so, and I'll need the scene rigged with lights by the time we get there."

"Yes, Detective. I carry portable light towers with me."

"Good. Collect whatever preliminary evidence you can and contact the county sheriff." Chatter from a police scanner droned in the background. "Wait. Remind me of his name?"

Our sheriff had a certain reputation around the state. He was known for picking and choosing which laws he would follow and for making up his own on occasion.

"Rhinehart, sir. Sheriff Dirk Rhinehart."

"Right, right. On second thought, I'll call the sheriff myself. Later."

That suited me fine. "Yes, sir."

"Sergeant? Blackthorne, is it?"

"That's correct, sir."

"Did you know the deceased?"

"Yes, sir. I grew up here. So did they."

"Any criminal history?"

"A few years back they both served time at the Eastern Oregon Correctional Institute for a range of offenses." I decided to wait to tell the detective in person about yesterday's attempt to cite the twins for poaching.

"You have a sense of who might have wanted to kill them?"

"Conceivably the list could be long. But I've got no specifics."

"We'll meet you there as soon as we can." Bach's radio crepitated madly as he signed off.

Before setting up the portable light towers, I phoned Sam Damon, the town funeral director and mortician. "Sam, it's Maggie Blackthorne."

"Evening, Sergeant."

Although I'd been his babysitter when he was in elementary school, Sam always referred to me by my rank.

"The medical examiner and a State homicide detective are on their way from Bend. Wanted to give you a heads-up that I'm going to need your services tonight, probably late, sorry to say. There are two bodies."

"Two, huh?"

"That's right. Anyway, I'll call you later once the ME gives the go-ahead." I planned to notify next of kin after the detective and Dr. Gattis finished their work at the crime scene. So I wasn't about to tell Sam which two bodies he was coming to collect. In addition to being the town funeral director and mortician, he was also the town gossip. No need to crank up the Dogpatch talking-circle any earlier than necessary.

"I'll be waiting for your call," Sam said.

Outside the wind had settled, making it easier to carry the light towers from my rig to the interior of the wigwam burner. After positioning the lights, I photographed the Ram 3500, the damaged livestock trailer, and the littered burner floor. I slipped on a pair of latex gloves and bagged the empty shotgun cartridges at the burner entrance and tossed the cigarette butts, gum wrappers, and can of Red Bull into separate plastic sleeves.

Steeling myself, I photographed the brothers from various angles and slipped their phone into an evidence bag. Then I waited in my rig, listening to Lucinda Williams and Tedeschi Trucks Band. I was about to doze off when my phone buzzed loudly. It was Hollis. I let it go to voicemail. I didn't feel much like having one of our little chats, but afterward, I listened to his message: their newborn son was healthy and beautiful.

The joy contained in Holly's voice was immense. But I wondered how I might reconcile the two events—the birth of his son and the death of the Nodine brothers—taking place on the same night, maybe at the same hour, out here on our solitary speck of Earth.

Shortly after nine thirty, the utility headlights from an OSP Ford Interceptor appeared in my rearview. I cut the Tahoe engine and greeted Detective Bach as he emerged from his vehicle.

He snapped shut the chinstrap on his down aviator hat and shook my hand. "I wish we could have met under more pleasant circumstances, Sergeant Blackthorne."

The man appeared to be in his mid-to-late fifties, slim

and fit, likely an indication of a tedious workout schedule. He'd probably been a handsome guy in his day, with a clean-cut military style that screamed self-assured and righteous. I also noticed the cross relief on his wedding ring. Old school, no doubt—Mormon or Catholic or something else regimental.

The medical examiner joined us outside the wigwam burner. She wore tall Frye boots over her jeans, a leather bomber jacket, and an expensive wool scarf. I had expected the doctor to be a man, of course, and I could see she had expected the same of me.

Bach took care of formalities. "Sergeant Margaret Black-thorne, this is Dr. Ray Gattis."

"Nice to meet you, Sergeant. Freaking cold out here, Al."

"I don't think this will take too terribly long, Ray," he said.

True to his reputation, Detective Alan Bach was all business. Apparently, though, he never wanted to be accused of making eye contact with a subordinate.

Speaking to his forehead, I relayed what I knew. Told him about the Nodines and the poached deer. Also explained they'd been driving the red truck when I attempted to cite them yesterday. "Neither man was the registered owner."

"Stolen?"

"Nothing reported, sir," I said. "It's registered to a Frank Sylvester with a Burns address."

He suggested we move on to look at the scene, and I led the way through the wigwam burner's open access door.

"My God, that smell," the doctor said.

"Mostly the remains of the deer they killed yesterday," I said.

She studied the iron mesh opening at the top of the structure. "I hadn't realized how large these things were."

"I hadn't either," I said. "They hid that huge one-ton and a livestock trailer inside. Never would've guessed it was possible."

"Pretty clever of them, too," she said.

"Until today, anyway," I countered, sans the usual snarky edge.

"I remember these old things," Detective Bach said. "They were used to burn sawmill wood waste up until the late seventies or so."

I pointed to the livestock trailer. "You can see the shotgun damage to the trailer's rear left wheel well, also the dead Rottweiler underneath. A different weapon killed the Nodine brothers."

"How'd you know where to look for them, Sergeant?" Bach asked.

"They called the station earlier this evening, asked me to meet them here."

"Time of the call?"

"Approximately five forty-five, Detective."

"And everything is the way you found it?"

"I took photos and collected the shotgun cartridges, cigarette butts, that kind of thing. I assumed you'd want to see where the shell casings landed near the bodies."

"Good thinking, Sergeant."

"I'd like to examine the two men now," the doctor said.

"Over here." I pointed to the second portable lighting tower erected at the far wall fifteen or so feet from the Nodines' vehicle and trailer. As we approached, the grisly scene unsettled me as much as it had a few hours ago. Even more so. The brothers' faces were now fully ashen, and rigor mortis had begun to set in.

"Jesus," the doctor said. "Whoever these two crossed was one pissed-off mother."

The detective crouched to get a closer look. "Seems they

were shot at close range, but I'll leave those particulars to you, Dr. Gattis."

"How thoughtful of you," she intoned. "I'll fetch my kit from the backseat of your SUV and get to those particulars, then."

"I don't mind getting your kit for you, Ray," Bach said, moving toward the access door.

The ME knelt and studied the dead men, removed a pair of latex gloves from her coat pocket, and closed their eyes. "What's your first name again, Sergeant Blackthorne?"

"Margaret. I go by Maggie."

"I loathe titles myself. Okay if I call you Maggie?"

"Yes, ma'am."

"I prefer Ray. Or Doctor, if you must. But never *ma'am*, all right?"

I made a mental note that *ma'am* had gone out of fashion. Probably explained its prevalent use by law enforcement types.

"I need to conduct the autopsies tomorrow, but there's not a morgue in the county, right?" Ray asked.

"Correct. I gave the local undertaker a heads-up we needed him to collect two bodies tonight."

"It'll take less than a half an hour to do what I need to here."

I stepped outside and phoned Sam Damon at home, let him know the ME would be ready for him by the time he got out here. Next I put in a call to the after-hours line at Whitey Kern's tow company, told him we needed his heavy-duty wrecker and a separate flatbed tow truck out at the old Seneca lumber mill site.

Bach returned with the doc's exam kit and his pack loaded with an assortment of crime scene tools. He asked me to join him at the Ram 3500. "Have the next of kin been informed?"

"No, sir. One of my troopers was with his wife at the hospital tonight about to have a baby. Our third officer is out on vacation."

"I see."

"And I thought I should be the one to inform the parents. I've known them since I was a toddler," I added.

"That could make it more difficult," he said.

"Not as difficult as finding the bodies of their sons, sir."

"I know it's the usual practice, Sergeant Blackthorne, but there's no need to call me *sir*." His invitation to be less formal was surprising. "How fresh?"

"How fresh?" Again, I was speaking to the man's forehead.

"The manure. How fresh is the manure?"

"Looks pretty fresh to me, but I'm not really an expert."

"Today fresh, if you had to guess?"

I squatted to examine the cow pies more closely. "I'd say it ranges from very recent to today fresh."

"And how many cattle would that trailer hold?"

"Typical size and weight, I'd say about five or six," I said.

"Five or six beef cattle worth much these days?"

"Up to ten grand for a full load, depending on the condition of the animals."

"Any recent incidents of cattle theft?"

"Not that I'm aware, Detective. But I did have a strange encounter earlier today with a local rancher. He was escorting a truckload of his Black Angus."

"Was he armed?" Bach asked.

"Mr. Trudeau's likely always armed. It was the truck driver I was interested in, though." I explained Jess Bennett was the cousin of the Nodine twins, and she drove for Frank Sylvester Trucking.

"Sylvester? The owner of our diesel pickup here?" he asked.

I nodded.

"Interesting. Is that just a coincidence, you think?"

"I'm not sure."

"And no citation was handed out?"

I shook my head. "None required."

The detective mulled that over a moment. "So there'll be no police report either."

It was hard to discern whether he was perturbed or not.

"Be sure to include that encounter in your incident report on the victims. I'm not finding much to go on in the vehicle except a few sets of latent prints. Although this might be something." He held out a small plastic evidence bag containing a sticky note with *BRADY* scrawled across it. "Found it in the glove compartment. Is that name familiar?"

"Might be a last name, a first name, a place name, a company name. Not one I recognize, though." I pointed toward the ignition. "Also, I noticed earlier the key was missing, possibly on one of the bodies."

"Would you mind dusting the passenger-side doors? I need to check for shoe and tire tread marks." He handed me his fingerprint kit and retrieved a can of aerosol dust and dirt hardener, along with a casting frame.

He indicated the burner floor. "I doubt I'll be able to recover any tracks in this muck of cow manure, but I've been surprised before."

While Bach attempted to find tread marks worthy of making a cast, I finished checking for prints. Afterward we bagged and labeled the paltry array of evidence we'd collected.

Frowning, the detective eyed the few items prepped for the lab. "Let's check on Ray."

Blood covered her smock and gloves, and she'd inadvertently wiped a two-inch streak above her left eyebrow. She removed her protective gear and gathered a pack of wet towelettes from her kit. "A fucking mess, Al. Semiautomatic handgun. And like you said, each shot twice at close range. The bullets caused extensive internal damage before exiting."

Bach pointed to another smear. "There's still a dab of blood on your forehead."

"Christ." She peeled off another towelette. "Both men had been roughed up. Hard to say right now if that occurred just before the shooting or hours earlier. But I'm certain they were killed where Maggie found them. They were undoubtedly forced to sit against the wall, so I'd rule out self-defense on the shooter's part."

"Did you find the truck key on either man?" I asked.

The doc wiped blood from her boots. "Damn it. These are practically brand new. And no, their pockets were completely empty. Not even a candy wrapper."

"Why would someone take the key but not the vehicle?" I wondered aloud.

"The shooter might have come alone. Possibly planned to come back for the truck and trailer later," Bach proffered. "Sergeant, you took photos of the shell casings before we arrived, correct?"

"Yes, Detective."

He removed a camera and a set of long tweezers from his pack, stepped tentatively around the bodies, and retrieved the four shell casings. "Please shine your flashlight behind the men, Sergeant."

As a result of Ray's examination, Dan and Joseph were now slumped forward and away from the wall. I aimed the Maglite beam behind them. Bach photographed the four slugs buried in the rusted metal siding and then used the tweezers to carefully remove the fragment of each bullet.

He placed the small plastic bag of slugs in the palm of his hand. "Nine millimeter."

We heard Sam Damon pull up and honk. I stepped outside and guided the hearse through the gate toward the wigwam burner. Sam and I placed the slain men in body bags, moved them onto separate stretchers, and carried them into the cold night air. The storm of purple had dispersed, and stars pricked the sky.

4

After the bodies had been loaded in the hearse, Sam offered to say a few words out of respect for the deceased. All of us stood in the night's showy brilliance as he delivered a benediction of sorts, one from a man simultaneously sickened by yet wholly dependent on ill-timed death. An aroma of dank pine and alkali drifted over us, along with the lingering fetor of blood and gunpowder.

As Sam drove away, the rest of us moved back inside the burner.

"What do you think happened here?" Ray asked.

"Something to do with beef cattle," I said.

"Well, there's definitely a lot of cow shit everywhere," she said.

"I would have suspected a drug deal gone bad, if it weren't for this." I nodded toward the Ram 3500 and livestock trailer.

"If we're talking about rustling, what's the link to our two victims?" the detective asked.

"I don't have a handle on any of it, including how they wound up with that expensive truck," I answered.

Bach started gathering up the items he'd removed from his pack. "Any known enemies?"

"Like I mentioned earlier, they probably acquired more than a few along the way. But no one in particular comes to mind at the moment."

Dr. Gattis collected the trash from her exams and placed it in a waste container. "Maggie, my guess is, Al will rely on you quite a bit during the investigation."

This was my first murder case, and solving homicides was not something I'd ever aspired to.

"That's a bit of pressure to put on a sergeant essentially operating on her own out here."

"And you're damned lucky you won't have to rely on that Sheriff Doofus person. Isn't that what you called him?" Doc Gattis asked.

I noted the wee smile from the detective. "Who's your district supervisor, Sergeant?"

"Jeremy Lake."

"What? The lieutenant up in La Grande?" Bach was incredulous. "That's more than a hundred and twenty miles from here. Asinine budget cuts. Politicians eliminate police positions but keep the same expectations for law enforcement."

"I know that dude. Lieutenant Lake—short, body-builder type, right? I was the responding ME when some old geezer fell through a rickety mine shaft. I found Lake to be about as cocky as they come," Ray said.

The good doctor certainly had that right.

"Let's gather up our gear, Ray," Bach said, reloading his pack.

She adjusted her wool scarf and lifted her exam kit. "Now, where the hell can I find a good steak and a stiff drink when we get to town?"

I eyed my watch. "I'm not sure about that steak. Things close down early around here. Except the bars. I'd recommend Club Paris. A block from where you're staying. Mack's Motel, right? Also a little classier. Even has a pretty good bartender."

"You're welcome to come along if you'd like."

"Thanks, but I need to wait here for the tow trucks and deal with the Rottweiler. Plus there's still notification of the family," I said.

"I'd appreciate you taking charge of preliminary evidence for the night, Sergeant Blackthorne. We'll meet you back at the station at zero seven hundred tomorrow morning."

"Jesus. Seven a.m.," Dr. Gattis said. "Today's been a long day, Al."

She had read my mind.

A raw wind flogged the wigwam burner's rusted metal siding and carried the scent of snow falling in the distance. Squatting near the soot- and manure-covered ground, I welcomed the gusts wafting through the open access doors. I'd been grappling with the Rottweiler's hundred-pound-plus carcass for several minutes in an attempt to remove it from under the livestock trailer. By the time I managed to place a tarp under the dead canine and drag it to my SUV, Whitey Kern had arrived.

Wielding my Maglite, I guided Whitey through the open gate and inside the burner. He hoisted the Nodines' diesel pickup onto the bed of his wrecker, the one he used to rescue disabled bulldozers and farm equipment. I helped him secure the red truck and handed him the permit authorizing transport to the State Police evidence warehouse in Bend.

"My gal Olive's on her way from Prairie City to pick up that cattle trailer," he said.

Whitey had the outsized face of an aging bulldog. Translucent skin exposed the blood vessels of his jowly cheeks and prominent nose, giving rise to a fierce countenance. But his gentle manner and easy laugh made him a man beloved throughout the county. "I'll help you load that poor old pup into your rig."

"I'd sure appreciate it."

We moved outside to my Tahoe. I opened the cargo door, laid a second tarp over the floor mat, and together we lifted the Rottweiler.

I covered the animal with a muslin game bag. "Don't suppose you ever spotted Dan and Joseph Nodine out and about in that vehicle?"

"I don't believe so, Maggie. But I did give 'em a tow last week. Their jeep broke down along Dog Creek Road."

"Were they living up there?"

"Not sure, but you might ask Ariel. She was with 'em."

"Ariel Pritchett?"

He nodded and climbed inside the cab of his idling tow truck. Last night at the Rifleman Club, I'd neglected to ask Ariel directly if she knew where the Nodines lived. And she hadn't volunteered the information either.

Whitey inched the wrecker and its one-ton load through the burner's access door, across the weedy concrete, and onto the roadway. I had known Whitey my whole life, too. He'd had nothing to say about the murder scene. Always friendly, but he tended to mind his own business. What with his tow company, Whitey had seen it all, including the head of his own son plopped down on hard pavement after a night of Hennessy, crystal meth, and fuck-all driving.

. . .

After Whitey's daughter Olive had come for the livestock trailer and I'd loaded the portable lighting towers in my Tahoe, I drove to Lynn Nodine's. The lights were out when I arrived. I knocked and called for her, watched for a lamp to switch on and for Lynn to emerge. I rapped on the front door and called her name a second time. I attempted to turn the knob. Locked. Same with the side door. No answer. Locked.

The blinds were shut, the curtains drawn. I shined the Maglite through the leaded glass window of the front door and into the darkened living room. The beam refracted off Lynn's antique mirror, rolled across her armoire and velvet-upholstered divan, and illuminated the flower-print wallpaper.

I directed my flashlight toward the wide-open garage. The orange VW bus was gone.

Aching with cold and a familiar sorrow, I sat on the top porch step and waited. Close to midnight Lynn turned into the driveway and parked.

"A second visit, Margaret? What the hell?" she said, moving up the walkway. "Like I said last night, I'm not in contact with my sons. On purpose. Do you plan to bother me every day about them poaching that damn deer?"

"Mrs. Nodine. Lynn. Sorry to bother you so late, but I need to speak with you."

"What is it, Margaret?"

"Please, can we go inside?"

Lynn walked up the steps to the front door and turned her key. I followed her into the living room, which shined with polish and carried the faint fragrance of rosewood, teak, and lime.

She settled into the divan, and I took the rocker across from her. "Are they in jail?" she asked. "Because if it's bail money you've come to talk about, I won't pay it. They can sit there and take it. Just like all the other times."

"No, that's not why I'm here, Lynn. I'm sorry to bring such terrible news." I gazed directly into her fiery eyes, an effort to borrow some of her spark and light up my own courage to say what had to be said. "Dan and Joseph are dead."

The mantel clock softly sounded out the seconds. "Did they wreck that old jeep?"

"I'm afraid they were shot to death."

"Murdered?" she whispered. "Murdered?"

"Yes, dear." I leaned into the space between us. The flame that burned from Lynn Nodine's core had been extinguished. She sat dazed and silent for several minutes, finally asking that I call her sister Beth over in Mt. Vernon. I offered to bring her a glass of water, some wine, but she stared at her hands folded in her lap until her sister arrived twenty minutes later.

"Thank you for coming to tell me in person, but you should leave now, Margaret," Lynn said.

I stood and put on my police Stetson.

"Have you been to see their dad yet?" she asked.

"I'm on my way to do that now." I briefly rested a hand on Lynn's upper arm. "I'll be in touch in the next day or two, but let me know if you need anything in the meantime. I'm so sorry it all came to this."

Driving to the Rifleman Club sometime after one a.m., it occurred to me that my parting comment to Lynn—*I'm so sorry it all came to this*—was an odd expression of sympathy, as if Dan and Joseph were simply unlucky and ill-fated, not in command of their own destinies and always bound to end up in a dark place, murdered in cold blood being the darkest place of all.

I informed Farley Nodine of his sons' deaths standing in the dusty back room that served as the tavern's office. The news was but another sad weight placed on his slumped shoulders.

"Well, I guess that's it, then," he said and moved back to the bar and set about mixing somebody's Moscow mule.

Ariel Pritchett stood stiffly in the middle of the barroom. She plucked a cigarette from her apron pocket and lit it, inhaled deeply. "What is it? What's wrong, Farley?"

"No smoking in here," he said.

She shifted her harried look toward me. The room was steamy with heat from the oil furnace and a full regiment of drunkards, but her hands were trembling. "Maggie? Please tell me what's going on."

"It should come from Farley."

Ariel dropped her cigarette and ground it out with the heel of her worn sneaker. She dabbed her nose with the back of a hand, took in the musty air. "Joey's been staying at my place most nights. We didn't have a fight or anything, but I haven't seen him since yesterday morning. We're supposed to go to Winnemucca next week and get married."

"Let's step into the office, okay?" It occurred to me that Farley might object, but he turned his back and poured a beer from the tap. I followed Ariel into the back room, closed the door, and placed my hat on the cluttered desk.

"You've got to tell me, Maggie, please. I really do love him."

"Dan and Joseph were murdered tonight." We both flinched at the severe edge to my voice, that move-your-motherfucking-ass-out-of-the-car tone I often resorted to with late-night inebriates. Which is why I lurched forward and clumsily wrapped my arms around her. "I'm sorry, Ariel. It's a terrible thing."

She quietly wept and slowly withdrew from my awkward

embrace, pressed her red fists over her hazel eyes. Dishwater-blond tufts dangled from her loosely tied ponytail. "I can't believe it," she said, shaking her head. "Joey and me, we really got along. And him and Danny were working on some deal that was supposed to set us all up for good."

Sorrowful moment as it was, I needed to press her for details. "What kind of a deal?"

"I don't know anything more than that. Danny was mad Joey told me that much."

"And you never saw them driving a brand new red Ram pickup?"

"You asked me about that last night. I don't think they could've traded their old jeep for a new rig. Besides, the jeep still belongs to their mom."

The twins owned no vehicles and hadn't bothered with driver's licenses after their stint in prison. Thus the lack of DMV addresses for either man. Must have been their way of staying on the down low. Which made the fact they were riding around in that snazzy one-ton even stranger.

Ariel fished in her pocket for another cigarette. "What happens now, Maggie?" she asked, lighting her Marlboro.

"We'll conduct an investigation and find the killer."

She took that under consideration.

"There's one thing you might be able to help me with. We need to search their belongings," I said.

She endeavored to compose herself. "Joey took his duffel bag with him when he left yesterday. That's all he ever brought with him to my place. Don't think he owned much of anything."

"A relative told me they were living near Seneca?"

"I've never been there, don't even know where it is exactly. Didn't seem like it was very homey, though."

"How long had Joseph been staying with you most nights?"

"About three months." She began to cry softly. "Danny would drop him off and then go to his girlfriend's house."

"Girlfriend?"

"Yeah. He'd been seeing Kat McKay."

Duncan McKay's sister. That caught me by surprise. "Did he stay overnight at Kat's?"

She shrugged. "I don't know for sure. Either there or the place near Seneca, I guess."

I touched her upper arm, in much the same way I'd placed my hand on Lynn Nodine's a half hour before. "Okay, Ariel. I appreciate you talking to me. I know this has been hard."

Between drags on the cigarette, she chewed at her lower lip.

"I'll need to follow up with you in the next few days," I said. "Can I give you a lift home?"

"Nah. Thanks, though. Farley will need taking care of."

We found him sitting at the bar nursing a tall tumbler of whiskey. He had closed the Rifleman Club for the night and was embarking on a path to grim inebriation.

I left Ariel and Farley to their grieving and drove to the station. Animal Services was closed at that hour of the night, so I had no choice but to wait until later in the morning to deal with the Rottweiler carcass. I stored the tagged items collected from the murder scene in our evidence locker, checked email, and listened to voicemail on my desk phone.

Lt. Jeremy T. Lake had made several attempts to reach me. Every one of his messages contained some version of *contact me ASAP*. It was past two in the morning, and I wasn't in the mood to email J.T. an apology for not being at his beck and call. Besides, for some reason he hadn't tried my cell phone, which left me wondering what asshole maneuver he was angling at this time to get me demoted or fired.

Back at my apartment, I unbuckled my holster and placed it on the dinette table, draped my peacoat over the back of the lone kitchen chair, and removed my boots and uniform. After tending to Louie and taking a long, hot shower, I shifted the stack of folded laundry from my bed to the dinette table, shut off the single bulb hanging overhead, and climbed between the ice-cold sheets.

Dorie's lights had still been on when I'd climbed the stairs up to my apartment. I'd considered stopping by, letting her know that Dan and Joseph were dead, yet there were procedures, a process to follow. Informing my landlord wasn't on the list. I knew Dorie was one of Lynn Nodine's few friends and would want to take over as the woman's caretaker, maybe call together a prayer circle. But there would be many dark days ahead for all that weeping and begging God almighty for solace.

Sleep, when it came, dragged me through the night until the electronic drone of my phone alarm sounded. I inhaled a turkey sandwich I'd purchased at Gas-n-Snacks some time back, dressed, and tied up my limp hair.

My first official task of the morning involved some torturous bureaucracy at County Animal Services. It was of little concern to folks that the State Police homicide unit was formally requesting the use of one of their deep-freeze lockers to store the Rottweiler killed at the scene of a murder. There were hoops to jump through, legalities to accommodate, and time to waste. Still, I managed all of it with a smile, and in the end, a couple of stocky workers even assisted me by removing the dead dog from the back of my Chevy Tahoe.

When I arrived at the office, I found a state-of-the art police vehicle, even newer and sleeker than Detective Alan Bach's Ford Interceptor, parked in my usual spot. Apparently, J.T. Lake had decided to pay a surprise visit. I straightened my shoulders, adjusted my badge, and opened the door to my trooper station.

"What the hell, Blackthorne?"

Standing almost as short as me in his extra-wide police Stetson and sickly mustache was Lt. Jeremy T. Lake, my supervisor and, it pained me to admit, my second ex-husband.

"I have to hear from goddamn regional that you were out wandering the hills and stumbled on two dead guys?"

Stupid of me not to assume he would show up sooner than later. I removed my hat and looked him square in his beady eyes. "It was obvious my first duty was to contact the murder squad, J.T."

"Not your call to make, Blackthorne. Not your goddamn call to make. From now on, I want to know your every move, and before you make it."

Mostly, J.T. could have given a rat's ass about police protocol or what I did with my time. His capacity for this kind of periodic bluster was always a wonder to me, since I knew from experience his only real power over anyone was a tendency toward intermittent cruelty.

"And I'm writing you up."

"What's this about, Lieutenant?" Detective Bach stood in the doorframe in a fresh uniform, lightly starched and pressed into exacting military creases.

He entered the office, followed by Dr. Gattis, who was dressed in designer jeans and a trendy flannel shirt cut to flatter shapely women. That, and her nicely coiffed golden-brown hair, were an indication she was not from around here.

Taken aback but nonetheless undaunted, J.T. stated his complaint. "Sergeant Blackthorne did not communicate with me, her supervising officer, regarding events of the last two days, sir."

"After finding the bodies last evening, the sergeant contacted regional to report a homicide. That's per protocol."

J.T. deserved to be pulled up short a lot more often in my view. But I knew better than anybody not to give out even the glimmer of a gloat. Also knew I wasn't exactly off the hook.

"Detective, Sergeant Blackthorne's second call should have been to me. That's also per protocol." J.T. crossed his muscular arms over his sculpted chest. Younger cock taunting the older rooster.

I noted he still sported that Rolex we went into hock for.

"You have a point there, Lieutenant," the detective conceded. "But I've kept her busy since she located the victims. Still, that oversight won't happen again, will it?"

"No, sir," I acknowledged.

Bach studied J.T. for a moment and then scanned the type of office that passed for rural law enforcement workspace. "I can certainly brief you on what we've discovered in addition to the bodies, Lieutenant Lake, which isn't a lot so far, but I would prefer to wait on that. Dr. Gattis and I arrived around nine thirty last night, and all three of us spent time out in the elements examining the crime scene."

"I understand, Detective," J.T. said.

But I knew he was seething.

"I've asked Sergeant Blackthorne to write her full report and have it to us first thing tomorrow morning. I'm about to head out to the scene and wrap up my initial investigation before traveling back to Bend. And the ME has to attend to her autopsies."

"First we need the keys to the evidence locker, Maggie," Dr. Gattis said.

J.T. tipped his big-hatted head toward Ray. "Nice to see you again, ma'am."

Apparently he hadn't heard the news that addressing a woman as *ma'am* was viewed unfavorably in some circles. Observing her reaction to J.T.'s salutation, I made a mental note to ask the doc for lessons on how to appear simultaneously disinterested in the person speaking and disdainful of what was being said.

I unlocked the bottom drawer of my desk and retrieved the keys to the locker. The detective and Ray moved past J.T., who stood as stiff as the dead Nodines, fists pressed into his thighs. Through some kind of minor miracle, he had been pulled up short twice in ten minutes. Being present for that was worth any future crap he'd send my way.

After Bach and Dr. Gattis closed the door to the evidence locker, J.T. turned and faced me. "I see how this all goes down, Maggie. The detective has your back today because he needs your help. But in the end, he'll go back to Bend, I'll head back to La Grande, and you'll still be stuck in this shithole."

My former beloved failed to realize the stupidity of that last statement. My shithole town was only marginally worse than his.

"I asked for this assignment, remember," I said, although sometimes it escaped me why.

"So, the names of the victims?" he asked.

"Daniel and Joseph Nodine."

"Brothers?"

"Twins."

"You know them?"

"Grew up with them."

"You ever fucked either of them?"

"That's a question you have no right to ask."

"You ever fucked either of them while you were married to me?"

"I only fucked one asshole while I was married to you."

J.T. smiled. "You always had a trashy mouth," he said and moved closer, nudging me backward toward my desk, pressing his groin into my thigh. "Watch yourself, Sergeant. I know your weaknesses."

"I know yours, too, dick face."

He closed in with a body clench across my chest, shoulders, and upper back. Moved his mouth to my ear and whispered, "How do you think your girlfriend there, that slut doctor, would feel about all them sloppy drunk blackouts back in the day? And the Boy Scout? He might think twice about your morals if he knew how many cowboys had you for a practice saddle."

Letting my body fall limp, I turned away from J.T.'s lead-weight hold, a handy tactical defense maneuver I'd learned as a recruit. But when I attempted to shove the palm of my left hand abruptly under his chin, he blocked with his right forearm and locked onto my wrist.

"I wish I'd pulled that fucking trigger when I had the chance," I said.

He released his grip, adjusted his oversized police Stetson. "There'll be none of that *have a report to us by tomorrow morning* bullshit—I want it emailed to me by end of day. And let Detective Bach know I appreciate his offer of a briefing, but I need to get on the road."

I massaged the exact spot on my right shoulder where I carried an ugly burn scar, a souvenir from our marriage.

J.T. walked to the door without a look back and left my

building. Yet the electricity of our violence lingered, in the way dust motes will.

"Maggie?" Dr. Gattis stepped back into the frame. "What the hell was that about?"

A person could reveal every page of their secret history and end up regretting the lack of prudence or guile. I was determined to prevent such a thing from occurring. Besides, how could I have described the black psyche of Jeremy T. Lake? That is, without calling into question my own soundness of mind for having stayed married to the bastard long enough to pick up a pistol and point it straight at his heart? What kind of a woman fell for such a yahoo, especially after it was clear his manly-man pretense was nothing more than a cover for impotence and a mile-wide mean streak? Not a woman like Ray Gattis, that's for sure.

"I'm not his favorite subordinate," I said.

"A compliment, no doubt," she countered.

I couldn't help myself; I had to laugh at that.

Bach carried the box of evidence and placed it on my desk. "I see the lieutenant is gone."

"He needed to head back to La Grande."

The doc slipped on her jacket. "And I need to get moving on those autopsies."

"I'd appreciate you giving Ray a ride to the undertaker's place, Sergeant."

"Of course," I said and relayed the gist of last night's conversation with Ariel Pritchett.

"I'm anxious to see your full report," he said.

"I'll have it for you sometime today."

"Thanks. I'll check it over and pass it along to Lieutenant Lake. I'm not sure that's per protocol, but let's just say it is." He peered at me intently, and directly for once. "Maggie. Are you and your staff ready to take on this investigation?"

Had he just called me Maggie? "I believe we are. I know this part of the state and the way of life out here—the good and the bad. Senior Trooper Jones is smart and a tenacious researcher. Plus our wildlife officer returns from vacation on Monday. He's the guy who keeps us organized. We're all good cops, Detective."

"I always prefer working with good cops."

The man actually tossed in a little smile.

"This case will test you, Sergeant. But I need your help, especially with all the recent cuts to my unit."

Bach paused to gauge my reaction. I nodded, hoping that was a passable signal I understood what would be required of me—of all of us—in hunting down a killer: instincts, enough clues, and some luck.

"You'll be officially in charge of the local investigation, at least for now, and working under my command. I want twice-daily updates, and if anything breaks, you'll call me immediately."

"Yes, Detective Bach." I'd known State Police resources were spread thin, but I was surprised to be given the go-ahead to investigate. It had become my practice to surreptitiously grant myself more authority on occasion, under the guise of pragmatism. But I'd drawn the line at homicide. Until now, that is.

He adjusted his hat and coat and lifted the box of evidence from my desk. "You do know that in all likelihood, a local citizen is the murderer?"

"I assumed so, Detective."

"I'll contact you if I find more evidence at the scene. And Maggie, in informal conversations, I'm fine with just Al." He gave me a short, firm handshake and a short, firm smile.

5

I delivered Dr. Gattis to Sam Damon's fancy funeral home, the Juniper Chapel Mortuary and Crematorium.

"Thanks for the lift," she said. "Can we meet for dinner afterward?"

"Sounds like a plan."

"I can't imagine it going later than seven."

"Sam closes at six."

"Maybe I can charm my way into staying another hour if I need to."

"Be careful, Dr. Gattis. Sam's a shy and tender bachelor. You turn on too much charm and he might think you're propositioning him and try to take you up on it, morgue full of bodies and all."

"I'll bear that in mind. And for God's sake, call me Ray."

On my way to Kat McKay's place, I noticed Hollis's Chevy Tahoe, one identical to mine, parked at our trooper station. I stopped in and found him at his desk in our musty office, thumbing through photos on his phone.

"Maggie, come see little man Hank."

"Look at all that hair," I said, leaning over Holly's shoulder.

"Lil and I want you to be his godmother, whatever that means these days."

"It means a lot to me that you would ask. But does it also mean I have to change diapers and shit like that?"

"Definitely. And that's just the beginning. So why didn't you return my call last night? I left you a voicemail, even invited you out for a beer."

"I should have, Holly. To congratulate you and Lil. But I wouldn't have been able to join you for a beer."

"Were you on a date?" He was incredulous.

"God, no. But I found Dan and Joseph Nodine."

It struck me how I tended to refer to the Nodines in the same name order. Maybe it was always that way with twins. You said the smartest one's name first, the nicest one's second.

"You found where they lived?"

"I found where they died."

"What the hell?"

"Right after you phoned and told me Lil was in labor, I had a call from Joseph. He was anxious to set up a meeting. Then I heard..." Recalling discovery of the bodies, I couldn't go on.

"Damn, Maggie." He rose from his chair and held me as I wept.

Minutes passed in our still and airless office before I could speak.

"Thanks for being my friend just now."

"Always," he said.

"They were killed before I could get there."

"Get where?"

I sat at my desk across from his. "That rusted wigwam burner up in Seneca."

"Any idea what happened?"

I shook my head. "Other than they were shot to death. A homicide investigator and the ME met me at the mill. But there's not much to go on yet. Which means we have to make this case a priority for the foreseeable future."

He took his seat. "We?"

"You and me. And probably Taylor, too. We're doing the legwork, reporting directly to Detective Alan Bach."

He smiled. "J.T. Lake will have a shit fit."

I laughed, relieved I was no longer crying. "I know."

"I've heard Bach is a good man. Strictly by the book, but rock solid."

"I don't even have a report for you to review, but I will by this evening. In the meantime, I'd like you to continue tying up some of those loose ends regarding the Nodines. That's more important than ever now."

"Will do."

"Damn, Holly. I almost forgot. You're officially on family leave now."

"Don't worry, we'll work it out. Lil and the baby come home from the hospital tomorrow morning. I'll put in my regular hours today, and if you can be flexible after that, I'll work whenever Lil doesn't need me around to help out."

"I know that's not what you want. Taylor's back from vacation in a few days, so no, take your leave like you planned."

"It's a murder investigation, Sarge. Lil will understand, unless it begins to eat up every hour of every day for months on end. And if that happens, the detective will see we're in over our heads."

"But we're not going to let that happen, right?"

"That's right. Now be quiet and let me get to work."

I knew I hadn't tried very hard to dissuade him. Which was pretty shitty of me.

. . .

As I turned down the street toward Kat McKay's house, a Land Rover whipped past at full tilt headed the opposite direction. I recognized the driver. Kat's kid, a boy named Rain who had the visage of one of the blank-eyed walking wounded I'd met volunteering at the Youth Authority's reform school. A practicum is what they called it at the police academy. Hell was more like it.

Kat and I were the same age. Like Ariel Pritchett, I'd known her since elementary school. As a girl, I always envied the handmade dresses Mrs. McKay sewed for Kat, stylish frocks out of quality fabric, not the ninety-nine-cent-a-yard gingham froufrou everyone else wore. We had never been close friends, though, and she lit out with Arlan Ferlinghetti after graduation, got married, and Rain was born a few years later. She divorced Arlan not too long after and had been living back in the area for more than a decade. She'd gotten rid of her married name, which stood to reason. But Rain was a McKay-Ferlinghetti.

Kat's small bungalow had recently been painted a deep brick color. I liked what she had done to the place, including the forsythia's gold buds bursting through the veil of frost. A sign spring was on the way.

The front door opened before I reached the porch. "Maggie. How are you?"

"Morning, Kat."

She had wrapped a pearl-white lambswool shawl tightly around her arms and torso. An elegant woman, but despite her carefully applied makeup I detected the dark circles under her eyes. Which shed light on what it might be like to raise a teenager alone in this two-horse town.

"Has Rain done something I need to know about?"

Sussing out Rain's mischief was not my purpose today;

maybe another time, though. "I'm here to ask you about Dan Nodine."

Kat opened the door wider and signaled for me to follow her into the frigid foyer. "I guess it doesn't surprise me that Dan's in trouble with the law again, but I don't know anything about it. Also, I ended it with him over a week ago."

"It's something else, I'm afraid. Dan and his brother were murdered last night." I waited for her to react, but there was nothing. "Would you like to sit down? Should I call someone for you?"

"No. It's a shock, of course. But I'm fine."

She was either the original Ice Queen or she must have been looking to dump Dan for a while.

"I'm hoping to talk to everyone who's had recent contact with either man," I said.

"Like I told you, I called it quits with Dan last Thursday."

I tried a different tack. "What was he driving when you last saw him?"

"He was in that army jeep, what else?"

"You tell me."

"He was driving that old jeep." She was emphatic. And annoyed. "He couldn't afford anything else. Didn't have a job, really. Picked up work whenever something happened along."

"Such as?"

"Odd jobs here and there, I think. All I know is he had money every now and then."

"How long had you dated?"

"Six months or so."

"Why'd you break up with him?"

"That's personal. And what's it got to do with anything, anyway?"

"Damn it, Kat. I'm not here looking for gossip to pass along. Someone just killed Dan and Joseph in cold blood."

"All right, all right." She clasped her long-fingered hands together. "It just wasn't working out for me. Most of the time I felt like I was dating my cousin or something. Then he stole money out of my purse, tried to say it was Rain. My son wouldn't steal from anyone. Especially me. We're really close, him and me."

Just the opposite, is what I'd heard. "Do you know where he lived when he wasn't staying with you?"

"With Joe somewhere, I guess, but I don't know where. And just to be clear, he never spent the night. I couldn't have Rain finding him here in the morning."

It was strange Ariel and Kat hadn't a clue where the Nodines called home. But maybe the brothers had kept certain info, such as their possible whereabouts, from the women on purpose.

"Most nights, Joseph stayed at Ariel Pritchett's," I said.

That got her attention. "Is that who told you I was dating Dan?"

Now I remembered why I always found Kat duplicitous. "Was it supposed to be a secret?"

"I'd prefer people didn't know. Anyway, Maggie, if you'll excuse me, I need to get to work."

Somewhere along the way, Kat had become a hair stylist and owned a successful salon.

I handed her my card. "If you think of anything."

Kat nodded and followed me to the porch. "Sorry if I was a bitch."

Did she mean sorry if she was a bitch to me or to Dan Nodine? I turned toward her. "One more thing. Did Dan ever mention a guy by the last name of Sylvester?"

"I don't believe so."

"How about anyone with the first name Frank?"

"Well, there's Frankie Jacoby, who helps out my brother at the feed store."

"I know Frankie Jacoby. This is somebody else."

"Then no."

"You have my card."

Kat tucked it in her pants pocket and nestled into the lambswool shawl. "I really do have to get to the salon, Maggie."

I couldn't figure out precisely what, but there was something off about Kat McKay, or at least her story. Since gut feelings weren't considered evidence—except in TV cop shows—I concentrated on writing my report. In the end, my account of events leading up to the discovery of the murdered Nodines and the info obtained subsequently was drafted, proofed, edited, and finalized before the end of day, as promised. The entire sordid manifesto amounted to a paltry five pages and bore not one substantive clue as far as I could tell.

I shipped it off to Bach and called Jess Bennett's cell number. I still hadn't circled back around to prod for more information on her twin cousins, especially the visit they paid her a couple of weeks ago. I barely recognized the recorded mumbling voice asking me to leave a message. I countered with my best cop bravado, leaving a brusque summons to return my call. If Hollis had been here, he'd have been razzing me with all kinds of shit for talking tough to a citizen. And I would've pointed out that the last twenty-four hours had put me in a mood.

After Doc Gattis completed the autopsies, we agreed to meet for dinner at the Blue Mountain Lounge, two blocks from Sam

Damon's funeral home. I locked up the trooper station, drove home, fed Louie, and changed into civilian gear.

I found Ray seated in the far corner booth, and as I expected, she hadn't waited for me to arrive before ordering a drink. Her specimen cooler and a chic leather duffel bag sat on the floor next to the worn vinyl-upholstered seat.

She looked up from her phone and tossed back her hair. "Maggie. I thought I'd been stood up."

I gestured toward her duffel bag. "You've checked out already?"

"Thought I might talk you into taking me to the airport from here."

"Sure. Sorry I'm late."

"You clean up nice."

I'd purposely put on my new boot-cut Levi's and the silk blouse I'd bought in Boise a while back. Even applied a spot of lipstick.

"I released the bodies late this afternoon," she said.

I slid into my side of the booth. "That's probably a relief for the parents."

"Sam said services were set for next Monday?" she asked.

I nodded and picked up the menu. Despite knowing there would be nothing new, or changed, or particularly enticing offered, I still scanned my options. Our server, a young woman the spitting image of Ariel Pritchett, stood over us at our table and smiled tentatively. Ray ordered another old-fashioned and the fried chicken dinner; I ordered a bottle of Bud Light and a cheeseburger, rare.

"Mind if I ask you a personal question?" Ray asked, observing our server as she drudge-marched back to the kitchen with our orders. "How the hell did you end up in this town?"

"Born and raised."

"Well, that's no excuse."

We both laughed, and I began to feel the 9-1-1 for alcohol. God, was that a line from some bullshit country western song?

"I lived in Salem for a long time, where the worldview's not quite as narrow. But how about you? How'd you get here?" I asked.

"You mean why do I spend my days flying to every ore deposit in this state to dissect dead bodies? I love central and eastern Oregon is one explanation, I guess. And I'm good at my job, if I say so myself."

"I'm good at my job too. If I say so myself."

"Oh, I believe it. But you seemed a little taken aback this morning when Al assigned you to the investigation," she said.

"I was surprised, I guess. Truthfully, though, there's no way I'd settle for not being involved. I found those men, and I want to find who killed them."

"I definitely understand that instinct."

Ray took a final swig of her first-round drink as her second round arrived. I briefly wondered if the booze might soon begin seeping from her pores, making it more difficult to convey the élan of wise physician, not to mention wiseass.

"Change of subject. Not to sound like your mother, Maggie, but you should be careful about ordering rare hamburger."

"Nah. The BM Lounge serves only grass-fed, hormone-free beef raised right here in our county. Not much of a timber industry around here anymore, but good beef? That's bank."

"Well, I'm still skeptical." She tipped back her second old-fashioned and drank slowly. "And the fucking bartender in this place should find a new line of work."

"Liquor Luddite is the term my cocktail-snob ex-husband would've used," I said.

"That's a good one. I might have to borrow it."

"He'll never know." I sipped my beer at a leisurely pace, to avoid treading the dangerous waters of personal history. "He lives in Portland."

"The two of you don't ever talk?"

I adjusted my collar. "Morgan and I talk pretty often. We're still close friends."

"I've never been married myself. Came close once, but it's not for me. That's nice you're friends with your ex, though."

"Well, the first one, anyway." Shit.

Ray smiled. "You have a second ex-husband?"

"Yes, one I don't like talking about."

"Got it," she said. "So let's talk about the first one. If you're such good friends, why get divorced?"

Why was she so nosy? Right, it had to be the bourbon. "Morgan divorced me. After he came to the realization he was gay."

Finally Ray Gattis had no quip at her disposal, so it was time for me to turn the tables. "How about you? Are you involved with anyone?"

"I can't decide." She paused. "Are you?"

I shook my head.

"But you've been married and divorced twice? Morgan, the gay guy in Portland, and who else?"

"Just another state trooper. It ended a while ago." I drank my light beer more assertively.

She peered across the table, her ardent blue eyes settling on their own piece of evidence. "Oh! It's that little prick lieutenant, isn't it? What's his name? Jeremy Lake, right?"

I waved for our server to bring me another of the same. "How did you figure that out?" I wanted that goddamn beer pronto.

"I guessed, of course. But the tension between you two this morning was obvious. Kind of like an angry divorced couple."

My second beer was delivered, and I ordered up coffee for the two of us.

"Isn't it against some protocol, your ex being your boss?"

"Probably." I had always dreaded the possibility of word spreading throughout the State cop community that I'd been married to that fool. Not because the news might affect my career. But the three or four people I gave a damn about would find out I'd once fallen that low.

"I'd like to drop the subject of second husbands, and I'd appreciate you not mentioning any of this to the detective. J.T.'s my supervisor, but he wasn't when we were together. And he really has so little to do with my life now."

"Other than making it miserable if he decides to."

"Good point."

"Not to worry, though. I won't say anything, mostly because I don't see a reason to. Besides, Al's a man who doesn't always follow the rules himself. As you've probably figured out."

I directed one of my blank stares across the dented Formica-topped table, which was met by her mischievous gaze.

She rested a lovely manicured hand over my chapped, nail-bitten left one. "Come on, Maggie. Surely you know how these things happen. Working death scenes with somebody, especially if it involves murder, tends to draw you together. Al and I have been trying to end it for months. Well, trying to keep it from going further is more like it. But we're making a mess of it. I'm making a mess of it."

I had definitely missed all of that. "He's not up for getting a divorce?"

"No. Despite his willingness to flirt around the edges of something possibly more exotic than hearth and home, Al's pretty committed to his beliefs," she said. "To his wife too, I suppose."

"What was that line from Dorothy Parker?" I asked.

"God, what was it?" Ray placed her drink on the table. "Oh, I know. 'Men seldom make passes at girls who wear glasses'?"

"I'm pretty sure Parker said that too, but I was thinking of the one that's a little more apropos: 'You can't teach an old dogma new tricks.'"

She tossed back her hair and laughed heartily. "Jesus fucking Christ. That is so true. Maggie, you're the first person of real intelligence and wit I've met for some time." Said in a manner that, alas, reflected the imbibing of two old-fashioneds rather than sincere admiration.

"Are you sure you'll be okay flying back tonight?" I asked.

She swallowed down the last of her supposedly disgusting drink. "Yes, because you're going to drive me to the airport and watch me board that little motherfucker of a plane. After I land, I'll take a taxi home and fall asleep in my own bed."

The Ariel Pritchett lookalike appeared with a tray carrying our supper and hastily placed the hot plates and coffee mugs on our table. Doc Gattis looked askance at my meal. And largely on account of the frozen entrées waiting at home, I lifted my lovely cheeseburger, cooked rare to perfection, and took my first bite. I took my chances. I always took my chances.

We ate quietly for several minutes. I knew I was famished, and I imagined Ray was too.

"This is delicious. You have to go to the country for good fried chicken," she said.

"For good fried anything, if you ask me."

"Maggie, there's a guy over there who's been staring the hell out of you. Got any idea what that's about?" I started to turn, but Ray said, "Tall guy with reddish hair?"

"Well, that describes a few people around here. Besides, it's probably you who's being checked out. The locals always give strangers a serious once-over."

"No, dear heart. He's not checking me out. I'd say he's pretty much ignoring everyone in the room *but* you."

Then I remembered. A couple of nights ago, Duncan McKay had filed a theft report. "Does he look like a retired bull rider?"

"You're blushing, for Christ's sake. And I don't know what a bull rider is supposed to look like, retired or otherwise." Ray sipped her coffee and checked her watch. "We should probably leave in fifteen minutes or so."

With no warning, Duncan appeared next to our corner booth, towering awkwardly above us. "Maggie," he said, "sorry to bother you."

"Oh. Hi. Um, this is Dr. Gattis."

He nodded. "Duncan McKay."

She shook his hand. "Pleasure to meet you, Mr. Duncan."

"McKay," he said.

"Sergeant Blackthorne and I were just finishing our meal before I fly back to Bend. Would you like to join us?"

"No, but thank you." He turned toward me. "Heard on OPB the Nodine brothers were murdered. Sorry you had to be the one to find them."

Ray eyed me over the rim of her coffee mug.

"Which means I haven't had much of a chance to look into your theft report," I said.

Duncan shrugged. "I guessed as much. The stuff will either turn up or it won't. Anyway, I saw you over here and thought I'd say hello before taking off."

I could feel myself blushing again.

"Nice to meet you, Dr. Gattis. I'll see you around, Maggie."

I grabbed the check and ordered a box for the rest of Ray's supper, and the two of us watched Duncan pull out from the curb in his delivery truck. I wondered once again why Dorie hadn't included him on her list of my prospects for romance.

Seated in the passenger seat of my Tahoe, Ray yawned and laughed to herself. "God knows I'm not an expert, not even remotely, but that Duncan guy seems like a good man."

"He might be."

She yawned again. "As someone said—I don't think it was Dorothy Parker, though—'A good man is hard to find, but a hard man is good to find.'"

Heading back from the airport, I mulled over the relationship between Ray Gattis and Al Bach. I wasn't sure why she'd revealed something potentially ruinous to their careers. Maybe like me, the alcohol and friendly chatter had numbed her sense of circumspection, but I suspected she knew I could be trusted not to betray them. And she was right on that count.

I stopped at my office before heading home and checked email. I half expected to find some diatribe from J.T. Lake. Instead I'd received a message from Bach: "Good report. Let's talk tomorrow. BTW, this a.m. at the murder scene, I stumbled on the truck keys. No other evidence, though. Also the team here in Bend found an unopened Hot Shot DXR 36 cattle prod in the lockbox of the Ram 3500."

The mysterious missing keys and, in all likelihood, one of the prods stolen from McKay's Feed and Tack. I sent a reply to the detective mentioning Duncan's theft report and sat in my office wrestling with our homicide case. Tomorrow, I decided, we'd begin assembling a murder board.

I treated Louie with a kitty snack and pampered myself with a scoop of vanilla ice cream and chocolate syrup, all of it carted to my bed in the corner. I read another page of *Libbey vs. Chase* and placed it on my nightstand next to the one wedding shot of James Patrick Morgan and Margaret Belle Blackthorne. The photo had been taken in front of our little cottage in Salem. I adored it. My first ex-husband resembled a buck-toothed penguin, and I looked like a fringe-haired prom queen. So unlike the wry comedy team we'd imagined ourselves to be.

Reaching to click off my mother's antique lamp, I opted to text Morgan instead. "What's up?" I thumbed.

He lived in a condo in Portland these days and owned a vinyl records shop, JP Morgan Retro. That ironic business name still made me chuckle.

"Out w William," he texted back.

"Who the hell is William?"

"Blab latr k."

I considered typing "fuk u k" but deferred to my hatred of the asinine deletion of letters in texting's bastardized form of communication. Kind of like removing connective tissue in one's brain in order to think more efficiently. Avoiding the use of vowels and diphthongs got you to stupid about as fast as hacking away at your cerebral cortex.

My phone chimed as I turned off the light. One last message from Morgan: "Nighty night, old lady." An inside joke from our married days, one that managed to leave me feeling a speck less testy and cantankerous about the world.

6

MORNING, FEBRUARY 23

Louie was reluctant to set paw outside and take in his daily constitutional. I'd had to pry him from his dusty cat pillow and carry him to the damp landing and down the narrow steps, where he tracked gingerly through Dorie's small patch of heather. He marked his territory unnecessarily and yowled to go back upstairs.

To make amends after his chilly gambol in the elements, I pulled him onto my lap and we sat together in my mother's worn granny rocker. Patty Griffin sang in the background, her voice lovely, pure, tinged with melancholy. Finally I rose and gently placed Louie in his cat bed.

"Hope you understand, buddy. I've got a murderer to catch."

I turned up the heat a notch and set out extra food and water. Kneaded Louie's head and neck the way he liked and listened to Patty's "Florida" track play all the way through before heading out to work.

. . .

The small alcove where we ate lunch or took our breaks at an old card table would make a passable hub to gather and begin putting together our murder board. It was tucked in behind four tall filing cabinets and largely hidden from public view.

I tacked up a map of Grant County on our bulletin board, empty but for last year's calendar and a few fluorescent health and safety notices. We were also outfitted with a chalkboard on which some kid had years ago drawn a house with square windows and lollipop-shaped trees in the yard.

After erasing the kid drawing, I stood on the vinyl-padded seat of a folding chair and wrote the names of the Nodine twins, along with the date and approximate time of their deaths at the top. Beneath that heading, I cordoned off three sections and labeled the first one *Unknowns* and the second one *Lab Analysis*. I labeled the last section *Possibly Related Events* and underneath listed off *2/20 anonymous poacher tip line call* and *Newer red Ram 3500 truck registered to Frank Sylvester, Burns*. Under *Unknowns*, I wrote, *Address of murder victims*.

"Morning, Sarge."

"Christ, Holly. I didn't hear you come in."

He palmed his eyes vigorously and yawned. "Yeah, I'm training to be light on my feet."

"So you can sneak up on your boss?"

"No, that's just a side benefit. It's for Hank. Little dude wakes up at the slightest rustle."

The man looked like shit.

I stepped off the chair. "What are you doing here, anyway? It's Saturday. I'm covering this weekend, remember?"

He poured himself coffee and stood beside the card table. "I still need to tie up those loose ends."

Hands on my hips, I considered the categories I'd arbitrarily selected. "I know I should have you put together a spreadsheet for this, but I like seeing everything laid out in front of me. Plus I wanted to get it started before Taylor gets back. He'd have us spend two days just designing the damn thing."

"I hear you. But we could slap it all up on the wall *and* build a digital version. Because you do know you'll run out of room on that chalkboard, right?"

I nodded. "Do we need more categories?"

"Nah. It's a good start. Might make sense to come up with more later on."

I filled Hollis in on the theft report Duncan McKay had filed and told him about the cattle prod found in the Nodines' truck. He snared a piece of chalk and entered the info in the *Possibly Related Events* section, but only after writing, *Jess Haney Bennett / Guy Trudeau / cattle truck (Frank Sylvester Trucking).*

"That's the spirit." I retrieved the keys to my Tahoe. "I'll be at McKay's Feed and Tack. I want to find out more about those cattle prods. Back in a half an hour or so."

I passed Lynn Nodine's place on the way. Her driveway and the street next to it were lined with cars, including Dorie's old Toyota Corolla, one fender covered with rusted primer, same as always. Prayer circle convened, check. Food enough for an army, check. Front room gossip, check. Cycle of life, check and double-check.

An electronic cowbell announced my entrance through the front door of Duncan's store. The odor of leather and grass seed mingled with the tang of oats, hay, and dry pine. He kept the establishment at exactly the same temperature as the out of doors—just this side of hypothermic.

His nephew, Rain, stood at the service counter dressed in a

seriously overstuffed down coat; its fur-lined hood, snapped tightly under the chin, framed the kid's ruddy face.

"Good morning," I said. "Is your uncle available?"

The boy passed me a dark glance and bounded through the open door behind the service counter. Duncan emerged moments later carrying a laptop.

"Can I help you?"

Was this the same friendly guy who made a point of saying hello last night at the BM Lounge? "Did I interrupt something?"

"Sorry. I've been inventorying stock in the storeroom all morning."

"How's that going?"

"It's a pain. But I haven't found anything else missing yet." He nodded toward the shelved merchandise in the sales area. "I'll know more after going through the rest of it tomorrow."

"Well, I might have some news. First I'd like to know if there's a way to track those stolen cattle prods? Some kind of unique identifiers?"

He chucked at his chin whiskers the way he had last night. "I'm not sure."

"Because an unopened prod, same make and model as the two stolen from your store, has turned up. I suspect it's yours, but is there a way to figure that out?"

"We attach barcoded labels to all our hard goods, and those are registered in the inventory system." He held up his laptop. "If I had access to that prod you're talking about, I could scan it and tell whether it's from my store."

He was wearing the same plaid wool shirt—loden green and black—he'd worn the night before and three nights ago standing in my police station. His version of a feed and tack uniform, I guess.

"I don't have possession of the prod, but if I could get a photo of the barcode, would your system read it?"

"It should, as long as it's from my inventory. Let me test it. I'll take a shot of some other label and scan the photo. But even if that cattle prod is from my store, where's the other stuff?"

"Only the one prod so far."

"Does it have any connection with the killing of the Nodine brothers?"

"I'm not sure what it's connected to yet."

Seemingly over his earlier irritation, he grinned. "That's a pretty good cop answer."

"It's the only answer there is right now."

Again I noticed the color of his eyes, nearly a match for the deep green of his shirt.

I picked up a can of snuff from a boxful on the counter, laid it in front of him. "Here, take a picture of the barcode label. See if your system reads it?"

"I don't tag small items like chewing tobacco or those pepperoni sticks over there. We enter that kind of thing by hand."

"How about the carton of jerky you reported stolen from your storeroom?"

"Oh, that. Turns out it wasn't missing after all."

"Damn good thing I didn't broadcast a statewide stolen jerky alert."

He almost laughed at my lame-ass joke before removing a set of pig snout pliers from a nearby carousel and photographing the barcode. He swiped the face of his phone across the register's scanner. "Yep. It picked up our price and merchandise info."

"I'll work on getting a digital shot of that cattle prod label to you later today. It might be tomorrow, though."

"I'm closed on Sundays, remember? But I'll be right here checking the front shelves for possible missing inventory. Just call or give a knock."

Rain reappeared, head down, gaze directed toward the floor. He eased a box of new sheep shears around the counter and behind me toward the front of the store.

"Don't set out any more than five packages of those, son," Duncan said.

I lifted my police Stetson from the counter. "Have a good day."

"You too, Maggie."

Despite a cloudless sky of sapphire and the promise of spring on the horizon, Arctic air rolled off the Aldrich Mountains and howled through the canyons and basins along the river. A cold pall held our valley in its polar vise. Which made me all the more grateful Hollis had stoked up the heat and turned our office into a cozy den.

I hung my coat and hat on one of the hooks by the door. "What's new?"

"Lil went into labor before I could check out Frank Sylvester or Seth Flynn, the manager of Sylvester's trucking business in Burns."

"Okay." I suspected I might be in for one of Holly's long, convoluted discoveries.

"Turns out Sylvester is a bedridden quadriplegic who can no longer speak. He's been set up with home health care. Apparently his wife's dead, and he has no children."

"Where'd you learn all this?"

"Oh, some stellar sleuthing on my part." He tapped a pointer finger on the office phone at his desk. "I called Flynn at the trucking company. He used to drive for the old guy but started managing the business eighteen months ago after Sylvester drove his three-wheeler down a cliff at his place out in Wagontire. Broke his neck. He's not expected to live much longer."

"Jesus."

"And before you ask, an accountant in Portland manages the financial side of the business. Flynn is the operations guy, and he let me know the accountant watches the profit and loss margins like a hawk."

"This accountant have a name?"

"I called her office. She's closed on the weekend."

"What did you think of Seth Flynn?"

"He was pretty open and genuinely surprised when I asked about the red truck. Said he knew nothing about it, complained that his company vehicle was a bucket of bolts, not some fancy mega cab pickup. Anyway, I verified Sylvester's condition with Sergeant Brown in Burns. No matter what, Sylvester's not our murderer. And Flynn seems far removed from the murder victims, even if the Nodines were cousins with one of his truck drivers. Speaking of Jess Bennett, I called her too, and she seems pretty skittish."

"Oh yeah, she's got a twitchy edge to her all right."

"We'll get a chance to question her in person. She's dropping by our office on Monday after the Nodines' funeral."

"So I'd say you tied up all those loose ends. Go on home to your wife and baby."

"Will do, Sarge, as soon as I check on one more thing. I pulled the VIN for the Ram 3500 from your report. I want to figure out where it was sold, but mostly, who bought it. If Sylvester's been a bedridden quadriplegic for a year and a half, it wasn't him."

"You can be sure it wasn't one of the knucklehead brothers."

While Hollis rooted around on the internet, I put in my first call of the day to Bach.

"Good morning, Maggie. Let me put you on hold while I close my door."

I waited, listening to Hollis in the background, the undulating drum of his keyboard being typed at maximum velocity.

When Al came back on the line, I mentioned the reply email I'd sent to him last night regarding Duncan's theft report.

"There's got to be a connection between the stolen cattle prods and the one my people found," he said.

"Absolutely. McKay's Feed and Tack is the only place this side of the state selling those. I'd like to arrange to get a photo of the barcode label so I can verify that's where it's from."

"Wait a sec." He tapped away on his keyboard in Bend, pretty much in harmony with Holly at his desk in our office. "Okay, done. I've ordered the photos."

I passed along the information Hollis had put together this morning. "Right now he's working on identifying who actually bought that red truck."

"Send me the State Police ID numbers for you and Trooper Jones. I can get you temporary access to OSP's higher-level security networks. Once in, you should be able to locate whatever info you need."

It was possible Hollis had already bypassed any firewall and searched said networks, but I let that thought go.

"I plan to make a trip back your way on Monday or Tuesday," Al said.

"The funeral is Monday. Were you thinking of attending?" It was hard for me to imagine Al Bach fitting in at one of our country-bumpkin funeral affairs.

"No, but you should."

"I intend to." Despite my eternal dread of the stoic singing of hymns and touching of caskets at one more goddamn gravesite.

"Good, and you'll want to strap on your cop antennae. Cases like this, especially in a small town, murderers often make an appearance at a victim's service. Mostly to avoid drawing attention to themselves by their absence."

"I did wonder about that." For instance, would Kat McKay show up? Or Guy Trudeau?

Bach was also adamant we needed to find whatever tent, cabin, or hovel Dan and Joseph Nodine had been living in part-time, where they stashed their shit and parked their jeep. "Find the place and the vehicle."

"I've already gone on one wild goose chase after Jess Bennett told me they lived somewhere around Seneca."

"There's got to be someone who knows exactly what everybody living within a hundred square miles is up to or where they're hiding out."

"Probably a few folks, but in this case, that's likely Cecil Burney. He owns the only gas station in Seneca, so he's generally the one source of fuel for miles around. And now that I think of it, there was talk of bad blood between the Nodine brothers and him."

Cecil had supposedly been in a long-running spat with Dan and Joseph—over what, only the three of them had known. I hadn't actually seen him since my own father's country-bumpkin funeral. But I knew everything he'd been up to lately, thanks to Dorie's senior membership in the county rumor mill.

"Go interview him today, Sergeant."

"I'll head there right away. Don't know why I didn't think of talking to Cecil before."

"Don't beat yourself up too much. You're relying on your

instincts, and that's a good thing. Just don't let that get in the way of looking at obvious sources."

That kind of oversight couldn't happen again. What if I'd stopped by Cecil's gas station two days ago? He might have gladly told me where to find Dan and Joseph, and maybe I could've gotten to them before the killer. On the other hand, Cecil had always been an alcoholic dickwad, someone who disliked the authorities more than anybody he might've had a vendetta against. A person like that never willingly told a cop a thing.

"Sergeant. Are you still on the line?" Bach asked.

"Yeah. Just mulling over some what-ifs."

"Well, stop that right now. The chance of you preventing these murders was next to nil."

"I'll call you this evening, report back on whatever I get from Burney," I said.

"Use my cell number. Oh, one more thing. The murder weapon. Ballistics folks ID'd it as a Kel-Tec PF-9."

Ah, cheap. And deadly.

I added the automatic pistol details in the *Lab Analysis* section of our murder board and wrote, "Who killed the dog with a shotgun?" under *Unknowns*.

I collected my keys. "I'll be back out in Seneca talking with Cecil Burney."

"Who's that?" Hollis asked.

"The crotchety drunk who's owned the Seneca gas station since forever."

"Oh yeah. I've had the pleasure of speaking with Mr. Burney a few times. He's a big, big fan of the police. Black officers in particular."

"He's a peach all right."

"I plan on going home to Lil and Hank after I finish my report. But you won't like what I've discovered so far. Records show Frank Sylvester purchased that Ram 3500."

"How's that possible in his condition?"

"I don't know how Mr. Sylvester bought it, and I don't know how the Nodines ended up with it."

"Maybe this will help. Bach is arranging our access to higher-level security networks."

He turned toward me. "Well, Maggie, I already have access to those higher-level security networks."

Just as I had suspected. "To make me feel better, when he sends us clearance, repeat your search. Officially, this time."

He nodded and flashed a guileless grin. "Sure."

I retrieved my coat and hat. "Give Lil and Hank my love."

"I'm supposed to invite you over."

"Sounds good. And go home."

He fake-saluted me. "Yes, Sarge." I turned off all the office lights, stepped outside, and shut the door. I could hear Holly chuckling.

I found no early signs of spring driving up Canyon Mountain and into Bear Valley, which sat at a much higher elevation than John Day and received, on average, more than three hundred and fifty feet of snow a year. A nasty tempest buffeted my Tahoe, drubbing the sidewalls and forcing the vehicle to buck along ice-sheen pavement. Still, navigating through wild weather didn't keep Frank Sylvester's supposed purchase of the Ram 3500 from nagging at me.

Somebody else had to be acting on Sylvester's behalf. Hollis said Seth Flynn was surprised about the new diesel truck, and I doubted the accountant was authorized to spend 50K on a fancy rig. But maybe a court-appointed guardian could—technically, anyway. For the time being, though, the only choice I had was to leave the conundrum sitting in the back of my brain.

The day had pulled past noon by the time I parked next to the Cecil Burney's gas station. His front office stunk of engine oil, vomit, and something else god-awful. I found him sitting next to an ice chest in the corner, fiddling with paperwork, smoking a hand-rolled cigarette, and drinking Milwaukee's Best. His eyes looked to have reached their serious state of glassy much earlier in the day.

"Afternoon," I said, standing at his cash counter.

He barely looked up. "Remind me who you are?"

"Sergeant Margaret Blackthorne. State Police."

"Thought you was some kinda teacher in the Willamette Valley somewhere."

He drew more liquid from his beer can, spilling some on his oil-stained shirt, a loud-colored Pendleton knock-off. Like Farley Nodine, he appeared to hardly bother with the state of his appearance or the thick white hairs protruding from his nostrils and ears and God knew where else.

"I taught elementary school years ago. I've been an officer stationed in Grant County for a while, though." Something I was sure he already knew.

"Well, teaching's an honorable thing, you ask me."

Cecil had probably disliked every educator he'd ever come across almost as vehemently as he hated the police. He was more of a vigilante libertarian sort of crackpot. A dime a dozen out here in Dogpatch west, where you trusted no one's authority and only called the law if the other guy had more weaponry than you and was aiming to harm you. Or something you cared about, such as your animals or your pickup tires. Outlaw pragmatism at its most virtuous.

"I've got a couple of questions," I said.

"Too bad about your dad. He was one of the good ones."

It was true, time virtually stood still in my county, but Tate Blackthorne had been dead more than twenty years.

"You happen to see Dan or Joseph Nodine the last couple of weeks? Maybe they bought gas, got a tire changed?"

"No, but I did hear somebody killed 'em." He spat out a tuft of tobacco. "I would sooner've sold gas to the devil himself."

"Maybe you saw them drive by your station?"

"No. And I'd tell you if I had. You can trust that."

I knew it wasn't smart to trust Cecil for anything. "What exactly was your beef with the Nodines?"

He pulled down the rest of his Milwaukee's Best. Belched loudly, the odor of which entered the chamber of horrid smells nearly undetected. "You can't live on the wind without paying your debts, is all I'm saying. There's bridges you can't burn behind you and still live a full and happy life."

"Explain what you mean by that."

"Them boys probably crossed too many enemies the wrong way. Maybe some friends, too."

"Is there something you know? Something you're afraid to tell me?"

"I ain't afraid of shit, and what I know is this—nobody gives a rat's ass they're dead. Except maybe their poor mama."

"I heard they were living somewhere around Seneca. I thought you might know where."

"Like I said, they was living on the wind."

It might have been his momentary consideration of Lynn Nodine, but he had backed off the harsh tone some. Cecil's way of showing sympathy, no doubt.

"But I got no idea who murdered 'em."

"Seems to me you pretty much have a finger on all the comings and goings around here, what with your gas station

sitting along one of the two real highways in this county. Plus
my daddy used to count on you for all the gossip. All the news
too, like who was cheating on their woman, who was robbing
who blind."

Cecil lifted another Milwaukee's Best out of the cooler,
popped it open. "I don't like cops."

Who knew?

"But my guess is old Tate done right by you. Taught you
justice weren't just for rich assholes."

As a matter of fact, that and shooting a hunting rifle might
be the only things my father ever taught me.

Cecil took a long, loud swig. "Ain't seen nothing directly,
but talk to all them big fancy cattle ranchers. I fucking don't
like them pricks either."

"Like Guy Trudeau, you mean?"

"That old bastard? He's broke as shit. Jesus, what kind of
police are you? Don't you know one of his kids stole all his
money and lit out somewhere years ago?"

He sucked down more of his fresh one. "No, I mean them
pure as the virgin Mary's twat, tree-hugging, organical
bastards who keep buying up land from ruined ranchers and
making bookoo selling their so-called natural beef."

A customer pulled up outside, and Cecil signaled it was
time for me to hustle out of his gas station. "We're done
talking now."

"No, we're not. I think you're lying about not seeing the
Nodine boys around. They were staying out here somewhere,
driving an expensive diesel hog, and yours is the only place
around to fuel up."

"You'll have to prove I'm lying."

"I'm prepared to arrest your ass right now. Withholding
evidence. Obstructing a homicide investigation. You name it."

"Fucking bitch."

From my duty belt, I pulled up my state-issued handcuffs, a pair previously worn by nearly every drunk in the county. Now it was Cecil's turn.

"I am indeed a fucking bitch. And I've been called worse than that, old man, so turn your ass around and put your hands behind you."

He looked toward the customer waiting outside. "Them boys never come here for fuel or nothing else. They wouldn't dare."

"What was your problem with Dan and Joseph?"

"I ain't never talking about that." He brought his wrists together, lifted them forward. "And you can haul me to jail right now for all I care, but I ain't never gonna say what that was about. Now they're dead, maybe I can get on with things."

"Where were you between five forty-five and six fifteen p.m. last Thursday?"

"Funny you should ask. I was at my first AA meeting. Methodist Church in John Day."

Given his current inebriation, he'd apparently skipped one or two of the twelve steps in the interim. Or he was just a deceitful motherfucker.

"I'll have to verify that." I returned the handcuffs to my duty belt.

"Go ahead. Verify away. You can start with Lynn Nodine. She sat beside me. We even went for coffee after."

"I'll ask once more. Did you know where her sons were staying?

"Not exactly. Just knew it was supposed to be up Logan Valley Highway somewhere. That's all I can tell you, I swear it." He bounded to the door.

"I might have more questions for you."

But Cecil had left the building.

7

As I headed east on Logan Valley Highway, heavy snow fell across the miles of meadows and stands of dark juniper. Taking Cecil Burney at his word on anything was troublesome, but I had no other clue where Dan and Joseph's place was. I chewed over Cecil's other claim that Guy Trudeau had lost all his money. That was news to me, but chatting up area cattle ranchers was already on my list, including old man Trudeau, broke or not. There had to be a link between those murdered men and somebody's cattle.

Driving slowly, I kept a look out for any sign of the Nodines' old army jeep and their encampment. After a plodding thirty minutes, I came to the junction with Starr Ridge Road. East of there, a mere twenty-five feet from Logan Valley Highway, stood Parish Cabin campground. Gated and closed for winter, that hadn't stopped someone from busting the lock and steering a vehicle through the entrance.

I parked the Tahoe and followed tire tracks into the deserted campground. Several grated fire pits had been placed here and there in the shade of thick Ponderosas. The tree canopy left the ground drier and the air colder. My wool peacoat and Thinsulate gloves barely kept me warm.

At the far most fire pit, an aged pickup camper sat directly on the ground. Next to it stood the Nodine brothers' brown-camouflage army jeep.

I contacted Whitey Kern's towing company and then cracked open the door to the unlocked camper. A down sleeping bag lay unfurled on a foam pad in the compartment built to fit over the cab of a truck. A second down bag had been rolled, tied, and placed on the small dining table. Next to it sat a Hot Shot DXR cattle prod still in its packaging.

The cupboards in the kitchenette were filled with boxes, bags, and cans of the usual poor man's fare. A green Coleman two-burner propane stove sat beside the small sink, along with a lighter, a pot, and a cast iron frying pan. Shirts hung inside a dinky closet set off to the side. A pair of jeans and some men's underwear lay folded on a shelf above the clothes rod. A full duffel bag, likely the one Ariel Pritchett had mentioned Joseph carried with him, sat beside the camper's small couch.

Entering the deeply chilled space, I inhaled the scent of mud and mold, but as I closed in on a small cooler sitting on the kitchenette counter, an oppressive scent of rot bloomed forth. I lifted the lid apprehensively, discovering a miasma of decomposing produce and the heart and liver of a game animal, no doubt the deer they'd poached on Wednesday, the day before they were murdered.

I clicked shut the cooler and opened the camper door, letting in the flash-frozen air. Hurriedly, I snapped photos of the cramped interior, along with shots of the sleeping bags, clothing, kitchen items, duffel bag, and the cattle prod and its barcode label.

I removed a pair of latex gloves from my pack and traded

out the Thinsulate ones. The duffel bag held a cache of dirty laundry, a belt, a pair of sneakers, and two books: a beautifully illustrated hardback copy of the *Rubaiyat of Omar Khayyam* and a worn paperback, Raymond Chandler's *The Long Goodbye*.

"What the fuck?" I'd never known either brother to be particularly bookish.

A photo slid from within the pages of Persian poetry. Lynn Nodine and her twins. Someone had written "Danny & Joey age six" in the white border. The boys were all smiles, and there was no trace of mischief, let alone criminality. Lynn's hand-printed name filled the space on the first page labeled *This book belongs to.*

I photographed the contents of the duffel bag, returned them, and closed the drawstring. Next I snapped shots of the vehicle and camper, gathered several large evidence bags from my Tahoe, and packed up the Nodines' sparse assortment of belongings.

Outside, I checked the jeep's glove box, where I found some gas receipts and seventy-eight bucks. I stashed the cash and the keys hanging from the ignition with the rest of Dan and Joseph's paltry possessions.

Waiting in the Tahoe's warm cab for Whitey Kern and his wrecker to arrive, my thoughts wandered to the photo of Lynn Nodine and her twins tucked inside the *Rubaiyat of Omar Khayyam*. In no mood to linger over their lives or mine all those years ago, I tuned in Band of Horses, turned up the volume, and pushed the image of Lynn and her sons from my mind.

.   .   .

"Hard to believe those boys could get themselves so low as to hide out here," Whitey said after we loaded up the camper and jeep.

I nodded. "I know you gave them a tow recently. Plus you said you hadn't seen them driving that red Ram 3500. But is there anything out of place you remember about either one?"

"I always try to mind my own business, Maggie. You know that."

"So is that a no? You never saw anything out of place?"

"Off the top, nothing comes to mind, but let me think on it. I probably spend more time in these middle-of-nowhere places than even you do."

"That's why I'm pressing you on this, Whitey."

He tipped his hat and climbed in the cab of his wrecker.

As I eased back onto the highway, the tires of my Chevy Tahoe spun over the snow-packed pavement before bumping back into four-wheel drive. I motored steadily back through Seneca and past Cecil's gas station. After a mile or so traveling north on 395, I passed Duncan McKay trudging along the opposite side of the highway, a nearly imperceptible limp in his gait. He carried a gas can, the universal sign of distress. I slowed, turned my rig around, and pulled up in the roadway beside him.

I adjusted the volume on Neko Case's "Margaret vs. Pauline" and lowered my window. "Out of gas, huh?"

"Yeah. My phone's dead too."

"Your luck's gone south lately."

"You got that right."

"How about I give you a lift back to your vehicle and siphon off enough fuel from the State of Oregon to get you on the road?"

"If you've got time, Maggie, that'd be great." He aimed a thumb behind him. "I'm parked up the way, about five miles down Harden Road. I'll pay for the gas, of course."

"A little free gas for stranded motorists is the kind of thing your tax dollars get you." In my opinion, anyway.

Duncan stashed the can in the back and climbed in front. He was too tall to sit comfortably in the passenger seat, yet he managed to adjust his legs and size-humungous work boots to fit available quarters.

After a mile or so of listening to the grind of rock salt and snow tires, he reached for the volume knob. "Mind if I turn up Neko? That voice is something." I acknowledged the sentiment, and he folded himself into the doorframe, rested his head on the seat back, and closed his eyes.

We passed a copse of quaking aspen and wild willow on the fringe of a narrow field just east of the roadway. An abandoned outbuilding tilted precariously in the wind. Mule deer and blood-red Herefords foraged in the distance. Otherwise there was nothing but rock and weather as far as the eye could see.

Duncan snorted awake. "Oh hell. Was I snoring?"

"A little."

He yawned and cleared the sleep from his eyes using his immense hands. How had any bull ever managed to buck under his grip on the rope?

"Were you making a delivery?"

"I was trying to." Duncan retrieved a cloth handkerchief from his pocket and blew his nose. "I forgot to check the damn gas tank before taking off. Total shit for brains sometimes. God. Sorry. I cuss too much."

Maggie Blackthorne, the near forty-year-old woman, barely contained her laughter hearing his cuss-word apology. But being Sergeant Blackthorne, I gauged the snow falling on the windshield. My half-assed wipers couldn't keep up when the flakes turned damp and dense. Maybe the Tahoe couldn't either. If I'd been driving the Nodines' one-ton instead, I'd have plowed on through like snow was dust.

We drove on, Lucinda Williams singing a raw ballad in the background, until we reached an elaborate gate blocking the entrance to a newly paved driveway. Bear Valley Cattle Company, lettered in wrought iron, formed an arc between two tall gateposts of lodgepole pine. A small wooden sign hanging beneath the cattle company emblem proclaimed, *Jesus Loves Grass-Fed Beef*.

"This is the place," Duncan said.

Automatic gate locks, security cameras, No Trespassing signs, and electric fencing created an impenetrable barrier around the place. But there was no phone number or call button to alert anyone visitors had arrived.

"Since when has there been a Bear Valley Cattle Company, and how were you supposed to make your delivery?" I asked.

"Not sure."

I parked alongside his delivery truck sitting on the shoulder near the ranch entrance, retrieved my siphon hose, and inserted it in the gas tank of my SUV.

"Here, I'll do that." Duncan sucked on the tip of the hose, yanked it out of his mouth, and let the liquid flow into the tank of his vehicle. Coughing, he spat gasoline residue across the snow-covered ground and reached inside his truck for a bottle of water.

"They're not particularly welcoming, are they?" I said, indicating the cattle company.

He drank a long swig of water. "I was damn disappointed earlier when I couldn't roust anybody on the other side of the gate."

I peeked up the drive. Three small double-wide mobile

homes were partially visible from where we stood, but it was hard to tell if anyone was within earshot. The snow had taken a short break, and waning sunlight sifted through the treetops, casting long, angular shadows. We waited in silence, an agitated breeze rattling through a stand of larch, until the delivery truck registered a quarter tank.

"Looks like you're all set."

"Thanks again, Maggie. Can I buy you coffee sometime?"

"I'd like that." I twisted my gas cap shut. "By the way, I found another cattle prod, same brand. And I've ordered a digital shot of the other one. I should have photos of the two barcodes to you later today."

"That was quick."

A black Prius in tire chains pulled up to the gate. I hadn't seen the driver or the teenage passenger around before.

"Is this the owner?"

Duncan nodded. "Asa Larkin and his kid."

"Would you mind introducing me?"

Larkin got out of his Prius and walked toward us. I tried to read the expression in the stranger's muddy blue eyes and on his long, chiseled face, a look of bemusement, indifference and hostility all in one.

"I thought you were delivering tomorrow." His lips were small, flat, and bloodless.

Duncan removed a slim rectangle of paper from his back pocket and unfolded it. "Twelve thirty today, according to the invoice. Plus we don't make deliveries on Sunday."

Larkin looked at his watch. "It's almost two. There was no need to stick around. Or call the police," he said, turning his attention to me.

"This is Sergeant Blackthorne. I ran out of gas and couldn't raise anybody at your place, so I walked to the highway. She gave me a lift back and some fuel."

"Mr. Larkin, is it?" I said.

He tilted his head slightly and blinked. "Yes."

We shook hands.

"The rumor mill must be out of commission. I didn't know new people had bought the Harden ranch," I said.

"We've been out here less than a year. Just me, my son, and my three hired men."

"You'll probably see me or one of the other troopers out and about patrolling on occasion."

That remark didn't register one way or another, so I decided to dig for info about this relatively new transplant to my county. "Move here from out of state?"

"No. Lake Oswego," Larkin said.

"You raised beef in Lake-O?"

"I practiced law."

The man didn't seem like an attorney any more than he seemed like a cattle rancher, but somehow that reminded me why I'd traveled to this part of the county in the first place. "Out of curiosity, did you know Dan or Joseph Nodine?"

A hint of color flushed across his pale cheeks. He passed a furtive glance toward his son. "The brothers found murdered a couple of days ago?"

"That's right."

"I passed that red pickup on the highway a few times, the one mentioned in the news. But that's all."

I sensed it was a lie, or at least a distorted version of the truth. No wonder he'd quit his law practice: the man had no poker face.

We all turned at the rough sound of an older green-apple Ford Bronco pulling in behind Larkin's Prius.

"I'd best open the gate so my men can get through and you can make your delivery, Mr. McKay."

"It's McKay. Last part rhymes with *sky*, not *hay*."

I liked Duncan's little speech on pronouncing his surname the way his Scottish relatives and most locals did.

"Good to meet you, Mr. Larkin," I called out as he walked back toward the Prius.

He climbed behind the wheel, hit the remote to open the gate, and drove onto his property, the Bronco following behind.

I caught a glimpse of the hefty driver and his hefty passenger bobbing in the rickety bench seat of the Bronco. Also noted the *Jesus Loves Grass-Fed Beef* sticker displayed on the back bumper.

"Don't go scaring off my paying customers, will you, Maggie?" Duncan said and laughed.

"I wouldn't think a man living in a fortress could scare that easily," I said, opening the door to my Tahoe. "I'll be expecting that cup of coffee."

A blizzard had kicked up, turning the gray sky a dark purple. Out of the curtain of weather, Guy Trudeau's ancient Torino drifted into view, traveling the opposite direction. Having dilly-dallied too long outside Asa Larkin's so-called cattle company, I ignored the decrepit heap's burned-out headlight.

Trudeau passed on my left, probably headed back to Big T, his ranch along the Silvies River. In the rearview, I watched the white sedan flip a cookie and ride the embankment. In slow motion, the old man managed to right the Ford's trajectory. His brake lights faded, disappeared.

My trip back to John Day had largely been slow going and utterly headache inducing. I stowed the Nodines' personal effects in the evidence locker and hunted for a couple of ibuprofen in my desk drawer. Hollis wasn't around, but I could see he'd added a few details to our murder board and left a sticky note on my desk phone. His message was categorically cryptic: *J.T.!!!*

When I put in my second call of the day to Al, he was distracted and took little more than a half-hearted interest in the new evidence. "Okay, Sergeant. Send out a report as soon as possible," he said and hung up.

Bach's friendlier attitude seemed to have vanished, but I hadn't the bandwidth to sit in my chilly, eerily quiet office wondering why. I typed up the report and sent it off to him, along with the photos I'd taken at the Nodines' encampment. I forwarded the shot of the cattle prod barcode his people had emailed me earlier in the afternoon to my phone and called it a day.

Louie was curled up next to his food and water dishes when I arrived. I replenished both, opened the freezer, and considered my instant dinner options—lasagna or three-cheese marinara. It was an easy hike to the Cave Inn for a salty pizza and a sugary, near-flat cola on chipped ice, but that struck me as no tastier and even less nutritious. I decided to wait on supper and hope for divine inspiration or possibly one of the delicious care packages Dorie regularly brought upstairs.

After a quick shower, I tied back my hair and pulled on some jeans, my ancient Jack Purcells, and a comfy sweater. I called McKay's Feed and Tack. Intelligently, Duncan had gone home for the night, so I dialed his cell phone.

"Hello?" Willie Nelson played in the background.

"Duncan. It's Maggie Blackthorne. Sorry to bother you at home."

He lowered the volume on Willie. "No big deal. I was just making dinner."

"This really could've waited, but I have shots of the

barcodes from the cattle prods. I'll text those to you so you can scan them through your inventory system tomorrow."

"No fence cutters or salt licks yet?"

"Nah."

"I'll check out those barcodes first thing in the morning and let you know."

"Talk to you then."

"Hey, just had a thought. I owe you a cup of coffee, but why don't you join me for dinner instead? We can catch up, whatever. Unless it's inappropriate or something?"

I never considered a meal with a citizen a problem, but I probably should've fibbed and told him I'd already eaten. Or that tomorrow would be another long day, and I'd have to take a rain check. I didn't, though.

"Sure, I guess. Sounds terrific."

Christ. Why had I said that last bit? Nothing more pathetic than squeaking like a fifteen-year-old accepting an invitation to her first date. Except maybe sounding like a lonely near-forty-year-old, two-time divorcée looking for a little nookie.

Since our little village had been spared the brunt of the mountain blizzard, I hopped in the Jetta I'd purchased more than a decade ago. I drove south through a narrow basalt gorge where Highway 395 ran parallel to the winding path of Canyon Creek, swollen now with snowmelt.

Duncan lived in a not-so-promising development project called Three Flags Landing. The whole affair comprised a tiny cul-de-sac with three modest houses plunked down on the edge of desolation. It might easily have been named Tumbleweed Estates or Juniper Junction. Except for the fact the development sat just off of 395, also known in this part of the state as Three Flags Highway, running as it did through Washington, Oregon, and California.

Duncan's house was the one occupied home on the cul-de-sac and the smallest of the three structures. In the beam of my headlights, I made out the plain two-story cottage, its dark green siding and white trim. A row of roses had been planted on one side of his nice little front porch. He'd even put in grass, but if it'd been up to me, the house would have faced east toward Strawberry Mountain, not smack into the other two homes.

He opened his door, oven mitt in hand, and waved me in, along with the frigid night air. It was a tidy, plain space, and I could see he shared my notion that Strawberry Mountain should be the focal point. Barely furnished, except for a dramatic wooden table set for two, the open great room was oriented toward the east-facing garden doors at the back of the house.

"Bet that's a nice view in daylight," I said.

"The prettiest mountain around."

"Dinner smells delicious."

"Baked trout with dill sauce."

God, what planet did this bull rider hail from? The way I remembered it, folks just rolled the damn fish in some flour and fried it up. But if Morgan had been here, he would have reminded me to be more positive in my thinking. He'd be right, of course. Duncan could've been shit-faced at the Rifleman Club, drinking Sonny Brook, and snacking on pickled eggs.

He lifted a bottle of wine from the counter. "Would you like a glass?"

"No, thanks, I'll pass for now." Willie Nelson still played in the background. "Is that his *Teatro* album?"

"Yeah. Nothing corny about that music, is there."

He invited me to take a seat at the table. I sat in one of the mission-style chairs, a furniture design I recognized from years of antique shopping in the Willamette Valley with Morgan.

"Nice place."

"Thanks. I like being out here. I'm close enough to the feed store, close enough to my folks' place in Silvies Valley, but not too close to either." He stood at the marble counter in the cooking area tossing salad in a myrtle wood bowl. He was graceful for a tall man, but that great shag of hair all but covered his lovely eyes.

I poured myself some ice water from a cut glass pitcher. "Have you gotten used to living in eastern Oregon again after being gone for so long?"

"Most of the time. I definitely don't miss Texas, but I'd give an eyeball for good barbecue." He added a paprika garnish to the trout. "And you? You like being back in Grant County?"

"I don't know yet. I've got no family here to speak of, and my oldest friend lives in Portland. Which might as well be Texas."

He stopped and tasted his wine, set the goblet back on the counter. "I was surprised when I heard you'd become a cop."

"I was surprised when I heard you'd stopped riding bulls."

"Well, that was bound to come to an end. I got beat up bad a couple of times."

Duncan placed the myrtle wood bowl and a ceramic casserole dish on the table and took his seat. He served the trout along with the chopped kale and hazelnut salad, laying the food out prettily on each plate.

He arranged a napkin on his lap and watched me take my first bite. "How is it?"

"Good. Really good."

The fish was tasty, but lately I'd had little to compare it to, save my frozen entrées and the cheeseburger I'd ordered the other night at the Blue Mountain Lounge. For sure, his meal could pass for fancy dining. I was mindful not to wolf it down and to hold my utensils the way Mrs. Simmons taught us during her 4-H class on the domestic arts.

"The dill sauce is a nice touch," I said.

"Glad you like it. Are you ready for some wine now?"

"Sure, I'll try a glass."

Duncan poured another goblet half full of wine tinged the color of dry grass, so cold it made the glass sweat. I sipped and winced at the fermented mix of sweet and tart.

He laughed and pushed a plate of bread my way. "Here. Cleanse your palate, then try another taste."

I did as he suggested, knowing full well nothing would ever persuade me the wine bottle's claim of *clean, crisp, Granny Smith character* was remotely accurate.

He smiled to himself and mixed some of the dill sauce with the kale. Pausing before tasting the green-on-green concoction, he peered across the table. "You've got a tougher job than I imagined."

"Most of the time all I do is scout around for speeding drivers, drunks, and scofflaws."

"But murder is something else altogether."

Master of the obvious, this man. Possibly an old flirt as well.

"It's unusual, I'd agree." I nibbled on the salad, picking out the hazelnuts on the sly.

"I suppose it's too early to know what happened out there."

"I really can't talk about the investigation." Nor did I want to.

We finished eating our fish and salad. A different album, this time Eva Cassidy, filled in the quiet.

"I do need to tell you something, Maggie," he said and

quaffed more wine. "I figured out my nephew, Rain, pilfered the jerky from my storeroom."

I guess that explained the dinner invitation.

"How about the other items?"

Duncan shook his head. "He was adamant he didn't."

"You need to establish whether those cattle prods are yours ASAP. Otherwise, I've got to question him about it."

"I thought that might be the case."

I poured myself some more water. The cut glass surface of the pitcher was an elegance I could get used to. "Why didn't you take all of this to local law enforcement in the first place?"

"You're the only real police we have around here. Everyone knows that."

I considered defending the sheriff's office and town police, but I figured Duncan suspected they would've hauled his nephew off to MacLaren Youth Facility before bothering to interview him about stealing from his uncle's store. I was also sure he probably had that just about right.

We finished our supper and talked about the weather, our similar taste in music, and hiking Strawberry Mountain next summer. We railed about our small-town high school years and the fact we'd each wanted to leave the place for good.

"I swore I'd never move back," he said.

"God, me too." Suppressing a yawn, I checked my watch. "Thanks for dinner, Duncan. It was tasty, more than tasty. But I should go home."

I stood and carried our plates to the sink.

"Maggie. I'd like it if you stayed awhile longer."

I was a fucking fool, that's all there was to it. I sat back down and handed him my mostly full wine goblet. "Could I get a gin and tonic? I can't stand this crap."

He laughed again. "What's your preference?"

"Tanqueray, if you've got it." Otherwise, brand didn't matter much. Gin was always my friend. Also my enemy.

"Ah. You like your gin London and dry."

Sure, whatever.

He rose, poured my drink over ice, and placed it on the table. "Drink slow. I wouldn't want you to get pulled over on your way home."

"How about a coffee chaser, too," I said.

He returned to the kitchen and turned on the one-cup Keurig next to the sink. Meanwhile, I texted him the photos of the barcode labels.

Duncan pulled his phone out of his pocket. "Thanks. I'll check these out first thing."

He placed a coaster and the mug of coffee beside my gin drink, took his seat, and poured himself more wine.

"There's something I need to warn you about," he said.

"Having to do with?"

"Dorie Phillips."

"Dorie? She was my mother's best friend, and she's my landlord."

"You live at the Castle Thrift Store?"

"In the apartment on the second floor."

"I had no idea."

"You don't follow the county breaking news alerts, I take it."

"No. That's how I keep my sanity." His deep voice had a lilt I hadn't noticed earlier. Probably the wine.

"So what's the warning about Dorie?"

"She was in the store last week. Told me you and I should get together."

I hadn't realized just how sly that ol' gal could be. Suggesting I think about a couple of dipshit romantic prospects but not mentioning Duncan.

He tipped his wine goblet toward my gin and tonic, and we clinked glasses. "Anything's possible."

"Not until I know your politics," I said.

"You care about that?"

"Damned straight I care."

"Conservative liberal. Does that work?"

"We'll see."

"You're tough."

"No, picky. I've been married and divorced twice."

"Twice, huh?"

"Yep. And some lessons have been learned."

"I hear you."

"I was happy the first time, until he wasn't. I took up with an ass the second time."

"And now here you are, sitting with me."

"But I really should be going."

He placed his goblet on the table. "I was in a grouchy mood when you first dropped by the Feed and Tack this morning. Then this afternoon when it was you who pulled over and offered me a ride, that made my heart jump."

"So much so you fell fast asleep, I noticed."

He smiled. I liked his smile, I realized.

"You're a lovely woman, Maggie."

Raw heat moved from my chest to my face. My entire body was flush, sweltering. Absentmindedly, I lifted a cube of ice and placed it on my florid neck. "I think I've had enough gin."

He brought an enormous hand to my cheek. "You do feel a little warm."

Slowly, his other hand moved to my opposite cheek. Then he took my hands, stood, and helped me up from my chair. We kissed.

"I have to say, you're the only woman in the county I'd

want to kiss. Or have dinner with. And it's not just because I get a little lonely sometimes."

"Not to mention a little horny."

"Is that a bad thing?"

I was certain it wasn't a bad thing at all, but desire had played tricks on me before. "There's a lot you don't know about me, Duncan. What I've done, what I've been through."

Duncan pulled me closer. "Here's what I do know. You're smart. Pretty. A good cop."

I brought my lips to his.

"And a good kisser," he said.

"And profane. Believe me."

"I traveled the rodeo circuit, remember?"

"I put all that cowboy shit talk to shame."

We kissed again and explored one another, carefully at first, then in a rush of roaming hands, his under my sweater, mine unbuttoning his jeans.

"Come upstairs with me," he said.

"Only if there's a bed up there."

"You're all about the comedy, aren't you?"

I pressed my body against his. "Not always."

Later, when Duncan walked me out to the Jetta, we stood in a long embrace, ignoring the cold, harsh dust-up of wind.

"Thanks again for dinner," I said.

"You're welcome to spend the night, you know."

I kissed him and climbed inside the car. While the Jetta warmed, I watched him amble back to his porch and close the front door. I regarded the small stand of Ponderosa at the edge of Three Flags Landing, the dark backdrop of Strawberry Mountain, and his little house.

"What the hell just happened?" I whispered beneath the loud flutter of engine noise.

Near midnight, I rooted around for my journal. I found it layered with a scrim of winter dust on a shelf next to the rocker, carried it to my bed, and opened to the most recent entry. February 4th, nearly three weeks ago: "Monday night. New moon, new mantra: I don't do desperate anymore."

"Remember that, Blackthorne," I said and nudged Louie from my side of our bed and back to his pillow at my feet.

Wind carried the toll and echo of church bells. Also the memory of Alligator Paulus, age sixteen. The two of us had lived for our Sunday morning ventures dabbling in religion. LDS, Nazarene, Assembly of God, First Baptist, St. Elizabeth of Hungary, Presbyterian, Episcopal, First Christian, and Methodist, we frequented whatever congregation laid hold of our fickle interests. We joined youth groups and went to Bible camps for God instruction, also to practice French kissing, making out, and feeling up. Church boys didn't care if we were smart, homely, or stupid, so long as we were willing to sneak from our cabin on dark summer nights and meet in the woods for a petting fest.

Alligator was a true friend. Beautiful, wild girl whose actual name was Alyssa, shortened to Ali, then lengthened to Alligator somewhere along the way. She died when her lawyer uncle crashed his piper Cherokee on Mt. Lassen. I got the news while away at college, and for a long stretch, her dying wrecked me. Wrecked me as much as Zoey's suicide or Tate's drunken fadeout. Like I'd plunged down on that ancient volcano with her, stranded and searching for a trail off the mountain, one that didn't double-back on itself.

I caught the deep chime of Church of the Nazarene's last peal of the morning. Dorie had ceased inviting me to join her there on Sundays. Although, I'd almost taken her up on it a couple of times just for the panorama outside the arched windows: long tabletop buttes and the John Day River slicing through a silver plain of alfalfa, cottonwood, and poplar. Not Duncan McKay's view of Strawberry Mountain, but a beautiful sight just the same.

I showered and put on a clean uniform. My breasts had been especially ripe and tender under the hot spray of water, a reminder of last night's surprise ending. A distraction I struggled to set aside. I was already working above my pay grade, and I knew I needed to find the killer if I wanted to keep the demons of self-doubt at bay. Preoccupation with an old grief and a new lover just had to wait.

Hollis and I planned to meet for breakfast, a routine we'd put on hold since the birth of his baby. First, though, I wanted to check in on Lynn Nodine. Dorie had spent the last few nights there, probably making a good-hearted pest of herself, if I knew both my landlord and Mrs. Nodine as well as I thought. But today Dorie would be at Sunday services, a habit I suspected Lynn had never adopted. All the other church ladies would be observing too, so I'd be free to speak to Lynn alone.

Her vintage orange VW bus was parked in front of her house. Farley Nodine was bent over the rear engine compartment, an oil rag over his shoulder and a toolbox on the ground beside him.

"Morning, Farley. How're you doing?"

He didn't bother looking up from his mechanic work. "'Bout like you'd expect, I guess."

"How's Lynn?"

"Same. 'Bout like you'd expect."

"She inside?"

"Yep. And glad to be rid of all them women."

Leaving Farley to his spark plugs or whatever, I tapped on Lynn's door.

She rose from where she sat in the front room and opened it. "Come in, Margaret. I've kind of been expecting you."

Inside, I was greeted by the dense, pleasant aroma of baked goods and coffee. Lynn offered some of both.

"No, thank you," I said as we sat. "How are you holding up?"

"I'm pretty numb." Which registered in the tone of her flat, hoarse voice. "After everything I've been through with those two, I should've figured it would end this way. But I wouldn't in a million years have thought they'd get themselves shot to death."

"No, neither would I."

"Can you tell me anything yet?" she asked.

I hesitated. "Can't really say much about the investigation. But it's my highest priority right now."

"Thank you, Margaret. You were always a good girl, a hard worker."

Lynn smiled. It had been years since I'd seen that. "I understand you found that old jeep. Since the title's in my name, State Police from Bend called about fifteen minutes ago, talked to me about filling out a claim form."

"I can get the form for you. Also, some of their belongings were at the same location out off of Logan Valley Highway. I'll drop by with the claim form for that too."

She nodded and sipped her coffee. "Logan Valley? Why out there?"

"I don't have an answer for that yet."

Cecil Burney had described the Nodine brothers as living on the wind. Maybe Logan Valley was nothing more than the place winter storms had blown them.

"Can you tell me what led up to the rift between you and your sons?"

She paused, hands trembling slightly. "All their thieving and lying, still they never disrespected me. Just left me ashamed. Until they stole the two thousand in cash I'd saved up for a trip. Nothing big. Just my sister Beth and me. A few days in Chicago, another couple in New York City. We'd dreamed of it since we were girls. Thing is, if they'd told me they needed money, for anything except bail, I would've given them the two thousand and never looked back."

"When did the money go missing?"

Lynn pursed her lips. "A year ago. About the time they quit coming around."

"When was the last time you saw them?"

"Last month. They were coming out of Chester's Market with a case of beer. They handed it over to some kid. I assumed they bought it for him."

"Did you speak with them?"

She shook her head. "I don't think they even knew I was there."

"Did you recognize the kid?"

"Afraid not. Maybe eighteen or so. Dark hair. That's all I remember."

"Okay, I'll let you be. I wanted to check in, make sure you were doing all right."

We both stood.

"Funeral's tomorrow," she said.

"I'll be there."

"You said they had some belongings?"

"Clothes. A couple of books."

"Books?"

"A Raymond Chandler mystery and a book of poetry."

"The *Rubaiyat of Omar Khayyam*?"

"That's right."

"A gift from my grandmother. It's where I'd stashed the two thousand dollars."

"There was also a photo inside. Of you and the twins when they were about six. Cute little boys."

"Yes. I remember."

"See you tomorrow, Lynn."

I arrived early at Erna's Café, the little hole-in-the-wall place Hollis and I both liked. Eggs, bacon, and ranch fries for $5.99, what was not to like.

Someone had left a copy of the *Blue Mountain Eagle* on my table, so I scanned it under the dim ceiling light. Duncan and his store were featured prominently on the business page. The photo of him was a tad blurry, but I liked his smile. I couldn't remember who had called him crotchety, but he seemed damn normal to me. And he certainly didn't make love like some ill-tempered men I could name.

Hollis scooted into the opposite side of our booth, knocking me out of my little daydream. "What's the gossip?"

He meant the "Cops and Courts" page, a log of last week's law enforcement activity and judicial decisions, complete with the names, ages, and towns of residence of those cited, accused, or sentenced.

"Forgot to check." I flipped to the log.

"Did you order breakfast yet?" His voice was deeper, crustier this morning.

I shook my head and sipped my tepid coffee. "Hope Lil's getting more sleep than you are. Maybe you should rethink delaying your family leave."

"I'll be okay."

Our waitress, a tall, busty woman with muscular arms, stood at our table. "Mornin'. Just the regular today?"

"Yep. But add a little salsa on the side, please," said Hollis.

She poured him a cup of coffee. "Sure thing. And what about you, hon?"

Calling a cop *hon* was probably verboten somewhere, but I liked it that she always did. "Can I get my eggs scrambled this time?"

"Comin' up," she said.

I handed Hollis the *Blue Mountain Eagle*. "Not much gossip, I'm afraid."

He checked the log and inspected the front page. "Any luck finding the Nodines' jeep or abode yesterday?"

"Found both. In a campground ten or eleven miles east of Seneca."

"So, not too far from the shuttered mill where they were killed?"

"Yeah, up Logan Valley Highway. Close to where they poached that doe."

"A few cattle ranches nearby, if I remember correctly," he said.

I nodded. "That reminds me. Met a guy new to the area while I was out there. Calls his place Bear Valley Cattle Company."

"Taylor told me about that. Some kind of hormone-free outfit, right?"

"Yeah. Cecil Burney went on a tirade about all the local

ranchers being bought out, taken over by the natural beef industry. Sees something criminal about making cattle into a profitable enterprise, I guess. Still, I take his point if this Asa Larkin guy is any example. Turned the old Harden ranch into a regular Fort Knox of the high desert. Electric fence. Security gate."

"A Texan?"

"A lawyer. Had a practice in Lake Oswego."

"And how was your visit with Burney?" Hollis asked.

"About as delightful as I thought it would be, although he did send me up Logan Valley Highway to look for that jeep."

I eyed a couple of customers entering the café. Two men in their mid-to-late forties, tall and rotund. Each wore a bulky jacket, cheap chinos, a straw cowboy hat, and a pair of slick black boots. I was pretty sure they were the two dudes in the green-apple Bronco who worked for Larkin.

"Don't turn around, but I think two of Asa Larkin's hired men just took a table."

Hollis stood. "I need to wash up."

On his return from the restroom, he tossed the men a glance before sliding back into our booth. "I've seen them around town. A couple of times at the hardware store. Once at McKay's Feed and Tack."

"They don't seem the ranch-hand type to me. Too much meat on their bones."

Our waitress placed the plates on the table. "Here you go, hon."

I forked up a wad of scrambled eggs and ranch fries and watched her toddle to the table where the two men sat. "Larkin's not particularly friendly, and he's apparently the religious type. His place even has a Christian motto, it seems. *Jesus Loves Grass-Fed Beef.*"

Hollis ladled a load of salsa onto his breakfast burrito.

"Lots of Jesus-loves-this and Jesus-loves-that kind of thing out here."

"Tell me about it."

After our meal, I spotted the green-apple Bronco in Erna's parking lot. "That's the rig those two men were driving yesterday."

Hollis surreptitiously snapped photos of the license plate and the bumper sticker with the cattle company motto, and I took a sly gander at the interior.

"What do you think?" I asked.

"I'm just following your instincts right now." He slipped on a latex glove and tried all four doors. "Who in this county locks up their vehicle?"

"Strangers? People with something to hide? Try the hatch in back."

He yanked the handle upward, clicking it open. "Now what?"

I surveyed the café. Gingham curtains blocked any view of the parking lot out of its few windows. "Go stand next to Erna's entrance. You'll think of a way to distract anybody coming outside."

"And what'll you be doing?"

"That was an order."

He smiled and handed me a pair of gloves. "Be careful."

I climbed through the open hatch and crawled hastily to the glove compartment. Nothing. Nothing under the front bench seat, nothing under the back. I edged back out through the hatch, eased it shut, and shook my head. Holly, standing nonchalantly by the café's front door, shrugged, and we walked to our cop Tahoes parked side-by-side in the lot.

· · ·

At my desk, I listened to voicemail. Whitey Kern had called late last night to say he'd delivered Dan and Joseph's jeep and pickup camper to the evidence warehouse in Bend. Earlier this morning, Duncan had confirmed the two Hot Shot DXR cattle prods matched the listings in his inventory.

"What's that smell?" Hollis asked.

"Probably the rotten meat inside the Nodines' cooler. Should have kept it on ice, I guess." I unlocked the evidence locker, moved the cooler to the freezer.

In the meantime, Hollis opened wide the office doors and turned on his computer. "Let's see what we can find out about the grass-fed beef guy. Asa Larkin, right?"

I nodded. "Drives a black Prius."

"Plate number?"

Hadn't occurred to me to check the plates.

"Maggie?"

"Didn't pull him over, Holly. Met him by happenstance."

"So you didn't check his driver's license either."

"Nope."

"Well, that's unfortunate, because there's no Asa Larkin listed on the Oregon

State Bar website or at the DMV."

I stood behind him, staring at the sites he'd pulled up on his two monitors. "What does that mean?"

"Name change? Alias? The man's a liar?"

That last had already occurred to me. And now that I knew the Nodines had been camped out not far from Bear Valley Cattle Company, he was high on the list of area ranchers we needed to talk to.

I scanned through close-up photographs of the Nodines' Ram 3500 and the livestock trailer that had finally been forwarded from the State Police lab in Bend. "Take a look at this." I turned the monitor toward Hollis.

"A livestock trailer?"

"It was parked beside the Nodines' red truck. See that?" I pointed to the bumper.

"That same *Jesus Loves Grass-Fed Beef* bumper sticker?"

"Think I'll let Larkin explain it to us. His false identity too," I said.

I pulled up the photos I'd taken on the night of the murder. I hadn't taken shots of the bumper or noticed the sticker. "Shit. I missed seeing it when Olive Kern loaded the damn trailer onto her flatbed tow truck."

"A lot going on that night, Maggie."

No excuse, I thought. "I keep blundering along, blind to one clue, stumbling across another. I think Bach suspects I'm not up to the task either. He was pretty cold over the phone last night."

"That's not why."

"What do you mean?"

"I left a clue for you."

"The cryptic sticky note you stuck on my phone, something about J.T.?"

He nodded. "So we knew J.T. would have a tizzy about Bach supervising our work during the murder investigation, right? Turns out he filed a complaint with Corporal Macintyre at regional. Made some case against you being fit to be a sergeant. Plus he thought it was inappropriate for our office to investigate murder cases."

"Fuck me dead. And fuck that son-of-a-bitch ex-husband of mine."

"What the hell? You were married to Lake?"

"Years ago. Lasted only a few months. It was a rebound thing after Morgan left me. Christ, can we talk about it some other time?" The last thing I needed right now was to chitchat with Holly about my love life.

"That explains a few things, but you don't have to worry. I've got your back, Maggie."

"I should've told you, though."

"It's none of my business who you've been married to."

We sat quietly. "How'd you learn J.T. filed a complaint?"

"I'd like you to think I have a secret source at regional, but I don't, unfortunately. That medical examiner, Dr. Gattis, left a voicemail on the mainline."

"Ray. She was probably trying to warn me."

"I think so."

"Well, no one's ordered me to stop investigating. Unless there's another voicemail you forgot to tell me about."

He shook his head.

"Before I get kicked off the case, let's go have a conversation with the dude posing as Asa Larkin. And if there's time, let's drive out to Guy Trudeau's place too."

Bear Valley Cattle Company's entry gate was wide open when Hollis and I arrived, which moderated somewhat the fortress vibe present yesterday. The black Prius was parked in the drive. The three identical mobile homes, for his hired men, I guessed, sat at the tree line about twenty yards from the newly painted ranch house.

Several minutes after I pressed the ranch house doorbell, a lanky teenager—presumably the son who sat in the Prius yesterday—opened the door a crack. Similar to his father, he looked both bemused and hostile, and he was high on a heavy dose of youthful wrath and white privilege. He wore a pair of expensive Ariat jeans, a double-pocketed Gitmon western shirt, some high-end cowboy boots, and a black felt hat, all likely ordered online from Shepler's or Langston's.

"Morning, son," I said, irking the boy with that diminutive tag. "I'm looking to talk with your father."

"Dad! That lady cop's back!" The kid opened the door wider, walked toward the back of the house and disappeared. "Dad! Did you hear me?"

"I heard you." Asa Larkin, or whatever the hell his name turned out to be, appeared in the front room, headed resentfully to the door. "Sergeant. Blackburn, was it?"

I extended my hand and we shook again. "Blackthorne. And this is Senior Trooper Jones. We'd like to talk to you about a couple of things, sir."

He eyed Hollis. The kind of once-over I'd observed locals make the first time they were introduced to the tall Black man who was my police partner and backup.

"All right," he said and led us further into the living room.

The décor was decidedly cold. Black leather wing chairs and matching divan with modern glass tables strewn about. The space had an icy, masculine flair.

We sat down, the cushioned seats crackling quietly beneath us. "What can I help you with, Sergeant?"

Hollis broke out his laptop and passed it to me.

"The Nodine brothers were in possession of this livestock trailer." I showed him the photo and waited for a reaction. "Here's a close-up shot of the bumper. Recognize that saying?"

"*Jesus Loves Grass-Fed Beef*, you mean?"

I nodded.

"Obviously I do. It hangs from my entryway outside. I recognize the trailer too. I reported it missing a couple of weeks ago."

"I saw nothing like that come across my desk. Did you, Trooper Jones?"

Hollis shook his head.

"I reported it to the sheriff's office. You're probably aware it's not a requirement to register a trailer that size in Oregon. I planned to anyway, but hadn't gotten around to it. Unfortunately."

"It was found at the scene of the Nodine killings and had sustained some shotgun damage." I paused for a reaction. Nothing. "For the immediate future, it'll have to remain at the evidence warehouse in Bend. To get it back eventually, you can file a claim with the State Police. With proof of purchase, of course."

"I see. So was that all, Sergeant?"

"I'll let the sheriff know the livestock trailer's been located." I stood, a signal for Hollis to do the same. "And the name you filed the report under?"

"Excuse me?"

"Trooper Jones did a bit of research. He found no Asa Larkin listed as a member of the Oregon State Bar. Nor is there an Asa Larkin in DMV records. Are you using an alias for some reason?"

His neck and face reddened slightly. "My legal name is Asa Wakefield. After my mother died, her sister and husband— David and Janet Wakefield—adopted me. They were killed in a car accident a while back, and I decided to change my last name to Larkin. It was both my mother and my aunt's maiden name."

Again I sensed his explanation was some distorted version of the truth. "Thanks for clarifying things, Mr. Larkin."

"I have petitioned to change my name legally."

I put on my hat. "I'll get back to you with that property claim form."

"Okay, what did you think of Larkin?" I asked Hollis on the way to Big T.

"He didn't seem particularly surprised the trailer was found at a murder scene."

"I thought so too. But he also strikes me as an imperious asshole, and maybe that flat affect is part of the package."

"Imperious, huh? Flat affect?"

I ignored Holly's teasing. "Let's figure out what kind of law he practiced, okay?"

"And did you notice he didn't name his biological father?"

"That's right. Good catch, H."

"You know me. Always suspicious of everyone."

Hardly accurate, but Hollis did have a knack for registering no surprise when it turned out someone was cagey, or a lawbreaker, or a royal fuck-up.

I changed the subject. "About Trudeau. He's not my fan. Called me a Podunk with a gun the other day. Might be good to have you doing the questioning."

"Sure, if you want me to. But he's not my fan either. Last time I stopped him, he was damned belligerent and had a pistol next to him on the seat. Besides, I like to watch you get these folks all riled up. That way I come off looking like Trooper Charming."

"I didn't really rile Larkin-slash-Wakefield, though, did I? He better have filed that theft report with the sheriff under one of those names, or his ass goes up on our murder board as a person of interest."

"I'll check with the sheriff when we get back from Trudeau's place."

9

At the junction with 395 we traveled about eight miles north, turned west on Izee Road, drove along the Silvies River, and finally headed north again toward the west side of the Aldrich range. I pulled off outside the battered gates of Big T.

The old man's Torino was parked in front of his dusty two-story house, and like the surrounding outbuildings, the house was a worn, weather-beaten mess. Sage, juniper, and cheat weed had overtaken the small orchard next to the barn, and the remains of fruit trees stood gnarled and wasted. The place appeared entirely absent of animal life: not a pig, a milk cow, a sheep, a chicken, or a dog. No beef cattle either.

We climbed over the locked gate and strode down a short ravine to the house. The Trudeau family had raised Black Angus out here for generations. So finding Big T in such a state of ruin was a true shock. I wondered if Cecil Burney knew just how broke Guy Trudeau was.

We knocked at the front door, called out for Trudeau, and knocked again. The weather had settled yet remained relentlessly glacial, despite sunlight filtering through the cloud mass. A frigid charge eased up my spine. I buttoned my peacoat and tried turning the doorknob to no avail.

"You check that side of the house," I indicated left, "and I'll take the other."

We each snapped open our holsters and slowly stepped off the porch.

I'd barely rounded the corner when Hollis called out, told me to meet him at the front door. "Man's hanging in the middle of his kitchen," he said and tried the knob again.

"Step back. I'll shoot the lock off."

"Try looking under the doormat first."

The key was hidden there, but the door was all but wedged shut by stacks of newspapers at least five feet high.

We could see more heaps of newspapers inside, along with magazines and livestock exchange reports covering the floor and the ancient furniture, filling up the stairwell and cluttering the hallway. Trudeau was broke and a hoarder too.

We zipped to the other side of the house hoping the key also worked on the back door, but it was locked from the inside. Around in front again, I squeezed through the small opening between the door and the piles of old news and pushed aside most of the crap blocking Holly's way.

In the kitchen, the table had been shoved to one side, a chair lay on the floor, and Guy Trudeau was suspended from the mounted light fixture. A belt had been cinched to the ceiling bolt and wrapped several times around the old man's neck.

Hollis took a small step back. "Shit. I always have a hard time with dead bodies."

"If there's any cell signal out here, call Sam Damon. Let him know we need his hearse pronto."

I fetched the digital camera from my pack and snapped photos: different angles of the body, the makeshift noose, the furniture arrangement, and the junk piled everywhere. I centered the kitchen table under the light fixture—a fake wagon wheel with globes made of milk glass—and placed a chair on either side.

"Sam's on his way," Hollis said, rejoining me in the kitchen. "Let's lower the body to the table."

At least a good foot taller than me, he stood on one of the chair seats, leaned the dead man's upper torso over his shoulder and began loosening the belt cinched around the ceiling bolt. Stabilizing myself, one boot on the second chair, the other boot on the table, I latched onto the dangling corpse.

We leveraged the body toward the melamine tabletop. The wagon wheel light fixture swayed, the globes trembling furiously, until gravity seized control of Guy Trudeau's lifeless remains. The old man's body thudded to the table, where his head—eyes open and glaring—landed on my boot.

"Good catch, Sarge."

"I see you got over your squeamishness." I moved my boot gingerly from under Trudeau's head.

"Not really. Think I'll find a blanket to cover him up until Sam gets here."

While Hollis looked for a blanket, I retrieved a pair of latex gloves and searched the kitchen. The larder was close to bare: salt, pepper, and a couple of other spices in one cupboard, a dozen cans of chicken noodle soup in the pantry. Bread, milk, and an apple in the refrigerator, along with a few beefsteaks and a venison roast in the freezer. Sparse as it was, I wouldn't have thought it belonged to a man headed for suicide.

Back with a coverlet polluted by filth, Hollis laid it over Trudeau's face and most of his body. "I've been thinking, Maggie. I'm not sure how the old guy could've wrapped that belt around his neck and lashed it to the fixture bolt."

"What are you saying, Holly?"

"Just seems odd is all. I think he'd have to be pretty strong to do both of those things standing on a chair. He'd have to cinch the belt tight around the bolt and tight around his neck for it to work. Plus he'd probably need to be taller."

I pulled a chair directly under the light, stood on it, rose up as high as I could, and reached for the ceiling bolt securing the light fixture in place. I was at least five inches too short.

"You think he had help?"

"I don't know about help, exactly, but it doesn't seem like he could do it on his own."

"Is this another murder?" I asked the stale kitchen air. "What the hell is happening in this county?"

I drew up my phone and hit Bach's number.

"You have to go outside for service and walk up the ravine to where we're parked," Hollis said.

"Start a search inside the house. I'll be right back." I hoofed it to my Tahoe, climbed inside, and punched in Bach's number again.

"Sergeant. I've been calling you for the last hour."

"Sorry, Detective. We're out in backcountry. Cell service is always spotty."

"I'm on my way to your office. The two of us need to have a conversation."

"Trooper Jones and I came out here to talk to a couple of ranchers about the Nodine brothers, but I'm afraid we found one of them hanging from his kitchen light."

"Dead?"

"Yes."

"Suicide?"

"We have questions about that. That's why I called. I think you should see this, Al."

"I'm driving Highway 20, about to make Burns and head north on 395."

"Good. You're fairly close, then." I laid out the directions to Big T.

"I'll contact the medical examiner, Sergeant," he said and clicked off.

Before heading back inside Trudeau's house, I made a hasty call to Sam Damon.

"Afternoon, Sergeant Blackthorne."

"Sam. We need to hold off on retrieval of the body for a while."

"I'm already about halfway there."

"Glad I caught you before you got any further. And sorry for the inconvenience. Think we'll only be a few hours more."

"I'm still billing the State for my time."

"Fine, but you need to keep quiet about Mr. Trudeau's death for now."

Hollis and I began searching the cluttered rooms, inspecting every cupboard, drawer, closet, bookcase, and gun rack. We sorted through heaping mounds of laundry—clean and dirty —examined every dun notice, receipt, legal document, and personal letter in his desk and file cabinet. And we looked behind and beneath the furniture and under every pillow and seat cushion. All of it pointed to Trudeau being a sad, dingy, bankrupt, and parsimonious old widower who was estranged from his children. A man who might kill himself.

"His ankles and wrists weren't tied. Don't you think he'd have been kicking, swinging his fists, fighting against whoever was trying to kill him? And wouldn't it have taken two people to wrap the belt around his neck, brace him up, and fasten the belt to that light fixture?" I asked Hollis. "*At least* two people."

"Let's say he was murdered. Whoever did it would need it to look like Trudeau offed himself. Wouldn't have tied his ankles or wrists, otherwise it'd be obvious he hadn't climbed up there of his own accord."

"Why wouldn't they just shoot him and make it look like an accident or a self-inflicted gunshot?"

"I don't know, Sarge. Cruel bastards? Or maybe they just meant to scare him some and things went haywire?"

"How'd they get in—or out, for that matter?"

"Back door, I'd say. He let them in, or they found it open. When they left, they locked the back door from the inside and closed it behind them."

"So you agree with me. If he was murdered, there was more than one killer?"

He nodded. "Assuming he *was* murdered."

"Which you're convinced happened, right?"

"Sure seems like it to me, but let's wait for the ME." He strolled from where we stood in the living room and opened the back door. "I need some air."

I followed him outside. "I know you question how he might have managed to get up there and hang himself with a belt. I don't disagree, but I'm having a hard time seeing it as a murder. And yes, I know Ray Gattis or whoever works this case will give us the answer to that."

"Why are you thinking it was a suicide?" Hollis asked.

"Trudeau was wealthy once. Owned a huge spread and a large herd of cattle. Then his wife died and all his kids moved away. Supposedly one of them later made off with his money. When I caught up with him the other day, he might have been hauling his last twenty-five or so head of Black Angus to the auction in Boise. All that starts to add up for a man like Guy Trudeau."

"Thought you said he was riding shotgun, making sure his

animals got to market. That means one thing to me. He was going to make sure he got his money. I doubt that's something a man would do if he planned to kill himself."

"Maybe he couldn't find a buyer in Boise after all."

"That's possible. Which would hold with your theory about him losing everything and deciding to kill himself."

"It's a question for Jess Bennett when we see her tomorrow. Did she make it to Boise with Trudeau's load of steers?" But as soon as I spoke the words, I sensed that no matter her answer, the three deaths were intertwined in some way.

Detective Bach, Hollis, and I stood in the front yard of Guy Trudeau's house where a vast garden of gladiolas, purple and bronze irises, and black-eyed Susan once thrived. Weeds, hard clay, and a rotted and wind-toppled cottonwood had replaced the flower plantings.

"First mistake you made was to move the body, Sergeant."

Al's officiously delivered statement was not to be taken literally; this was definitely not the first mistake I'd made in the short time the man had known me.

Hollis, who had only just been introduced to Bach, stepped in behind me. "It appeared to be a clear case of suicide when we arrived, sir," he said.

"Doesn't matter." Al brushed a swath of dirt from the military crease of his slacks. "Procedure is clear. You wait until the medical examiner arrives before moving the body. Did you take photographs, at least?"

"Of course." I hoped I sounded as indignant as I'd intended.

"I'll look at those after I've seen the body."

"In the kitchen, but through the back door, not the front. You'll see why when we get inside," I said.

Bach moved toward the rear of the house.

Hollis nudged my shoulder. "Procedure or not, Maggie, I don't think we did anything wrong. The nearest damn ME is two hundred miles away. Were we supposed to just leave him hanging there?"

I signaled my agreement, and we followed Al to the kitchen. He stood over Trudeau's body lying on the table, slipped on a pair of latex gloves, and examined the purple-red contusions ringing the dead man's neck. "Extensive bruising."

"Fingernail scratches too," I said.

"Probably trying to loosen the belt as he swung." Bach checked the contents of Trudeau's pockets, exhumed a tattered wallet and a folded scrap of paper. After looking through the wallet and removing a driver's license and three one-dollar bills, he unfolded the paper.

I scanned it. "An invoice from Wilson's Animal Clinic."

Several days before I'd pulled over the semi load of Trudeau's cattle, Jen Wilson had written a prescription so the old man could treat his steers for something called Moraxella bovis. Sounded ghastly.

"I don't suppose he left a note?" Bach asked.

"Didn't find one. We searched the first floor pretty thoroughly, although we still have to go through the attic."

"Leaving no note doesn't necessarily mean anything. How about any evidence of despondence?"

"His wife died several years ago. Children, two sons and a daughter, no longer live in the area. He's supposedly penniless, which shows in the condition of his ranch. Plus there's the mess everywhere in the house. Put all that together, and it says something about the shambles his life was in," I ventured.

Al paced the first-floor rooms and surveyed the makings of Trudeau's hoarder obsessions. "I see what you mean about the state of the house. I'll take a look at those photos now."

He spent a good ten minutes scrolling back and forth through the shots I'd taken of Trudeau's body suspended from the kitchen light, examined the fixture itself, and pulled the coverlet aside, exposing the corpse.

"It is suspicious how he might have managed to hang himself with that belt."

"Hollis is more convinced it's murder than I am."

"At least until we hear from the ME," Hollis said.

"Speaking of that, Dr. Gattis is arriving at the airport in about an hour. I'd appreciate one of you picking her up and driving her back out here."

Hollis volunteered to go, in part to allow me the courtesy of a private dressing down, which I was certain Bach was itching to hand me. I also knew it would give Holly an opportunity to check in on Lillian and the baby before he fetched Ray from the airport.

I tossed Hollis the keys to my Tahoe. "It probably needs gas before you collect Dr. Gattis."

He nodded, departed through the back door, and trod quickly up the ravine.

Al suggested we inspect the rest of Trudeau's property before finishing our search of the house. The outbuildings were on the verge of collapse, except for the family's monumental and once-famous barn. A masterpiece built out of fir and juniper, it had been featured in a ranch journal touting the great utilitarian architecture of the 1800s.

As a young girl, I had toured the barn with my 4-H club and found it palatial, grand even. Years later after Zoey died, I fantasized about moving out of Tate's tiny Nashua at the trailer park. I imagined living alone in the barn at Big T, secreted away in some obscure enclosure or dark corner of the hayloft.

"I remember reading about that old barn," Al said.

"Looks a bit haggard now, but it was really something once."

The pasture spreading out from the barn was overgrown with thistle and surrounded by lax and forlorn barbed wire fencing that sagged between the listing posts and tumbledown rock jacks. We inspected the chicken coop and shop quickly and spent about an hour inside the barn. Finding nothing of note, we walked back to the house and sat on the porch steps in the sparse warmth of late winter sunlight.

Bach plucked a long blade of grass from the dry sod. "You might have heard. Lieutenant Lake filed a complaint."

There it was, out in the open. Perhaps it was merely the long shadow cast by Trudeau's massive barn, lit now by a slant of sun, but Al appeared drained, less assured. Less angry, too.

"I wish you'd told me you once had a personal relationship with Lake."

I wondered why it had been deemed my responsibility to declare the possible conflict, not J.T.'s. "The whole thing was over long before he became my supervisor."

"More significantly, Lake questioned your leadership."

"I passed the sergeant's exam. With flying colors."

"I know. I saw your file. But according to Corporal Macintyre, the lieutenant alluded to past bouts of severe depression."

For the second or third time in recent days, I wished I'd pulled the trigger and shot that motherfucker when I had the chance. But the violence in our short marriage remained our little secret. One neither of us would ever speak of. I'd never disclose hitting rock bottom for a time or how I came by that scarred-over wound on my right shoulder. He'd never cop to his own brutality or his hatred of women.

"I passed the police recruits psych exam too," I said.

"Yes. Corporal Macintyre ordered me to review your full personnel file."

"And?"

"It sparkled. But me assuring the corporal about your character and police skills didn't assuage his doubts. Your file has been flagged for the foreseeable future."

"Meaning what?"

"No more promotions or choice of assignments until top brass removes the flag."

"And I have no recourse?"

"The OSPOA would invoke your rights to due process."

"My union? You do know what organization we both work for, don't you? And union or no union, invoking my rights is one thing, but representing me, being on my side, is quite another. Lady cops aren't supposed to be mucking around in real police work. And if those bastards hear the words *severe depression*, I'll become the butt of every 'she's always on the rag' joke they ever tell."

Bach's face and neck had reddened several shades, but he didn't lash out. "Why do you care about all of that?"

"Because I'm a damn good cop and I don't plan on messing that up if I can avoid it. There will be no complaint to my union. I'll tough it out. I've toughed out worse before."

"I believe it."

Desperate for something profound to utter and lessen the unease, I channeled Buddha. "Life follows a strange path sometimes, doesn't it, Al."

"It does. We just have to do what we can to do right by our actions. But it's not always easy."

"I think I've disappointed you."

"Because of circumstances beyond our control, Maggie, I took a risk handing you a lot of authority in the Nodine matter. And you took some risk accepting that challenge. But you haven't disappointed me."

"What about the investigation?"

Bach shook his head. "Macintyre didn't force me to take you off the case. And I would have argued against it if he had. The corporal is smart where his troops are concerned, so I have to assume he recognizes Lieutenant Lake's...own issues. I'll leave it at that."

I stared at the stinkbugs excavating the matted earth near my feet. "Sorry about the inappropriate language."

"I'm pretty sure you've said worse."

"What?"

"I read your complete file, remember. You only had a single past complaint filed against you. One of your fellow recruits at the academy accused you of verbal abuse."

"Barnes, right?" He had been my partner on some exercise, and I'd warned him to get his ass in gear, or words to that effect.

"I don't believe I've ever read a complaint with that many profanity redactions."

It was past time to change the subject. "I think I'll search the attic now."

"I'll join you." He rose and followed me to the back door of the house.

The attic was a roomy space filled with light, dust, forgotten furniture, and memorabilia. It contained two sets of bunk beds and looked to have been used as the bedroom for Trudeau's two sons. Their photographs, 4-H awards, and sports team photos graced the walls and dresser tops. There was nothing indicating the old man had set foot there in the last twenty years, let alone used it to carry some of the weight of his cache of hoarded newspapers.

We rummaged through the dressers and the two antique wardrobes that still held several articles of male adolescent clothing. I secretly coveted the Grant Union Prospectors letterman's jacket with a chest patch that read "Pete," indicating Trudeau's oldest son. Other than that, we found nothing connected to the father's death or his life these last several years among the brothers' leftover personal effects or in the shelf of novels that stood in the far corner.

The daughter's room on the first floor had been left similarly undisturbed, as if the old man and his wife—while she was alive—had chosen to preserve the last remnants of their children's childhoods so as to not crack the illusion of sustained kinship.

While we searched the attic, we discussed my own childhood growing up in what Bach referred to as "God's country." We also talked of him being the oldest child in a large family from Twin Falls, Idaho, a clue that he'd grown up Mormon. So, I avoided hot-button topics, meaning politics and religion. I could smell conservative and God-fearing from a mile off, and he was both. His little affair with Ray Gattis aside, Al Bach walked the straight and narrow, and I needed to stay on his good side. Besides, I didn't care what he believed as long as he was fair and professional.

"You find bodies in the damnedest places, Sergeant Blackthorne," Ray said when she and Hollis met up with us.

"It's becoming my specialty," I answered.

Inside Trudeau's grimy kitchen, Doc flipped on every light possible and examined the old man's body. "Trooper Jones tells me there's some question this is suicide?"

"That's right," I said.

"I know procedures say to leave everything in place until the ME arrives, but first officers on the scene of a possible suicide often forget that. Except on TV, of course," she said, drawing back the coverlet. "A great deal of bruising, not necessarily uncommon in suicide by hanging. Are there photographs of the body as it hung?"

I showed her the digital shots. "These will be clearer when viewed on a larger screen, Ray."

"I'm going to need better lighting to establish cause of death. Has Sam Damon been notified? I'd like to use his mortician's table."

"Yes, but I called him off until you arrived."

"I'll give him a heads-up," Hollis said, stepping out.

"Nothing official, but what do you think, Ray?" Bach asked.

"I can see why there might be a question about it. A complicated way to loop the belt around the light fixture and his neck. And no note, right?"

"Correct," I said and explained Trudeau's family troubles and financial demise. "I mostly come down on the side of suicide, but Hollis believes murder is more likely."

"Any thoughts on who might have a motive to kill Mr. Trudeau?" Al asked.

"Like the Nodines, he might've had a few enemies," I said.

"But you still lean toward it being a suicide?" Doc Gattis asked.

"I do. That's why I'm glad you're here to answer the question."

"Any sense of the time of death?" Bach asked Ray.

"I'd estimate sometime within the last six to twelve hours. I need to run a couple of tests, though."

"I passed him on Highway 395 just yesterday. About two

thirty or so in the afternoon," I said. "Heading toward his ranch, I assumed."

Hollis reentered the kitchen. "Sam should be here in forty-five minutes."

Ray removed her latex gloves. "Would you mind taking me back into town now, Trooper Jones? I didn't have time to pick up lunch before the flight, so I'd like to get something to eat before I start the autopsy."

"I'll take you back, Ray," Bach offered. "I need to check in at the motel and do some work from my laptop."

"You're spending the night?" she asked.

Al nodded, buttoned his coat, and turned to me. "You have the contact information for next of kin?"

"I found an old address book. I'll start there."

Dr. Gattis picked up her kit. "Since there was ill will between Mr. Trudeau and his children, let me confirm cause of death before you contact them, Maggie."

"Will do. And I'll swing by the funeral home later to pick you up."

"Say between five thirty and six?"

Al put on his cap and extended a hand to Hollis. "Nice meeting you, Trooper. I'll see both of you tomorrow morning."

10

Hollis and I waited on the front porch for the undertaker. When he arrived, I walked up the ravine and opened the gate, directed him to the back door of the ranch house. The three of us wrapped the corpse in a body bag, placed it on a stretcher, and loaded it in Sam Damon's hearse.

As he'd done when he'd come to collect the Nodines, Sam asked for a moment of silence. Only the magpies objected, clamoring from the roof of the barn.

I followed Sam's hearse to 395 and down Canyon Mountain, dropped Holly off at the office, and headed to my apartment to check on Louie. When I opened the door, he wheezed from his pillow. Alarmed by the sound of his purr and his lethargy, I dialed the emergency number at Wilson's Animal Clinic.

After no one picked up, I tried Jen Wilson's home phone listed in the twee local phone book. She didn't answer that either, and I didn't know her personal cell number, so I moved Louie and his pillow next to the heat vent and refreshed his food and water.

I slipped downstairs to Dorie's thrift store.

"Maggie. How have you been, girl?" she said.

"Working hard. How about you?"

"Thank goodness Lynn's sister is staying with her tonight. I've about run through my repertoire of chicken recipes. Take a load off?" She nodded toward her small living room.

"No, I can't. But could I ask a favor?"

"Of course."

"Louie's sick. Didn't even eat the food I set out for him. I had no luck reaching Jen Wilson at home or at her clinic, and I don't have her mobile number. Would you mind checking on him once in a while over the next few hours?"

"Sure thing. I'll see if I can track down Jen's cell number too."

"Thanks." I gave her a little smooch on the cheek and climbed back in my Chevy Tahoe. I was surprised she hadn't offered to call together a prayer circle on Louie's behalf. More surprising was the fact she didn't seem to have gotten word yet about Guy Trudeau's death.

The office was quiet but for the beat of the analog clock hanging above the file cabinets. Hollis had left a second sticky note on my desk phone.

"God, not another J.T. Lake clusterfuck," I said to the still air.

I snatched up the note: "Larkin filed a theft report with the sheriff. Asa Wakefield is listed in the OR Bar directory. Practices elder law." That still didn't prove that Larkin and Wakefield were one and the same.

Retreating to the alcove, I stared at the Nodine murder board. There were so many lines of inquiry, I couldn't keep track. We needed to pick one and go with it. But the list of unknowns was already too long, and there might be Trudeau's death to factor in. And what did *BRADY*, the name found on the folded sticky note in the glove compartment of the Ram 3500, have to do with anything? Maybe nothing, maybe everything.

Who was the kid Lynn Nodine had seen the twins handing over a case of beer to outside Chester's Market? Dark hair, eighteen or so, maybe older. I could draw up a damn list of twenty or more boys who'd fit that description, including Duncan's nephew, Rain McKay-Ferlinghetti.

I was exhausted, mostly of spirit. I hadn't felt this vulnerable and at risk of failure in some time, and I was too wrung out to start the Trudeau report. The last five days had left me edgy and oddly bereft.

And then there was Duncan, suddenly in my life or a passing fling? Either way, I was losing my grip, the ironclad trap on my heart—the one I always counted on to keep honest emotion at bay.

All of it made me fearful my well-practiced self-control would slip away in the middle of tomorrow's funeral.

I drove to Sam Damon's Juniper Chapel Mortuary and Crematorium and found Ray in the chapel. She had turned the blond oak rostrum used by reverends and other funeral speakers into a makeshift desk for her laptop. The large Bible typically displayed prominently on top had been removed to the floor.

With the cross and candle-lit altar behind her, the doc might have passed for a beatific figure in some ethereal sanctuary. She glanced up from her laptop as I entered the room and flashed a doleful smile. "You couldn't wait another week to find that old man's body?"

"That would have been even more unpleasant."

"For you, maybe." She massaged her temples. "Al and I called it off last night, and supposedly for good this time. So I could have used *at least* another week before being in close proximity, especially out here in the middle of nowhere in a motel room three doors down."

"Fate. It always tests a person."

"Fuck fate."

"You've got that right."

"Good to see you, though."

"You too. So what can you tell me about Mr. Trudeau?"

"Strangled with that belt. Foreign skin cells under his fingernails, and some of the bruising indicates he fought his killer."

"Murder for sure, then?"

"Yes, and I'd speculate a large male, given the length of the belt. Mr. Trudeau was too lean to wear a size forty-six. But he was muscular for his age, which indicates he was too strong for even a really buff woman to choke him to death and haul him up there on her own."

"But a strong woman could assist, though?"

"So could any healthy teenager."

"Strangling a senior citizen's not my idea of anything healthy."

"See, that's why I like you, Maggie. A lady cop always ready with a smartass retort, even when the subject is gruesome."

"A cop who didn't need another damn murder in her district."

Sam Damon appeared in the aisle between the ten or so rows of pews. The kid I'd babysat had grown into a thin, reedy man who always seemed joyless and strangely sneaky. Never a good combination.

"Excuse me, Dr. Gattis, Sergeant Blackthorne. I need to set up the sanctuary for tomorrow's funeral."

"I'm finished for the time being, Sam. But I'd like to run another test tomorrow after the service."

On the way out of the building, Ray suggested we go to dinner.

"God, if I tell you I have a sick cat and need to check on him, would you think me pathetic?"

"Yeah. But I have an old Scottie dog, and I'd do the same. I suppose breakfast tomorrow morning is out too?"

"I might have to take Louie to the vet first thing. And then there's the funeral."

"Oh, yes. The funeral." She paused for several moments. "I'm flying back tomorrow afternoon. Four o'clock. If you or Trooper Jones has the time, could you give me a lift? I prefer not to ask Al. This is already hard enough."

"One of us will get you to the airport."

Ray Gattis was the embodiment of sadness and regret when I dropped her off at Mack's Motel. In my rearview mirror, I watched her pull a pack of cigarettes from her purse. She lit one and began to smoke it, leaning against the door of her room. Bach's Ford Interceptor was parked less than ten feet away.

Dorie met me outside after I parked next to her store and handed me a slip of paper. "Jen Wilson's cell number."

"Thanks, D. How's Louie?"

"Tired of me bothering him, I think. He doesn't seem any better or any worse than he was earlier, but he still didn't eat anything."

"I really appreciate your checking on him."

Inside the apartment, Louie didn't move from his pillow but offered up a brief tail wag. I picked him up, and we sat in the granny rocker. I added Jen's number to my contacts and hit call.

"This is Jen."

"Hi, Jen. Maggie Blackthorne. Sorry to bother you on a Sunday, but my old tabby is under the weather. Listless, croaky purr, can't get him to eat."

Always a pleasant woman, she put me through a litany of questions regarding Louie's symptoms. No runny nose or eyes, no vomiting or diarrhea, just the serious rasp, lethargy, and lack of appetite.

"Remind me, how old is he?"

"Sixteen."

"I was just about to sit down for supper, but I could meet you at my clinic in an hour."

Jen had built her animal clinic not too far from her house on acreage off Highway 26 along the John Day River.

"Great. See you around seven thirty, then."

Even a treat from the kitty cupboard didn't interest Louie. "What's up, old boy? I've never seen you turn down one of these."

Jen Wilson was a gregarious woman who saw the world as largely good and kind, except where the mistreatment of animals was concerned. She was physically everything Ray Gattis was not: muscular and broad chested with short, platinum hair. Jen also sported tattoos and nose rings and always dressed in Carhartt coveralls.

"Poor guy." She plucked Louie from my arms and fetched a thermometer. "One-oh-four. Yep, he's got a fever. Look at those droopy eyes. Dehydrated too. He's definitely sick, Maggie."

"How sick?"

"I don't know. Considering his age, I want to keep him overnight and get him hydrated. I'll check out the possibilities after that."

"Louie will have a fit about all of it."

"Not to worry, they don't call me the cat lady for nothing."

I'd heard her referred to as the dog lady, the horse lady, and even the sheep lady, never the cat lady.

"Don't let this get around, but calling me any kind of lady is pretty far off the mark." She laughed wildly at her self-deprecating joke, and I tried to muster a chuckle too.

I watched her place Louie in a large cage.

"He'll be okay, Maggie."

I put on my police Stetson. "Be sure to say hi to Vicky."

"Will do. She's on fancy steroids right now, getting ready for IVF."

"In vitro fertilization?"

"Yep. Should turn out great. Hell, I've done hundreds of them on heifers. Works most every time." That was about as much as I wanted to know about the procedure, but I was sure Jen and Vicky would be outstanding moms if all went well.

Around nine o'clock back at the office, I set about contacting one of Trudeau's kids listed in that address book I'd uncovered. Pete, the son with the snazzy letterman's jacket, was a teacher in southern Oregon last I'd heard. I tried the two numbers hen-scratched inside the front cover of the address book next to his name. After no one answered, I tried the single listing for the daughter, Melissa, just a year older than me. Her number was no longer in service.

The same for Ronny, the middle boy, who always reminded me of the Nodine twins, except for having more money, more of everything, including an even greater affinity with bad behavior and petty crime. I figured him to be the one who'd absconded with his father's money, if Cecil Burney's rumor bore out.

I put in a call to regional dispatch and made a request for an officer in southern Oregon to deliver the next-of-kin notification, assuming the address listed for Pete Trudeau in Medford was still accurate.

It didn't help my earlier mood any when I got to my apartment and found it was dark, oppressively cold, and empty. The milk in my refrigerator had gone sour, too, the odor seeping into the spare box I called home. I opened the front door to let in fresh, icy air, turned the heat on full blast, and buttoned up my peacoat. Next I poured the milk down the drain and rinsed the carton.

The only calories I'd taken in were the breakfast at Erna's and a pathetic grab-n-go sandwich for lunch. I was famished, but there was shit nothing to eat. Which meant I had to avoid the half bottle of red wine on my counter and the pint of gin in the cupboard.

Unexpectedly, Duncan stood at the open door holding a pizza box. Was I hallucinating?

"Maggie?" he said. "Are you trying to warm the outside air or chill down your apartment?"

I wasn't about to explain my cure for getting rid of sour-milk smell. "No, but you're right on time." I indicated the pizza. "I'm starving."

Duncan crossed the threshold into my apartment, closing the door behind him. He placed the steaming pizza box on the table and brought my cold, chapped hands to his warm lips. "I'm hungry too."

Midnight wind, the grizzled juniper battering my kitchen window, Duncan moved quietly from the bed. He dressed and carried the cold, half-eaten pizza from the table to the refrigerator. I pulled on a long flannel shirt and a pair of wool socks, swept up the two wine glasses, empty but for the magenta dregs of Merlot, and placed them in the sink. We kissed and he sat in the chair beside the small dining table, lacing his boots.

"Sexy outfit," he said.

"Next time I'll keep my uniform on and break out the handcuffs."

"I'm serious. You look sexy. And I'm glad to hear there'll be a next time."

"On one condition." I gathered a hank of his unshorn hair between two fingers. "Let me trim this mess."

His full laugh surprised me. "God, you're fun. I can't understand why one guy would let you get away, let alone two."

"Let's just say neither had a good sense of humor." Which wasn't true in Morgan's case, but I was for damn sure not going to stand half naked in my kitchen and explain the motivations of my ex-husbands to the man who had singlehandedly recharged my batteries. And I didn't mean the triple As loaded in my vibrator.

"Tell you what. I'll let you cut my hair if you let me take a broom and dustpan to your apartment."

"Whoa. That's a deal. Shake on it?" I peered into his green eyes and extended my hand.

He nodded toward Louie's cat pillow I'd shifted from the

end of my bed to the floor. "You have a pet?"

"An old tabby cat. He's under the weather, so I took him to see Jen Wilson this evening. She kept him for the night."

"This county would be in bad shape without Jen."

"Especially the pets and livestock."

"Come here." He coaxed me gently onto his lap. "Sit with me for a few minutes. Then I have to take off, let you sleep. Tomorrow—today rather—could be a tough one."

He meant the Nodines' funeral and its aftermath.

"Can I ask you something personal?" Duncan asked.

"Depends."

"The scar on your shoulder, how'd you come by that?"

"It's a long story."

"After you became a cop?"

"Yes. But it had nothing to do with being a cop, okay?"

"Okay. Sorry to pry. Let's get you tucked in and I'll be on my way."

"I'd rather stay right where we are for another minute," I whispered.

"You got it."

Mark Taylor's spotlessly clean Ford F-150 pickup was parked next to our police station when I pulled up around eight a.m. Taylor was a generally uncomplicated guy who took his job as a fish and wildlife officer with the Oregon State Police very seriously, and he saw his role as husband and father as the culmination of the good life.

He was the kind of fellow I probably should have married. But no. Sincerity and naiveté were suspicious qualities to my mind, and Taylor had both to the bone. A good cop, though.

"Welcome back, Mark. How was Disneyland?"

"Great. We were smart to go before spring vacation. No

long lines. The three-day pass is pretty cheap. And we got a heck of a deal at the Disneyland Hotel." He held up a chubby digit with each example of just how smart they'd been.

"I'm glad you had a good time."

"You should plan a trip there your next vacation. It's more fun for adults, really. The kids got bored, wanted to hang out at the hotel pool all day. Ellie and I, though, we couldn't get enough of Splash Mountain. *The* bomb."

Did anyone else use that dated expression these days?

"Hollis and Lillian's little boy was born while you were away," I said, hoping to shift the conversation to a topic about which I gave a care.

"Also, we drove down to Seal Beach, south of Anaheim. It's the damnedest thing. The sand has to be hauled in from the desert."

Jesus Christ, the play-by-play was already tedious. "Did you hear what I said? Hollis and Lil had their kid."

"Heard that, yeah." He indicated a small, gift-wrapped package on his desk. "Brought back some baby Mickey ears for the little tyke."

I opened my computer. "Have you heard about the murders?"

"The Nodine twins, right? I saw your display back there by the break table."

"That's our murder board. Turns out we're going to need another one. We found Guy Trudeau's body yesterday. Someone tried to make it look like he'd hung himself, but the medical examiner pronounced it a homicide."

"Is that so, Sarge?" Hollis had arrived.

"Morning, Hollis. Congratulations," Taylor said.

"Thanks, Mark. Glad you're back. We could really use your help around here." He settled in at his desk. "So, Dr. Gattis determined Trudeau's death was no suicide?"

"Yep. She still needs to run a few tests, I guess."

Taylor placed a small package on Holly's desk. "Go ahead. Open it. Ellie and I couldn't resist. It's for...What's your baby's name?"

"Henry. We're calling him Hank, though." He picked up the package. "I think I'll take it home so Lil and I can open it together."

"Nah. Open it now. I want to see the look on your face."

Taylor reminded me of a good-hearted kid, overly eager to please but never quite getting there.

"Actually, I think it's time we all got to work. I have a homicide report to finish before the funeral," I said.

"Funeral? Is that why you're all dressed up?" Taylor asked, referring to my mourning outfit, the one suit I had ever owned. Black, wool, and out of fashion.

"The Nodine brothers' service is this morning."

"Speaking of the Nodines," Taylor said. "I saw you'd written something about Kat McKay dating one of them. Dan, maybe?"

"Yeah," I said.

"I cited her about a month ago up Murderers Creek. She was doing target practice inside the state wildlife area. Blasting away with a nine-millimeter handgun. The same kind you've got listed on your murder board."

"A Kel-Tec PF-9?"

He nodded. "She had that kid of hers along too."

"Rain."

"Right. Right as rain." Taylor chuckled.

Hollis placed the baby gift on his desk and made his way to the murder board. He noted the Kel-Tec 9 and Murderers Creek beside Kat McKay's name, added "Rain" in parentheses.

Taylor scrolled through email and hummed "It's a Small World After All," prompting me to call Jen Wilson.

"Maggie," she answered cheerfully. "Louie has perked up nicely, but I think I'd like to keep him around for the day. Will that work for you?"

That news perked me up as well, despite Taylor's incessant humming in the background. "Whatever you advise here, Jen."

"All right. I'll see you this evening. We close at five, but just give me a heads-up if you're going to be later than that."

"Will do."

I finally set to work on the Trudeau homicide report. Although I managed to describe the details of the old man hanging dead in his kitchen, by the time I'd fully related our discovery of the body and the ensuing search of his property, I felt like I was on a sickening fast track to becoming an expert at recounting murder scenes.

Al Bach opened the station door as I stood at the printer waiting for it to spit out my pages. I had already set him up at the extra desk, empty since the second fish and wildlife position was cut from our budget.

"This will work fine, Sergeant. I brought my laptop along," he said, placing it on his temporary desk.

After describing the layout of our office and directing him to the supply closet, I introduced Bach to Taylor, who thereafter refrained from regaling us with Disney songs and stories of his SoCal adventure. OSP brass often prompted Taylor's timidity.

To ease his discomfort, I asked him to listen to the recorded tip line call reporting the Nodines poaching deer out in Logan Valley.

"See if you recognize the guy's voice. Hollis and I didn't,

but you might. Also, would you pull up the Kat McKay citation you mentioned?"

"I'll get on that right now," Taylor said.

Bach followed me to our back alcove and spent a few minutes studying the murder board. "Pretty compelling, Maggie."

"A lot of data, though."

"Better that than too little, I promise you. After the funeral, let's look at some of the threads you've got listed and see if anything ties together."

"I like that idea." I was relieved he was on my side again. Yesterday's conversation had gone better than I'd expected, and his disdain for J.T. Lake turned out to be a side benefit.

Juniper Memorial Chapel had filled with family members, locals in mourning, and likely some onlookers hoping for a view of the murdered men. But Lynn and Farley had wisely gone for a closed-casket affair.

On the church organ at the front of the sanctuary, Dorie played "All the Way My Savior Leads Me" while the last of the funeral-goers filed in and sat in the pews. I stood in the back next to Sam Damon, who closed the doors at precisely 11:05 a.m. Reverend Bill took the podium and led us in prayer. Afterward, Brian Clancy, a former classmate of mine and of Dan and Joseph, read the eulogy. Then Alice and Dave Hanover sang "The Old Rugged Cross," mostly hitting the harmonies.

Al had reminded me to note who attended and who didn't. Dorie, all of the other church ladies, and any husbands were present, of course, along with every relative still living in the John Day Valley and their cousin Jess Bennett from Burns. Ariel Pritchett sobbed from the front row seated next to

Whitey Kern and his girl Olive. But I didn't know what to make of Cecil Burney. He'd cleaned himself up for the occasion, despite his supposed hatred of the Nodine brothers. Conversely, Kat McKay was conspicuously absent.

After the funeral service, most of us climbed in our vehicles and followed Sam's hearse, now loaded with the two caskets, three miles up 395, turned left at East Road, and drove to the cemetery grounds. The fast breeze had faded to a flutter, and we stood in warm sunlight before the twin graves, a view of Strawberry Mountain Wilderness directly southeast and the broad river valley to the north and west.

Graveyard rites turned out to be an abridged version of the observance we had attended earlier, with a final send-off prayer from Reverend Bill. Alice and Dave Hanover sang a song Lynn had requested, Clapton's "Tears in Heaven," which echoed from the hilltop cemetery, across the valley, and trailed the course of the river. Finally, a hymn I knew and understood.

After the service, I made my way across the wet blades of grass to hug Lynn and say goodbye. "Afraid I have to pass on lunch at the Grange hall."

"Thank you for coming, Maggie. Wish I could take a pass on lunch. I'll be glad when all the fussing comes to an end."

"I know, Lynn." I placed a hand on her shoulder. "Everybody means well."

"Oh, I get that. It's just not my cup of tea."

I smiled and brushed aside a strand of my hair.

"You'll let me know when you find out who did this," she said.

"Of course. As soon as I can."

I crossed the cemetery grounds toward my Tahoe parked in the line of vehicles. My mother and father were buried a few rows over, not side-by-side, but near one another. They weren't divorced when Zoey drove herself headlong into the river, but their marriage was long over, and Tate had been living alone in his trailer house for years.

I was fifteen when Zoey committed suicide, and I found Tate's emaciated body shortly before my eighteenth birthday. I hadn't visited their gravesites since the funerals, and I didn't plan to begin practicing that custom anytime soon.

The service and burial rites for Dan and Joseph had left me rheumy. I wanted to clear my head, take a drive east past Prairie City to the wayside overlooking the John Day Valley. The view was stunning from there—river and canyons, peaks and desert, fossil scarp, and a vast range of scrub and forest, all in one expansive vista. It could almost make a heathen believe in the possibility of a higher power. Yet it was the sea-green and vermilion earth and the pewter-blue swath of sky that embodied the divine and sacred in my eyes. No obligatory text or enigmatic ritual required.

These days, though, a modernist replica of Conestoga wagons, symbolizing the Oregon Trail, tainted the wayside. Homage to brave souls crossing into unknown territory, it was also a reminder of slaughter and bondage: Lillian's people, Holly's people, and all of those who found themselves in the path of white ignorance and so-called manifest destiny.

This was all too pensive a reflection to dwell on, especially in light of the post-funeral scene now playing out several yards from the twins' freshly dug graves. Farley Nodine and Cecil

Burney swaggered and circled one another, heading for a bust-up.

"Hey!" I shouted as Farley gave Cecil a hard shove.

My dress boots had already collected mud on their spikey heels and were otherwise not built for peace officer duties, making for a difficult and slightly treacherous trot across the wet grass back to the gravesites. By the time I caught up with the fracas, Farley had pinned Cecil on the ground and had his hands around the old drunk's neck.

I yanked Farley's collar and managed to lift him off Cecil. "Fucking stop this shit right now."

But Farley was fired up and wrenched free of my grasp. As he aimed a kick toward Cecil, I stepped toward it, and Farley reluctantly pulled up. Both men's raspy breathing filled the air.

"Help him up, Farley."

"I don't need the bastard's help." Cecil jerked himself up and brushed at his blazer and Wranglers. "You owe me thirty-four bucks for the pants."

"You owe me a lot more than that, Burney."

"What's this all about?" I said and waited for one of the old men to speak. "Answer me, damn it."

"I don't figure it's any of your concern, Maggie." Farley bent down and snatched his cap up from the wet earth. "An old feud, is all."

I zipped up my knee-length down jacket. "All right. I assume Lynn knows. I'll just ask her."

Cecil stepped toward me. "You will not go bothering Lynn about this."

"She's got enough on her mind. Besides, she won't tell you neither," Farley added.

But I was certain there was someone who would tell me, and I had no doubt she knew all the details. Dorie.

"I'm going to stand right here and watch the two of you walk to your vehicles. And if either of you falls victim to some *accident* anytime soon, I'll know who to fill out an arrest warrant for." I watched both men drive away as Sam Damon and his helper lowered Dan's and Joseph's caskets, settled them into the earth, and began filling the two pits with rich, black soil.

I stopped at home and changed into my uniform, then high-tailed it back to the office.

Taylor was holding down the fort. "How were the services?" he asked.

"Long."

"Say, I placed a copy of Kat McKay's citation in your inbox. And I listened to the poacher tip line call. I didn't recognize the voice either."

"Didn't sound much like a local, did he?"

"No, but that doesn't really mean anything I guess." He logged off his computer and cleared his desk. "I'm making part of my back country rounds this afternoon. South Fork Road, up Murderers Creek, and down into Fields Creek. "

"Sounds good. Be sure to take your lunch break."

"Headed home right now." He fetched his coat and hat. "I'll radio if I see anything interesting. Oh, and Hollis and Detective Bach should be back about one thirty."

"Take it easy out there." I perused email and got the word that Trudeau's son Pete had been notified about his father's death.

I paced the alcove and thought about Kat McKay out in the Murderers Creek Wildlife Area shooting off that Kel-Tec 9. I wondered how Duncan might react if I ended up arresting his sister for murder. He'd be pissed, of course.

"Nothing in this world is without goddamn complication, is it?" I said aloud to myself.

Trudeau's murder board needed its own place in the alcove, so I left off mulling over the fate of my budding love affair. At the front counter, I dug around for tape and markers, crouched down and searched the bottom shelf for a chart pack.

I heard the front door open.

"Hello?" A chirpy, girly voice called out. "Trooper Jones?"

I rose to find Jess Bennett standing in our waiting area. She'd also changed out of her funeral wear and was sporting a short skirt with geometric designs running along the diagonal. Her phosphorescent pink bustier shone through a sheer white blouse.

"I thought I'd find the other officer, Senior Trooper Hollis Jones," she said. "He called me the other day?"

I pulled Taylor's chair next to my desk. "Have a seat. Trooper Jones is out for lunch."

Disappointed, but resigned to having to deal with me instead, she sat.

"I called you the day after your cousins were murdered and left a voicemail. You never called me back," I said.

"I know, ma'am, and I'm sorry. I was on my way to Winnemucca and out of signal range. By the time I listened to your voicemail, I'd already heard the news about Danny and Joey."

"That wasn't why I was calling you. When I stopped you Thursday, you said you were taking Guy Trudeau's twenty-seven head of steers to Boise. That didn't happen, though, did it?"

"No, ma'am."

"Where'd you deliver them?"

"I don't think I'm at liberty to say. You should ask the old man."

"Ms. Bennett. Maybe you misunderstood Trooper Jones when you talked to him a few days ago. This is not a friendly chitchat over coffee. This is a murder investigation."

"Do I need a lawyer?"

Jess Bennett no doubt had a better sense of whether she needed legal representation than I did, but I said nothing.

"You gotta believe me, I'm not supposed to give out that information. It's up to the owner to tell you. Mr. Trudeau could sue our company if I did."

"Trudeau is dead. Strangled."

"Jesus." The woman's pallid complexion turned more ashen.

"Where did you haul Mr. Trudeau's cattle?"

There it was again, her westward glance for an answer. "I can't say."

"So the answer to your question is yes, you need a lawyer. I'm arresting your ass. Taking you to our shithole county courthouse, where the sheriff will lock you in a holding pen along with all the drunks and meth heads who call the place their second home."

"What kind of bullshit is that?"

"The kind of fucking bullshit I'm suddenly inclined to resort to."

"You actually think I might have something to do with the murders of my cousins? Or that old man?"

"I don't know. You have a link to all three, and you better tell me where the hell you delivered those cattle."

Hollis had returned from lunch in time to interrupt my tirade. "Ms. Bennett, I'm Trooper Jones. We spoke on the phone."

She nodded.

"I'd recommend you answer Sergeant Blackthorne's questions. She's kind of lost her sense of humor about multiple murders in her State Police district. Me? I'm just here to help her figure out who killed your cousins and Mr. Trudeau."

Jess sighed and faced me. "All right, ma'am. The twins were supposed to return six head of Black Angus steers they'd stolen from Trudeau. They were gonna meet us at nine on Thursday morning so we could load them in my cattle truck. Everything was supposed to be square after that. Trudeau wouldn't press charges. But they didn't show. So the old man and I finally loaded up the last of his steers and took off."

"How did you know it was the twins who stole the livestock?" I asked.

"The old man let it slip while we were waiting for them to show up. I let on like I didn't know who the Nodine twins were. And I was glad they never came. Might have pissed Trudeau off more if he knew I was their cousin."

I wasn't sure I bought that part of the story, but I let it go for the time being. "Where'd you head to after I pulled you over last Thursday?"

"Instead of Boise, Trudeau led me to some ranch not too far from where you stopped us. When we got there, three big guys stood at the cattle chute, loaded for bear. The buyer argued with Mr. Trudeau and wouldn't let us unload. And with those three armed guards there, he had to do what the owner said. So I hauled the steers back to the old man's pasture land and then drove back to Burns."

"Could you identify on a map where you tried to deliver the animals?"

"I'll try, ma'am. I'm truly not out to hinder prosecution or whatever. I loved those boys to death. Shit. Didn't mean to phrase it that way."

"Follow me." I led her to the topographic map posted on

the alcove wall next to the murder board, Hollis following behind. "Here's about where I stopped you."

She studied the map.

"On Thursday, you said Trudeau was carrying a gun," I said.

"He was, ma'am. He damn well was. More than one, I think."

"But not enough to take on the men you said were *loaded for bear*."

"No way. They were armed with Beretta M9s. And that's just what I saw."

"Are you a collector?" Hollis asked.

"Collector?"

"You recognized the specific weapons. How is that?"

She shrugged. "Late-night TV. Gun shows. Online auctions. It's not rocket science."

"No. Just social science," he said.

Holly's snarky remarks were so much more sophisticated than mine.

"I think it was near here." Jess pointed to an area slightly north of Seneca. "Weirdest thing I ever saw, too. No wranglers. No dogs. Just those men with guns and some suit in fancy clothes. The place had a different-sounding name, too. Wasn't called a ranch."

"Bear Valley Cattle Company?" I asked.

"That's it," she said, a tinge of relief in her voice.

"Okay, Ms. Bennett, we're done for now, but we might have more questions later."

"Ma'am, could you just call me Jess? *Ms. Bennett* reminds me of that idiot I used to be married to. Plus Seth and I got married in Winnemucca last Friday. I go by Flynn now."

She put a worn denim jacket on over her sheer blouse, tugged it tight across her chest, and closed the pearl snaps.

She placed her petite truck driver hands on my desk across from my equally diminutive cop hands.

"For Aunt Lynn's sake, you need to find who killed my cousins."

"I hear you, Jess," I said.

Al returned from lunch with a bag of green grapes to share and joined Hollis and me at the card table in the alcove.

"Do you both believe the Bennett woman?" he asked after we described our visit with her.

"Her last name's Flynn now. And yeah, I think I believe her. How about you, Hollis?"

"I definitely believed her about the armed men."

"Okay, then. I'd like to interview the ranch owner. What was his name again?" Bach asked.

"Larkin. Asa Larkin. Legal surname's Wakefield," I said.

"Right. Adopted by an aunt and uncle." Al pushed his chair away from the table. "Let's head out there right now, Sergeant."

I turned to Hollis. "Dr. Gattis needs a ride to the airport around four o'clock. We might still be out at Larkin's, and Taylor might not be back before then."

He nodded. "I'm on it."

"I'll text Ray and let her know, pass along your number," I said.

Hollis plucked a couple of grapes from the bag. "In the meantime, I'm going to make another attempt to contact Frank Sylvester's accountant."

"What's that about, Trooper Jones?" Bach asked.

"That Ram pickup the Nodines were driving," Hollis answered.

"I remember. Registered to Frank Sylvester, who owns the trucking company in Burns."

"Sylvester's been bedridden ever since he broke his neck a year and a half ago. Don't think he could have gone to a dealership and bought it, or charged it online, for that matter. Sarge and I want to find out if there was a proxy buyer. Anyway, the manager of the Sylvester's company gave me the name of their bookkeeper, an accountant at some firm in Portland."

Bach gathered up his computer and retrieved his jacket from the back of his chair. "If you get nowhere with the accountant, I know a guy you can call in Portland."

I slipped on my peacoat and police Stetson and followed him to his rig.

Would never have guessed Al liked to blast old-time honky-tonk while driving around in his Ford Police Interceptor. Classical or the Mormon Tabernacle Choir seemed more his bent, not Ernest Tubb and Hank Williams.

He turned down the music a couple of decibels. "You're lucky you have a good team to work with out here, Maggie."

"Don't I know it."

After several miles, I turned the volume down even more and came back to yesterday's conversation out at Big T. "Do *you* question my leadership?"

"Maggie, I'm well aware whose leadership should be in question. Perhaps it *is* being questioned, but I'm not privy to that information. This is the reality of a career in any paramilitary organization. We all follow someone's orders, move on to the next thing, and don't look back. Now if you don't mind, Patsy Cline is one of my favorites."

He nodded toward the volume toggle, and I bumped "I Fall to Pieces" up a notch or two. I had to admit that voice was fine.

"Our junction is up ahead on the right," I said.

He slowed the SUV. "Here?"

"Yes. The place is about five miles in."

We arrived at Bear Valley Cattle Company and found the gate locked.

"There's no call button or intercom." I checked my phone for bars. "And no service."

Al switched on his secondary siren, giving rise to a deafening wail.

"What the hell is that?"

"The Federal Signal Q. Two-hundred-watt PA," he bellowed. "It seems to have done the trick."

Larkin, in a down jacket, stepped briskly from the porch of his ranch house and walked toward the gate. Al shut off the siren, zipped his coat, and stepped out of the Interceptor. I trundled behind him.

When Larkin realized it was a couple of cops, one of whom was visiting him for the third day in a row, he pulled the automatic gate opener from his coat pocket, activated it, and we walked through the entrance.

"Good afternoon, Mr. Larkin. I understand you've met Sergeant Blackthorne already. I'm Detective Alan Bach, Oregon State Police homicide unit." He handed Larkin his card. "We have a few questions. If we could step out of the elements, we can be in and out in no time."

"Certainly. Follow me."

Larkin led us to the same room in which Hollis and I had sat questioning him yesterday. I could sense his greater unease this afternoon. A homicide detective had that effect on folks.

"Sergeant Blackthorne had an interesting conversation

earlier today with a driver for a company called Frank Sylvester Trucking."

Larkin moved his glance from Bach to me.

"The driver claims to have tried to deliver twenty-seven steers to you last week," I said. "She was escorted by the owner of the cattle. She also said there were three armed men standing guard at your loading chute."

"Does this have something to do with the killing of those two brothers?" Larkin asked.

An odd question, I thought. "We don't know if it's connected to the Nodine murders."

"Let me explain, Mr. Larkin," Al slipped in. "We're interested in the truck driver's story because of the man who tried to sell you those steers."

"Guy Trudeau?"

"After Trooper Jones and I visited you yesterday, we found Mr. Trudeau dead. Another homicide," I answered.

He flinched. "How?"

"The medical examiner hasn't released a report yet," I said. Which, technically, was true.

"Regarding Mr. Trudeau, you ultimately refused to buy his cattle?"

Bach was gifted at redirecting an interview.

"Trudeau agreed to deliver thirty-three animals in healthy condition and ready for pasture-finishing, not twenty-seven malnourished and sick ones."

Ah, thus Jen Wilson's prescription to treat whatever Moraxella bovis might be.

"Sick?" Al asked.

"A number of his stock were underweight, listless, and had serious eye infections. I wouldn't let him unload, let alone pay him. That's why my hired men were there. And armed."

"All right, Mr. Larkin. Thank you for your time. I think you answered our questions for now. But we'd like to speak to your men," Bach said.

"They're away from the ranch today."

Al stood. "Another time, then."

Larkin looked at his watch. "I need to drive to the highway and pick up my son at the bus shelter."

"Your boy goes to Grant Union High School, right?" I asked.

"A senior. Headed for U of O next year. Now if you'll excuse me, I should get going."

We followed Larkin's vehicle back toward Highway 395, without the honkytonk blaring this time. Both of us silent, watching the man steer his shiny, black, tire-chained Prius over the ice-packed and grooved road.

"Is Seneca too small to have a high school of its own?" Al asked, breaking the low hush that had settled in the cab of his Interceptor.

"Yeah. High school–age students, which includes all the ranch kids from around Seneca, go to Grant Union in John Day."

"And back there, Mr. Larkin said something about pasture-finishing. What is that?"

"It's supposed to guarantee beef cattle raised only on grass and hay aren't fed grain before being sent to market. Something like that, anyway."

"I don't eat beef myself, but I know I prefer my chicken pasture raised."

It was interesting how he let banal personal information dribble out like that.

"We need to figure out what happened to those twenty-seven steers Trudeau tried to sell Larkin," he added.

"And the six others the Nodines had supposedly stolen from Big T."

"We're certain the woman truck driver was being truthful about all of that?"

I sighed. "We've probably got to be open to the idea there's more to her story."

As we approached the junction with 395, Larkin pulled off the roadway alongside a school bus shelter. The son, already waiting to be picked up, stepped from under the shingled roof, glared rancorously at his father, and jerked open the passenger-side door.

I nodded to the boy, a gesture meaning nothing more than howdy in this part of the world. But his return glower exhibited the contempt and utter disdain he felt for hick cops. I made a mental note to find out everything I could about the rude little bastard.

"What do you know about Mr. Larkin's son?" Bach asked.

"I was just thinking about that myself. Not much is the answer. Not even his name."

When Al and I arrived back at the office, Hollis was about to leave for the day.

"Glad you got here before I left," he said. "I've got news about the bookkeeper-slash-accountant. A woman named Sarah Anderson, but her maiden name was Wakefield. She's Asa Larkin's sister by adoption."

Bach placed his pack on his temporary desk. "How'd you track that down?"

"Started with the state's list of certified public accountants. I verified on a couple of other systems."

"Did you speak with her?" I asked.

"No. I wanted to talk to the two of you before getting in contact."

"Are you absolutely sure about what you found, Holly?"

"As sure as I can be without the Anderson woman's first-hand confirmation."

"Good work. Especially figuring out her maiden name," I said.

He shrugged "I was hoping to take it to the next level. Figure out who might be a legal proxy for Sylvester."

I peeled off my coat and tossed it over my desk chair. "When you do talk to her, don't let on you know about her relation to Larkin."

"Nah, I wouldn't do that, but maybe I should try to reach her now."

"It's too late in the day. Contact her tomorrow, and go home like you were about to."

"I'm with Maggie. Spending time with your wife and newborn is important right now."

"You've got kids, Detective?"

"Five daughters. And Hollis, you're welcome to call me Al whenever we're not with the public."

"Appreciate that. And I agree with both of you. I definitely need to spend more time with Lil and the baby. Let's solve these murders so I can do that." He donned his police Stetson and walked to the door. "Night, Maggie. Al. I'll be at home if you need me. Oh, I almost forgot. Dr. Gattis canceled her flight plans. There was some problem with the autopsy or something. They were booked up at Mack's, but she was able to get a room at the Best Western."

"Have a good night, and let Lil know I plan to drop by in the next day or so. I have a little something for Hank," I said.

"She'll like that."

. . .

I put in a call to the school district administrative office at the high school hoping to catch Zan Wilson before he left for the day. He'd been the district superintendent for almost twenty-five years. After his wife passed away, he finished raising his daughter, Jen, alone and sent her off to veterinary school. But when she returned to start her practice with her girlfriend—now wife—in tow, his Christian fundamentalist heart broke in two. Supposedly, Zan and his daughter hadn't spoken in years, but maybe that would change if Jen and Vicky had a kid.

He answered after a single ring.

"Zan. It's Maggie Blackthorne."

"Maggie! I was going to call you. I want you to come talk to students when we hold our career fair next month. Born and raised in this town, went off to college, and moved back years later as a sergeant with the Oregon State Police. That's a good story."

"Kind of sounds like the story of a loser to me."

"There's a lot of respect for law enforcement among our student body."

Couldn't help but roll my eyes. "Maybe, but they probably won't be too impressed with me moving back to the place where I grew up. You know how most young people are, itching to break free of their hometowns."

"But you'll speak to them anyway, right?"

"You bet, Zan. Happy to."

"Good. Now, what can I do for you?"

"I'm trying to get some information on one of your seniors."

"I believe I'd have to see a note signed by a parent or some kind of warrant for that."

Did you suddenly forget about Zan Wilson's ethical compass, Blackthorne? Still, I pressed him. "Even if it's just a name?"

"I can't imagine a student in the entire district whose name you don't know."

"I'm surprised myself, but I don't. He's new. I believe his last name's Larkin, but it might be Wakefield."

"Did you read the latest *Blue Mountain Eagle*?"

"I skimmed it a few days ago."

"You checked out the sports section?"

"No, but I take it I should have."

"There's only one new senior this year. Name's in an article on our basketball program."

I didn't see the difference between just telling me the name and pointing me to an article that includes the name, but whatever. "Appreciate all your help, Zan."

"Thanks for taking time out for our career fair. I'll have the guidance counselor get in touch."

On second thought, a career fair gig was an assignment right up Mark Taylor's alley. Maybe he could throw in a story or two about Disneyland.

I opened the *Blue Mountain Eagle* website and scoped out high school athletics. The Grant Union Lady Prospectors basketball team was doing well, probably going to state. Their male counterparts weren't even close.

I found what I was looking for in an article describing the boys' team's recent one-point loss to the Burns Highlanders. Asa Larkin's kid was in the grainy photo flanked by teammate Rain McKay-Ferlinghetti and captured in a mid-air dunk shot —cocky in his Lake Oswego–styled mane of coal-black hair. The boy had kept Wakefield as his last name, but his first name was Brady.

12

I turned toward Al Bach's temporary desk, excited to think I might've solved the mystery of the name on the sticky note he'd discovered in the glove compartment of the Ram 3500. But he was involved in a phone discussion, as animated as I'd seen him. Voice higher, cadence less resolute, not mad or sad or happy, perhaps remorseful. Possibly talking to his wife, lonely at home in Bend, tired of his trips into the wilderness investigating the murderous tendencies of some of our state's outback citizenry.

When he clicked off his phone, I rolled my chair in front of his desk. "So about Asa Larkin's son."

"Yes?"

"His name's Brady."

"Dear Lord."

I'm not sure why, but that response made me laugh. Loudly. "Sorry, that's not what I expected you to say, I guess. What's our next move?"

"Wait and see, unless you have a sense that Larkin and his kid might be ready to pick up and leave."

"I have no idea, really, but I don't think so."

"All right, then. Add it to your murder board for now, and let's take Dr. Gattis out to pizza or a nice supper. That was Ray on the phone just now. She's starving. As am I. Bet you are too."

"Nah. I'll eat later. I have the Flynn woman's phone number. I'd like to get her back in the office. Hopefully she hasn't gone back to Burns already. I want to ask her what happened to those twenty-seven beef cattle, because they sure weren't at Trudeau's ranch. And I'd prefer to talk to her in person and in my police station."

"I'm not ordering you to come to supper, Maggie. But I'd appreciate it. And I think Ray would too."

"Sure, then. Supper it is." Again, I spoke to Bach's forehead.

"Tell you what. Try phoning Ms. Flynn, and if she's still in town, we'll interview her together."

I dialed Jess and waited while it went to voicemail. I let her know we had more questions and told her not to ignore my message this time. Then I phoned Ray and asked her to meet Al and me at the Blue Mountain Lounge.

"Oh, for Christ's sake, Maggie. He's the last person I need to see right now."

"Yeah, that's right, where we ate a few nights ago. I've got an urge for another cheeseburger. See you there in five." I hung up and put on my coat. "Your rig or mine?"

"Mine."

I planned to request Patsy Cline for the short drive there and back.

Dinner with Ray Gattis and Al Bach turned out to be a sober affair, which was not to say somber, but definitely without alcohol. Less profanity too, at least on my part. I tried not to let my quasi chaperone status get in the way of conversation, but in order to keep everything simple and on a platonic plane, I took on the role of provincial nerd, jabbering about the success of the Grant Union Lady Prospectors basketball team.

"I never would have seen you as a fan of high school sports, Maggie," Ray said when Al got up to use the restroom.

"I haven't been to even one game. It was just something to blab on about. Now that we're alone, tell me how you're doing."

"I don't feel like talking about it yet, but if you keep finding corpses at the rate you're going, then we might get around to the conversation by this time next year."

"That bad, huh?"

"That fucking bad."

Bach returned and paid for the meal. "Ray, I meant to ask earlier, but I was so engrossed in the story about the local girls' basketball team, I forgot."

Doc and I both laughed.

"Al Bach, did you just make a goddamn joke?" she asked.

Red-faced and flustered, he also laughed. "Sorry, Maggie. No offense."

"It's okay. I was just telling Ray I've never attended any of their games, so I can't be much of a real fan."

"What were you wanting to ask me?" Ray said.

"There was some kind of problem with Mr. Trudeau's autopsy?"

"Not really. There was evidence of malignancy. The lung, the liver. That's not what killed him, of course, but it soon would have. It did complicate the autopsy. I wasn't sure I could finish before my flight, so I canceled the reservation."

. . .

Ray headed back to her motel room, and Bach dropped me off at my office. Jess Flynn hadn't returned my call, and since it was only just past seven, I drove to Lynn Nodine's place, where I suspected the relatives had gathered after the Grange hall funeral feast. It was a stretch, but Jess might still be in town, working at comforting her aunt. When I arrived, the place was dark and Lynn's Volkswagen bus was the only vehicle parked outside the house, half in and half out of the garage.

It seemed she had finally gotten what she wanted. To be left alone, so I left her alone too, turned up the heater in my Tahoe, and continued on up the street, across the bridge over Canyon Creek. I would have been surprised to find Farley Nodine or Ariel Pritchett working at the Rifleman Club tonight, but I stopped in anyway. The owner, a transplant from some town on the coast, was substituting for Farley at the bar, but Ariel was serving drinks and bar snacks.

Some stragglers from the funeral had pushed together a few tables. Relatives mostly, but not Jess Flynn. The jukebox sat silent, and I could hear them talking, their voices low, solemn. I took a booth in the corner.

Ariel wandered over. "How can I help you, Maggie? A beer? Maybe a mixed drink?"

"Seltzer water with lime would be nice."

"Got no lime. Want it over ice?"

"Sure."

When she returned with my drink, I asked if she had time to sit and go over a couple of things with me.

"After I put on some music. I don't need the customers or the owner listening in."

I watched her select several songs on the jukebox. A kind woman who'd done nothing more nefarious than live a harder life than some in our backwater county. She was already beginning to stoop under the weight of her limited choices. Resigned to forking over her scant shekels for the ironic accoutrement of poverty: cigarettes and a shitload of TV channels. She sat across from me and leaned over the table, balanced on her rawboned elbows.

"Thanks, Ariel. I'd like to follow up on some things."

"Okay."

"First, how're you doing?"

"Well, I was pretty much a basket case at the funeral. I'm only working tonight 'cause I need to keep my job."

"You should check with Dorie. I think she's looking for somebody to help her in her thrift store." A fib, really. But it was in the realm of possibility, I figured.

"No tips at the thrift store, though. You said you wanted to follow up on some things."

"Did Joseph ever talk about anyone named Brady?"

"That rancher's kid?"

I nodded.

"He's new around here. I know he's trouble, though. Got too much money for his own good. Always tryin' to get Joey and Danny to get him beer or weed, or plotting something."

"Plotting? Like what?"

"I don't really know. I just knew something was up with him ever' once in a while."

"Did he have anything to do with the deal you talked about?"

"Like I said the other day, I didn't know details. Joey said nobody could know, so I doubt they'd involve some kid. Especially that Brady shit."

"Unless he's the one who cooked up whatever it was they were involved in."

She sighed and shrugged, folded her arms across her chest.

"We're working our tails off, chasing every lead, Ariel. So

this is important. Could it have been Brady they were working a deal with?"

"I know you're tryin' to find the killer, Maggie, but I'm flustered. I miss Joey a lot."

"You mentioned the boy was interested in beer and weed. Maybe Brady wanted to work as the middleman selling to other students, and he was looking to Dan and Joseph as the source?" A theory I pulled out of my ass.

"You know dang well it's always been easy for teenagers to get beer around here. Pot too, even when it was illegal for everybody."

"Maybe he asked them to commit some other kind of crime. Something more serious."

"Any of that might've been hard for the kid to get away with. His old man's pretty strict, I guess. Religious nut."

"So I gathered. Okay, that's all for now, Ariel. But I need to ask you to keep our conversations confidential. I have to be able to trust you on that."

She shook her head repeatedly. "I'd never tell anybody nothing that might hurt your case. You gotta believe me."

"I know you wouldn't mean to, but we live in a dinky, boring town. Gossiping and spreading rumors is built into our genetic code."

"Which is why I put on that damn music, remember?"

If the woman was going to repeat our conversation about Brady Wakefield, there was nothing I could do about it. I reached across and patted her upper arm. "I know how you felt about Joey."

"No. Don't think you really do. But it don't matter. I just want justice for both of 'em."

"I do have one other thing to ask you about."

She looked over at the tables where the funeral-goers sat

drinking. Seemed like everyone needed a refill. "I should get back to work."

"What's the beef between Farley and Cecil Burney all about?"

"Maybe gossip and spreading rumors ain't built into your whatever kind of code after all."

I glimpsed the hint of a smile.

"Old Cecil's got the hots for Lynn. And even though they're divorced, it pisses Farley off every time Cecil comes around. Specially today at the funeral."

Maybe Cecil's animosity toward the Nodine twins had something to do with Lynn. It seemed unlikely given the venom tainting his outrage. But it reminded me he'd said he was at an AA meeting seated next to Lynn last Thursday evening. I still needed to verify that.

Parked in the lot behind the Rifleman Club, I dialed Jen Wilson's number. I was late getting back to her about Louie, and although her clinic was a short walk from her house, even Jen might've been hard-pressed to appreciate my call. Sure enough, she came on the line without her usual sunny disposition.

"Sorry to call after hours, Jen."

"Maggie. Louie's ready to go home, but can it wait til tomorrow? Vicky and I just turned on *Fargo*."

"Sure thing."

"Come by anytime."

I briefly distracted myself wondering about Jen's seeming lack of cheerfulness, and then I let that go. It wasn't my job to make sure the civilians in my territory were happy. My job was to make sure they were safe.

. . .

Just after eight, Hollis texted and invited me to drop by. Lillian and Hank were still up, and it was a good time to visit. I stopped off at my apartment to fetch the small wrapped package on my dresser—a red hat I'd crocheted from baby wool—and jumped in my Jetta.

Last time I'd been to their home on Airport Road, Lil and I had sat on the front porch out in the weather. I'd admired the view of the John Day River Valley to the north, but tonight I understood even more why they'd chosen to buy this house in particular. The picture window in the living room faced south-west toward the Aldrich range. I also liked how they had decorated the place—a mix of their separate cultures overlaid with infant paraphernalia. It all exuded pride. And love. And baby smells.

"Damn," I said, "he's the most beautiful newborn I've ever seen." Which I could count on one hand, truth be told.

Made sense, though. Hollis and Lil were both physically attractive, stunning even, and their child had inherited a gorgeous meld of Paiute and African ancestry—almond-shaped eyes, thick dark hair, and creamy brown skin. He lay in his swaddling blanket inside the papoose carrier that Lil had woven. I noticed he wasn't wearing Taylor's Mickey Mouse ears.

Unwrapping Hank's hat, Lillian held her breath. "It's incredible. Red stands for faith and happiness. It's handmade, right?"

I nodded.

"You made that, Sarge?"

"Yep."

He bent forward and crushed me with a bear hug.

"We're honored, Maggie," Lil said, joining in our embrace.

"Gosh, Mr. and Mrs. Two Moons-Jones." I wasn't certain

they used that hyphenate anywhere out in the real world, but I thought it fit their kid nicely.

Shortly after I arrived, Lil carried Hank and herself off to bed.

I turned to Hollis. "I think I solved the Brady conundrum, or at least the person who owns the name."

"Did you want me to guess?" he said after a conspicuous pause.

"Asa Larkin's kid. And he apparently regularly hit up the Nodine twins for beer and weed. Ariel Pritchett also told me he was always 'plotting something.'"

"Did she have any details?"

"I don't believe Ariel's much into details."

"Maybe she should be encouraged to get more into details, then."

"I think it helps for her to stew on things. But I know she's also cautious about ratting out Joseph and his brother in any way."

"No way to rat them out now."

"She's scared she'll reveal something about herself, I suppose."

"Ariel was about to elope with Joseph. Doesn't she pretty much have to know more than she's saying?"

I knew Holly was probably right about that. Also knew I'd avoided pressing her for more information.

"There's a good chance, I'd say. And some possibility she's taking advantage of our childhood connection."

"I never noticed that working for anyone else around here."

"Even so, the next conversation with her, I want you to be there."

"Or better yet. Detective Bach."

· · ·

Halfway up the stairs to my apartment, I stopped, walked back down to Dorie's place, and pulled the clapper on her strange antique doorbell. She emerged from her residence in back of the thrift store.

"Maggie. You don't have to ring, just come on in," she said, opening the door.

I followed her to the living room and sat in the overstuffed chair next to an oak table, forgetting this was the corner where she left her treacly sandalwood incense burning.

Dorie sat across from me and fetched a quilting project from the satchel full of fabric sitting at her feet. "It's for the Jones baby. Henry, right?"

"That's right. They're calling him Hank, though."

She proceeded to baste together the layers of stitched squares of gingham, the batting, and the flannel backing.

"It's lovely, D. Hollis and Lillian will appreciate it, especially since it's handmade."

"I talked to Lillian at Chester's Market just last week. She's a sweet little thing."

I knew Dorie better than I knew anyone, and this was code for not being sure Lil was sweet at all.

"Have you eaten dinner?" she asked.

"I had a cheeseburger at the BM earlier."

"I bet those people wish they'd never named that place the Blue Mountain Lounge. I have some pie in the kitchen. You're welcome to a piece."

"No, thanks. I wanted to ask you about something."

She placed her quilting hoop back in the satchel. "Shoot."

"Farley and Cecil Burney got into a row after the funeral. Do you know what that might've been about?"

"Oldest story in the world."

"Somebody told me Cecil has a thing for Lynn. And apparently Farley gets riled up about it even though they've been divorced for years."

"Decades, but that's only part of it. Lynn and Cecil had an affair while she and Farley were still married."

"God. I find it hard to believe Lynn would have anything to do with that filthy old drunk. But I guess Farley's pretty much in that same category." The same category Tate had been in.

"Lynn was a regular wild girl when she was young and drank quite a bit herself. She stopped before the twins were born, but she and Farley split up not too long after. If it weren't for her Forest Service job, and AA, of course, she'd be a sadder case than she already is."

I'd never thought of Lynn Nodine as being a sad case.

"I've prayed and prayed for her."

"Kind of like you've prayed and prayed for me?"

"Exactly like that. And I noticed one of those prayers was answered."

"Meaning?"

"I saw your pizza delivery guy come by last night, and I heard him leave early, early this morning." Dorie flashed one of her wry smiles.

I rose to leave. "It's time for me to be going. Thanks for the old gossip."

"Sit for a while longer. I'm going to get us both a piece of pie."

She stood and ambled to the kitchen. I sat back down and pushed the burning incense to the far side of the table.

When Dorie returned with our desserts, we sat quietly, chewing.

"Apple pie is my favorite. So good," I said. "Back to our conversation a moment."

"The part about Duncan?"

"No. Let that rest, would you?"

"Oh, sure I will."

"The affair with Lynn, is that why Cecil despised Dan and Joseph?"

"I don't know. Maybe indirectly? There were rumors for a while that Cecil was the twins' actual father. I never asked Lynn about it and never will. But I didn't think those boys resembled Cecil, or Farley either, for that matter. I always just thought they looked like each other."

"They reminded me of Lynn, except for the eyes. Whether or not Cecil was their father or knew he was or wasn't, the wrath he still has for those boys is..."

"Murderous?"

"I was going to say beyond the pale. Especially now that I know about his feelings for Lynn."

"Well, Dan and Joe brought Lynn a lot of pain over the years."

"There is that."

I carried our plates to the kitchen, and Dorie resumed basting together the layers of Hank's quilt.

On the way out, I bent down and kissed her on the cheek. "Good night."

"The world sure has a way of spinning out of control sometimes. Even our little bit of it."

Her little pseudo metaphysical pronouncements always amused me. "Isn't it all simply God's grand plan?"

"You're a cynic, Maggie. But I love you."

At the base of Aldrich Mountain, the river cuts a slow, indelible arc, winds along the silver plain of alfalfa toward a copse of blue sage and the Widow's Creek Bridge. To kill herself, Zoey rammed our jeep though the railing and plunged thirty feet into a surge of black water. Tate found her pinned against the pilings. Ruined and lost as it left him, he'd have been better off to lie down beside her and float among the crawdads, avoid the years wasted pickling his liver.

I woke in the grim murk of death rituals, grief's general mindfuck. Brought on by yesterday's funeral for those wild boys from my childhood and by today's anniversary: twenty-five years ago, three days before my fifteenth birthday, my mother committed suicide.

I clicked on the antique lamp, drew back the coverlet, and stepped into the chilly room, turned up the heat, and started my day. After a shower, I scrambled a couple of eggs and made toast. Surprised at how tasty breakfast turned out, I decided that when things calmed down, I'd check out some recipes and start eating healthier meals. Give up frozen entrées altogether. That trifling bit of resolve improved my disposition some, so much so I tossed an aging apple and an energy bar into my pack for lunch.

The trill of my phone startled me out of my little self-help session. A text from Duncan: "Morning! Got time to drop by the F&T for a visit?"

"I'll do my damnedest. Yesterday was crazy"

"So I heard. Be careful out there okay"

Before I could thumb a flirty response, Lynn Nodine rang through.

"Margaret, I found something, and I think you need to see it."

"I'm on my way."

Lynn opened her door before I reached the front steps. Even though her voice over the phone had lacked urgency, seeing her standing there, anxious, waiting for me to arrive, I knew she'd found something important. I followed her inside, through the living room, to the glassed-in porch at the back of her house.

"I like to sew or knit in this room. Sometimes I come out here and read."

"Nice space."

"I kept the copy of the *Rubaiyat of Omar Khayyam*, with the two-thousand dollars tucked inside, over there in the credenza."

Another one of Lynn's lovely antiques.

"Last night I opened it to put something away and noticed a large manila envelope lodged between my mother's family Bible and a book of Shakespeare sonnets I bought recently."

"What was inside the envelope?"

She retrieved it from the credenza's middle drawer and placed it on the marble countertop. "Five hundred in cash and a note from my sons."

I pulled on a pair of latex gloves and removed a folded sheet of lined paper from the envelope. "I may have to claim the letter and money as evidence."

"I know that, Margaret. That's why I waited until this morning to call you."

"But at the very least, I'll make sure the note is returned to you."

"I knew I could count on that too."

We both sat as I read it:

Dear Mom, Sorry we've been such shits, and even more sorry we took your money. Hope this makes up for some of it. We have to leave the state. Don't know for how long, but we'll get in touch down the road. Not that he'll care, but let the old man know we left. Also Joe wants you to pass along word to Ariel Pritchett. We decided it would make things worse if he went to see her before we left. Take care of yourself.

. . .

Each man had signed his name and left a personal endearment.

I took off the latex gloves and stroked Lynn's hands folded in her lap. "And just to make certain, you recognize the handwriting as theirs?"

"Yes. And I have other samples if you need them."

I shook my head. "I'm glad you found the letter."

"It doesn't help much right now, but it might later," Lynn said.

"I've had a couple of discussions with Ariel. I'll pass along the message from Joseph."

"Ariel's a nice girl. I saw how upset she was at the funeral."

"She told me that she and Joseph were about to get married."

Lynn considered that news.

I cleared my throat. "I have a few questions, if you don't mind. Do you remember when you bought the Shakespeare book?"

"At the LDS Temple's annual book sale, Saturday before last. Five days before Dan and Joe were killed."

"So sometime between that Saturday and the following Thursday, they left the money and the note."

"And their wallets, with a long-expired driver's license inside each one. I found them tucked behind the Bible." She stood and collected the worn leather billfolds from the credenza shelf. "I assume you knew these were missing."

"Yes." But I couldn't make meaning of why they had stashed them here. Or, for that matter, how they might have come up with the five hundred dollars. Or how they were planning to survive on the run with only seventy-eight dollars between them.

I put the latex gloves back on and lifted the wallets from her outstretched hands. I placed the note back in the envelope stuffed with bills and slid everything into an evidence bag.

"I have another question."

"What's that, Margaret?"

I knew her well enough to discern she'd nearly reached the limit of her patience, if not her stamina.

"Cecil Burney says he sat next to you at an AA meeting last Thursday evening. At the exact time the twins were killed. Can you vouch for that?"

"That old man doesn't understand the meaning of anonymous, does he?"

"Apparently not."

"Well, he was there, but he didn't exactly sit next to me. And he came in late."

"How late?"

"The meeting usually runs from six to seven thirty. He probably arrived fifteen or twenty minutes into the opening testimonials. And I remember we chatted a bit during the coffee social afterwards."

I decided to forgo asking about her past relationship with Cecil, but I did want her insight into his dislike of her sons. "Why did he have so much animosity toward Dan and Joseph?"

"I'm sure you heard your mother talking about it at some point, but years ago, Cecil and I had an affair."

My blank stare was legitimate. Zoey was many things, but a gossip? No.

"Anyway, the boys could've had some kind of an altercation with Cecil over that. But if it ever happened, it was a long time back. Maybe when they were in high school?" she said.

I considered our time in high school together. The Nodine brothers fought with dozens of boys and even some men, but I couldn't remember any tales about them duking it out with Cecil or anyone else tough enough to stand their ground against both twins at once, not to mention pack heat and be willing to use it. Twenty plus years ago, Cecil Burney had been such a man.

"Thank you for calling me this morning, Lynn."

I stood and put on my police Stetson. She stood as well. I reached to hug her, but she stepped back.

"I'm going to lie down now, Margaret."

She moved from the sun porch, turned down the hallway, and walked toward her bedroom. I let myself out and made sure the door latched behind me.

13

MORNING, FEBRUARY 26

Low on fuel, I parked the Tahoe alongside a pump at Gas-n-Snacks, asked Shorty Denton to fill it with regular, and handed him my State credit card. While the tank was filling, I spied Bach's Ford Interceptor parked across the street next to the Best Western where Doc Gattis had spent the night. Without thinking it through, I pulled out my phone and punched in her number.

On the fourth ring, she picked up. "Maggie?"

"Good morning. I'm on my way to the animal clinic to pick up my cat. Would you like to join me, get out of your motel room for a while?"

"Sure, I'm just waiting around for a call from my office. Can you give me ten minutes, though?"

"I'll be parked outside. Join me whenever you're ready." I signed the credit card slip, moved onto the street, and drove around the block. By the time I pulled into the motel parking lot, Al's big SUV was gone.

I clicked on the radio. KJDY's usual playlist was the same honkytonk Bach preferred. Instead a nineties favorite from R.E.M., "Losing My Religion," hailed from the speakers. I turned it up and sang along. Nearly drowned out the sound of my phone buzzing.

"Is that R.E.M in the background?" Duncan's voice sent a charge through me.

"On KJDY even. Can you believe it?" I lowered the volume.

"Let's meet for an early lunch. How does that sound?"

"I would like that, but I need to fetch my cat from the vet."

"Supper, then?"

"That would be nice. Unless Louie needs some extra attention this evening."

"Louie's your cat, I hope."

I laughed. "Yes, Louie's my cat."

"See you about seven, my place? Or would you like to go out somewhere, go on a proper date?"

"I don't think I've been on a proper date in my entire life."

"Me neither."

"Why start now, right? I'll see you at seven at your place." I clicked off the phone and the radio and absentmindedly rested a finger on my bottom lip. I needed to contain that little thrill if I wanted to make it to seven o'clock.

Ray opened the passenger-side door and stepped into my rig. "What are you smiling about?"

She sounded considerably less despondent this morning.

I shook my head. "Nothing, really."

"Maybe it's the weather. It's a beautiful day."

She was right. Forsythia, Lenten rose, and viburnum bloomed under a cloudless cyan sky. We pulled out of the lot and drove east.

"You seem more like yourself this morning," I said.

"Yes, I was just this side of bitchy last night."

"So I noticed."

"I'll ignore that crack," she said as we turned into the drive at Wilson's Animal Clinic.

I introduced Jen and Ray, and we all took a seat in Jen's office.

"Before we get to Louie, I wanted to ask you about the prescription you wrote on Monday of last week to treat Guy Trudeau's livestock."

"Gosh. Was that only last week? Let's see. Oh, right, Moraxella bovis.

"What the hell is that?"

"A bacteria. Causes bovine keratoconjunctivitis."

"Pinkeye?" Ray guessed.

"Yep. And it's nasty stuff, and it had spread through his herd."

"How is it different than conjunctivitis in humans?" Ray asked.

"It involves flies and extreme pain. Untreated, it can lead to blindness and weight loss."

Doc Gattis grimaced. "Lovely."

"And for ranchers, all that equates to less value at market."

"About Louie?" I interjected.

"He's a prize. Very healthy for a feline of his age, particularly now that he's bouncing back from his bout with early-stage pneumonia." With one hand, Jen rolled a thick strand of her platinum hair. In the other hand, she held the tortoiseshell spectacles she'd removed and toggled the frame back and forth as she spoke.

Doc Gattis's phone rang, and she stepped outside to take the call. In the meantime, Jen and I made our way to the kennel at the back of the clinic where I retrieved Louie.

He purred calmly as I cradled him and even when I placed him in his carrier. "Together again, old boy."

"I'll miss you, Louie," Jen whispered into the carrier opening.

I gathered up his medication and placed it in my coat

pocket. "Say hi to Vicky."

"Will do."

After dropping Ray off at the Best Western, I backtracked to my apartment, got Louie settled in, and made my way to the office.

Bach sat at his temporary desk. He had shut down and packed up his laptop. "Good. You arrived before I had to take off."

I pointed toward his laptop case. "You're leaving for the day?"

"I'm headed back to Bend and then to Paisley. A terrible domestic violence case. Multiple homicides. I'm in charge of the preliminary investigation."

I'd seen the bulletin last night. An unemployed trucker shot his ex-wife and two daughters to death. He didn't have the courage to turn the gun on himself, though.

"Mrs. Nodine called me to her house this morning. Sometime between Saturday the sixteenth and Thursday the twenty-first when her sons were murdered, they stopped by her house while she was out. Left a note, their wallets, and expired ODLs, and five hundred dollars."

"Nothing of substance in the note?"

"Just that they had to leave the state for a while."

"And the mother found these items when?"

"Last night. After the funeral."

Al slipped on his coat. "Might she know more?"

"I'm certain she doesn't. She and her sons had been estranged for some time. But I'm less certain about Ariel Pritchett."

"The fiancée?"

"I'd hoped you might come with me to talk to her. Hollis is

convinced she has to know more than she's let on. I'm afraid I've been reluctant to press her more. She's already quite emotional."

"Take Hollis along."

"He's taking some time with his family today."

He checked his watch. "You're better at this than you think. If she knows more than she's told you, you'll be able to push as hard as you need to."

Hopefully, he was right about that. "So you're off to Paisley. Home of the annual mosquito festival?"

"That's right."

"About the same number of working poor citizens as Seneca, right?"

"And also a former timber town."

"Rural poverty stinks."

He nodded. "I was on the phone with Dr. Gattis right before you got here. Ray's accompanying me back to Bend, and possibly Paisley. She asked me to tell you that she'd talk to you soon. She also said you need to find some way to stop the bloodshed in your county."

"A good start might be to end rural poverty."

"Good luck with that," he said, pulling on his jacket. "I'm leaving the Nodine and Trudeau investigations in good hands, Sergeant."

Before Al reached the door, Jess Flynn opened it and stepped into the muggy room carrying a toddler on one hip. A guy I presumed to be Seth Flynn, her new hubby and manager of Frank Sylvester Trucking, accompanied her.

"You wanted to talk to me again?" she asked.

"Yesterday," I said.

"Today will have to do."

And here I'd thought we ended our last discussion on such good terms.

"Sir, this is Jess Flynn. And this is Detective Bach, State Police homicide unit."

Jess shifted the child to her other hip.

"Have a seat, Ms. Flynn," Bach directed. "We have a few follow-up questions."

She handed the baby to the man who had arrived with her and sat where Al indicated.

I stood over her. "In our discussion yesterday, you claimed you delivered Mr. Trudeau's steers back to his place after the prospective buyer refused them."

"Yes, and that's what I did."

"You returned the steers to Big T, Trudeau's dilapidated ranch?"

"Well, near there. I hauled them back to the BLM grass-lands acreage where he had a grazing permit. Same place I picked them up, out along Izee Road."

"I'll need directions to the drop site."

"I met Trudeau at the Bear Valley guard station. Then he led me to the loading chute."

"I can get you the exact location," the guy holding the toddler offered. He handed the baby to Jess. "I'll get my laptop."

"And you are?" I asked.

"Seth Flynn. I run Frank Sylvester Trucking," he said.

He extended a hand, and I shook it.

"I track all of our trips on a spreadsheet, pick-up to delivery."

Flynn went out to the parking lot to retrieve his laptop, and Bach asked me to step into the alcove.

"I need to head out now, but let's plan on having a discussion early tomorrow morning. Before that if we need to. Also, take one of your troopers with you if you go check on Trudeau's steers."

"Good luck in Paisley. I'll talk to you tomorrow."

Jess was gently rocking her toddler when I returned to my desk. "What's your baby's name?"

"Sophia."

Like Hank, Sophia was a reminder of time rolling forward and my aging gametes in diminishing supply. And the child Morgan and I might have loved fiercely and raised together now lost in the mist of past history.

Seth Flynn returned with his laptop and began clicking through the layers of his trip spreadsheet. "Okay, let's take a look. Last Thursday, February twenty-first. The loading chute at milepost thirty, Izee Road west, near the junction with South Fork Road." He directed the screen toward me.

I pointed to the column labeled *Destination*. "Says they were to be delivered to Caldwell, Idaho. Not Boise."

"Caldwell's a suburb of sorts. It's where the stockyard's located," Seth clarified.

"I don't know why the old man ordered up a trip to the Boise area when he didn't plan to go that far," Jess said, "but I was following behind him, remember? And he led me to that weird-ass cattle company place."

"Hon, you might want to watch your language," Seth said.

Despite that bit of patronizing, his affection for Jess was obvious.

"It's not a problem," I said. "I sometimes use profanity myself. May I hold Sophia for a sec?"

Jess handed the sleeping baby to me. She had the same pale skin and dark hair as her mother. And me, for that matter.

Reticent, the woman took the child back from me. "Everything's okay, right?"

"If you're asking whether everything is all right with your little girl, I'd say she's just about perfect."

Jess smiled.

"Thank you both for your time," I said to the couple.

After I finished the apple and energy bar I'd brought for lunch, I rummaged around the office for snack crackers, apparently having abandoned this morning's resolve to adopt healthier eating habits. The Ritz box was empty, and the Triscuits were too stale even for me. Hungry, I thought about the pizza in my refrigerator at home, left over from Duncan's visit the night before last. And then I thought hungrily about the man himself, an indulgence abruptly interrupted by Taylor's noisy entrance through the front door of our trooper station.

He usually went home for his meal breaks, often arriving back at the office smelling of garlic or onions or some exotic extract his wife, Ellie, had learned to make through the online extension service. Today, I detected the scent of chocolate nougat and caramel. It made me wish I had a Snickers bar stashed somewhere.

"Mark, before you take off your jacket, we're taking a little trip. I want to find Trudeau's missing cattle."

"Where're we headed?" He handed me my peacoat.

I slipped the coat on and grabbed my pack. "Izee Road."

"Out near Murderers Creek, then."

"Yeah. He was apparently pasturing them on BLM property."

Taylor locked the station door, and we climbed in my Chevy Tahoe.

"Wouldn't Trudeau have pastured them at his ranch?" he said.

I shook my head. "Big T's in quite a state of disrepair these days. Pasture's gone to pot, along with all the outbuildings."

We pulled out of the parking lot, gravel sounding a metallic ping.

"He was down to about thirty or so head of cattle, right?" Taylor asked.

"That's right. All steers," I answered.

"How does anybody get a grazing permit for so few livestock?"

"He'd probably had the permit for years, originally for a much larger herd. My guess is he was selling them off a few at a time."

We drove south on 395 past Canyon Mountain until we reached Bear Valley and the Silvies River drainage system, stretching over a massive plain on the backside of the Aldrich range.

Eight miles or so north of Seneca, I cut west on Izee Road. Not far from Big T, we passed the ranch where I had worked as the cook's helper. The summer I turned fifteen, I spent my mornings mastering the art of sourdough biscuits and my evenings watching the sun set, the rosy alpine glow spreading across the mountains and streaming through broad stands of Ponderosa.

Off to the north, Dead Point—a needle-like basalt batholith—loomed above the high desert, an eerily apt reminder of the three murders that had occurred a relatively short distance away.

At milepost thirty, a loading chute had been built into the fencing next to a gate. There were no cattle to be seen, and the property beyond the fence was thick with juniper. From there, the land sloped sharply up a shale escarpment.

I shut off the engine and retrieved my binoculars. "Let's take a walk."

Outside, Taylor zipped up his jacket and pulled on the

damn Pendleton earmuffs he always talked to me about ad nauseam.

"Dang, Maggie. It's freezing."

I reached across the front seats to the glove compartment, lifted out a gray wool scarf and my Thinsulate gloves, and bundled up. I climbed over the gate, and Taylor followed suit.

Traipsing uphill over slippery terrain, I wondered why the acreage was labeled grassland cattle forage. Seemed more suitable for bighorn sheep and wild horses—that is, until we reached the summit. We'd hiked up a small ridge that looked over a creek-basin pasture of native bluebunch wheatgrass and Idaho fescue where a small herd of Black Angus grazed.

I brought up the binoculars and recognized the Big T brand, a capital *T* superimposed on a larger capital *B*. I counted thirty-three animals, six more than Jess Bennett had hauled in her livestock truck, and all carrying the Big T brand.

"Trudeau's cattle all right, but I count more steers than I expected to find." I passed the field glasses to Taylor. "Double-check, will you?"

He aimed them in a slow swath across the pasture. "Thirty-three?"

"Uh-huh."

"How many were expecting to find?"

"Twenty-seven," I said.

"How'd the extra steers get here?"

And then I understood. Dan and Joseph had brought the six animals back to where they'd stolen them. Just like they said they would.

Taylor stood awkwardly on the loading chute gate. "I'm pretty sure you're right, Maggie. The Nodines returned the steers they stole from Trudeau. But why didn't the truck driver or

Trudeau realize the six missing steers were up there in the pasture?"

"The twins were late and Trudeau and the woman headed out before they arrived?"

"Guess that makes sense." He hopped off the gate and dragged a burlap bag out from under the loading chute. "McKay Feed and Tack? Didn't they recently have a theft?"

I put my hands on my hips. "Yeah, but one of the stolen cattle prods was found in the Ram 3500 the Nodines were driving. The other one was in their old camper."

Taylor opened the burlap bag. "Wasn't other stuff missing? As in, two forty-pound salt licks. And one, no, two fence cutters?"

I peered inside. "Goddamn, Mark. Good work."

"Nothing but luck. The sack was camouflaged in the shadows underneath the chute. I could've easily missed it."

"Well, I missed it completely."

"You think it was the Nodines who took all that stuff from the Feed and Tack?"

"Seems like it. Probably left the burlap bag here when they brought back the steers."

He nodded and loaded it in the back of the Tahoe. We took off over the worn macadam. Bordered on either side by scrubby lodgepole pine and dry sagebrush, the surface of Izee Road was a mix of riven asphalt and chesil underlay. Like the land was reclaiming the old ranch route bit by bit.

Again in the distance, I saw the Aldrich range and the Palouse-like hillocks of soft gold transforming to deep green in the slow release of winter's icy paralysis. Despite the strange beauty and tranquility, all the little jaunts to backcountry were taking time away from attending to the list of questions still needing answers. For one, Kat McKay. She was due another visit so we could talk about that semiautomatic pistol of hers.

. . .

The drive back to town was quiet, even after I clicked on local news and weather. There wasn't much new to report on either front until the voice of Sheriff Dirk Rhinehart broke through the otherwise mundane broadcast. In a statement delivered from the steps of the courthouse, he warned the citizenry of Grant County that the Oregon State Police had yet to apprehend the killer or killers of the Nodine brothers and Guy Trudeau.

The sheriff went on to assure the populace that he, the officers on his force, and the contingent of five dozen volunteer deputies were prepared to form a search party to hunt down whoever had murdered the three men, should it come to that.

Taylor sighed. "He's not kidding either, is he?"

"Afraid not." I shut off the radio. "Don't know how you can take a search party out looking for a killer if you don't know who the killer is."

I plugged in my iPod and put on Emmylou Harris.

"Got any Taylor Swift?"

"Definitely not."

"I like to tell people she was named after me."

I pointedly turned up the volume, silencing the man until we parked at our police station. He hauled the burlap bag to the evidence locker while I checked messages at my desk.

I'd received a statewide update on the murder investigation down in Paisley and a short voicemail from J. T. Lake asking me to contact him first thing tomorrow morning. His tone had lost some of its incivility. I wondered if someone had given him the word to back off during the homicide investigations. Nah. Would never happen.

"You want me to contact Duncan McKay? Let him know

we found the rest of the stuff from his store," Taylor offered.

"I was just going to do that," I fibbed.

He moved off to his desk.

"On second thought, go ahead and make the call. I actually need to go talk to someone else." Kat McKay. A conversation I wanted to have without the distraction of flirting with Duncan beforehand.

"Sure, right after I check the fish and wildlife log."

On the way to question Kat about that automatic pistol, I'd barely made it to the high school at the border between John Day and Canyon City when Asa Larkin's black Prius passed me on the left. Doing so in a no-passing zone was an infraction, not to mention idiotic given the car had sped up and swerved wildly around my State Police vehicle. I flashed my lights and sounded my non-emergency siren, signaling the driver to move to the shoulder.

Brady Wakefield—Larkin's son—was at the wheel, and Rain McKay-Ferlinghetti was his single passenger. The Wakefield boy rolled down his window.

"License and registration, please," I said. "Did you know it's a violation to pass when the lane lines are solid? Plus you were speeding in a school zone."

Brady shrugged, removed his license from his hip pocket and the registration from the sun visor.

After the numbers came up clean from DMV, I wrote out a citation and watched both dark-haired young men through my windshield.

Brady's window slid down as I walked back to the Prius.

I handed him the registration, his license, and the ticket. "I've cited you today for the two traffic offenses. Your court date is on the bottom of the form there."

He pressed the automatic window button in his door panel and began closing the window.

I knocked on the glass. "Hold on. I'm not finished."

Brady jerked his head and eyeballed me maliciously. "Fuck off, lady!"

I opened the driver's-side door. "Unlock the rear cargo hatch and step out of the vehicle."

He hit the hatch lever and moved out of the Prius.

"I'm sorry I lost my temper, ma'am. It's just, my dad will be pissed I got a ticket."

I'd noted the birthdate on his driver's license. He'd just turned nineteen.

"You mouth off to a police officer again and your dad might have to bail you out of the local hoosegow."

"For what?" Rain stood next to the passenger door. "What would you arrest him for?"

"Do you know what I might find in the rear cargo area?" I asked him.

"I have no idea."

"Then you're better off minding your own business. Get back inside the vehicle."

As I moved to the open cargo hatch, Brady following behind, a dozen or more black-and-white magpies lifted from the juniper-infested hillside and swept overhead, shrieking in Corvidae furore.

The cargo area was empty. Well, of course. Brady was smart enough to hide his contraband, booze or otherwise. I rolled back the protective mat and popped open the lower storage compartment. I found a set of tire chains and a folded tarp. Under the tarp lay two seven-round magazines loaded with nine-millimeter cartridges and a Kel-Tec PF-9 automatic pistol, same model handgun used to kill the Nodine twins.

Maybe I was finally getting somewhere.

14

AFTERNOON, FEBRUARY 26

After Brady Wakefield denied knowing about the gun in the back of the Prius, I took possession of the key fob and his phone. Visibly shaken, he agreed to wait quietly in the backseat of my Tahoe. I'd convinced him that was how he could avoid being placed there in handcuffs.

I called Hollis at home, and he joined me within minutes, arriving just before Duncan drove up. The Prius, the two Tahoes, and the Feed and Tack delivery truck were parked end-to-end facing south on the shoulder of Three Flags Highway, directly in front of the high school.

Duncan met up with us, his buckaroo's limp more pronounced this afternoon. "Maggie. Hollis. What's the situation with Rain?"

The boy had called his uncle the moment he saw Brady slide into my police rig.

"I'll need to talk with him," I said.

"What about? Over the phone, he told me it was Brady who was in trouble."

"Other than a couple of traffic citations, no one's in trouble until I say so."

Rain had moved from the Prius to the front seat of the delivery truck. "Come with me," Duncan said.

He opened the driver's-side door. "Sergeant Blackthorne needs to talk to you before we can go. And that means you need to answer her questions, do you understand?"

The boy nodded, and I slid into the driver's seat and closed the door.

"I saw your picture in the *Blue Mountain Eagle*. The one from the basketball game."

Rain ignored my comment. "When do you read me my rights?"

I ignored his drama. "Where were you and Brady going in such a hurry?"

"No place special. That's just how he drives everywhere."

It was remarkable how much he resembled his father, Arlan, and not just because of the thick hair. With those fierce eyes, wiry frame, and the same Ferlinghetti remove, Rain was a gene copy of his dad.

"You boys were out cruising the gut?"

"No, driving to my mom's house."

"Do you know why Brady is sitting in the backseat of my police vehicle?"

Rain paused and bit his lip. "You found something in the back of his car?"

My blank stare, again purposeful.

"Alcohol is my guess," he said.

"I'd be issuing both of you a Minor in Possession charge if that were the case."

"Then I've got no idea what you found."

"You're free to leave with your uncle. First I need ask you about something. You were with your mother when she was caught target shooting in Murderers Creek Wildlife Area?"

"Yeah. But I never shot anything."

"Really?" A boy learning to shoot was practically a requirement in Grant County.

"I don't like guns. I think the target practice was an afterthought or something. Driving out to Murderers Creek was Kat's idea of a mother-son outing."

It was never a good sign when a kid started referring to a parent by their first name.

"An afterthought?"

"Kat's never been a gun person either. I don't get why she decided to buy a pistol."

A question I was eager to have an answer to myself.

I rejoined Hollis and Duncan. "I got what I needed from Rain."

"Did he behave himself?" Duncan asked.

"Yes. He's free to go. But before you take off, did Mark Taylor contact you?"

Duncan shook his head.

"We found the other items taken from your store. I think the salt lick and the fence cutters were pilfered at the same time as the cattle prods. And probably by the Nodines," I said.

"They would've had to break into my place, then, and I've had no break-ins that I know of. I banned them from the Feed and Tack more than a week ago."

"Why?" I asked.

Duncan rearranged his cap over his thick swath of hair. "They'd been swiping little stuff for a long time. Packs of gum, a can of chewing tobacco, some pin screws, a hacksaw blade. I did stop them at the door and made sure they handed over the hacksaw blade. But they came back a week later and tried to palm an expensive bottle of pinkeye spray. Mostly I'd ignored the other puny thefts, but this time I saw the truck they were driving. That massive red gas hog. I decided they could probably afford to pay for whatever they needed.

Anyway, I told them they weren't welcome in my place anymore."

I wished he had shared this news with me earlier. "You should've called the town police and had them arrested."

An expression new to me darkened his face. Was he embarrassed? Irritated?

"I already told you what I think of our police. But given what happened after I kicked the Nodines out of my store, I should've called you guys. And I probably should've wondered why they needed pinkeye spray, but I didn't."

It was all I could do to refrain from offering Duncan some affectionate sign of reassurance. But I needed to hold myself in check standing in public view.

"The pinkeye spray, that's for cattle, right?" I asked.

"Most all livestock."

"If you could pinpoint when they tried to steal a bottle of it, that might help us."

"Saturday the sixteenth. We were in the middle of a big sale."

"Thanks, Duncan. We should get going," I said.

"Me too. I left Frankie in charge of the store." He extended a large, warm hand, first to me, then Hollis. "Be seeing you."

"Sorry about calling you back to work today, Holly. I know you wanted some time at home."

"Once you mentioned the Kel-Tec 9, there was no question about staying home. Just glad I was there long enough to take care of Hank so Lil could sleep in." He pointed toward the backseat of my Tahoe. "What are we doing about Larkin's kid?"

"He said he didn't know the weapon was there, and I'm pretty convinced he didn't. His cocky façade went south as soon as he saw the gun in the storage compartment. And when I asked to see his conceal carry permit, he about lost his shit."

"It probably belongs to his father, don't you think?"

"That's a question we'll have an answer to soon. Apparently one of Larkin's men is driving him into town to pick up his Prius. He's meeting the boy and us at the station."

Once inside our office, Brady sat nervously in the single plastic deck chair we'd placed in the all but nonexistent waiting area. He picked vigorously at the lint on his expensive black shirt and then rolled up one sleeve and went after a scab on his elbow with the same vigor. When Asa Larkin arrived, the boy stood and snapped shut the pearl-buttoned cuff of his sleeve in one action.

His father avoided looking directly at the kid, instead inscrutably casing the interior of our office until arriving at some unknowable conclusion. "Have you arrested my son, Sergeant?"

"He's been cited for two separate traffic violations. No arrest, though."

Larkin reached into his back pocket and pulled out a folded checkbook. "How much are the fines altogether?"

"Those are paid to the court. You can find the information on his citation."

"So we can go?" Larkin asked, returning the checkbook to his pocket.

"There's a matter I'd like you to clear up, but I think it would be better if your son waited for you in the car."

I handed Larkin the key fob I'd confiscated earlier, and he tossed it to Brady. "I'll join you shortly. And just so there's no question, your driving privileges are suspended indefinitely."

The boy straightened his shoulders and opened the front door.

"Brady, don't forget your coat," Hollis called after him.

"Thank you." Brady collected his charcoal-gray Canada Goose parka and shut the door.

I invited Larkin to take the seat next to my desk. He did so reluctantly.

"The 'matter' you wanted to ask me about?" he asked impatiently.

Larkin's dismissive attitude was getting old, but I decided to forgo any snark. I explained that I'd found a Kel-Tec PF-9 automatic pistol and two magazines of ammunition in the cargo-area storage compartment of his Prius.

He didn't miss a beat. "I have a concealed weapons permit."

I heard Hollis opening up his computer.

"But your son doesn't. In fact, he appeared stunned a weapon was inside the car at all."

"I neglected to remove the pistol and ammunition before giving Brady permission to use the car," Larkin said.

I patiently waited for the man to say more.

"I usually keep the gun in my safe at home. Brady doesn't know I keep a weapon there, nor does he know the combination."

"What made you decide to carry the gun in your car?"

"Three murders a few days apart, for one thing. But as I already explained, I'm not usually in the habit of taking it with me, so I forgot to lock it back in the safe."

"Mr. Larkin," Hollis broke in. "Records show your carry permit was issued in Clackamas County."

"What? Does that matter since I'm still an Oregon resident?"

"In Oregon, permits are issued by each sheriff in the

county of their jurisdiction," I said. "We'll need to check with the sheriff's office, see if they have any restrictions on permits issued by another county."

I glanced at my watch. A few minutes past five o'clock. "I'm afraid their office is closed now. That means I'm putting a legal hold on your weapon for at least forty-eight hours."

That bullshit move nearly elicited a smile from Larkin before he stood and slowly turned.

"Don't forget Brady's phone, Mr. Larkin."

He lifted the baggie containing his son's device from my desk and left our building.

Hollis stared at me for several seconds, rose and walked to the front window, and watched the silent Prius pull out of our parking lot. "Jesus, Sarge. That was something. You know damned well Sheriff Rhinehart has no conceal carry restrictions. He'd likely designate Larkin as one of his volunteer deputies, too."

"You were the one who brought up the conceal carry being issued in another county. That was good timing, by the way."

"Larkin's an attorney, remember?"

"Well, he's a shitty one if you ask me. He didn't even try to call my bluff."

"He could be back with an injunction first thing tomorrow morning," Holly reminded me.

"There's got to be some way we can arrange to get forensic ballistics on that gun."

I picked up the landline and dialed Bach's number. When he didn't answer, I called the State Police lab. Gone for the day.

I slammed the receiver. "Shit."

"When I was with Burns OSP, they used a retired forensics guy a couple of times. Harry Bratton. He's got a spread near Silvies," Hollis said.

"Why am I just now hearing about this?"

"When have we needed a faster turnaround than we can get from the State lab? Plus I don't think Harry is equipped for every possible scenario."

"Silvies is close," I said.

"About halfway between here and Burns."

"And in our county, so part of our police district. In case that comes up when I ask Bach for the go-ahead to contact Bratton."

I tried Al's office phone again. When he didn't answer, I radioed his Interceptor.

"Evening, Sergeant Blackthorne," he said, road noise and loud honkytonk in the background. "Let me shut off the music."

I waited for Hank Williams's yodeling to quiet. "We've come into temporary possession of a Kel-Tec PF-9 belonging to that rancher you met yesterday."

"Temporary possession?"

"I'm holding it for forty-eight hours on a technicality."

"What kind of a technicality?"

"Asa Larkin's conceal carry permit is registered in Clackamas County, not here. I told him I needed to confirm that Sheriff Rhinehart's office is kosher with him holding an out-of-county permit."

"Which you and I already know is yes," Al said.

"Of course. Hollis even suggested the sheriff would designate Larkin as a special deputy."

"That's mighty witty of Trooper Jones, but I don't see what that has to do with the forty-eight-hour hold. Which, by the way, conceal carry issue aside, doesn't strike me as strictly enforceable."

"We needed to buy some time. I'd like to run the weapon through a ballistics check. The problem is, by the time we get it to the lab in Bend, or any of the other labs around the state, it'll take more than forty-eight hours," I explained.

"I'm listening," Bach intoned.

"Hollis knows about a retired forensics expert who lives nearby. I guess Sergeant Brown in Burns used the guy for ballistic exams in the past."

"Harry Bratton?"

"That's right. I'd like your okay to call him."

"Harry's one of the best forensic technicians I've ever worked with. But I'm not sure you've given me a reason to give the go-ahead."

"Larkin is a peculiar bird, living in that fortress with armed bodyguards. But the fact that he owns a Kel-Tec 9 is what makes him a person of interest in my book."

"All right, Maggie, go ahead and give Harry a call. I'll get a message to the State lab folks, make sure they provide you remote access to whatever you might need."

"Thanks, Al."

I clicked off the radio and made the call to Harry Bratton. He just happened to be in John Day visiting relatives and agreed to stop by. I hoped the timing of Bratton's family get-together signaled our luck was changing, that we might know by tomorrow whether Asa Larkin's Kel-Tec 9 was the murder weapon or just one of many such guns floating around out there.

Who was I kidding? Larkin could present us with an injunction canceling the forty-eight-hour hold before we learned shit.

Waiting for the forensics guy, I paced the office, dusted file cabinets, and mulled over the Asa Larkin conundrum. Any connection to the Nodine twins and old man Trudeau was seemingly random, but there had to be something to it all. Starting with Trudeau's attempt to sell his sick steers to Larkin, the proximity of Dan and Joseph's camper to Bear Valley Cattle Company, and now the Kel-Tec PF-9 automatic handgun found in Larkin's Prius.

And there was a new goddamn wrinkle to consider. The twins had obviously tried to make off with a bottle of Duncan's pinkeye spray because they'd already stolen six steers from Trudeau. But that was five days before they were killed, so where had they pastured the cattle? For sure not in the wigwam burner, despite all the cow pies. Had they managed to sneak them onto a patch of some rancher's acreage?

Around five-thirty, Duncan interrupted my ruminations with another text. "Working late. Dinner out @ 8:00 okay? I'll pick you up"

His message was calming, temporarily blocking out the barrage of murder-mystery twists invading my headspace and reminding me that Duncan's sudden appearance in my life was worth taking a momentary breath for, especially since I was sure I would end this long day making love to the man.

I sent him the thumbs-up emoji and continued my office walkabout, this time sweeping the floor while cogitating over Asa Larkin. What about all the signs pointing to some kind of dealings between the quadriplegic Frank Sylvester and him? And what about Larkin's cousin/stepsister/whatever being the accountant for Sylvester's long-haul trucking business? Was she the proxy buyer of the Ram 3500?

I'd also begun to entertain the possibility that Larkin might be Frank Sylvester's court-appointed guardian and conservator. Elder law was Larkin's legal specialty, so he would have considerable cover should anyone come sniffing around. More to the point, Larkin would have control over Mr. Sylvester's assets.

"Are you all right, Sarge?" Hollis interrupted. "You seem bewildered by something."

"Sarah Wakefield Anderson. Who hired her to do the books for Sylvester's trucking company?"

Before Hollis answered, Harry Bratton arrived. He had a thin face, broad forehead, and high cheekbones, all of which magnified his bug-eyed expression. He reminded me of Steve Buscemi, maybe Walton Goggins. Like the characters those actors usually played, Harry was, by virtue of his physical appearance, simultaneously compelling and peculiar. He was also straightforward and personable. I liked him immediately.

After retirement, he had built a forensics lab on his property near Silvies and put the word out to rural law enforcement agencies throughout the Great Basin. He came to our meeting equipped with the formal paperwork needed to take temporary possession of Larkin's Kel-Tec 9. He'd also come prepared to upload the ballistics files Hollis had pulled from the State lab's website.

He scooped up the business cards Hollis and I had placed on the table with our cell numbers scribbled on the back. "This should be all I need. I might have findings to you tomorrow sometime. Maybe even first thing in the morning, but let's plan on talking by the end of the day for sure."

After Harry left with the weapon and data, I laid out the Asa Larkin quandary Holly had observed me stewing over, all of Larkin's explicit and fuzzy links to the three murdered men and Frank Sylvester.

"I'm not sure we'll ever know where the Nodines pastured the six steers, but I see your point about the other connections. I'm in the office awhile longer. I'll do some more digging into the trucking company. Sarah Anderson, too. See if I can find out who hired her to be Sylvester's bookkeeper."

"I'm off to chat with Kat McKay again. I want to know why

she got herself a Kel-Tec 9." I slipped on my peacoat and hat. "Will I see you tomorrow, Holly?"

But he was already swimming in the digital sea.

One of Kat's neighbors must have been hosting a Tupperware party, leaving guests to take up every available parking space. I found a spot a couple of streets over near the historic Episcopal church and walked to Kat's place.

Instead of conversing in her foyer, this time she invited me to join her in the living room.

"Your home is lovely," I said, and I meant it. She had an eye for decorating, finding just the right hues and furnishings.

"Thanks. I like being surrounded by nice things. So Maggie, Duncan already talked to me about your little run-in with Brady Wakefield. He said you also had a talk with Rain. Is that why you're here?"

"Actually, I dropped by to ask about your recent citation. Discharging a weapon in a protected wildlife area."

"I paid the fine," she said meekly.

"No, that's not the issue. Rain told me he didn't understand why you wanted to buy a pistol. Said you weren't 'much of a gun person.'" And she'd raised her kid alone without ever owning a gun. Why get one now?

"Is there some law against me owning one?"

"You don't have a criminal past, so no. But I'm curious why you got yourself a semiautomatic weapon rather than a single-action handgun?"

"Why are you asking all these questions?"

"Because I just found the Nodine brothers blown to bits. By a Kel-Tec 9, like the one you shot up the wildlife area with."

"I borrowed the gun, Maggie."

"Borrowed it?"

"And I took it out for target practice. But that was asinine to go to a wildlife area. Anyway, I gave it back to the owner after your game warden guy wrote me a ticket."

It occurred to me Kat and Larkin might've been friendly, perhaps more than friendly. I could see why they might strike up a romance. She had aged, but in a way that suited her, made her more attractive. It was possible she'd even become a woman Larkin could consider a tolerable stand-in for all those Pilates-addicted fortyish gals from Lake Oswego. Especially given most of the other options available in my county. If Larkin had shown an interest in her, there would be little wonder why she dumped Dan Nodine.

I cocked my head slightly to one side, and I hoped imperceptibly. "Let me guess. You borrowed the gun from Asa Larkin."

"Who on earth is that?"

"Brady Wakefield's father."

"I've never met the man."

I wasn't sure I believed her, but I had nothing much else to go on. "Okay, Kat. Thanks for your time this evening."

"Sure, Maggie. You're always welcome to drop by."

Now that last statement I did not believe.

Walking the few blocks to my rig, constellations and asterisms shone brightly in a now cloudless sky. I inhaled the cold, sweet air, climbed in my Tahoe, and circled back by Kat's house. Larkin's Prius was parked in the driveway behind her Land Rover.

I straightened the apartment, moved the cat pillow from the end of my bed, replaced the sheets, and waited in the rocking chair for Duncan to arrive. Finally, I took Louie in my lap and picked up *Libbey vs. Chase*. I'd managed to get beyond page eighty, but barely. I was having a hard time getting into a story with two such despicable main characters.

Close to eight thirty, I heard McKay's Feed and Tack delivery truck pull up outside. Still holding Louie, I opened the door and waited on the landing.

Duncan brought a bag of groceries out of his rig and held it up. "Steak dinner."

A man after my own heart.

He climbed the stairs and took Louie and me in one of his bull-rider arms and hugged us against his broad chest. "Jesus, I thought about you all goddamn day."

I'd mostly thought about Asa Larkin all goddamn day, which was, for one thing, not that productive. And for another, not sexy.

"Louie's flattered you thought about him all day."

Duncan scratched Louie under his chin. "Nice to meet you, old boy."

"What kept you so long at the Feed and Tack?"

"I'm behind on my billing." He indicated the grocery bag. "Rib eyes, potatoes to bake, salad fixings, and something to drink."

"Nice. Might be interesting preparing all that in my dinky, spice-poor kitchen, though."

"We'll make do, I think." He placed the bag in the refrigerator. "So did I blow it by not reporting the Nodines for stealing the pinkeye spray?"

"I wouldn't say you blew it. I'm glad you told us, but it still goes into the hopper with everything else we know. Just could have gone in there sooner."

"Would it have made a difference?"

I gave that question a few seconds of thought. "No. Now let's dispense with the shop talk and get cooking."

"If you say so, Sergeant."

I took his hand and led him to my bed. I lit a candle. Slowly we explored each other's warm body and removed our clothing.

"I'm afraid I can't get enough of you," he whispered in my ear.

"Don't be afraid," I whispered in return, even knowing I was. And also thrilled. With my fingertips I traced his brow, his soft mouth, his strong jaw. "You have nice eyes."

He pulled me closer and gently drew my hair from my face. "You're just damned beautiful."

No man had ever called me that or even pretended to find me beautiful. I considered thanking him but kissed him fully on the lips instead.

"And like I said before, a good kisser," he said.

He enfolded me in his muscular arms, and I wrapped mine around his naked waist. Our embrace gave over to a fierce desire.

Later, bodies still buzzing, Duncan and I made supper in my little kitchenette, broiling the steaks, baking the potatoes in the microwave, and putting together a salad. We carried the little square dining table a few feet, placing it next to the settee, and sat side-by-side eating our dinner on mismatched plates.

I poured each of us a glass of the fancy beer he'd bought to go with the meal and took a bite of my steak. "Perfect."

"Not too rare?"

"Is there such a thing?"

He smiled and put his arm around me. "A woman like you. That's rare."

"You're kind of unusual yourself, Mr. McKay."

"I'll tell you what's unusual. Watching you question my nephew this afternoon."

"That's the problem with being a cop in a small town. You might have to interrogate your lover's nephew."

Duncan leaned into my shoulder and bumped me lightly. "I've been elevated to lover?"

"Is that okay?"

"Works for me." He gave me a little peck on the cheek.

"About Rain, how did he seem when you drove him home?"

"Worried about why you took Brady into custody."

"Brady went home with his father. Dad will pay his ticket, and everything will be fine."

"He said you found something in the back of the car?"

I leaned closer and kissed him. "Maybe a late supper after making love isn't a good time for work talk."

"Yes, ma'am."

We finished our meal, cleared the dishes, and nestled together on the settee. I was beginning to like all the domesticity more than I probably should. I wondered if he felt the same.

"I need to take off soon," he said.

"Before you go, there's something I've been dying to ask you about," I said.

"Is it all right if I don't want to answer?"

"Of course."

"Then ask away."

"What happened between you and your wife?" That hadn't quite come out as I'd hoped, but it was too late now.

"Slippery slope there, Maggie. If I answer, you'll have to do the same."

"About the second one too?"

"Yep."

"Well, I guess it's a deal." One that made me nervous as hell, but I was the person who'd started all of this.

"She liked messing around with other women. For a long time I tried to make room for that, but after a while I didn't see much difference between messing around with other women and messing around with other men. I might've kept it up if we'd had kids. That was never going to happen, though." He paused for a moment. "Your turn."

"Hubby number one and I adored each other. That might be a fantasy, but I don't think so. We had a lot of fun. A little house in Salem. Plans. We wanted kids. All that. And we're still close."

"What happened?"

"Interesting that your wife liked women."

"Preferred women."

"Morgan finally understood he was gay. And even though I always fancied myself as having good intuition, I hadn't seen it coming. Anyway, that was that. Marriage over."

"But you're still friends?"

"We were married for ten years. Happily, I think. So yeah, we're still friends."

"Casey and I were married for fifteen years. Let's just say we're not friends, but I wish we were. That's a long time to be with someone and never see or speak to them again."

"With Morgan, I was devastated. I just couldn't believe it. And I was pregnant."

I might have lost it altogether, the conversation having strayed to treacherous terrain, but Duncan put his arm around me and pulled me close.

"That's enough past history for tonight," he said.

"Way more than enough."

15

MORNING, FEBRUARY 27

In the pale light, Louie eyed me from across the room. I lay in bed listening to his deep-throated purr, the low tick of my alarm clock, and Dorie's vacuum cleaner laboring away downstairs in her thrift store.

Duncan had stayed until eleven thirty last night. Once he left, I slept deeply despite our parting conversation. He could've taken it further, all the way to my heart's dark core of regret and sorrow. Instead, I told myself, he'd sensed that was a place I wasn't ready to go.

I sat up slowly and studied my reflection in the retro mirror anchored above the settee. For a moment I saw the old Maggie Blackthorne staring back, the one who felt safe giving over to passion, love even. I liked seeing that gal again.

"You look tired, Sarge," Holly said before I'd even hung up my coat and hat.

I yawned. "Yeah, the long days are getting to me." Late-night nookie didn't help either.

Hollis filled my mug with coffee, brought it to my desk,

and took the chair Asa Larkin had sat in yesterday afternoon. "You'll want to hear my news bulletin of the day. Frank Sylvester. His first wife died of some kind of cancer, leaving him to raise their young child on his own. The child, a boy, was adopted by the wife's sister and her husband when he was two years old."

I felt a chill rise up the back of my neck. "This story is beginning to sound familiar."

"The boy's name was Asa Sylvester."

"And he was called Asa Wakefield after the adoption?"

"That's right."

"Jesus, Holly. You've outdone yourself this time."

"I just started with what he told us on Sunday, that Larkin was the maiden name of his mother and his aunt. Then I turned over a few more rocks. But I can't figure out why he goes by Larkin and not Sylvester."

"My suspicion about Larkin being Sylvester's guardian and having conservatorship over his money, business, and land holdings? Maybe it's more than a suspicion, and maybe he doesn't want to raise red flags by using the same last name," I said.

"As Sylvester's son," Hollis began, "couldn't he still be appointed his guardian and conservator?"

"Yeah. But he'd more likely avoid raising red flags if he continued going by Wakefield."

"Like I said, switching his name to Larkin doesn't make sense."

Hollis went into processing mode, jiggling one leg and tapping a pen on my desk. I turned pensive and anxious for the jolt of caffeine to hit me.

"Unless switching names has something to do with the stepsister. A way to avoid spotlighting his personal link to Sylvester Trucking's bookkeeper?" I finally said.

"Well, it wasn't that hard to figure out Sylvester is actually Asa Larkin's father. Or that Sylvester had adopted him out to the Wakefield couple. Or that the stepsister is Sarah Wakefield Anderson, for that matter."

"For you it wasn't difficult, Holly. But most cops or anyone else investigating Larkin's dealings don't have your smarts, or they don't have your access to data. Or don't have either the smarts or the access."

He cleared his throat. "Just don't ask me for too many details, all right?"

I pretended not to hear that, walked to the alcove, and stood in front of the murder boards. Jumble of facts, feasibilities, tangled abstractions. The dross of three dead men. I blew air through my pursed lips.

"Maggie?" Hollis had joined me.

I nodded toward the lists that made up our murder boards. "What are the similarities between the two murder cases?"

"Similarities?"

"Commonalities? Like circumstances?"

"Beef cattle. Frank Sylvester, at least his trucking company. Jess, the female truck driver. Location."

"Location?"

"Near Seneca." Hollis stepped to the map and measured with a ruler. "Here's the deserted mill right outside of Seneca. Here's Big T, around sixteen miles away."

"How far away is Larkin's cattle company from each crime site?"

Again, he marked the distance using the ruler and referred to the map legend. "Six miles or so to the wigwam burner. About twenty to Big T."

I shrugged. "I suppose that means Larkin's place is relatively close to both the mill and Trudeau's ranch, but so what?"

Hollis sighed. "I'm not sure what to make of it."

"Another shiny object?"

"Yeah. I have to watch out for those all the time."

"Speaking of shiny objects, what about the sign on Larkin's gate and the bumper stickers on his livestock trailer and that old green Bronco?"

I pointed to the catchphrase we'd listed on the Nodines' murder board, *Jesus loves grass-fed beef*. "I've never gone online to check it out. Have you?"

"Not until now," he said, and we moved to his desk.

I stood behind Hollis as he googled Larkin's adopted motto. The first site listed was an outfit called Sonshine Sustenance Group. It was a mix of evangelical philosophy and cheesy advertising for their organically grown fruits and vegetables, raw milk, and the consortium of ranches supplying the free-range chicken and grass-fed pork, beef, and lamb offered for sale. Products could be purchased online or at the general store they operated on their property along the Snake River.

In addition to hawking wholesome dietary offerings, Sonshine Sustenance Group welcomed all-comers to their annual heavenly host prayer and music festival. And families interested in having their children educated in a Christian environment were invited to check out the Glorious Lord Academy. Hollis took us to the Academy page, where smiling, beatific kiddies and teens engaged in instructional games, Bible-story theater, and the milking of stout dairy cows.

"Isn't that Larkin's kid, only a little younger?" He pointed to the dark-haired boy in a photo captioned "Brady W. plays *Mathaliscious*."

I moved closer to the screen. "That's him all right. Click on the link to the consortium of ranches."

Five large spreads in Oregon, Washington, and Idaho supplied the beef. Larkin's Bear Valley Cattle Company wasn't one of them. But we did find those bumper stickers and metal signs touting Jesus as a lover of grass-fed beef, along with other kitschy paraphernalia, all of it priced cheap to make spreading the word more consumer-friendly.

"How would you characterize this place if you had to?" Hollis asked.

"Part hippie, part holy roller, and part huckster?"

"What might it have to do with Larkin, other than his kid attending school there?"

"Maybe his aim is to join the Sonshine brotherhood."

"He doesn't strike me as the brotherhood type. Conservative Christian, maybe. Certainly conservative."

"I meant he might want to be part of that consortium raising grass-fed beef. So at the risk of meandering down another dead end, I'm going to call the Sonshine Sustenance Group and see what I can find out." I picked up the receiver on Holly's phone and dialed the number on their homepage.

"What are you looking for, Sarge?"

"What they might know about Larkin and his ranch."

It turned out the owners were a chatty and effusive married couple, and with the exception of a proclivity to praise God or Jesus at the end of nearly every sentence, their take on religion reminded me of Dorie's. Plus they were good witnesses, in the secular sense: open, candid, and more than willing to help an officer of the law.

"Well, that was interesting," I said after hanging up.

"Sounds like they know all about Bear Valley Cattle Company," Hollis said.

I nodded. "The husband and wife who founded the place put me on speakerphone, told me it was unfortunate but they hadn't welcomed Asa Larkin into the Sonshine fold, or rather their ranch consortium. Guess his approach to raising animals doesn't meet their standards because he supplements with grain until his calves are yearlings. Only after that does he move strictly to pasture and hay."

"Not purely grass-fed, then."

"Yeah, I guess. Anyway, Larkin was apparently pissed as hell when they told him his cattle and methodology weren't acceptable. Even after praying about it all together."

"He's not much of a businessman, I take it," Holly ventured.

"He argued they owed him their allegiance."

"Let me guess. He's spent a pretty penny on tuition and board, plus he's been a big contributor to their cause?"

"Yep. My working theory is Larkin sent his son to an isolated compound along the Snake River because he wanted the boy to grow up having the kind of country life he'd missed out on," I said.

"So why isn't his kid doing senior year at the Glorious Lord Academy instead of Grant Union High School?"

"That's just how angry Larkin was. Yanked his kid out, and his money with it." Which might explain Brady's general bad attitude, not to mention the icy covenant between father and son.

"Interesting gossip, but how does that help us?" Hollis asked.

"Good question."

The blinking light on my desk phone indicated I had voice-mail waiting. I could see from the number that flashed on the screen that I'd missed another call from Jeremy T. Lake. I'd forgotten to get back to the bastard first thing.

"Sergeant Blackthorne." J.T.'s voice dark and cutting. "I'll follow up with an email, even though Corporal Macintyre would prefer I speak to you directly. But since you can't be bothered to return my calls, the email will have to do."

I opened my inbox and read the subject line of J.T.'s email: *Senior Trooper Hollis Jones*. "I've recommended Jones be promoted, and Corporal Macintyre agreed. He'll be contacting Jones in the near future, but he wanted me to let you know ahead of time."

"Fucker," I whispered.

Mostly to piss me off, J.T. had always been dismissive and condescending when it came to Hollis. And now my asshole ex-husband had managed to do the one thing he could ever do to hurt me.

A promotion would mean Holly's transfer for certain. The loss of my police partner and one true pal out here. Which was why I hadn't made the recommendation myself. One of my most selfish dick-moves ever.

I needed some air. "I'll be back in an hour or so."

The idea of Holly's promotion depressed me more than the cluttered murder boards we'd cobbled together. Even though I was sick to death of driving all over the county looking for answers and finding only more questions, I needed to get out of the office.

Since finding the Nodines' bodies, I'd passed by the Seneca mill site several times without stopping to check the scene, something that was six days overdue. It was close to noon when I arrived, and the temperature had bumped to a balmy thirty-eight degrees, despite the mass of gray overhead. A steady wind whipped across the frozen plateau of sagebrush, lashing against the metal siding of the rusty wigwam burner. Inside the precarious structure, someone was busy scanning the expansive wall with a flashlight.

"Hello!" I called out, making my way toward the burner.

Ariel Pritchett slipped from the shadowy interior. "Maggie?"

"What are you doing in there?"

"I wanted to see where it happened."

"Dammit, Ariel, this is a crime scene. As the tape across the entrance clearly says."

She swept the windblown hair from her face. "I know I shouldn't have gone inside, but I was careful not to disturb nothin'. Someday I'd like to put up a little memorial out here, unless that's illegal or something."

For Christ's sake, this wasn't the scene of a fatal car accident.

I moved closer. "You have to stay off this property until I say otherwise."

"All right, I got the picture." She zipped up her hoodie. "I was gonna stop by your office after this."

"Oh?"

"I need to get somethin' off my chest."

"Something you neglected to tell me?"

She nodded.

I pointed to the Tahoe. "Let's talk in my SUV."

Once inside, she fixed her gaze through the front windshield and watched the junkyard grasses wafting in the breeze.

"What did you want to tell me, Ariel?"

"I knew about that red truck. Joey even took me for a ride in it."

Shit. Another goddamn note to stick up on the murder board.

"Why'd you think you needed to lie to me twice about it?"

She shrugged. "Afraid I'd be in trouble, I guess."

"Why? Were you there when they stole it?"

Ariel shook her head. "That ain't what happened. It was part of that deal I told you about."

"Who was the deal with?"

"Wish I knew. Don't know what they had to do in exchange for it neither."

"How long had they had the truck?"

"About a month, I think," she said.

"Did you know they stored it here?" I indicated the wigwam burner.

"Inside that thing?"

"It was found parked near their bodies."

"I don't understand."

"They must have figured they could keep it hidden here. Until they had to skip town, that is."

Her expression was grave. "Skip town? What are you sayin'?"

"They left a note for Lynn. Told her they had to get out of the state for a while."

"But Joey and me was gettin' married, Maggie, I swear."

"I believe you, but something must have come up suddenly. I know they were afraid of somebody. They even called and asked me to meet them here. But it was too late. They were dead before I arrived."

Ariel pitched forward abruptly as if she were about to vomit on the floor of my police vehicle. Instead, she sobbed violently.

I lifted a packet of tissues from the center console and placed it on the dashboard. "In the note the twins left for Lynn, Joseph asked her to let you know they were leaving. Sounded like they planned to come back, though."

That seemed to calm her some, and she was able to

whisper a question. "You asked me about some guy the other day?"

"Yes, Frank Sylvester."

"Nah. That ain't the name. It's some rancher."

"Mr. Sylvester lives out in the country south of Burns, but he's not a rancher."

"I overheard Danny and Joey once. Whatever the deal over the red truck was about, it had somethin to do with a cattle rancher. Somebody I'd never heard of. And I've racked my brain tryin' to remember his name."

I started to suggest Larkin but stopped myself. I needed Ariel to recall the name on her own. "Think on it for a day or two."

She nodded.

I thought of another question. "Last Thursday when I brought you the news about the killings, you said you hadn't seen Joseph since the previous morning. Was that unusual?"

"Yeah, we'd been together every night since about the time we decided to get married."

"And you assumed he'd be there when you got home from work on Wednesday?"

She became teary once more. "I did. Why're you asking?"

"Just trying to nail down a timeline."

If I believed what Ariel was telling me, and I did, the last time she saw Joseph was last Wednesday morning. Did something happen that day to prompt the Nodines to get ready to skip town? Something besides poaching a deer that evening.

She looped the strap of her handbag over her shoulder. "I should get to work."

"Call me anytime if you remember that rancher's name. Night or day."

"Okay, Maggie. I will."

Ariel drove her battered little Datsun pickup back toward

John Day. After a few minutes of watching the sun sear through the clouds and light up the spire of Dead Point and the indigo mountains west and east, I followed her back down Canyon Mountain.

Shortly after I arrived at the office, Taylor came and stood warily at my desk.

"Cecil Burney is here. Says he needs to speak to you right away."

"Tell him I'll be with him shortly." I turned to Hollis, deep into his excavation of some website. "Did you hear that?"

He came up for air. "What's up?"

"Cecil Burney is paying me a surprise visit."

"Hell must have finally frozen over."

"Well, if anyone would know, it'd be him."

On purpose, I kept Cecil waiting for about ten minutes. I found him sitting patiently in the plastic deck chair next to the row of coat hooks.

He stood as I entered the waiting area, his fierce, bleary eyes trained my way. "Need to talk to you somewhere private."

The choices for private conversation were limited: the storage closet, the evidence locker, the lavatory, and the alcove now taken over by murder boards. I led him to the storage closet, pulled the chain to turn on the single bulb overhead, and set up two folding chairs. He closed the door and we sat, stuffed awkwardly in one another's air.

"Sorry, Cecil, this is the best I can offer," I said, hoping to quell any desire he might have to bolt.

He peered round the space, the boxes of blank forms, utility pencils, and paper towels. "I've talked to cops in worse places."

I noticed his trembling hands. His body was fighting

coming off the booze. "You here to tell me about that trouble between you and the Nodine boys?"

He nodded, leaned forward in his chair wincing, his head hung barely above my lap. "Their mama. She and I had a thing way back when. It was Lynn who ended it, said I was a worse drunk than Farley."

I already knew this part of Cecil's story, but I sat quietly.

"Then somehow them sons of hers found out and started makin' my life hell. First vandalizing my place, then slicing my pickup tires, stealing tools. Finally caught me passed out in my rig, drug me out to the pavement, and kicked the living shit outta me. I woke up, took myself to the hospital, and after that, bought myself a shotgun. I started takin that long-barreled hog with me everywhere."

Like a lot of people out here, Cecil slipped his word endings now and then, made up improper contractions on occasion, and used the incorrect verb tense sometimes. But that habit was a nod to local custom, not necessarily a sign of poor aptitude. A rural Oregon affectation, so to speak.

"Why didn't you go to the police?"

He winced again. "You know why."

Tobacco and cheap scotch alone wouldn't account for the baleful rasp in his voice.

"Because you fucking hate cops."

Cecil grunted. "You might be the exception."

"Finish what you came here to say to me."

"When those boys was shipped off to prison for a while, I didn't have to worry about them intimidating me or messing with my stuff."

"Didn't have to worry about shooting them with your long-barreled hog either." The closed-in space was becoming intolerable. "But then they got out of prison."

"And left me alone at first. Then about six months ago,

they gut-shot my border collie with a goddamn thirty-aught-six."

Cecil juddered in his shoulders and flailed, trying to catch his breath. Finally overcome, he could do nothing but bawl into his open palms and shake his head. "Those fucking shits killed my Billy."

He wept quietly. Even though I had to keep a firm grip on my professional judgment and even knowing this man might be a murderer, it was all I could do not to wrap my arms around the old bastard and weep with him.

After several minutes, he lifted himself out of his grief and breathed deeply. "Okay. I'm ready to tell you the rest."

"The rest?"

"Last Thursday, I was locking up my gas station, about to leave for the AA meeting, I seen the Nodines pass by goin' north on 395. They wasn't driving their army jeep but that fat, red monster truck you asked me about. Anyways, I took off, hanging back so they wouldn't notice me. Then they turned down the road to the old sawmill."

He paused, his hands quavering.

"Did you follow them?"

"I pulled to the shoulder and parked. Don't know what I was planning, and I had to get to gettin' if I was going to make the AA meeting. But while them fucks drove down the highway, I'd watched that Rottweiler standing in the truck bed. Bobbing around, howling and barking. And I thought about Billy. Killed for no reason."

He shifted his face toward the ceiling, closed his eyes.

"What happened next?"

"Got Billy as a pup. He was all I had. So I started my pickup, went slow down the dirt road, stopped just past the gate behind a wide clump of junipers. I grabbed my shotgun and inched toward the wigwam burner. I saw 'em in there, one on the phone, one yelling shit. While the Rottweiler pranced around free. I stepped quick to the opening, raised the shotgun. I blew a hole in the trailer and gut-shot their dog. Then I run, sure they'd go after me with that thirty-aught-six they had in their gun rack. But they didn't."

"You know I have to charge you with a felony. It could mean time in jail, prison even."

"I know. Deserved. Not because of the Rottweiler, neither. I should've come forward earlier, told you what happened after. If I had, maybe Lynn could've found some peace and stayed on the wagon."

I was tiring of his capacity to string out the plot. "So tell me now. What happened after?"

"To get back on 395, I would've had to drive back past the Nodines and their rifle. So I decided to keep on the mill road, take the long way to John Day. I was about to pull out when Kat McKay's Land Rover flew around the corner and ground to a stop."

Rain had been the one applying a lead foot to the Land Rover the morning I went to Kat's place to tell her about Dan Nodine's murder.

"Did you recognize the driver?"

"It was Kat all right."

"Did she see you?

"Pretty sure she had no idea anybody was parked behind that patch of junipers."

"Keep going, Cecil."

"I nosed my pickup out from behind the trees and watched her climb over the gate and beat feet to the wigwam burner. Then I took off for that AA meeting. Like a fool, I wanted Lynn to notice I'd made it there this time."

"Why should I believe all this, that you only killed the Rottweiler and not the Nodines too?"

"Because all I wanted was revenge. Wanted them two to feel the same hurt I had over Billy."

"What proof did you have the twins killed your dog?"

"I seen Dan do it with my own eyes."

If true, it was the most vicious accusation I'd ever heard concerning Dan Nodine.

"Lynn said you came in late to the AA meeting."

He paused, put his hate-the-cops face back on. "Did the killer use a shotgun? 'Cause that's the only weapon I own."

Somehow I could almost believe him. Cecil was sly, but it was hard to imagine he could make up a story like the one he'd just told me. Still, I'd be a fool to trust the man completely. Tears for his dead dog notwithstanding, there was every possibility he had a cache of assault weapons somewhere. Also nothing to say that he didn't have a change of heart when he got back to his pickup and pulled out a Kel-Tec 9 semiautomatic pistol stashed under his seat, returned to the wigwam burner, and murdered the Nodines.

"I could get a search warrant within the hour, verify the shotgun is the sum total of your arsenal."

"Go right ahead."

He clearly longed to add *bitch* to his dare. And just like that, we were back at a place of mutual animosity. I was certain we both preferred it that way.

Someone knocked at the storage closet door. I stood and opened it.

"Harry Bratton is on the phone," Hollis whispered.

"We're done here," I said. "Follow me, Cecil. Trooper Taylor will take it from here."

Cecil shuffled behind me, the two of us inhaling fresher air in phlegmy unison, and I motioned for him to sit in the chair across from Taylor.

"Place Mr. Burney formally under arrest for withholding

evidence in the Nodine murders. Also, cite him for first-degree animal abuse for shooting their dog."

Taylor finished writing down my directives. "My pleasure."

I knew withholding evidence in a homicide investigation was hard enough for Taylor to stomach, but Cecil's killing the dog would bring out Taylor's righteous anger.

16

Harry Bratton had identified three distinct sets of fingerprints, none of which were in LEDS. His ballistics exam also determined that Larkin's Kel-Tec PF-9 semiautomatic handgun was the weapon used in the Nodine murders.

"No question about it," he had said before ending the call.

By the time I'd finished my discussion with Harry, Mark Taylor had put together Cecil Burney's citation and arrest warrant. He'd also gotten my signatures and delivered the old drunk to the county jail.

"I'm supposed to pass along a message to you, Maggie," Taylor said.

"Let me guess. 'Go to hell.'"

"No, he told me to tell you that it's on you to get her back on the wagon. I asked who he meant, but he said you'd know."

"Thanks, Mark. Message received." I turned to Hollis. "I want you to be in on this call with Bach."

As I dialed the number, he placed his laptop on the card table next to the speakerphone.

"Homicide," Al said, answering on the other end.

"Afternoon. Maggie Blackthorne. Hollis Jones is on the

line too. We want to fill you in on a couple of things, get some direction on how to proceed."

Bach shuffled papers in the background. "Is this about the forensic exam?"

"Partly. Harry ID'd Larkin's Kel-Tec PF-9 as the murder weapon and lifted three sets of prints, none of them in LEDS. And something else has come up. We have a witness—Cecil Burney, the owner of the Seneca gas station I talked to last Saturday. He claims to have seen Kat McKay enter the wigwam burner shortly before the Nodines were killed."

Hollis gave me a look. I hadn't had an opportunity to tell him about Bratton's phone call, the details of Cecil's visit, or my latest chat with Ariel Pritchett.

"How reliable is the witness?" the detective asked.

"Generally speaking, not very. In fact, Trooper Taylor just checked him in at the county jail. I've charged him with withholding evidence and felony animal abuse. He shot the Nodines' dog."

"Whoa," Bach called out.

"What the hell?" Hollis mouthed.

"I believe we have to check out Burney's story right away." I reminded Bach that Kat McKay had been dating one of the Nodine twins up until a week before their murders. "I spoke to her last night, and she admitted borrowing Asa Larkin's Kel-Tec PF-9 to target shoot. Claims she got it from his son, though. Says she's never met Larkin."

"You found the weapon in the man's vehicle yesterday, so she obviously returned it at some point."

"We need to figure out when," I said.

"Have you verified with Larkin that he lent her the pistol?" Al asked.

"No, but he did tell us he usually stores it in a locked safe and that his son doesn't know the combination, doesn't even know a gun is kept there."

"Brady seems like an intelligent kid," Hollis offered. "The kind who's tenacious enough to figure out the combination to his father's safe."

"Good point," I said.

"So we have other possibilities to explore when I see you later today," Al said.

"For one, Hollis figured out Frank Sylvester is Larkin's biological father."

"Can't wait to hear more. Right now, though, I'm late for a meeting. I do have one more question. Any progress on the Trudeau murder?"

Oh, that. "Nothing more than what Jess Flynn told us about the altercation between Trudeau and Larkin over those steers."

After Bach signed off, Hollis and I remained in the alcove stewing in our own thoughts.

"Cecil Burney. He's something else," Hollis said finally.

"Crazy old bachelor. Practically lives in that trashy gas station of his."

"And Kat McKay. I've only spoken with her a few times, but she's not really friendly, is she?"

"No. And she could be lying about not knowing Larkin. Shortly after I left her house last night, I drove back by, and his black Prius was parked in her driveway."

"I hope you have more evidence than that if you're ever called to testify," Holly teased. "Besides, if the car is the only thing you saw, it could've been his kid hanging out with her son."

"What?" I was caught sideways for a moment, mostly

because I'd stupidly not thought of that. I managed to come up with a retort anyway. "If you recall, he was in our office when Dad suspended his driving privileges."

Holly rolled his eyes. "What was the message all about, the one Mark delivered to you from Cecil?"

Shit. I needed to take care of that. "Thanks for reminding me, Holly. Honestly, it's a private matter. I'll be back shortly"

I stuffed the speakerphone back in its cubby, grabbed my coat and hat, and hurried out the door.

I parked in front of the Castle Thrift Store. Lynn Nodine would no doubt reject any attempts by me to rescue her from hooch, and she'd definitely spurn that gaggle of church ladies swooping in. But Dorie was her friend, the one and only. More than that, Dorie was willing to put up with all of the drunken venom Lynn might spew and still be there when Lynn crawled up from the dark hole again. Dorie would save Lynn from herself. The same way she had saved me years before.

Entering the store, I heard the usual electronic ting, a muffled chime alerting her to customers. I wiped my feet on her flower-print doormat and removed my police Stetson.

Dorie stepped from her living quarters at the rear of the building. "Maggie. You don't usually drop by in the middle of the day."

"I wanted you to know Lynn has started drinking hard again."

"You saw her?"

"No. Somebody who cares about her enough to let me know."

"Cecil Burney?"

"Doesn't matter who, but I know if anyone can help her right now, it's you."

"You're right, it doesn't matter who you heard it from. And thanks for coming to fetch me." She gave me one of her sweet, God-loves-you hugs, collected her coat and purse, and hung the *Closed* sign in the front window.

I followed her out and watched her drive away toward Lynn's house in her rusted-out Toyota Corolla. I'd missed lunch earlier, so I charged up the stairs to my apartment, checked on Louie again, and heated and inhaled one of the last frozen entrées in my freezer.

Before I finished quaffing a glass of water to wash it all down, Hollis rang. I swallowed and answered, "Just heading back."

"A Mr. Pete Trudeau is here to talk to you."

Guy Trudeau's oldest son.

"Christ on a crutch, they're crawling out of the woodwork today."

"I'll let him know you're on your way."

Pete must have driven up from Medford to put his father's affairs in order and make funeral arrangements. I hadn't seen him since the summer before I started high school and he left for college. Quiet, serious, and hell-bent on getting as far away as he could from ranching life and his old man, so the gossip went.

The dented Volvo parked outside the police station had to belong to Pete, the proper vehicle for a middle school math teacher. The man even looked like a middle school math teacher: gray face, eyes, and hair. He rose from the plastic deck chair in the front corner of our office, and we shook hands, his grip hardier than I would've expected.

"My condolences," I said.

He nodded. "I haven't been to Big T in years, Maggie.

What the hell happened to the place? That beautiful old barn practically destroyed."

I refrained from suggesting he might know how the family ranch had fallen to rack and ruin if he'd bothered visiting his father a long time ago.

"I hadn't been to Big T in several years either before I drove out to speak to your dad this past Sunday. I'm not sure how long it's been in the state it's in."

"Can you tell me why you went to see him?"

"He'd had some dealings with Dan and Joseph Nodine right before they were murdered. We wanted to question him about that."

"What? When did that happen?"

"A week ago tomorrow."

"And you suspected Pop was involved?"

"We planned to question him about a couple of things, but that's pretty much all I can share with you at this point."

Pete shook his head. "He was a mean old bastard, but I don't know about murder. Anyway, have you figured out who did kill the Nodines—or Pop, for that matter?"

"Not yet, I'm afraid. We're chasing every angle, though."

He didn't appear convinced, and why should he? A nearly week-old double homicide followed by his father's murder a few days later, and we had no solid leads on either.

"I'm staying at the Best Western for a few days. I'm hoping to get things in order with his estate," Pete said.

"Do you plan on a memorial service?"

"Melissa and I decided on no services. He'll be cremated and the urn placed next to our mother's in Sam Damon's mausoleum."

His sister, Melissa, always a strange bird, had been a year ahead of me in school. "How's Melissa doing?"

"Fine, I guess. Divorced a couple of times. Has difficulty keeping a job."

"And Ronny?" Their brother who had run in the band of wild boys along with the Nodine twins.

"We haven't heard from Ronny in a long time. He was always Pop's bright, shining star, and then he crashed to earth on meth and opioids."

Pete seemed to be confirming my notion that Ronny was the one who took off with the old man's money.

"My sense is your dad had been selling off his cattle little by little. I'm afraid there are only about thirty head of Black Angus remaining."

Pete inhaled deeply. "Well, I didn't expect to inherit much anyway."

It was hard to tell whether he really gave a damn about Big T or his father's death, but who was I to judge. I delved into what snippets of info I could offer, telling him where the small herd was pastured and about the issue of pinkeye among the animals.

"Okay. I'll arrange to get the cattle treated and possibly sold while I'm here."

"The ranch itself is a crime scene at this point."

He nodded. "I saw the warning signs when I was there yesterday. I'll probably come back in the summer, put it up for sale. Assuming things are resolved by then."

I took his hint. He wanted his father's murder case wrapped up by summer. Probably not as much as I did, though.

"God, life is just so weird, isn't it? Strange to come back here for the sole purpose of arranging Pop's cremation and dealing with his leftover animals."

I wrote down the location of Guy Trudeau's grazing land and added my office phone number. "Give me a call before you head back to Medford, and I'll let you know if we have any new information."

"Thanks. It was good to see you, Maggie, all grown up and official. You look great, by the way."

I ignored his parting comment and walked toward the alcove. There was no way in hell Hollis or Taylor would mention Pete's flirty little compliment, not directly, anyway. But sooner or later, one or both would attempt to slide some smartass remark into our conversation.

Hollis, looking a little ragged around the edges, followed me into the alcove. "I'd like to take off for home by four. Hank's a bit colicky."

"And Lil needs a break."

"She does."

I cleared my throat. "And you need one too. I'm beginning to rethink you delaying your leave time."

He gave me an ominous look. "We've already talked about this, Maggie. I'm here. Until these murder cases are called—solved or put on ice—I'm here."

"So noted." I tacked a blank chart pack page beside the Nodine murder board and wrote *Timeline* at the top. "We know time of death was sometime between five forty-five and six fifteen in the evening, right?"

Hollis took the marker from me and scribbled the TOD range on the fresh page.

"Cecil Burney says he set out for John Day at five thirty to make his six o'clock AA meeting but took a detour to the old mill following after them."

"How do you spell *Burney*?"

I spelled it out for him, and he added the name and departure time.

"While I was on the phone with Joseph, I'm sure I heard Cecil shoot the Rottweiler. That was at about five forty-five. He claims he ran back to his vehicle and watched Kat McKay speed by, park, and enter the wigwam burner. Says that's when he took off for the meeting. And for the moment, I believe him. Mostly because someone I trust told me he arrived at the AA meeting twenty to twenty-five minutes late."

And being sober when she told me, I had no reason not to take Lynn Nodine at her word.

"Why was he so late getting there?" Hollis asked after adding *AA meeting ETA 6:20.*

"Says he didn't want to risk being shot by the Nodines as he drove back by the wigwam burner, so he stayed on the mill road and drove the back way into town."

Hollis measured the distance on our map. "It's a longer route and unpaved and graded, which would definitely make the drive time ten or fifteen minutes more."

"So what normally takes about half an hour on Highway 395 would've taken forty or forty-five minutes. Which means, given Cecil's ETA at the meeting, it's unlikely he killed them."

"Plus he'd have to have access to Larkin's Kel-Tec 9. And as much as I think Burney's capable of murder, I doubt he managed to get ahold of that gun."

"I agree," I said.

"Did he express remorse for shooting the Nodines' dog?"

"No. He felt guilty about not coming forward earlier with the information about Kat McKay is all."

"He doesn't seem like a person who'd be bothered too much by guilt."

Holly's on-the-nose assessment aside, Lynn was Cecil Burney's one weak spot. Her lapse back into booze had gotten to the old man.

"For now, let's assume he shot the dog and took off to his AA meeting driving the mill road just like he said."

"So that leaves us with Kat McKay as a suspect?"

I had to admit it. "She's a suspect now for sure, especially since Larkin's pistol is a match. Larkin's a suspect too, of course."

We sat quietly studying the timeline. Hollis checked his watch.

"You should get going," I said.

"In ten minutes or so."

"Kat may turn out to be our prime suspect, but something about that notion bothers me."

"Because she's a woman?"

"Hell, no. It's something her kid, Rain, said. He was surprised she was interested in having a gun around at all."

Holly drew a line at midpoint across the page. "Maybe her viewpoint changed."

"Maybe she really was afraid of Dan Nodine." I was grasping at a plausible straw.

"We have to figure out when she returned Larkin's pistol. Showing up at the murder scene around the time the Nodines were killed, that's pretty compelling evidence," Hollis said.

"I know, I know."

He sighed. "Let's think through the possibility she left the scene right away and someone else arrived just after."

That tripped a wire in my tired brain. "What if the murderer didn't reach the wigwam burner after Cecil and Kat had taken off. What if the killer was there with the twins the entire time?"

"That's at least possible." Hollis wrote *Suspects* below the line he'd drawn.

"When Joseph called me, he said they were in bad trouble, had messed up big-time. They knew somebody was coming after them. And from the sound of his voice, they were scared shitless." I turned to our timeline. "I just can't wrap my head around Kat being a killer."

"I can tell. Maybe it's a little too close to home. It's not easy to think someone you grew up with could force those men at gunpoint to sit in the dirt and then shoot them in cold blood."

Reality kicked me in the gut. Emotion had blunted my instincts, clouded my judgment, and sent me into denial. I'd been under the delusion that Duncan would see I was just doing my job if Kat was arrested for the Nodine murders. But I knew the truth. If that happened, our short romance would be just that.

"Speaking of close to home," Hollis broke in, his way of ending my brooding, "I'm about to head out."

"Okay. Thanks for helping me work through some of this."

"We'll get there, Maggie."

I nodded and smiled, a small ruse to camouflage my burgeoning distress. Duncan had appeared in my life after a long and loveless drought, and I wasn't in the mood to fuck up a good thing.

Before Hollis could gather his things and scram, his desk phone rang.

"Let it go to voicemail."

He looked at the number on the screen and picked up. In the meantime, my phone sounded too, and Bach's name popped up.

"I'm just now managing to get on the road," he said. "So I'd like you to meet me at the junction to Larkin's ranch. What's it called again?"

"Harden Road."

"I'll be there as soon as I can."

"Drive carefully, Al. They're calling for snow at higher elevations tonight."

Taylor was standing at my desk when I finished the call.

"Can I help you?" My snide tone caught us both by surprise.

He dropped his chronic smile. Evidently I had nicked Taylor's ego a smidge.

"Sorry, Mark. That sounded pretty officious. I'm a little on edge."

"It's okay, Maggie. I just wanted to tell you I'm on my way home."

"See you tomorrow."

Hollis threw me that look, the one that meant Mark deserved more respect, but he didn't take it any further.

I pointed to my phone. "That was Bach just now. I'm meeting him out at Harden Road in a few hours."

He pointed to his phone. "And that was Bach's detective friend in Portland. You wanted to find out who hired Sarah Anderson to be the accountant for Frank Sylvester Trucking."

"Asa Larkin?"

"Yep. He's Sylvester's guardian-conservator. No surprise, he also authorized the purchase of that Ram 3500, supposedly on Sylvester's behalf."

"I was sure it was something like that. And speaking of the Ram 3500, Ariel Pritchett told me it was part of the deal the Nodines had going. She thinks with some rancher."

"What? Didn't she tell you before she knew zip about the red truck?"

"Twice. Said she was afraid she'd get in trouble. Thing is, she couldn't remember the rancher's name."

"You gave her a clue, right?"

"Almost. But then I decided to let her come up with the name all on her own, in case *the rancher* turns out to be someone else. Like one of Larkin's hired men."

Hollis shut down his computer. "Ah, another shiny object."

I tossed my keys brusquely in the desk drawer. "Dammit, weren't you going home?"

"I'll see you in the morning."

"Good night, Holly," I said, listing Larkin's and Kat's names in his new *Suspects* category.

"Breakfast at Erna's tomorrow? Maybe that will help your mood."

"Maybe."

It was snowing heavily, the kind of snow I had been crazy about as a girl sledding down Starr Ridge, a long, steep scarp on the backside of Canyon Mountain. Always with a gang of other kids pulled behind somebody's snowmobile, the entire earth radiant under a full sun. But for tonight's purpose of driving into the foothills of the Aldrich range to Bear Valley Cattle Company, such weather was a fucking torment.

I parked on the shoulder of Harden Road and waited for Al Bach, Susan Tedeschi's hypnotic brand of blues sounding from the speakers. Mind wandering, snow shushing over the windshield of my SUV, I thought of Duncan. His sea-green eyes, that shock of auburn hair turning sandy, the sound of his voice, and how he carried himself with serious but amiable confidence. I thought of how he touched me.

I wondered what the hell I was doing falling in love in the middle of two homicide investigations. One of which might involve Duncan's sister.

Bach slowed his Ford Interceptor and flashed his headlights, signaling me to lead the way to Asa Larkin's ranch five miles up the snow-laden road. The drive was ponderous, but at least the blizzard had subsided some.

When we arrived at the cattle company compound, the interior of the main house and the three double-wide trailers were all fully lit, creating strange angular shadows over the shared courtyard. And given the collection of dwellings crowded together, I could've imagined a clan of Mormon polygamists converging here and laying claim to the place.

With the entrance locked and no cell service or way to communicate, Al switched on his emergency lights and activated his blaring Federal Signal Q siren to once more alert Larkin the State cops had arrived. His hired men rallied from their respective double-wides and tracked through the snow toward us. They had tramped halfway across the courtyard when Larkin opened the lock remotely.

Less emboldened, the ranch hands/bodyguards/whatever stood three abreast and watched warily as we passed and made our way to the front porch of the main house.

"It's late, officers," Larkin said from his open doorway.

Once inside, Asa Larkin's sleekly decorated front room should have made me feel all cozy with its rustling fire and the aroma of fresh-cut pine, but the icy chrome-and-glass tables and the cold black leather divan and wing chairs belied any sense of hospitality and warmth.

He invited us to take a seat. "I assume you're here to return my pistol."

Bach placed a digital recorder on the glass-topped coffee table, turned it on, and noted the date and subject of the interview. "We've had your Kel-Tec PF-9 tested by a forensics expert. We know it was the handgun used in the homicide of Nodine brothers."

Larkin barely flinched. "I've rarely even shot the thing, but I'm not saying another word without my attorney present."

"We'd be happy to contact a lawyer to meet us back at my office in John Day," I offered.

He scarcely avoided a sneer. "I already have one on retainer. He's worked for me a good long time."

I had to wonder why someone working in elder law would

need an attorney on retainer. Then again, most lawyers I'd known were cynical, wary, risk-averse creatures.

"Give him a call," Al said.

Larkin paused and cleared his throat. "His office is in Portland. He lives near there in Happy Valley."

"Then you'll need to take Sergeant Blackthorne up on the offer of contacting someone local."

Larkin's face emptied of color. Something had finally rattled the man. "You assume I'm willing to drive to John Day at this hour."

"Make no mistake, we assume nothing of the kind. That's why we have the authority to arrest you and take you there in handcuffs, Mr. Larkin," Bach said.

That shut him up, leaving me room to take the discussion in another direction. "The day before the Nodines were murdered, I encountered them driving that red Ram pickup. The vehicle was brand new and registered to Frank Sylvester at his trucking business in Burns."

"What does that have to do with me?"

"Why don't you tell us?" I needed to rein in my enthusiasm for snark.

"Sylvester's my father, at least by birth."

"And you had yourself appointed as his guardian, correct?" I asked.

Larkin couldn't hide his astonishment. "Yes."

I pressed further. "And that's how you have access to his assets."

He nodded slowly. "I'll inherit it all at some point, anyway."

"What's the date of Sylvester's most recent will?" I was on a roll, and I planned to keep it up until I was ready to pass Larkin back to Bach.

"He contacted me a few years ago. Let me know he'd

drawn it up. I was to inherit everything. That was before his accident."

"And after the accident, you got yourself appointed as his guardian and the conservator of his estate. That's when you began making large purchases, but not necessarily in the interests of Mr. Sylvester," I said, my voice calmer than my nerves.

I tried to gauge the flat affect he'd taken on. "We put people in prison for that, too. Also people who aid and abet criminal wrongdoing. Such as your stepsister, Sarah Anderson."

The comment about his sister was the spark that relit Larkin's flame. "Sarah has no idea about guardian-conservatorship law. She keeps the books and writes the checks when I tell her, and that's all."

"I'm not sure that would convince a jury," Bach chimed in.

"And I'm curious," I said. "How did the Nodines have possession of the Ram truck?"

"They stole it."

"Before or after stealing your livestock trailer?" I asked.

"Both went missing at the same time. So yes, that's when they stole the truck."

"You reported the missing trailer, why not the Ram 3500?"

"Because technically, it wasn't mine to file a report on."

"Technically, nothing. You didn't want the police following the path back to your misuse of Mr. Sylvester's assets." Al had gotten tired of Larkin's evasions. "More to our reason for calling on you this evening, the theft of that diesel truck represented fifty grand worth of those assets and perhaps an excuse for murdering the men who took it."

"I wasn't happy when I spotted them driving around, but I'm a Christian, and I do not cheat, steal, *or* kill."

I'd had about all I could take from this hypocrite. "So if

you don't steal, how do you justify siphoning off your father's estate?"

"I took some of what will soon belong to me completely. But for the wrong reason. I did it out of greed. Avarice, cupidity, covetousness. A desire for material possessions. I was about to run out of my own funds, and I lusted after that pickup truck the way I never had about anything or anyone in my life."

"So when it was stolen, God was teaching you a lesson?" I asked.

"Yes, and I've prayed for forgiveness." He breathed deeply before going on with his sob story. "I'd left my unlocked truck in the parking lot—key in the ignition, the trailer hitched to the back—while I made a deposit in my bank account."

Who knew God was ironic when meting out retribution?

"Let's get back to your Kel-Tec PF-9," Bach ordered.

"Again, I've barely ever touched it. Only started carrying it with me in the car a few days ago. I already told the sergeant, three murders in one week had me on edge."

"That's hard to believe, coming as you do from a metropolitan area," Al shot back.

Larkin ignored Bach's skepticism. "I usually travel with one of my men. They help with ranch operations, but they also act as my security team, I guess you'd say."

Al prodded. "You need bodyguards? I'm really struggling to see why you've put all these security measures in place. Locked gates, electric fencing, and a semiautomatic pistol."

"Protection, obviously."

"From what? Unless you're a serial defrauder of other infirm and incapacitated clients like your own father. Or perhaps you keep more in that safe than a handgun."

That finally pushed Larkin into silent mode. The three of

us sat for a full minute in a deathly hush. Then it was my turn again.

"Did you recently loan your pistol to a woman named Kat McKay?" I asked.

Larkin erupted in derisive laughter. "Absolutely not."

"What is your relationship with her?"

"I don't know a woman named *Kat* anything."

"She claims to have borrowed your handgun so she could learn to shoot," I countered.

"What? I would never loan anything to a stranger, let alone a firearm."

"I guess I'll have to confirm that with her."

"Please do, Sergeant."

What might have been confirmed was that Larkin's kid had loaned Kat the gun, just as she'd told me yesterday. And if that was the case, Brady also knew the weapon was stored in his father's safe and knew the combination.

"Mr. Larkin. I'm not quite ready to arrest you for murder, but you've already admitted to a crime." Bach stood and snapped the handcuffs from his duty belt. "You're under arrest for criminal mistreatment in the first degree, a Class C felony, punishable with up to five years in prison."

"Yes, I'm fully aware of the length of punishment. I'd like to be able to call my attorney in Portland first."

Al clipped the handcuffs around Larkin's wrists. "You can make that call from the county jail."

"What about my son?"

"He's over eighteen and no longer a minor, but I can call juvenile authorities, request an exception so he can be placed in foster care tonight," I said.

"God, no. I'll ask one of the men to sleep in the main house and make sure he catches the school bus tomorrow."

I rose from the leather chair. "It's better if we do the asking. Anyone in particular of the three?"

"John Vickers in the mobile home closest to the main house. He understands how to keep Brady in line."

"I'll speak with your hired man," Bach said. "In the meantime, Sergeant Blackthorne will deliver you to authorities at the county jail, and they'll take it from there."

Before I'd climbed in the front seat of my Tahoe to haul our prisoner off to the pokey, Al and I agreed to meet at the office at seven the next morning. We would drive to Kat McKay's house from there. He thought having a homicide detective arrive unexpectedly might demonstrate how seriously we were looking at her as a murder suspect. I didn't disagree, particularly since the only space available for an interview at my trooper station was the storage closet.

"And I'd like to get to the bottom of a few things before Larkin posts bail. Otherwise, there's every chance he'll light out of here, despite all that Christian poppycock," he added, actually employing air quotes.

One man's abiding faith was another man's Christian poppycock, it seemed.

The drive to the county jail in Canyon City was uneventful, as was the handoff to the sheriff's deputies. I suspected Larkin's attorney would fly in tonight and he'd be out on bail by late afternoon tomorrow. The attorney might eventually even find a way to kick the charge down to Class A elder abuse, a piddling violation that would amount to Larkin having to fork out a whole two thousand bucks or so to the State of Oregon.

Frank Sylvester could be dead by then, turning Asa

Larkin's lame justification for spending Sylvester's cash assets in advance of inheriting them into a matter of ethics and morals rather than fusty legalities. With all that in mind, it heartened me to see him plopped in a jail cell alongside some of our more unsavory local denizens.

After Larkin was tucked in, I checked messages. Duncan had called twice earlier in the evening and later texted: "Seems police business has you working overtime tonight. Be careful out there. Hope to see you tomorrow"

Tomorrow. I drove straight to my apartment and crashed under the covers, exhausted and desperate to avoid thinking about Duncan or what might play out in our interview with his sister Kat in the morning. I peeked at *Libbey vs. Chase* lying on the nightstand. I could continue reading or just admit I'd grown weary of the novel's bad cop/bad cop antics some time ago. I turned out the light and fell into a restless sleep.

I rose without disturbing Louie. Pulled on my wooly slippers, adjusted the heat, and filled a glass with ice-cold tap water. I turned to the microwave's fluorescent clock face: early in a day that promised to be long.

Craving more sleep, time to think, to sort out the meaning of this past week, I tore through my morning regimen none-theless, arriving at the office at six twenty. I fired up the coffeemaker and refilled the sugar bowl.

Hollis arrived shortly after, joining me at our break table in the alcove, where the two of us waited fretfully for the day's first shot of caffeine.

When the brew signal chimed, he poured each of us a mug full and returned to the table. "A trip to Erna's this morning?"

"Nah. The visit to Asa Larkin last night ended late."

"The guy will start thinking we suspect him of something."

"He's definitely got the picture now."

"Is he under arrest?"

"Yeah, but not for killing the Nodines. At least not yet." I sipped the hot coffee. "Larkin's charged with a Class C felony. I think we were already on the verge of putting this together, but he's been dipping into Frank Sylvester's assets for his own benefit."

Hollis yawned and palmed one eye. "So, some possible prison time. Couldn't happen to a nicer guy."

"We're heading to Kat McKay's place in the next little bit. She's still a suspect in the Nodine case, especially given what Cecil told me yesterday."

"How does that sit with you this morning?"

I'd gone to sleep last night aching to warn Duncan his sister could be on the brink of being charged with murder. Thinking about it now brought on a niggling headache.

"Not great. But neither does an unsolved murder case."

It occurred to me I could be straight with Holly, explain my objectivity was being tested and why. But even with my police partner, I wasn't about to share certain weaknesses.

Detective Bach coughed. "Good morning," he called to us.

"Coffee?" I inquired.

"No, thanks. Brought along some chamomile tea." He and his thermos joined us in the alcove. "How's your newborn, Hollis?"

"He's got a healthy set of lungs."

"That's a good sign."

Hollis smiled, collected a third chair, and placed it next to our cluttered, cramped break table.

"I filled Hollis in on last night's visit to Mr. Larkin. The arrest part, anyway."

Bach's voice was throaty from lack of sleep. "Where do we want to start with the McKay woman?"

I sipped more coffee, praying it would hurry up and burn through the brain fog. "My thought would be to start with the romance angle, rather than the weapon."

He lifted his thermos and poured a cup of urine-colored tea. "Romance? You mean with Larkin? He was adamant about not knowing who she was."

"No, I'm talking about Kat's relationship with Dan Nodine. It couldn't have been a happy love affair."

"Seems a smart place to start," Hollis added. "Largely because of the Kel-Tec 9. Did Dan know she was borrowing another man's gun?"

I all but winced at Holly's chance double entendre. "Exactly. Goes to motive. If he knew, did he throw a fit, react violently, or threaten her in some way? Or maybe he was making it hard for her to move on quietly without him."

"All right, we'll start the questioning there," Al said, examining his watch. "Zero seven hundred. We need to get on it."

Kat McKay. Not someone I'd ever thought of as a murderer. I saw her as a lonely woman, hitting forty, and stuck in a waste-land of available options. I could relate to that.

"Maggie," she said, opening her front door. "You're back." Even in her pink beautician's uniform, hair pulled up in a ponytail, and but a tad bit of makeup, she was lovely. For the first time, I saw a resemblance to Duncan, the same large green eyes.

"Good morning, Kat. This is Detective Alan Bach with the State homicide unit. We have a few questions."

"May we come in, Ms. McKay?" he asked.

"This is about the murders of Dan and Joe, isn't it?"

"Yes," he said.

"I don't understand. I already spoke with Maggie about all that."

"Something else has come to light," I said.

"All right." She led us to her dining room.

Once again I appreciated her taste in décor. The room was charmingly spare. A simple antique pedestal table of dark oak, a matching sideboard, and four ladder-back chairs stained a deep burgundy. No gewgaws or doilies.

When we were all seated, Bach turned on the digital recorder, attested to the purpose of the interview, and dove right in. "How long were you involved with Dan Nodine, Ms. McKay?"

Kat gathered together the planes of her body, a sort of protective armor. She then rested a manicured hand at her throat. "Like I already told Maggie, six months."

He opened his Portage police notebook. "And while you were in a relationship with Mr. Nodine, you borrowed Asa Larkin's semiautomatic handgun?"

"Remind me, is that Brady's father?" she asked me.

I nodded.

She turned toward the detective. "His son lent it to me. He's a good friend of my boy, Rain. Brady's over here a lot, and I mentioned once I was thinking about buying a handgun."

"And he brought his father's Kel-Tec pistol by so you could test it out?" I asked.

Kat paused. "Brady made it seem like the gun was his, and I was interested in that model."

"And that's the weapon you took to the wildlife area for target practice, correct?" Bach asked.

"Yes. I'd only ever shot a hunting rifle before. Once when I was younger. I didn't like it, though, the kick of the rifle butt. But I'd never used a pistol."

"How'd you do?" Al asked.

"I'm not sure what you're asking." There it was in her voice: that trace of ice.

"The target practice. Were you a good shot?" Bach clarified.

"I was doing all right, until Maggie's fish and wildlife officer came along."

"Kat, you said you were interested in the Kel-Tec. Did you research different brands and makes of handguns?" I asked.

"Yeah. On the internet."

"How long ago was that?" I continued.

"A while back."

"But while you were dating Dan?"

"Well, a few months before last week. So yes."

I leaned closer. "Had he threatened you? Is that why you decided to buy a gun?"

Kat smiled. "No, he was always nice enough, just not my type in the end."

Did she mean the Dan Nodine I knew, the scumbag who gut-shot Cecil's dog?

"You didn't see him as nice when he stole money from you," I reminded her.

She seemed to have forgotten that. "It was already pretty much over between us by then."

"He was more than a petty thief, Kat. And I can't help wondering how jealous he got when you borrowed the pistol from Brady."

"Brady's just a kid."

"He's nineteen. Wealthy by comparison. The kind of young guy Dan Nodine wouldn't want loaning his girlfriend anything," I pressed.

She removed a nail file from her pink beautician's smock. Tapped it lightly on the tabletop. "You're trying to get me to tell you something bad about Dan, aren't you? Well, let's see.

Poor hygiene, lazy, I guess—but he was always sweet to me. Boring, but sweet."

"I loved him like a brother when I was a kid, but he grew up to be sneaky, dishonest, and mean. Nobody could have missed that." By rights, I could have called the man an asshole, but with Bach present, it was best to avoid using profanity during an interview with a civilian.

I nudged further. "And you didn't answer my question. Was he jealous when Brady lent you that gun?"

"Dan had no idea I had it. But even if he'd known, he wouldn't dare question me."

"Mr. Nodine wouldn't cross you even if he'd wanted to, right?" Bach asked.

She held his gaze and absentmindedly filed her nails.

He continued, "Otherwise you might have ended things."

She shrugged. "I really don't know if he understood that, Captain Brock."

"Bach. *Detective* Bach," I corrected, even though Al's name tag was clearly visible.

"My apologies."

"I'm having a hard time believing Dan never got angry with you or said a cross word," I said.

"All right. He was pissed when I told him it was over between us."

"Did he threaten you then? Or harm you physically?"

"No. But he wasn't happy when he left."

"What day was that?" I asked, despite having already noted the date on our murder board myself.

"Like I told you, Maggie, a week before someone killed him."

"You didn't have much of a reaction when I gave you the news."

"Not everyone reacts the way you think they should, Maggie."

Hardly anyone reacted the way I thought they should, but that was beside the point. Kat hadn't reacted at all.

Al broke in. "Were you relieved when you learned Dan Nodine was dead?"

"I wouldn't say relieved, exactly, but...This is going to sound cruel. I felt bad for Ariel, is all."

"His brother's fiancée?" Bach asked.

"Yes. She really cared for Joe."

So Kat was capable of empathy. That was something, at least.

I decided this was a good time to share Cecil Burney's story. "What if I told you we have a witness who says you seemed pretty agitated when you marched into that wigwam burner last Thursday evening?"

"And Ms. McKay, I want to remind you. Last Thursday—February twenty-first—the Nodines were murdered inside the wigwam burner. Sometime between five forty-five and six fifteen p.m."

"Around the time you were seen there," I added.

She stood. "You don't honestly believe I killed those men, do you?"

Al and I said nothing.

"Maggie, you've known me forever. We've been close at times."

Pure bullshit.

Kat went on. "And I happen to know you've got a little crush on my brother."

I was surprised she knew of my days-old fling with Duncan, but I held my edge. "None of that has anything to do with why we're here."

"One more thing, Ms. McKay. The murder weapon has

been positively identified as Asa Larkin's pistol. The same one you borrowed."

She sat back down. "What? I returned it before they were killed, I swear."

"We know the gun was returned," I said. "We just don't know when."

She placed a fist over her lips, thinking through her answer. "Before the shootings, I know that."

"You need to be more specific," I said.

Bach planted his elbows on the table and leaned forward. "While you're reflecting back on when you returned the gun, tell us why you went to the wigwam burner that night."

Beyond the garden window, her starkly bare locust tree glinted in the sun. Mottled shadows fell across the room. Winter sending mixed messages again.

Kat exhaled. "I was looking for my son. He hadn't come home after basketball practice. It pissed me off. He had a major test the next day. Brady's not the best influence on my son, but I thought if I found Brady, I'd find Rain."

"How did you know to check at the old mill?" I asked.

She paused briefly. "I'd overheard Brady telling Rain he'd seen his father's stolen truck inside that decrepit burner. It sounded like he would've driven off with it, except the key was missing."

"Why drive out there the back way on the mill road?"

"Apparently that's the route Brady prefers. Probably a better chance for undetected speeding, I guess."

I needed to remember to put the mill road on our list of byways to cruise on a regular basis.

"Why didn't he just tell his father about the truck, Ms. McKay?" Bach asked.

"I don't know."

"Why didn't you tell his father, Kat?"

"Supposedly his father already knew who had it and where it was. I don't know him, don't know why he never called the police. That wasn't any of my business. Just Rain. Rain was my business."

"Kat, you keep saying you don't know Mr. Larkin, but I spotted his Prius parked in your driveway night before last. *After* I dropped by and spoke with you about his gun."

The nail file slipped from Kat's hand and bounced lightly on the tabletop. "Tuesday night? Rain had gone to bed early. Later I thought I heard voices. It might have been Brady. He could have come through the back door and I didn't notice."

No doubt Hollis had been right. Brady had sneaked out of the ranch house despite Larkin suspending his driving privileges a few hours before.

"Do you know if Brady was friendly with the Nodines?" I asked.

"I guess Brady had been paying the twins to buy his alcohol for a while. Dan let that slip. I confronted Brady about it, because of Rain. He told me my son didn't drink, but I didn't believe him. I made him promise not to get Rain in trouble. He can't be caught drinking. He'd lose his basketball scholarship."

"Ms. McKay. When exactly did you return the weapon to Brady Wakefield?" Bach asked.

"Three days before Dan and Joseph were killed."

I couldn't help but feel relieved she'd passed the semiautomatic back to Larkin's kid before the murders. Which was both self-serving and quite possibly premature.

"How is it you're now certain of the exact day, when earlier in our conversation you weren't?" Al continued.

"I just remembered it was on Monday of last week. My shop is closed on Mondays. That's when I do my grocery shopping and run errands. I was out for a couple of hours, I guess.

When I got home at about two, both boys were here, not at school where they were supposed to be. It made me angry. Brady can afford to skip school, but Rain can't. He could lose his basketball scholarship for that, too. I took Rain back to school and drove Brady and the handgun to his father's cattle ranch."

I sat back in my chair. "What happened when you arrived at the wigwam burner?"

"It was pretty dark inside, but I saw Dan and Joe on their hands and knees with a flashlight. They were trying to coax their dog out from under the red truck. I left before they saw me." She lifted a tissue from the pocket of her pink uniform. "I heard later the dog was found under the pickup, shot to death."

"This is important, Ms. McKay. Was Brady or Rain inside the wigwam burner?"

"No."

"You're positive?" Al's voice had taken on an edge.

"I didn't see anyone else."

"Which is not the same as *they weren't there*, is it?" I put in.

Kat directed her gaze at me. "Rain was home when I got back. And I didn't see Brady or anyone but the Nodines inside the burner or anywhere near it."

"And why didn't you tell me about going to the wigwam burner when I brought you news of the murders last Friday?"

"Being there had nothing to do with the killings, Maggie."

"Except that it makes you a possible suspect."

"Is that true, Detective?"

"Until we learn more, you're a person of interest," he said.

"I did not kill those men."

For the first time, I believed her completely.

Bach shut off the recorder and rummaged through his daypack. He sighed. "I don't have a statement form with me. Do you happen to have a blank copy with you, Sergeant?"

"Afraid not, Detective."

"We'll need you to follow us to the police station and fill one out, Ms. McKay."

Kat nodded.

"And after that, you're not to leave Grant County until we give you the go-ahead," he added.

"The go-ahead for what?" It was Duncan. He and Rain had entered the house through the back door without being noticed, and now they stood in the arched passageway between the kitchen and dining room.

Rain's expression of sheer distress was even more pronounced than usual. It was a look I'd interpreted in the past as severe anxiety, possibly a sign of emotional abuse. But after our little chat the other day, I'd come to view it as something else. A thoughtful, introverted boy sorting out his place in the world.

Duncan looked past me toward Kat. "The go-ahead for *what*?"

I rose from my chair. "Detective Bach, this is Duncan McKay, Kat's brother. And her son, Rain."

Al stood and shook their hands. "Alan Bach, State Police homicide unit."

Duncan removed his cap. "My nephew was concerned his mother was about to be arrested."

"Ms. McKay has agreed to follow us to the police station and make a formal statement," Bach said.

"About?" Duncan asked.

Kat eyed Rain cautiously. "My relationship with Dan Nodine. We dated for a while."

Given Rain's obvious astonishment, it was plain she had kept her son in the dark about her romance with Dan. Still, it was better he'd gotten word of it from her before the story made its way through the rumor mill. Kat understood that, and if nothing else, she would always be pragmatic.

Whatever Duncan's views on Kat dating Dan Nodine might have been, he kept them close to his vest. "I'll make sure Rain gets to school," he said.

"Thanks." She turned to Al. "Shall we get on with it? I'd like to open my salon on time."

Everyone moved from the dining room to the foyer. Kat fetched her coat out of the front closet and followed Bach out the door.

I faced Rain. "Sorry we had you worried about your mom."

"It seemed pretty serious when I noticed her talking to you and that detective."

Duncan nudged him toward the hallway. "You should finish getting ready for school, son."

I stepped to the porch and turned to glance back at Duncan before he closed the door. He smiled and winked. A wave of longing and tenderness left me blushing. I returned a smile just as Al Bach tapped the horn on his Ford Interceptor.

Once Kat McKay's statement was signed and out of the way, Bach got caught up in some long-distance coaching of the team investigating the multiple murders down in Paisley. He sounded weary as I listened in the background. Too many killings in a short period could scramble any ordinary cop's brain, but if it started to get to an experienced homicide detective, you had to know justice was in trouble.

I was anxious for us to corner Brady Wakefield and, with any luck, to do so before his father made bail. On the drive back to the office from Kat's place, I'd contacted Zan Wilson, principal at the high school. Three days ago, when I asked him about the name of Larkin's kid, Zan had given me the runaround, using the lack of parental permission as an official barricade.

That was before I knew Brady was an adult, legally speaking. And before I'd begun to wonder about his interactions with the Nodines and his access to the murder weapon. This time I told Zan that a State homicide detective and I would be showing up at the high school this morning at ten o'clock, and he needed to have Brady waiting alone in an office. We'd soon know if that bit of bluster worked.

After Al hung up, he gathered his laptop and thermos and loaded them in his pack. "I have to get to Lake County, straighten out a couple of detectives on the protocol for questioning a murder suspect."

"I'm going to talk to Brady Wakefield. But I'll take Hollis with me."

He nodded. "I trust your judgment, Maggie. If I didn't, I wouldn't be heading for Paisley right now. But if I'm not around, make sure Hollis or Mark is alongside you every step of the way from now on. You got that?"

"Of course. I trust your judgment too."

He smiled tiredly and gathered his coat and hat. Sometimes the sweeping, radiant beauty of remote Oregon locales didn't compensate for the paucity of State Police resources.

After Al left, I gave Hollis the rundown on our interview with Kat and told him the two of us would be heading to the high school in fifteen minutes to meet with Brady Wakefield.

He slipped on a latex glove. "Why isn't the McKay woman under arrest?"

"She claims she returned Larkin's pistol three days before the Nodines were killed."

Hollis carefully slid Kat's empty water glass into a plastic bag. He had offered it to her as she'd stood at our counter signing her official statement. "Prints."

"Gotcha." I checked my watch. "If Brady says it was three days, then she's probably off the hook."

"What about her being at the wigwam burner?"

"Kat didn't deny it. Says she went there looking for Brady *and* Rain. Wherever Brady goes, Rain goes, I gathered. Says all she witnessed was Dan and Joseph dealing with the wounded dog."

"Did they notice her?"

"Guess we'll never know."

Hollis removed her water glass to the evidence locker.

"We should get going in about five," I called after him and then gathered a few blank statement forms, tucked them inside my pack, and made sure my Tascam digital recorder was charged.

Hollis retrieved his wallet and phone from his desk

drawer. "Did Kat know the Nodines stowed the Ram pickup at the deserted mill?"

"Her story is Brady had found it there."

"Why didn't he just drive it home?"

"No key."

Hollis rolled his eyes and followed me to the waiting area where our coats hung.

"Mark, we'll be at the high school," I said to Taylor, standing at one of the filing cabinets.

"Anything you want a heads-up about while you're there?" he asked.

"Yeah. Text me if the court calls to say Asa Larkin's out on bail. Or for that matter, if you hear from him or his attorney directly," I said.

Alone with Hollis in my Tahoe driving to the high school, I felt strangely satisfied we were going to be conducting the interview together. "What's your sense of Brady Wakefield?"

Holly massaged the dark stubble sprouting from his chin. "He's an enigma with an odd father."

"Nineteen is kind of old to still be in high school. He must have been held back a grade somewhere along the way."

"Lots of students are nineteen when they graduate. Me, for instance." Hollis turned down the volume on an old Willie Nelson song. "Do you think the kid's involved in the Nodine murders somehow?"

Sunlight breaking over Canyon Mountain pierced the cobalt sky, lit up the cottonwoods, nearly blinding me. "Jesus," I said, slipping on my sunglasses. "I'm not at the point of naming Brady a suspect, but he knew Dan and Joseph and had dealings with them."

"And if he did murder those men? What'll happen to him?"

"Even Larkin can't buy away a homicide conviction. If Brady did it and we can prove it, his life is pretty much fucked."

"Despite his age and no criminal history?"

"You know the answer to that, Holly. Aggravated murder. Unless his attorney can convince a jury it was self-defense. I could envision that, I guess. The Nodines were good-sized men. They might have jumped him, he got spooked and killed them."

"Except, according to the ME, they were probably forced to sit against the burner wall before they were shot."

"Except for that."

I turned into the parking lot at Grant Union High School. The historic part of the building had stood in a small basin in the shadow of juniper-covered hills since 1936. Canyon Creek cut behind the two-story structure just off of Highway 395 next to the short stretch of road between John Day and Canyon City.

It was eerie entering the doorway of a building I'd walked into at least a thousand times over twenty years ago. The place had stayed pretty much the same, but it had changed too. For one, there were fewer rich kids and more poor ones. Although it was apparently still unusual to spot a person of color, especially a tall Black man holstered up and official. Hollis hadn't seemed to notice, or gave up noticing a long time ago, but I found all the teenage looky-loos annoying as hell. Plus it meant by the end of the day, everyone in town would know we'd dropped by to pay a visit to Brady Wakefield.

We found our way to administrative services, and I announced our appointment with Zan Wilson to the receptionist.

"Sure, Maggie. I'll be right back."

I had no idea who the woman was, but she seemed to know me. That kind of moment had occurred several times since moving back to town. More than once I'd stood in the middle of Chester's Market, chagrined by my lost knack for recognizing faces, all the while some old schoolmate or their sibling or parent regaled me with memories of me as a kid.

"I apologize," I said once the receptionist returned and asked us to have a seat. "I'm afraid I don't remember your name."

She laughed. "I've only lived here for a year or so, but my husband grew up here. Randy Buckley."

I knew the Buckley family, but no Randy.

"You might remember his dad, Mike," she added.

My God, Mike Buckley was only a couple of years older than Duncan, and he had a married son? Maybe a grandchild?

"Sure, I remember Mike."

"And everyone knows who Maggie Blackthorne is. You too, Trooper Jones, although I don't know your first name. You didn't grow up here, I guess. How's your wife and baby doin'?"

Hollis smiled and was about to answer Mrs. Randy Buckley when Zan appeared.

He signaled for us to step into the hallway leading to his office. "I thought you said you'd be accompanied by a homicide detective," he whispered.

"He was called away on another case," I whispered in return.

Zan took a moment to weigh his choices, but strictly speaking, he didn't have more than one. "Brady's in my office. He thinks you're here because of his father."

"Is he upset about that prospect?" I asked.

"I can't tell. He's pretty opaque."

I removed my police Stetson. "Is he a good student?"

"Above average. Barely."

"But enough to get into U of O, I hear."

Zan pointed east. "My office is at the end of the hall."

I knocked and opened the door. Out of the large window, the canyon was stunning, especially on a day like today, cloud-free, the indigo mountain shimmering. A nearby thicket of scrub junipers neatly framed the view from Zan's desk and hid most of the crowded parking lot.

"Nice to see you again, Brady," I said. "You remember Trooper Jones."

He acknowledged Hollis and turned to me. Someone had landed the boy a doozy of a shiner.

"What's this about?" he asked.

I placed my recorder on the table where he'd waited for us. "I'm here to ask you more about your father's handgun. The one I found in the Prius."

"All right."

I understood what Zan meant about Brady's opaqueness. I didn't think it was an act, more like learned behavior. Maybe a survival skill.

We sat across from the boy. I clicked on the recorder and clarified for the record today's date and why we were questioning Brady Wakefield.

I decided to avoid any attempt at coyness. I wasn't very good at it, anyway. "You loaned the Kel-Tec PF-9 to Kat McKay?"

"So?"

"Rain was surprised his mother was thinking about buying a pistol and that she actually tried out your father's weapon," I said.

Brady eyed me for a moment. "His mom does what she wants and doesn't really care what Rain thinks."

"Did Rain tell you that?"

Brady shrugged. "No. I just gathered that from conversations. Anyway, what's the big deal about loaning her the gun?"

Hollis moved forward in his chair, signaling he had a question. "Do you know the combination to your father's safe?"

"Of course."

"I thought so. You remind me of me at your age. Except for sports, I didn't care much about school, grades, all that. I liked puzzles. Solving them. Liked scoping out computer logic, complex systems, networks."

Brady scoffed. "You were a hacker?"

Hollis smiled faintly. "When you unlocked the safe, what did you find?"

"A bunch of papers and the nine-millimeter Kel-Tec."

Brady had dropped the innocent act he'd played me with after I pulled him over and found the gun.

"How long did it take you to figure out the combination?" Hollis asked.

Brady leaned back in his chair and crossed his arms over his chest. "No time at all. Deep down, Asa's a simpleton. I used his simpleton reasoning. It had to be something biblical, so I ran through a few of his stupid morning affirmations. Then I tried the acronym for that crap adage he tacked up on our gate. J-L-G-B. And ta-da!"

Hollis leaned in a tad. "J.L.G.B. *Jesus loves grass-fed beef.* Something he picked up while visiting you at the Glorious Lord Academy?"

"Good job on the Google search."

I paged through my spiral notebook until I found my jottings from two days ago. "'Tuesday, February twenty-sixth. Brady Wakefield denies knowing about the Kel-Tec

PF-9 automatic pistol in the rear lower storage compartment of the Prius.' And here you are bragging about breaking into your father's safe and finding the very weapon."

"I denied knowing it was in the back of the Prius because I didn't know it was there."

"Why don't I believe you?"

He started to respond, probably some smartass remark, then he changed the subject. "Can I have some water?"

"I'll get it," Hollis volunteered.

"Thanks," Brady said and faced me directly. "I don't tell lies."

Which wasn't exactly the same thing as not being a liar. "Good to know. Now, when did you loan the gun to Kat McKay?"

"Maybe a month or so ago. I don't remember exactly."

"Clearly she'd returned it by the time I pulled you over for reckless driving."

Brady removed his phone from his back pocket, scrolled through his messages.

"What are you looking for?"

"I'm trying to figure out when I loaned her the gun, Sergeant."

Hollis returned carrying a glass of water. He'd placed a napkin around it to absorb drips and to make sure the surface was clear of his own fingerprints. "Here you go," he said, handing Brady the glass and removing the napkin.

The boy drank it all in one long gulp, then checked for dates on a series of text messages. "I loaned the Kel-Tec to Rain's mom on February second. A Saturday. Rain was working at his uncle's store, so I took it to him there."

"And she gave it back to you when?" I asked again.

"Sometime early last week. Monday, I think. Yeah,

Monday. That's the day she caught Rain and me skipping school. I took it home and shut it in the safe."

Just as Kat had told Bach and me—she gave the gun back to Brady three days before someone used it to murder Dan and Joseph.

"Were you friends with the Nodine brothers?" I asked.

"I paid them double for beer. If that's a friendship."

I decided to keep the questions focused on his relationship with the dead twins. "Did you know they'd stolen your father's Ram 3500?"

For a full half minute, the room was silent but for our combined breathing and the low roar of students roaming a hallway far from Zan's office.

"Asa told me they took it. Said it was a warning from God."

I moved the recorder closer to Brady. "Was that an acceptable explanation?"

He laughed. "Acceptable? I don't get to challenge Asa's explanations. No, I was sure he'd stolen it somehow before the Nodine brothers managed to."

"Explain that," I said, even though I was sure I knew the answer.

He pushed the palms of his hands together and forcefully rubbed them slowly against one another. The first tic he'd let slip.

"I'd figured out setting up the ranch had about drained all of Asa's funds, but then he showed up in that brand-new truck. I'm not sure how he paid for it."

"When did you discover the Nodines had been stowing it at the abandoned mill in Seneca?" I asked.

Brady fiddled with one of Zan's pencils. "I think I'd like another glass of water."

"We're almost done here. When did you find the Ram 3500?" I repeated the question.

"The day I put the Kel-Tec back in the safe. Early that evening I drove by the mill and noticed the Nodines' army jeep parked along the shoulder of the road near the gate. They were backing Asa's truck inside that teepee-looking thing."

"Did you talk to them?

"Nah. I kept going before they could make out the Prius."

"Did you tell your father what you'd seen?" I asked.

Brady shook his head and removed his Canada Goose parka from the back of his chair. "I thought we were almost done."

"Kat overheard you say you'd found your father's stolen pickup," I said. "But you didn't have a key, right?"

He turned ashen, then scarlet. "What do you mean she overheard me?"

I shrugged. Why had that question touched a nerve?

"I scoured the ranch house for the extra key. Asa probably tossed it after he came up with his 'warning from God' rationale for not going to the cops. Besides, if he'd reported it, he might've had to explain how he got it in the first place."

Brady was pretty smart for a student performing barely above average. He was either bored with school, lazy, or both.

I switched the subject. "I saw your Prius parked at Rain's house two nights ago, just after your father had taken away your driving privileges."

"If I can crack a safe, I can sneak out of the house. Do it all the time."

"So you went to see Rain?"

He nodded. Confirming that Larkin hadn't been visiting Kat on Tuesday night.

"Do you know a man named Frank Sylvester?"

"What? How do you know about him?"

I shared one of my blank stares with the boy.

"The papers I saw in the safe had something to do with some guy by that name."

I wanted to explain it all to Brady. That Sylvester was his grandfather, and he'd sent his toddler son Asa to live with an aunt and uncle after his wife passed away. I believed he deserved to know. But who'd died and made me the kid's social worker? Besides, I needed to test his *I don't lie* declaration one last time.

"Where were you between five forty-five and six fifteen last Thursday evening?"

He folded the parka across his lap, combed his fingers through his ink-black hair. "The night the Nodines were killed. Asa caught me skipping out on basketball practice. We argued. I said something about being nineteen, that I should be able to skip practice if I wanted. He gave me the usual BS and sent me to my room for the night."

"Your father. Is that how you got that shiner?" I asked.

He gingerly touched the dark lump below one eye. "Yeah. After you handed me that ticket a couple of days ago."

"My father was really strict too," Hollis said. Since returning with the water, he'd quietly taken in the back-and-forth between Brady and me. "I'd get so angry sometimes. But I'd usually find some way to pull one over on him, make the whole thing worth it."

Brady slipped on his parka. "That's what I do while I'm supposed to be hanging out in my room, reading the Bible and praying."

I wanted to hear more about all of that, but it would have to wait. "So last Thursday evening, what did you do instead of read the Bible and pray?"

Again with the tic of rubbing his palms together. "Sneaking out of the house is easy. Once I was out, I got on my fifteen-speed and rode to the highway. Stashed the bike inside the bus shelter for safekeeping and ran to the old mill."

He yanked up the zipper of his parka. "Dan and Joe's jeep was parked by the open gate just like a few nights before. But this time they were inside the teepee thing."

My heart sped. We were getting close to something.

"Okay, Brady. What happened once you got to the mill?"

"I told you, I don't lie."

He looked at me for acknowledgment, so I nodded.

"I didn't kill them. I went to barter for the truck. If I could sell it somehow, set up my own stash of money, that might be my ticket out from under Asa's thumb. He wasn't ever going to report the theft. Ever. And I thought there was some chance I could convince the Nodines to hand over the keys and everything would be forgotten. No more joyriding in Asa's turbocharged crew cab pickup, but no prison time either."

Hollis and I sat stock still, barely breathing. I caught his glimpse. We knew we were there.

"And how'd that go?" I asked.

"I didn't get a chance. They were..." The boy wept quietly.

I slid Principal Wilson's box of tissues closer and waited for Brady to regain his composure.

"Joe was talking all worried on his phone. Dan was agitated, pacing back and forth, shouting for the dog to shut up. He yelled at me to get the fuck out of there."

"Take a breath, son," Hollis said, his voice low, soothing.

"The driver's-side door was wide open, so I ran to the truck hoping to grab the key from the ignition, thinking I'd come back for it later. But one of the twins had the key. About then I noticed some old dude standing in the opening of the teepee. He had a shotgun aimed toward the Nodines. I jumped in the truck, dove through the space between the two front seats to the bench seat in the back, and dropped to the floorboard."

"I'll get more water," Hollis offered.

"How long did you lie there, Brady?"

He shrugged. "Until after it was all over and then some. Maybe twenty minutes or so."

I placed my hand on the table near him. "Let me tell you what happened next. Joseph had been on the phone with me, asking for my help. He was interrupted and clicked off after the old dude fired a couple of rounds from his shotgun, killing the twins' Rottweiler. After that, the old dude ran back to his rig and hightailed it out of there. But not before witnessing Kat McKay speed by and park next to the gate. She'd driven out there looking for you and Rain. She ran—"

Brady interrupted me. "Rain wasn't there. He was probably still at basketball practice, but he wasn't at the mill with me."

I nodded.

Hollis returned with a small pitcher of water and another couple of glasses for the two of us. He filled all three.

"Thanks," Brady said.

I sipped from my water glass and continued. "So, Kat ran to the wigwam burner—some people call it a teepee burner. She saw the Nodine brothers dealing with their wounded dog. All the while, you were crouched on the floor of the backseat. And after that, somebody murdered the Nodine brothers."

The kid exhaled. "I think there were at least two people there, yelling about some steers, ordering them to sit down. I was so freaked out, I could be wrong. Lying there in the dark, hearing all the screaming, I was losing it."

He wept abruptly, a loud, deep howl. "God. They were begging. I can still hear that, can't get it out of my head."

The tension was breathtaking. We all stood on a ledge, waiting for a net to appear.

Brady went on. "*Pop, pop, pop, pop!* It stunk like sulfur and smoke. And then nothing but doors slamming and loud engines pulling away. I couldn't move. It was dark and freezing, so I finally forced myself to get up and run all the way to Harden Road and bike back to the ranch."

Hollis broke in. "You said loud engines?"

"Yes, two."

"The two loud engines pulling away, is that why you thought there were at least two people?" I asked.

"Yeah. And it seemed like different voices—no, it was definitely different voices—threatening Dan and Joe."

Hollis leaned forward. "Male?"

"Yes."

"Did you recognize them?" I asked.

He considered the question. "I used my parka to muffle the noise. The screams echoing from the teepee walls, I thought my ears would bleed."

"When you left the burner, did you notice the jeep still parked beside the gate?"

Brady shook his head. "I didn't notice one way or the other. Sorry."

"There's one other thing I need to tell you," I said.

The look on his face: complete exhaustion. "Okay."

"Your father's Kel-Tec 9 was the murder weapon."

I expected him to break down again. Instead he held his breath for a moment.

"Then I think I might know who did it." He pulled up his phone, opened the photo app, and scrolled through before turning it toward Hollis and me. "John and Ruben Vickers, two of Asa's hired men."

Hollis and I looked at one another. I knew what he was thinking: What the fuck?

19

I stepped out to the reception area, asked Mrs. Randy Buckley to order lunch for Brady, and returned to Zan's office. "Why didn't you talk to us about all of this before now?"

"Would you have believed me?" Brady said.

"We believe you now. And it might have helped us solve the murder."

He closed his brown eyes tightly and raked a hand through his dark, wavy hair. "I was so scared. I couldn't. I didn't know what to do."

Again, I slid the box of tissues toward him.

He opened his eyes and retrieved one of the tissues. "Finally I talked to Rain."

"You told Rain?" I asked

Brady nodded. "Two nights ago, when I snuck out of the house."

"Did he suggest going to the police?" I asked.

"To you specifically. But I didn't."

"Yet here we are. It's all out in the open. Right?"

He sighed deeply. "I've told you everything I know."

"Does it take some of the weight off?" Hollis asked.

"It does."

"Because you'll have to talk to the district attorney and testify at the murder trial," Holly explained gently.

"God," Brady whispered.

"I do have one other question," I said. "Why do you think the Vickers men might have killed the Nodine brothers?"

"Well, John's a dick," Brady said, looking over at me. "Sorry."

"I know what a dick is, son. Most of them only make other people miserable, but they don't necessarily commit murder."

"He caught me opening Asa's safe a while back. Threatened to tell Asa, knocked me around. I ended up telling him the combination."

Mrs. Randy Buckley tapped on the door. Hollis stood and opened it. She carried Brady's lunch tray and placed it on the table.

"Thanks, Mrs. Buckley," Brady said.

I watched the boy tackle his meal, reminded myself that he really was just a kid. "Why did you end up giving John Vickers the combination?"

He finished chewing his large bite of fish sandwich. "Why do you think?"

"You tell me."

Brady was incredulous. "Because John is capable of more than just knocking me around. He gets a kick out of shooting jackrabbits, ground squirrels, gophers, anything that wanders onto the property."

I didn't want to be the one to break it to him, but that's what a lot of folks around here called a sport.

He opened his carton of chocolate milk and chugged half. "That mentality. That's why Asa hired him and his dim-bulb brother in the first place."

"How about the other guy?"

He took another bite of his sandwich. "Wayne Smith? He's just somebody Asa knew from Lake Oswego. Not too smart either, but nice enough."

Brady drank the last of his chocolate milk, finished off the square of apple cobbler, and pushed his tray to the side. "Are we done now?"

I shut off the recorder and handed him a statement form. "Yeah, after you sign and date this."

"What is it?"

"Your official statement saying you gave us this information voluntarily."

"Voluntarily?"

"And that it's accurate to the best of your memory."

Brady skimmed over the form, signed and dated it. He retrieved his lunch tray and got up to leave.

I stood and opened the door. "We may need to talk to you again."

He winced. "Again?"

"This is a murder investigation. We'll talk to you as many times as we have to."

Holly and I were both a little buzzy when we hopped in my Tahoe.

"Jesus H. Christ," I said, smacking the steering wheel with both hands. "We're so close I can taste it. Can't you?"

He massaged his temples. "That was exhausting."

"But exhilarating."

"And now we know John Vickers had access to the Kel-Tec 9."

"All those papers referencing Frank Sylvester, too," I said. "And don't you think the second loud engine Brady heard had to be Dan and Joseph's jeep? Obviously driven away from the mill by someone who knew where they parked their camper."

"Makes sense."

"Like a lot of rural folks, the Nodines probably always left the keys hanging in the ignition. Which made it handy for whoever dropped the jeep back at the campground."

"The jeep keys are still sitting in our evidence locker. I'll make sure Harry Bratton takes a look at prints right away."

Pulling into the parking lot, I recognized the dented Volvo stationed in front. "Pete Trudeau. Maybe he's uncovered something useful."

"Maybe he just enjoys your company."

There it was, the playful little dig aimed at Pete's flirtatious overture yesterday.

Inside, Taylor and Pete were having an animated chat about fly-fishing, mostly about tying their own flies, throwing around quirky terms for the different whatevers they used for catching trout. Hollis strolled to the evidence locker, Brady's water glass in tow.

I was eager to touch base with Al, but I paused at our service counter across from Pete.

"Maggie, I found this in a storage unit Pops rented," he said, referring to a large, wrapped rectangular package he'd placed on the counter.

"What is it?" I asked.

"Some painting I've never seen in my life. A Frederic Remington, at least by the signature."

I turned to Taylor. "Would you mind tracking down Detective Bach for me? Let him know it's crucial we talk right away."

I ran my fingertips across the top of the covered painting. "I was an art major for about half a minute a long time ago.

But I should warn you I can't authenticate anything except my own amateur dabbles."

"I'm more interested in finding out where he got it and how long he's had it. He opened that storage unit account the day before he was killed."

"Interesting. How'd you find out about the storage unit?"

"Chester's Market. I was buying a few groceries and ran into Terry Moore, one of my buddies from high school. He manages the storage rental place these days, had heard about Pops, and wondered what to do about the unit."

"Gotta love a small town. You were careful when you uncovered it, right?"

"Of course. I'm just a math teacher, but even I know that."

I'd inflicted a wound to the man's ego and I wasn't even trying.

I put on a pair of latex gloves, untied the twine holding the packing material in place, and slowly unwrapped the painting. An Indian brave seated on a muscular gray mustang held aloft a red blanket with one arm and his rifle with the other. Clouded sky, the horse stood on a hillside that could have been one of those surrounding our little burg during the exaggerated heat of late summer, every arid stick of grass vividly golden.

Guy Trudeau had definitely gotten his hands on a painting that was either a genuine Remington or its good facsimile, and probably not long ago, given the timing of the storage rental. And what the hell did it mean?

"I can't say for certain if it's a Remington original or some-one's hand-painted reproduction."

"What was he doing with it?"

I shrugged and signaled for him to follow me to my desk, where I keyed in *Frederic Remington*. One of his paintings, *Cutting Out Pony Herds*, had sold a few years ago at the Reno art auction for more than five million dollars. A copy of the same work, hand-painted on museum quality canvas, was available online for around three hundred dollars.

I entered *The Blanket Signal*, the name of the piece laid out on the counter. Strangely, there were two slightly different Remington paintings with that title. The original of the one Pete brought in was painted in 1896 and worth about four million.

"So Pops had come by an expensive masterpiece or a cheap knock-off?"

"Seems like it."

"News to me. I can't see how he could afford either one."

I redid the packing material and put the painting back in its box.

"Far as I can tell, Maggie, that old man had turned into a hermit, not an art collector."

Truer words were never spoken.

"It's got to be stolen, right?" Pete added. "Or maybe he found it?"

"Nothing's been reported missing as far as I know. We'll do some research, see about any recent art thefts. And we'll put out a statewide bulletin. In the meantime, I'd like to keep the painting in our evidence locker. I'll give you a receipt for it, of course."

"Followed by dinner tonight?"

"Way too much going on right now."

"Maybe another time, then?"

"Aren't you married or something?"

"More like 'or something.'"

Taylor came to my rescue. "Detective Bach on line one."

"Thanks." I pointed to the package. "We're storing this here for a while. Write out a receipt so Mr. Trudeau can be on his way. Then send out a bulletin looking for the possible owner of a lost Remington painting."

Taylor picked up the package. "Sure thing. Follow me, Mr. Trudeau."

Pete trudged after Taylor toward the service counter. "Nice to see you again, Maggie."

I ignored that last remark and lifted the receiver. "Afternoon, Al."

He was still on the road making his way to Paisley, the usual highway noise in the background. I ticked off the main points of our long interview with Brady Wakefield.

"I take it you and Hollis found the boy's explanation plausible."

"I think so. And he also corroborated parts of Kat McKay's story. Right now Hollis is busy digging up background on the Vickers men."

"It's significant that one of them had the combination to Larkin's gun safe."

"Couldn't agree more."

"Has Larkin made bail yet?

"Typically bail hearings are set for later in the afternoon."

From his desk, Hollis waved two eight-and-a-half-by-eleven-inch pages he'd retrieved from the printer.

"Hold on a sec, Al. Hollis is trying to tell me something."

Holly handed me the printouts.

"Rap sheets for John and Ruben Vickers." I scanned through the pages. "A couple of charmers. Assault and battery, auto theft, bilking homeowners through faulty roof repairs, theft of antiquities, the list goes on."

"Any serious violence?" Bach asked.

"The worst's an Assault II. And they were charged together in every incident."

"Any prison time?"

"A year in 2011. Eighteen months in 2014."

"Given how all three men greeted us last night, I assume they carry weapons."

"Definitely."

"You could pull the Vickers men in for that, but hold off if you can. I'd feel better if I was there when you confront them. I hope to have this mess in Paisley cleared up by end of day and be back up your way tomorrow. In the end, though, it's up to you."

"Got it."

"What about the other hired man? Did the boy say anything about him?"

"Name's Wayne Smith. Brady thought he was okay, but Hollis is running the name through LEDS." I went on to share the story of Pete Trudeau discovering the Remington painting in his father's rented locker. "Could be worth a lot of money."

"My wife and I own a replica of *Against the Sunset*. It's a favorite of mine." In the background, regional dispatch called for him over the radio. "I'll check in with you later this afternoon."

The office was quiet except for Hollis querying LEDS and printing out the results. Pete had skedaddled, and Taylor was out somewhere. It was already two o'clock, and I was starving.

"Holly, I'm headed to Prairie Maid. You want anything?"

He held a ten-dollar bill aloft. "BLT, with a salad. No red onions. Ranch dressing on the side. And one of their huckleberry milkshakes."

I repeated his order back to him, and he nodded.

"Did you find anything on Larkin's other hired hand?"

"Not yet. A name like Wayne Smith makes sleuthing a little harder. Nothing on the fingerprints either."

"Speaking of fingerprints. The keys to the Nodines' jeep?"

"Mark volunteered to take them to Harry Bratton. Also the water glasses from this morning."

"Thanks for that."

"Don't thank me." Holly's little nudge telling me to be nicer to Taylor.

I called in our lunch orders and drove to Prairie Maid, Tedeschi Trucks' bluesy rock blasting from the speakers. I parked and sat listening to "Midnight in Harlem," scrolling through the *Blue Mountain Eagle* online. No news was good news? Except maybe word of the local mule deer count, lower than the year before, which had been the lowest in a decade. Song over, I stepped out to the order pickup window, paid for Holly's BLT, salad, and milkshake and my quarter-pounder cheeseburger cooked rare.

The new owner, a woman from Helix or Heppner or some other H town in the rural depths of Oregon, handed me the bags and tall drink cup, along with my change. "You have a nice day, officer," she said as I put a few bills in the tip jar.

She started to close the window but changed her mind. "Can I ask you a question?"

Lunch, mine especially, smelled lovely. "Sure."

"If I saw something, but don't really know what it means, would it be worth telling you about? In case it has something to do with one of those killings last week?"

I searched for a name tag. "Of course, Ms....?"

"Angie. Angie Dennis."

It was hard to get a real look at the woman, but I could see she was dressed like a normal person: jeans and a plain T-shirt.

"What do you think you might have seen, Ms. Dennis?" I

placed the bags and shake on the small counter in front of the pickup window.

She made certain other customers weren't pulling into her parking lot. "That Mr. Trudeau. He was a regular, always ordered a small burger and a cola, no fries. He stopped by right after I opened up—so around eleven—on the day the police found him."

"My partner and I."

"I thought so. Your partner's the African American officer, right?" she said and indicated the tall, lidded cup. "He likes the huckleberry shakes."

My damn cheeseburger was getting cold. "What do you think you saw the other day?"

"When Mr. Trudeau drove away, a silver SUV followed him out of my parking lot. No one from the SUV had come to the window to order or pick up. I think they might've been waiting for him."

"Did you see the driver?"

"Tinted windows. I couldn't see anybody or whether there were passengers."

"Besides the color, did you notice anything else about the SUV? License plate? Make and model?"

"I didn't pay attention to the license plate, and I know squat about makes and models. But their bumper sticker caught my eye, even wrote it down." She removed a blank order slip tacked to a bulletin board next to the pickup window and slid it my way. On the back, in perfect D'Nealian cursive, she'd written, "Jesus loves grass-fed beef."

"Why didn't you come talk to us about all this before?"

"I guess 'cause I'm not a gossip, and I didn't think much about it at first."

"But you wrote down the message from the bumper sticker?"

She giggled. "Oh, that's to remind myself to figure out where I can buy it online. For my brother. He's a Jehovah's Witness."

There was nothing conclusive about Angie Dennis noticing the SUV following Guy Trudeau out of her parking lot. Also nothing conclusive in her spotting Larkin's adopted motto. Still, I asked her to come to the office and make a formal statement. Her survival depended on a so-called lunch crowd plus Grant Union students stopping in after school for treats, but she agreed to drop by our office between four thirty and five.

Driving back with our lunches, my starving gut sent word. If that silver SUV did trail Trudeau out of Angie's parking lot, it had something to do with Larkin or his men.

The huckleberry milkshake had nearly melted to over-flowing by the time I placed it on Holly's desk. My cheese-burger was in need of a heat-up in the micro, but that would've only turned the bun rock hard and overcooked the meat. I was too famished to care one way or another, so I sat at my desk and scarfed my cold meal.

"Here." He passed me the red onions Angie had neglected to omit from his salad.

"No, thanks. We still have people to talk to this afternoon."

While we ate, I told him about the silver SUV that had followed old man Trudeau from the Prairie Maid.

"That bumper sticker. It's like Larkin's calling card."

I nodded. "Angie Dennis is coming in sometime between four thirty and five to make her statement."

Hollis sucked on the remainder of his shake, sat the empty cup on his desk, and turned back to his computer.

"Take a break first. Go home and see your wife and kid."

"After I finish here."

"Some might find your refusal to follow my instructions insubordinate."

He wiped his hands with tiny white napkins. "Some might think you're full of it."

No doubt about that, but Holly saying it only made me smile. "The silver SUV, without a plate number or even the make and model, can the owner be ID'd?"

Hollis tossed his trash in the garbage can. "I'll start with Larkin and his crew."

"I need to pick up my dry cleaning. Back in half an hour." I cleared my desk of lunch mess, grabbed my jacket off the coat hook, and opened the door. Light poured in, brightening the dull of our workspace.

"Damn, Holly. The sun's out *and* it's warm. You really should take a breather and step outside for a while."

"When you or Mark get back," he said and clattered away on his keyboard.

I drove through town past the dry cleaners and headed for McKay's Feed and Tack. I hadn't answered his messages from last night, forcing myself to wait and see what would come of our interview with Kat.

The place was hopping when I arrived. All the parking spaces were full, and inside, a line of customers waited to check out.

I pulled to the curb and sent a text. "The store's crowded?? What's up with that?"

He replied as I parked back at the station. "Don't effing know. Dinner at my place?"

"I might be late," I wrote back.

"It's never too late for tacos and beer"

"Si"

. . .

"Didn't you just leave?" Hollis said.

"Long line at the dry cleaners. You should take that break since both Taylor and I are here now."

He ignored me. "I was about to call you. Wayne Smith owns a silver 2012 Nissan Pathfinder."

"This is our Wayne Smith for sure? Larkin's ranch hand, henchman, whatever?"

"Yep. Address matches. He's got a pretty clean driving record and no rap sheet."

I shuffled back and forth across the crowded space between my desk and Holly's. "The Vickers brothers and maybe this Smith dude. Might they all be involved in the Nodine killing *and* Trudeau's murder?"

"Are you asking me or telling me?"

"Yes," I said.

"Well, if you're asking me, I'd say it's possible. Especially since John Vickers was able to strong-arm the safe combination out of Brady. But if you're telling me one or all of those men are involved, I need a few more dots connected."

I continued to pace. "I'd like to interview the lot of them right now."

"Bach wants to be there, right?"

"Yes. I wish to hell he hadn't been called back to Paisley."

"I know, but I say we wait and see if he makes it back tomorrow before we drive out and question them."

"He left it up to me to decide."

"And I'll do whatever you tell me to do."

"Except take your break."

Hollis passed me one of his special smirks.

"Okay, tomorrow, then. With or without Bach." The desk phone startled me. "Al?"

"No. This is Sergeant Brown from Burns."

"Of course, Dave. What can I do for you?

"I just saw your bulletin about the Remington painting. It might belong to that guy out in Wagontire you asked us to check on."

"Frank Sylvester?"

"Yeah, I guess he's a collector. Or was, anyway."

Were some goddamn wayward strands finally falling into place?

"Interesting. That might help solve a conundrum in one of our homicides."

"Glad I got right back to you, then."

"Thanks. I owe you one, Dave."

"You're welcome, Maggie. Tell Hollis I said howdy."

"Will do." I hung up and went back to roaming our bit of floor space. "Dave Brown says howdy."

"What's the news from Burns?"

"Here's another dot to connect. Frank Sylvester's an art collector."

"Ah, the Remington painting. And there's one other dot I forgot to share with you. The fingerprints on the Kel-Tec 9. Just as we thought. Larkin, of course, but Harry also matched Kat McKay and Brady from those water glasses."

"That was fast."

"Harry's just that good."

"How about the jeep key?"

"He's still working on it."

Taylor peeked over the bank of file cabinets where Hollis and I sat at our desks. "Whitey Kern is in the waiting area, Maggie. He'd like to have a word."

"Send him on back," I said.

He pointed to the blinking light on my desk phone. "And Mr. Larkin called from the courthouse while you were out. Left you a message."

"Okay."

Whitey ambled toward me and stood with his cap in hand. "Afternoon, Maggie."

I indicated the extra chair beside my desk. "Have a seat."

A short fellow, Whitey sat his thin rear on the front edge of the chair. "The other day you asked me whether I'd noticed anything out of place recently. You know, while I was out in my tow truck."

I didn't recall that exactly, but I nodded just the same.

"The day before the Nodine boys...the day before they passed away, I was called out to rescue a guy stuck just off Logan Valley Highway."

"What was so out of place about this rescue?"

"The guy had slipped down one of them nasty gullies. And he was driving Chet Harden's green Bronco. I know 'cause I must've towed that thing a dozen times."

"This guy have a name?"

He pulled a receipt from his shirt pocket, laid it on my desk, and worked to decipher the signature. "Well, I can't read it exactly."

Whitey had the nervous habit of smacking his lips together where they met on the left side of his mouth. Twice. The sound of two little kisses randomly punctuated his delivery as he spoke. It was a quirk I'd always found peculiar but charming.

"Let me have a look."

I lifted the receipt. Although the signature was sloppy, I could see someone had signed the thing *Asa Larkin*.

I wanted to know it was Larkin for a fact. "Can you describe what the driver looked like? Tall? Slim? Overweight? Short?"

"He had dark hair, I think. But it was more'n a week ago, and I don't remember skinny or fat, tall or short. You see, I was already tired from making too many runs that day. Olive was out with all-day morning sickness. She's expecting my first grandkid."

"How old would you say the guy was?"

He shrugged. "Don't know."

"Try harder, Whitey."

He squirmed in his seat. "I should've brought this to you sooner. He stole Chet's green Bronco, didn't he?"

"No, but you're certain it was the same rig Chet Harden used to drive?"

"That's why I come in, Maggie. I had Olive look back through our records. License plate's the same."

I stood. "Mind if I make a copy of the receipt?"

He indicated he didn't mind, but I was already on my way to the copier.

"Here you are." I handed him the original.

"You're sure the Bronco wasn't stolen from ol' Chet?"

Hollis had confirmed Asa Larkin owned the Bronco after taking photos of it in the parking lot of Erna's Café last Sunday. "I know for certain it's registered to the rancher who bought Chet's place."

He nodded and stood to leave. "Well, whoever slid down that gully was pretty unfriendly, if that helps."

"Wait a sec. I've got a couple of photos for you to look at."

I snared the Nodine binder out of Holly's in-basket and placed the mug shots of Larkin, the Vickers men, and the DMV printout of Wayne Smith's driver's license photo on my desk. For good measure, I threw in the blurry newspaper photo of Brady playing basketball.

"I know you were tired, but might one of these be the guy?"

Whitey took a few minutes to size up the photos. His hands shook slightly, hovering above the table. He placed his index finger on one of the shots of Larkin taken yesterday at the county jail. "Him, I think."

"This is all really helpful. Thanks for coming in."

"If I think of anything else, I'll let ya know," he said and wended his way to our front door.

His story might be worth bupkis, but Whitey and his tow truck rescued drivers from all kinds of isolated places where all kinds of backwater illicit shit could be going on. It wouldn't do for him to curl up inside his protective shell again and never pass on another speck of information, useful or not.

I examined the receipt again and faced Hollis. "We have Larkin's signature around here somewhere, right?"

He nodded. "On the *acknowledgment form* you conjured up.

The two of us are meticulous about following the procedures we invent."

"Just let me see the damn signature."

Holly chuckled and took the Nodine binder from me, found the man's acknowledgment form I'd made up on the spot after confiscating his Kel-Tec 9, and handed it over.

"Seems like it matches the one on Whitey's receipt."

Hollis scooped up the receipt and the form. "Yeah, I'd say the signatures are the same all right, but what does that tell us?"

I shrugged. "*P-chuh?* No idea yet."

"Your odd little noise there reminded me. Does Whitey always make that double-smack sound out of the corner of his mouth when he talks?"

"Yeah. He's kind of a nervous guy for a tow truck driver. Nice old bird, though."

I listened to Larkin's voicemail. It contained a strange mix of outrage over how I'd managed to confiscate his Kel-Tec 9 and concern for his son. His own attorney had advised him that our county sheriff recognizes conceal carry permits from another county or state and that my seizure of his pistol was done illegally and under false pretenses. Plus he'd learned that we'd interviewed Brady at the high school yesterday morning and without a lawyer present. So he planned to sue the State of Oregon and me. He left out the part about his handgun being a murder weapon.

I listened to the recording several times. "Well," I said to Hollis, "Larkin is pissed and threatening to take legal action."

"Being angry and litigious might be the least of his worries," Hollis said.

"But that's not even the most interesting part." I turned on the speaker and played the message. "Does that voice sound familiar?"

"Play it again." He listened more intently. "Sounds like Larkin."

"Exactly. And it sounds like Mr. Anonymous from the poacher tip line report on Dan and Joseph."

"I'll pull up the MPEG file."

We listened to the poacher tip line message and this morning's voicemail.

"I think you're right, Maggie. In the tip line call, he sounds a little nervous, and in today's message, he just sounds irritated."

"I'm not sure it's worth knowing whether or not he was the tipster. But if he was, I'd like to know why he was out there and so far from the paved roadway."

"Maybe he spotted that red truck and decided to tail the Nodines. Then called the poacher hotline and turned them in."

"Could have happened, just not in that fancy Prius."

"No, not in the Prius. But he could have been driving the green Bronco. That would explain how he could off-road and follow them."

"And witness them kill and butcher that doe. Holy shit, Holly. Here I was about to bump Asa Larkin's name further down on the list of murder suspects."

Taylor's phone interrupted the silence that had settled in, the three of us working quietly at our desks.

"That was the court clerk. Larkin made bail," he announced.

"Not surprising, I guess. By the way, Mark, I meant to tell you earlier I appreciate you delivering the water glasses and jeep keys to Harry Bratton."

Taylor was dumfounded, but it wasn't like I *never* thanked the dude. "Sure, you're welcome. Harry says it's harder to lift a print from a metal key, but he thinks—"

An infant's loud cries interrupted his prattle. Lillian and Hank had arrived for a surprise visit. We left our desks and joined the kerfuffle at the front counter.

Taylor took the baby and held him like a professional dad. When it was my turn, I cooed and cradled Hank like an amateur, and like most inexperienced cooers and cradlers, I made the whole thing worse. Finally, Hollis lifted his agitated child from my arms.

"I'm just dropping him off for an hour or two," Lil said. "You don't mind, do you, Maggie?"

"Sure. A gal has to get her mani-pedi on schedule, right?"

"Absolutely," she said, moving in close to Hollis and her infant son.

"That's a beautiful baby, you two," Taylor said.

I brushed my fingertips along his tiny arm. "His skin is amazingly soft."

My desk phone rang.

"You should get that. It could be Detective Bach," Hollis said quietly.

I raced to my desk, where Al's name flashed across caller ID. "Detective."

"Maggie. Just checking in. Things in Paisley are squared away, and I'm on my way back to Bend."

I spent ten minutes or so updating him—the information from the Prairie Maid owner, Wayne Smith and his silver Pathfinder, Sylvester being a collector of Remington art, and possibly establishing Larkin as the anonymous poacher-hotline tipster.

"Well, I see why you're anxious to interview Larkin again, and his hired men."

"Search the ranch property too."

"I agree. But more than ever, I need to be there when you do that. For your benefit as well as the efficacy of the investigation."

Efficacy? I was getting used to Bach's occasional patronizing slip. I suspected that was his way of mentoring.

"Got it, Al. Should I contact Lieutenant Lake and let him know we plan to interrogate the four men and search the cattle company tomorrow?"

"No. He won't be of any help up in La Grande. And I've about had it with his interference."

"How about Sheriff Rhinehart?"

"Heavens, no. But we will need a warrant to search all out buildings, residences, and vehicles."

"I'll put Mark Taylor on that right away."

"I'll call you in the morning before leaving from Bend."

I was home earlier than I'd been in more than a week. The welcome warmth of the day had carried into evening, allowing Louie a weather-free exploration of Dorie's side yard and the tan hillock at the back of the building. His short illness days ago had left him less spry but seemingly more grateful for his time padding across the bright new grass of late winter.

Off to the east, dark, sullen clouds had begun to gather against the twilight, pinned in by the Strawberry range and precursors to a new storm. If it had been summer, the air might have taken on the thick scent of dank clay and pine pitch.

Louie, possibly sensing the damp to come, signaled it was

time to go back inside. I carried him up the stairs, changed out his food and water, and tossed in a kitty treat.

After my shower, I opened the closet and surveyed my meager collection of regular citizen wear. Besides the funeral suit and the silk blouse I'd worn to dinner with Ray Gattis last week, I owned a red V-neck sweater, a wool plaid Pendleton shirt, and a couple of tees and sweatshirts. No dresses, but plenty of jeans. While I stood in front of the open closet gauging the best option for my dinner date with Duncan, he texted.

"Ready whenever you are"

"There in 20"

I slipped on the V-neck sweater and some jeans. I didn't own a pair of Frye's or other sexy boots, so it had to be my ten-year-old Jack Purcells. Rarely did I bother with makeup, but I dabbed on some mascara and a spot of lipstick and scrounged around for something besides my mother's pearl post earrings. I found the few baubles Morgan had given me, put on the dangling silver hoops he'd picked up during a trip to Santa Fe, and called it good.

Duncan opened the front door before I even made it to his porch. "I like your nice police uniform okay, but I have to say, that red sweater's a good look."

"Thanks. You look pretty snazzy yourself."

He'd traded in his Feed and Tack shirt for an aqua-blue button-down that intensified the green of his eyes and all but melted me before I had even stepped through the door. I longed for dinner and small talk to be over, for the dishes and the jokes to be put away.

He took my hand and led me to the dining area. "Supper's on the table, except for the pot roast."

"What happened to tacos and beer?"

"Couldn't find any damn fresh tortillas at Chester's Market, but they did have a nice roast. Speaking of which, have a seat and I'll serve it up."

He doled out slices onto each plate, which were already affixed with a baked and buttered russet. I tonged the salad into our salad bowls.

"Jesus, we're like an old married couple," I said.

"Ha!" Duncan turned pink at the neck and squeezed my hand. "On the other hand, my folks just heat up Hungry Man dinners and sit in front of the TV."

"I haven't seen them around town for a while. Are they doing all right?"

"Pretty good, I think. Traveling some in the little RV they bought. Dad's arthritis acts up a lot, so Mom does most of the driving."

"Is that why you moved back, to be around to help take care of them?"

"Mostly. Plus they needed someone to take over running the business. Also, I wanted to be around for Rain." He took a masculine bite of beef, chewed, and swallowed. "And you? Why'd you decide to come back?"

I shrugged. "I think I wanted to make some kind of peace with my childhood, if that makes sense. I've always been haunted by it."

His look was solemn. "I don't understand, I guess."

"Poverty. My mother's suicide. My father's long tumble into the bottle."

"I'm an idiot, or I didn't pay attention. As a kid, I never realized any of that was going on."

I almost attributed that to privilege, yet I knew my shame as a girl had taught me to hide behind a mask, the pretense of Zoey and Tate's deep devotion to their one and only child.

"Well, you were just a kid," I said.

"And have you made peace with all of it?"

"That'll never be completely possible. But I'm turning forty soon, and I understand I'll suddenly gain great insight and find tranquility."

"Oh, sure. Happened to me when I hit forty a few years ago. I was immediately calm and composed, not to mention wise."

"Wiseass, maybe."

"Yeah, that too," he chuckled. "When do you turn forty?"

I looked into his great green eyes. "March first."

"What? That's tomorrow. Doesn't give me much time to shop."

I reached across and traced his jawline with the tips of my fingers. "You've already given me the best gift of all."

Duncan smiled and waited for an explanation.

"A bit of normalcy in the midst of the chaos of these last many days."

"I hoped you were going to say something about my skills in the bedroom."

"That's been a bonus for sure."

He stood and scooped up his plate, salad bowl, and utensils. "Let's put the leftovers in the fridge and dump the dishes in the sink. Then we'll wander upstairs, okay?"

"Shouldn't we load the dishwasher?"

"Hell no."

I woke in Duncan's bed. His back toward me, he rose and fell, rose and fell in the soft sigh of breathing. I slowly lifted the covers and sat up, placing my bare feet on the cold floor. I pulled my bra from the pile of clothing next to the bed and slipped it on.

"Hey," he said. "Don't leave."

I leaned across the bed and kissed his forehead. "I have to go."

He pulled me back under the sheet and against his nakedness. "No, you have to come."

He slid his large, warm hand over my soft belly. With his other hand, he unhooked the bra. A surge of heat arced through me, and I tore off the garment.

Light from the crescent moon beamed through the window. In the stillness, skin to skin, our explorations and murmurs. Charged and urgent, we rocked and cried out, alone and together, alone and together.

Later, I drifted back toward sleep, aware some threshold of intimacy had been crossed. In the aftermath, I was euphoric but apprehensive. It stood to reason. I liked the man. I knew I could come to love him. Maybe I already had. And so, the unease. Yet, wrapped in Duncan's arms, I let the tricky feelings go. Soon enough, tomorrow would arrive.

At first light, I drove to my apartment. Louie was at the door, ready to be let out. We trod outside under a clear sky. The high desert breeze was fresh on my warm skin, despite the chilly temperature. It felt good to be alive. I carried my old tabby back into the apartment, where we sat in my mother's rocker.

"Well, Louie, what are your plans for the day?"

His left ear, the one he'd injured in a long-ago catfight, flitted at the sound of my voice.

"More of the same, huh? Me too, I'm afraid."

. . .

Hollis was engaged in a serious phone call when I pulled up to my desk across from his. He listened intently to whoever was on the other end, repeating, "Yes, sir, I understand. I will, sir."

Christ, I thought, was that Corporal Macintyre letting Holly know he'd been promoted? I fired up my desktop and prepared myself for the news.

Hollis finally hung up. "Hey, Maggie. Guess what?"

I smiled that fake smile I'd learned from Zoey. "Got no clue."

"Harry's identified a print from the jeep key. One that doesn't belong to either Nodine." He tossed me a wide smile.

Occasionally Holly's convoluted setups were tedious. "Okay, I'll bite. Whose fingerprint?"

"Ruben Vickers."

"Holy fuck."

Whatever corruption was festering out at Bear Valley Cattle Company, I deemed it an unfit place for Brady Wakefield to return to. Finding a safe house for him had occurred to me yesterday sitting in Zan Wilson's office, the boy crying on the other side of the desk. I wished I'd done then what my instincts told me. There was no question about it now that we planned to confront Larkin and his hired men.

Where, though, and with so little time to make it happen? Not with Dorie, bless her heart, and for sure not any of the church ladies. He could use some time with an openhearted guy, but Zan Wilson was a holy roller, and Brady seemed fed up with that ilk. The world could use more men like Duncan, the way he cared for Rain. No preaching but a gentle nudge when necessary, stepping back when it was called for.

I retrieved my hat and coat. "I'll be back shortly, Hollis."

• • •

Duncan looked up from his laptop as the Feed and Tack's electronic cowbell sounded.

"Hey." He moved from behind the service counter and kissed me. "Happy birthday."

I checked the aisles for customers, but we were alone. "Are you hungry?"

He placed his hands on my back, moved them lower, and pressed his body to mine. "Yeah, I'm hungry."

"For breakfast, guy," I said. "And that's the second time you've used that joke."

He smiled. "Sergeant Maggie Blackthorne, enforcing the law and policing my sense of humor."

Still holding me, we swayed together a few beats. God, the lilt of my heart. I had to snap out of it.

Taking a small step backward, I inched out of his arms. "I was thinking we could try the waffles at Erna's Café."

"Sounds great, but can I take a rain check? I'm here all by my lonesome this morning."

I took his hands in mine. "I've also come to ask a favor."

He led me to the storage room behind the counter. "We can have some privacy in here."

The large open room contained rows of shelves, which held meticulously labeled and organized stock.

"I need your help with something really important," I said.

"Here, take a seat on that crate of horse blankets." He pointed to a nearby wooden box stored on the floor against the wall.

He sat down beside me. "What's up?"

"It's a strange request. And I'm afraid I can't give you many details."

"Okay?"

"It has to do with Brady Wakefield. He needs a safe place to stay tonight while we take care of a police matter."

"What kind of police matter?"

"I can't say any more than that."

"Will you be safe?"

"As safe as I ever am."

"Well, Sergeant Blackthorne, that fucking answer is not very reassuring." He wasn't joking.

"Dammit, Duncan. This is my job."

"Yes, I know. And I want you to be safe." We heard the electronic cowbell. "I'll be right back."

Maybe it had been a mistake to ask Duncan for this favor. But I knew that wasn't the real problem. It was the risk that came with police work. If he couldn't handle that now, he might never be able to.

"Maggie. I apologize for getting pissed. I have no right." He sat beside me and extended a long, muscular arm around my shoulders. "I'm falling pretty hard for you. And I know, it's too soon. There's plenty we don't know about one another. Blah, blah, blah. But all that doesn't mean it's not real."

I kissed him and tucked a stray strand of his thick, sandy hair behind his ear. "I feel the same way."

He drew me back into his arms. "I need you to be safe, all right? And yes, Brady can stay at my place. I really like the kid. But even if I didn't, he'd be welcome to stay."

"Thank you. I actually thought of you because of how good you are with Rain."

"Speaking of Rain. Brady spending the night at my place could be complicated."

"What are you trying to tell me?"

"This is confidential, okay. Rain and Brady are in a relationship."

"They're intimate?"

He smiled. "That's an old-fashioned way to put it, but yes, they're intimate. Like we're intimate."

"Please tell me Rain is eighteen."

"Rain is eighteen. And when he learns Brady is staying with me, he'll want to spend the night too."

"Kat?"

Duncan shrugged. "Rain hasn't told her, as far as I know. But she's not an idiot."

"Well, as long as it doesn't interfere with his basketball scholarship, she'll probably be fine."

He nudged my shoulder. "Aren't we catty?"

"I'll stop at the high school, let Brady know I've arranged for him to stay at your place tonight." In this instance, I decided I could afford to ignore Al's instruction to bring Hollis or Taylor along every step of the way from now on. Inventing my authority again.

"Have him meet me here at the store after basketball practice."

The electronic cowbell signaled another customer.

"I'll let you get back to work."

He stood, pulled me up from the crate. We kissed and held one other.

"Oh, excuse me." Jen Wilson stood in the entrance to the storage room in her veterinarian smock. "I was hoping you might have some Bar-Guard-99 syringes in stock."

He cleared his throat. "Yep. Follow me, Jen."

I trailed him out of the storage room and caught her eye.

She shrugged and handed me a knowing grin. "Lambing season."

I didn't understand what that meant exactly, but I nodded. "Nice to see you, Jen."

"How's Louie?"

"Much better. I'll bring him by your clinic soon." I moved toward the front door.

"Take it easy, Maggie," she said.

Which, if I'd bothered to think about it, I might have interpreted as some kind of warning.

Zan Wilson's office was unavailable, so Mrs. Randy Buckley led me to the crowded, messy, windowless space used by the school's guidance counselor and went to fetch Brady from his math class. The posters on the office wall were ubiquitous epithets encouraging good habits of mind and body, or they displayed healthy, vigorous teens about to march off to mundane college campuses to begin their academic studies. A military recruiting poster was also taped to a file cabinet, as if the guidance counselor had displayed it under duress.

Brady closed the office door a little too hard. He wasn't happy to see me.

I pointed to the chair on the opposite side of the counselor's desk. "Have a seat."

"Do you know how much crap I got for meeting with you yesterday?"

"From?"

The kid tossed me a nasty look. "Lots of people."

"How about John and Ruben Vickers?"

"I didn't go home last night."

"Where'd you stay?"

He shrugged. "With a friend."

"Your father didn't have anything to say about you not coming home?"

Brady fiddled with the guidance counselor's paperweight. "He was pissed, but mostly at you. He didn't like spending a night in jail. Anyway, I told him I had to cram for a history test."

I turned on the recorder, placed it on the desk. "Why do you suspect the Vickers men killed the Nodines?"

He counted out the reasons. "One, John knows the combination to the safe. Two, they're scuzzy ex-cons who boss me around and make lame jokes about my clothes. And three, they ratted me out to Asa a few times."

"Nothing specifically related to the Nodines, though?"

He shrugged. "No. Other than John being able to nab the gun out of Asa's safe if he wanted to."

"They ever threaten or physically assault you?"

"Like I told you yesterday, John knocked me around. And he pushed me up against a doorframe once, told me he'd beat the shit out of me the next time I opened my smart mouth."

"Did you tell your dad?"

He sneered contemptuously.

"What'd they rat you out about?"

"The Nodines buying me beer, the times I snuck out of the house, that kind of crap."

I took a different tack. "Are all of the hired men authorized to use that old green Bronco?"

Brady paused. "Wayne has his own SUV. Pretty much just John and Ruben drive the Bronco."

"How about your father?"

"A couple of times, maybe, when he has to drive somewhere the Prius can't go."

"How about you?"

"I'm not good with a stick shift, but I might drive it if Asa's out in the Prius."

"Have you ever driven it?"

He took a moment to answer. "Just around the ranch. Why all these questions about the Bronco?"

I ignored his question. "Are you planning to go home tonight?"

He shook his head. "I can't breathe there. And something weird's going on."

"Weird?"

"Asa's coming more unhinged every day. And John's basically running the place now."

"Are you staying with the same friend tonight?"

"His mother said I couldn't."

"Kat McKay?"

He nodded. "I'm not worried. I'll find a place to stay."

"I can probably arrange somewhere for you to go for the night."

Brady tilted his head slightly. "Why would you do that for me?"

"For your safety. I probably should've arranged to place you yesterday."

"Place me? What do you mean by that?"

"You're an adult, so I don't mean foster care. And you can say no."

He chewed his upper lip. "What've you got in mind?"

"How about Rain's uncle?"

The boy's demeanor softened. "Will he do it, do you think?"

"I spoke with him earlier. You're welcome to stay at his place. If you say yes, he'd like you to meet him at the Feed and Tack after basketball practice."

Brady smiled for the first time since entering the counselor's office. "Rain says he's a good guy."

"So that's a yes?"

He nodded. "Are you going back out to Asa's ranch?"

I clicked off the recorder and had him sign and date a second statement. "You're free to go to class now."

"If you do go back out to the ranch, you'll probably need the access code for the gate. There's a keypad attached to the gatepost. Punch in the letter *J* and three, one, six."

"John 3:16?"

"What else."

"That's helpful, Brady."

"As long as the code hasn't been changed." He stood. "Tell Mr. McKay I promise I won't be in the way."

"Just remember to mind your manners and eat whatever he fixes for dinner. I hear he makes a mean pot roast."

Bach was still on the road when I radioed with an update. "I hope this is our last foray to Bear Valley Cattle Company, Al."

"Couldn't agree more. See you in half an hour."

Hollis, at his desk across from mine, had listened to my side of the conversation. "How might all this go down when we get out there?"

I tried to read my partner's thoughts. "Are you worried?"

"Sure, a little."

"Me too. Only a fool wouldn't be."

I noticed Taylor sorting reports at the print station. "Mark, I'll need you to join us when we question Larkin and his men today."

A smile cracked his wide face, like a kid who'd finally been picked for the team.

"In the meantime," I said, "you two should take an early

lunch. My guess is Bach will want to move in on Larkin's place soon after he gets here."

"What about you?" Hollis asked.

"I'll slip next door for a slice of pizza," I answered.

"Come on, Sarge. We can shut down the place for an hour," Hollis countered.

"Nah. We'll be closed for the duration once Bach gets here. Besides, I need to think through some things," I said.

Taylor gathered his coat and hat. "Back in an hour."

Hollis continued working at his desk.

"I mean it, Holly. Take your lunch."

He closed out his document and pulled his keys from the drawer. "Make sure you get something to eat, okay?"

"Yep."

But I wasn't hungry. I sat in the alcove and stared at the Nodine murder board. The room was dim and cloyingly small. I exhaled, added "John and Ruben Vickers" to the list of suspects. Beneath that, I wrote Wayne Smith's name. I considered tacking "Cecil Burney" up there for good measure, but I just didn't buy it, especially knowing Larkin's automatic pistol killed the twins, not the old man's shotgun.

I needed some air and stepped outside to the pizza window across the parking lot. Nearly froze my ass off while a couple of tellers from the bank around the corner got the rundown on topping choices.

I was in a mood by the time I sat back at the card table chowing down my single slice, an all-meaty with spicy peppers, warmed up to about the same temperature as my cup of diet cola on ice. But mostly it was the murder board and not my trip to the pizza window that had set me on edge.

My cell phone buzzed, and Morgan's name flashed on the screen. There was a time not so long ago when his calls made my pulse race. "Sergeant Maggie Blackthorne here."

He laughed. "Happy birthday! I meant to send a card, but you know how it is."

I didn't really know how it was with him, but it didn't matter. He'd remembered to call, and he still had the sweet voice of the always chipper. That cheered me up.

"God, I've been so busy, I almost forgot about my birthday."

"Yeah, I heard about your backcountry crime spree. Are you doing okay?"

"I'll be doing a lot better when we solve the murders."

Al Bach appeared at the entrance to the makeshift alcove.

"Hey, Morgan. I really do appreciate the call, but I've got to go for now. I'll get back to you sometime this weekend."

"Take care of yourself, and do get back in touch soon. I've got a lot to tell you."

Al sat down in one of the folding chairs lined up around the card table and pointed to the list of names on our murder board. "Prime suspects?"

I turned toward him. "In the Nodine case, the Vickers brothers for sure. John knew the combination to Larkin's safe, and Ruben's prints were found on the Nodines' jeep key. We should keep Larkin on that list, too. And possibly Kat McKay, but unless we learn something new, I don't think so."

"I agree with you about the McKay woman. How about Larkin's son?"

"Brady's a little lost and confused, angry with his father. But I've seen nothing yet to make me suspect he's the killer."

"And how about the Trudeau murder?" Bach asked.

"Again Wayne Smith and the Vickers men."

He placed his thermos on the card table and spread out the contents of his sack lunch. "Anyone else?"

I thought about the possibilities. "Maybe the Nodines, if

they'd been alive. Their father, Farley, I suppose, but that's a long shot with zero evidence."

He lifted his sandwich from the table. "So Larkin, Smith, and the Vickers brothers."

"And if I'm wrong?"

"We'll work our way through the next rung of suspects."

Bach's plan was to caravan to Bear Valley Cattle Company. Taylor would ride with him in the Interceptor, and Hollis and I would take my Tahoe.

He laid out the rest of it. "Maggie, you're more familiar with the terrain, so you'll lead. Try to find a place to park about a quarter mile or so from the ranch compound."

I nodded. "Think I know just the spot."

"And assuming all the men will be there, we'll frisk each for weapons and have them wait in the main ranch house. Mark, you'll stay with the men while the rest of us search the three mobile homes. We'll check the main house last and question them one at a time," Al clarified.

"Larkin will want his attorney there for sure," I said. "The rest of them might too."

"If we have to, we'll take them into custody and bring them back here." Bach briefly inspected our sparse digs. "Remind me, does the courthouse have an interview space? Doesn't seem like the State of Oregon has set you up for that."

"Yeah, the courthouse has a spare office for interviews. It's only marginally better than our storeroom," I said.

"The difference is there's a handy jail cell just up the stairs," Holly noted.

I swirled the dregs of my coffee. "There's that."

"I'll call over and give them a heads-up," Taylor offered.

"Could get tricky if we bring in all four at once and want to separate them."

Bach stood and stretched. "We'll work it out. I've interrogated suspects in almost every tiny courthouse in the state, including this one. Sometimes you have to get creative. Before we take off, I'd like to assure everyone we're going out there as part of a murder investigation. This is not a tactical operation with sharpshooters on standby. We're not confronting the posse comitatus, we're visiting a ranch to question the owner and his hired hands."

I wondered about the purpose of this little talking-to. Was it to bring down the tension or ratchet it up?

"I think we all understand that, Detective," I said.

"Good. Let's move out."

Tall clouds, pure white and immense, roamed the pale sky. The climb up Canyon Mountain toward Bear Valley had been quiet, the thrum of tires and the heater's rattle in the background. Mostly I found the churn of road noise strangely soothing, but Al's parting admonition nagged at me.

We all knew we were heading into a situation that could go south in a hurry. Maybe we should have called in the sharpshooters or at least been geared up for that. In the end, though, I had to trust Bach's judgment.

I glanced over at Hollis. "Hey, does Lil know this afternoon could turn out to be a deal?" Cop code for a fucked-up mess.

"No. Does Duncan?"

I hadn't expected that, but all right. Things were out in the open, at least. "He knows something's up. Mostly because he agreed to take in Larkin's kid."

"That so? I had a feeling Duncan was one of the good ones."

I knew I didn't need to make that same pronouncement about Lillian Two Moons. Holly understood that was a given. Plus he was merely handing me his blessing where Duncan was concerned.

Then I remembered his promotion. He'd soon be transferred. A stab of rage swept over me, that old hatred and bitterness revived. J.T. Lake. I'd kill that dickwad yet.

Hollis interrupted my mental tirade. "What's up, Maggie? Are you practicing your tough face?"

"What?"

"You look mad as hell."

"It's this case." I really wasn't very good at lying.

"Sure. I thought you only brought out that face for J.T. Lake."

"As a matter of fact, I *was* thinking about that asshole."

"Can I give you some advice?"

"Can I stop you from giving me some advice?"

"You need to move on from all that baggage between the two of you. It's not healthy."

Pondering his good counsel, something else occurred to me. I needed to get over myself, quit the self-absorbed bullshit attitude where his promotion was concerned. At least try, for Christ's sake.

"True dat, Holly. Being chronically pissed at the man is an exercise in futility."

"*True dat*? You posing as Outkast or something?"

"Just throwing around some urban lingo, my friend."

"Yeah, from the nineties. You're just showing your age, my friend."

I shoved my right hand toward him, palm forward. "Talk to the hand."

"Oh, snap. You got me there, Sarge," he said and chuckled.

· · ·

We passed Starr Campground, just off 395. The Aldrich Mountains spreading west, the Strawberry Range spreading east, we drove across the plateau between. Scrub juniper and pine battled for sparse water on the dry foothills and rangeland until we reached Bear Valley Meadows. Its sweet creek composed a narrow swath of high desert lushness. I tapped the brakes and signaled right. Checked the side mirror to make sure Bach had seen I'd turned down Harden Road toward Larkin's ranch.

I kept the speed low. The road was graded, not paved, and likely prone to dust, even this time of year. About a mile in, I pulled off next to a knot of larch, verdant with new growth and surrounded by juniper and sagebrush, making sure Al had room to park beside my Tahoe.

I figured we were within a quarter mile of the entrance to Larkin's fortified cattle company. Tucked next to the trees, our vehicles would be largely hidden from the ranch house and the compound of mobile homes and outbuildings.

As I cut the engine, my phone rang. It was Ariel Pritchett. "I need to take this."

Hollis nodded and climbed out of the SUV.

"Ariel?"

"Two strangers—big guys—were in the bar last night. I couldn't hear everything they was sayin', but they griped about their boss a bunch."

I glanced at the others waiting in the weather for me to join them. "Okay?"

"Their boss is named Larkin. I wrote it down. Don't know if this guy's who Joey and Danny had the deal with. But it's the same name, I'm sure of it."

"Thanks, Ariel. That really helps us a lot."

"I'm glad, Maggie."

"I have to go now, but you take care." I decided to keep

Ariel's news to myself for the time being. If it was true, what did the Nodines agree to do for Larkin in exchange for the Ram 3500?

Bear Valley Cattle Company stood on a mesa, the two mountain ranges on either side. The high winds of afternoon bore down on the four of us gathered between the two rigs, silencing our phones and double-checking our nerves.

His voice barely audible against the windy bluster, Al asked me to lead the way to the entrance. Beyond the electric fencing, we caught sight of dozens of Black Angus feeding at an elaborate covered cattle crib filled with hay. It was easily fifty feet long and double-sided to accommodate a large number of animals. The usual aroma of sage, pine, juniper, and clean air had been overtaken by the raw stench of cow manure, now blown far and wide across the prairie and yellow-green hills.

Behind the cattle crib stood a sizable new metal barn, probably erected after Larkin bought the place from Chet Harden. Parked next to it was a small fleet of three-wheelers, a hay wagon and bailer, an ancient Allis-Chalmers tractor, and the old green-apple Bronco.

When we arrived at the entrance, I found the keypad, held my breath, and entered the code Brady had passed on to me this morning. The gate waved open slowly. Unlike the visit Al and I had made out here two nights ago, the hired men didn't rouse from their mobile homes. The sound of our movement had found cover in the gusty whip-snap of tree branches, but that didn't make us invisible. We were standing at the wide-open entrance of the compound in broad daylight.

Larkin's black Prius was parked in the gravel driveway, but Wayne Smith's silver Pathfinder was nowhere to be seen.

Bach pointed toward the main ranch house. "Let's start with Mr. Larkin."

In most scenarios, four State Police officers approaching the well-preserved thirties-built farmhouse might have piqued someone's curiosity. But we managed to make it to the front porch and ring the doorbell without causing a stir.

Several minutes passed before Asa Larkin opened the door. "What is it now?"

Bach held up the judge's order. "A warrant to search your property, including any vehicles, outbuildings, and all residences. In the meantime, we need to pat you down for weapons."

"You already have my pistol."

Hollis stepped forward and conducted the body search. He nodded to Al.

"We'll also be questioning you and your men," Bach announced.

"Wayne's in Burns buying supplies." There was a childish testiness to Asa Larkin's voice.

"We don't mind waiting," Al assured him. "Now, would you summon the Vickers men? You'll all wait here with Trooper Taylor while we search the mobile homes."

On a panel next to the front door, Larkin punched two call buttons labeled "J.V." and "R.V."

"Let's move into the next room, sir." Taylor walked toward the dining room to the right of and behind the living room. I nudged Larkin forward and followed after.

The dining room was a good choice. White walls, black marble dining table, and six black Windsor chairs that looked uncomfortable as hell. A space even more sterile and cold than Larkin's ultra-modern living room, except for the framed artwork hanging on the east wall. I hadn't noticed it before: Frederic Remington's *The Fall of the Cowboy*.

There was something to consider in that choice of painting, its dark hues, the image of two free-roaming drovers
resigned to a fenced-in world, the implication of that
metaphor. But I would have afterward to chew over Larkin's
perceptions of the world.

Larkin sat in one of the Windsor chairs without protest.
"I'll need to call my attorney. He's staying at that historic hotel
in Prairie City."

"Of course, sir. Give me his name and I'll make the call."

I had to admit, Taylor really was good at this.

John and Ruben Vickers, wearing their stiff Western hats
and their cheap lookalike outfits, entered the main house.
Something in their faces telegraphed an utter lack of surprise
at finding two cops in the living room and another two in the
adjacent dining room.

"What's going on?" John Vickers finally called out to
Larkin.

"Ask the homicide detective there." He indicated Bach.

The brothers exchanged glances. "What's this about,
Detective?" John, apparently the more talkative one, asked.

"Search warrant." Al held up the document.

Vickers notched up the volume on his baritone. "Based on
what?"

"John," Larkin said, "let's just get this over with."

"The judge granted a warrant to search everything on the
ranch premises. Are your mobile homes unlocked?" Bach
asked.

Both men nodded.

Al pointed to the dining room. "You'll wait in there with
Mr. Larkin."

Hollis and I each frisked one of the Vickers men. Again,
something in their demeanor made me think they weren't

surprised the cops had shown up. Not resigned to it exactly, but always open to the possibility.

Taylor drew two empty Windsor chairs slightly away from the table. "Make yourselves comfortable."

"And for the present, all of you need to turn over your phones to Trooper Taylor," Bach said, nodding toward Mark.

22

Al led Hollis and me outside to Larkin's front porch, where the wind had settled into a light breeze punctuated by intermittent gusts. "Any thoughts about Mr. Larkin or the Vickers men just now?"

"Did anyone else think the brothers seemed kind of blasé about four cops showing up?" I asked.

"I'm not sure that was it, but there was something," Hollis said.

Bach shrugged. "Let's get on with it. I'll take the first mobile home, Hollis you take the second, and Maggie the far one."

We all donned latex gloves, and Al handed out evidence bags.

A tabby cat the spitting image of Louie scrambled outside when I opened the metal door of the third double-wide. Inside it smelled of fried eggs and bacon, a cover for the litter box odor and the extra-full trash can in the kitchen corner. The double sink was piled with dirty dishes, which were also stacked and strewn about the countertop. I opened and inspected the cupboards and the mostly empty drawers.

I noted the bills, recipes, and snapshots pinned to the refrigerator by magnets. One photo showed Wayne Smith standing between two young women, maybe his daughters or nieces.

The small dining table was largely free of debris except for a small stack of *Blue Mountain Eagle* newspapers all turned to the crossword puzzle page. Unless the man had cheated, I could see he was pretty good at word sleuthing. I browsed every issue, looking for any articles that might have been circled or cut out. Finding none, I moved on.

Multiple coats, hats, and boots were stored in the closet between the kitchen and the living room. I checked pockets, looked under hats, and shook the air out of his boots and a couple of empty shoe boxes.

The living room itself was much cleaner, less littered, and nearly bare of furniture, as though he mainly occupied the kitchen/dining room. The section of the built-in entertainment center where a television was supposed to be ensconced sat empty. I'd noticed the main house didn't seem to have a TV either. Maybe Larkin had banned them or refused to shell out for a satellite dish.

Down the hallway was a second door to the outside and a small bedroom, empty and obviously unused. The main bathroom across the hall included a laundry closet with a washer and dryer, but otherwise appeared to be for guests only.

The master bedroom at the back of the double-wide was where Smith slept and dumped his clothes. I inspected the articles of clothing strewn about and examined the few items hanging in the large closet.

I hesitated to explore the master bath given Smith's lack of tidiness in the kitchen/dining area. By comparison, it was barely messy and came equipped with a separate tub and shower, a double sink, and a relatively clean toilet. In the adjoining linen closet, he stored towels, toiletries, cleaning supplies, a locked file box, and a loaded Beretta M9.

With no other rooms left to search, I placed the semiautomatic handgun in my evidence bag and carried it and the file box to the front door. Through the door's small window, I watched Wayne Smith shuffling, head down, toward his mobile home and away from his Pathfinder parked on the gravel driveway. He couldn't have missed our police vehicles where we'd left them a quarter mile down the road.

I set the evidence bag and file box on the floor and unsnapped my Glock holster. Opened the front door and stepped outside. "Mr. Smith," I called.

He peered up from his study of the frozen earth beneath his feet and stood stock-still. The look on his face was one of both surprise and curiosity. "Why are you on my porch?"

Smith didn't appear to have noticed Hollis and Al approaching from his left.

"I'm Detective Bach, Oregon State Police homicide unit." He pointed to where I stood on the small deck outside Smith's front door. "This is Sergeant Blackthorne and Trooper Jones beside me."

Smith jerked and faced Bach. "What's this about?"

"We have a warrant to search the premises of Mr. Larkin's ranch, including your mobile home and vehicle." Again, he held up the warrant. "We're going to check you for weapons and then sequester you with the other men in the main house."

"You said homicide? What are you looking for?"

"Mr. Smith, place your hands above your head." Hollis patted him down. "Come with me."

While Hollis delivered Smith to the dining room of the main house, I joined Al in the yard.

"Anything?" I asked.

He shook his head. "Nothing of interest in either of the other double-wides."

Hollis stepped from the front porch of the ranch house and rejoined us. "Detective Bach probably told you we came up empty. How about you?"

"A loaded Beretta and a locked file box. I left them inside Smith's place for the time being."

"The Beretta's interesting, anyway," Hollis said.

"I figured the file box might be locked for a reason." I scanned the three double-wides. "Did you check the exteriors?"

They indicated they had.

"I was about to do that when I saw Smith walking across the yard."

While Bach and Hollis went through Smith's Pathfinder, I searched his back porch and his front deck. But we all found nada.

I pointed toward the new metal barn and the green-apple Bronco, a good hundred feet away. "I'm going through their rig again."

Bach didn't ask about the *again* part, and we all marched to the Bronco. Even with a legal, more professional once-over, it came up clean.

With our rigs parked a quarter of a mile away, we agreed it was safer to leave the evidence bag containing Smith's weapon and file box inside his double-wide. All three of us were anxious about the time, eager to get the interviews underway, but Al wanted to search the ranch house first.

The four men detained in the dining room appeared restless, or in the case of Wayne Smith, flummoxed. I pulled Taylor aside and asked how things were faring.

"Mr. Larkin's attorney hasn't responded to my phone calls yet, and he apparently checked out of his hotel room."

"Is that making Larkin nervous?"

"Oh, yeah. Also, everybody wants to use the facilities."

"You go first, then I'll watch the others while you escort them one at a time. Search the bathroom while you're in there, then search it after everybody's done their business," I said.

Al and Hollis had paired off to comb through the second floor. Once Larkin and his men were all back around the dining table and Taylor had given the all clear on the main-floor bathroom, I began my search of the dining room.

I'd never been in such a home, every space meticulously clean, the walls painted white, all of it in line with Larkin's cold, sterile, and expensive preferences for furniture and art. The Remington in the dining room might have been the exception, not for its muted grays but because it was anything but contemporary in the extreme.

"Be careful with that," Larkin said as I inspected *The Fall of the Cowboy*.

"Is it an original?" I asked.

He hesitated, as though he'd never thought to wonder about its authenticity. "I believe so."

After inspecting the massive black china hutch in the dining room, I moved to the adjoining kitchen. I examined drawers, cupboards, appliances, and the separate pantry. From the pantry, I slipped out the back door to the old-timey wrap-around porch. There were no fancy Roche Bobois deck pieces, or austere sculptures, or anything futuristic. Just one of those tan plastic containers near the hose bib made to resemble a wooden box, including the molded, wood grain effect. I lifted the lid. Lying atop the requisite green garden hose were two more Beretta 9s.

Hauling the guns in an evidence bag, I followed the porch

around to the front door, where I reentered the ranch house, turned a swift right to cross through the living room, and began hurriedly climbing the stairs to the second floor.

I heard the shattering of glass at the top of the staircase before the shot registered. The shooter had missed me but killed the black Euro light sconce on the wall above me.

Hollis and Al drew their weapons, giving me cover as I crawled the rest of the way to the landing.

Where was Taylor? What had happened to Taylor? Fuck, what had I missed bolting to the second floor?

"They have Mark's Glock somehow," Hollis whispered.

I pulled myself up from the floor of the wide landing. The weapon hadn't been fired before the sconce was blown away, so Taylor hadn't been shot, at least.

"Trooper Taylor!" I shouted down to the first floor.

"His gun is being pointed barrel-first at his skull." By now I recognized the cultivated lilt of that voice. Larkin.

I caught the thud of a wallop to the gut that followed, Larkin crying out in pain, and an expensive Windsor chair splintering against the hardwood floor of the dining room.

"For the time being, Officer Tootles is coming with us," one of the Vickers men called from the living room directly beneath the second-floor landing.

I looked at Al, shook my head, and pulled my gun from its holster. "That's not how this is going to play out, Vickers."

"Then we've got a big problem."

Bach, Hollis, and I stood at the edge of the landing braced against the banister, our weapons held in plain view. We could see that John Vickers indeed had the Glock pressed against the back of Taylor's head. Ruben Vickers stood behind them.

I leaned cautiously over the railing. "I'd say it's you two with the problem."

The brothers conferred quietly.

John Vickers stepped further out into the living room to give the three of us on the landing a better view of captor and captive. Taylor, with his hands laced at the back of his neck, walked ahead of Vickers.

"They jumped me after hearing you go out the back door to the porch, Sergeant."

Vickers jabbed Taylor in the back with the gun barrel. "Cut the fucking chitchat."

Ruben Vickers stepped cautiously toward the front door.

"My brother is going to pull up in Wayne's Pathfinder. Meanwhile, Officer Tootles and I are going to follow him slowly and wait by the door."

"Put the gun down and release Trooper Taylor," Bach directed.

"That's not happening." Vickers pressed the pistol to Taylor's ear.

"Are you doing okay, Mark?" Bach asked.

"I've been better, sir."

"Me too, son." Al leaned across the banister, his Luger held at arm's length, both hands wrapped around the butt, his head angled slightly, sighting his target. He fired the pistol, its sonic timbre radiating outward.

Below us, Ruben Vickers howled, clutched the wound on his left thigh, and fell in a heap next to the front door.

Reflexively, Al took aim at John Vickers. Hollis and I followed suit. But in an instant, shot after shot rang out as the man fired Taylor's Glock semiautomatic toward us on the second-story landing.

Bach managed to get one round off before the three of us dropped to the floor. The ranch house fell quiet except for the faint sound of falling debris. Bullets from the semiautomatic had shattered several of the landing's safety rails, leaving daggers of clear-grain fir.

Al and I sat up slowly and brushed the wood dust from our hair and uniforms. We moved to the rickety, bullet-riddled banister. John Vickers lay dead in a sprawl on the living room floor.

"Mark," Bach called down, "if you're able to retrieve the weapon, glove up and bag it."

"Yes, sir. After I come up with a compress for Mr. Vickers's leg."

"Hey, Maggie," Hollis whispered hoarsely. "I think I've been shot."

It took a moment to grasp that he was lying on the littered floor to my right. "Goddamn it all to hell!" I removed the outer carrier I wore over my duty shirt and turned it into a temporary compress. After applying it carefully to the wound in his side, I spread my peacoat over his torso.

I shouted for Taylor. "Hollis has been shot. If you have service, call the Seneca ambulance."

"Already did that!" he shouted back. "They're about ten minutes out."

"I'm going to go get the emergency kits from our vehicles." Bach tossed me his keys, and juiced by adrenalin, I vaulted down the stairs and grabbed the Pathfinder keys where they lay on the floor beside Ruben Vickers.

"Larkin and Smith?" I asked Taylor.

He indicated the kitchen. "They were shoved inside the broom closet, then the door was blocked shut."

"Secure them to a couple of dining room chairs." I handed Mark my handcuffs, raced out the front door, drove the quarter mile to our police vehicles faster than I could have run, pulled the emergency kit out of Bach's interceptor, and floored my Tahoe back to the ranch house.

I handed Taylor one of the emergency kits. "Send the EMTs to Hollis when they get here."

Dashing upstairs with the other kit, I moved two stairs at a time. Al had elevated Hollis's head and was helping him sip water. I fetched a gauze compress from the emergency kit and replaced the makeshift one I'd slapped together using my outer carrier, now soaked through with an appalling amount of blood.

Bach stood. "I messed up. We could have taken it slower, even let them leave. I doubt they would've gotten very far."

"I don't know, Al. They were threatening to kill Mark. I think they easily might have."

He turned pale. "I made a mistake. One that comes with a price."

I couldn't tell if he was being philosophical, thinking about his church teachings, or what. "We'll have an opportunity to debrief everything later."

"I'm going downstairs to check Mr. Vickers's leg wound."

Hollis turned to me. "Sorry to get blood all over your stripes, Sarge."

I held the compress firmly to the wound. "Shh."

"Lil. Tell her I love her and Hank very much."

"You can tell her yourself."

"Please."

I nodded.

"And don't call her until I'm on my way to the hospital. Or to Sam's mortuary."

He was perspiring and shivering at the same time. I snagged a blanket from an upstairs bedroom and a damp washcloth from the attached bath. I placed the blanket over him and used the washcloth to dab his forehead.

"Holly. The ambulance will be here any minute, but there's something I need to tell you."

"Something I need to tell you too." His voice was weak, harsh in the throat.

"You go first."

"I'm not taking the promotion, but thanks for the recommendation."

"What? No, that's not—"

Mark Taylor placed a hand on my shoulder. "They're here."

I hadn't heard the siren or Taylor and the EMTs climbing the stairs. The technicians moved in quickly, dressing Holly's wound, carrying him to the ambulance, setting him up with IVs, and ferrying him to the hospital.

One of the EMTs stayed behind to patch up Ruben Vickers's upper thigh. The bullet had done little more than graze him, which meant there was no need for hospitalization. The EMT initially green-lighted Vickers for transport to jail, but once he turned hysterical at the sight of his brother's body lying on the floor under a hastily arranged coverlet, the EMT consulted by phone with a physician in John Day.

Over my objections, the medical director at Blue Mountain Hospital demanded Vickers be brought in for observation and dispatched another ambulance to take him to the hospital. Al seemed disinclined to intervene, so I lobbied to interview Vickers before the second ambulance arrived. The medical director vetoed that too but agreed to at least have a security guard installed in Ruben Vickers's room.

I found it all frustrating. "In his state, he might have told us all we needed to know to solve these homicides."

Bach eyed me. "That's not how this works, Maggie. You know that."

Hollis had smiled as the EMTs closed the door to the ambulance. He was still alive, and I told myself he would stay that way.

I dreaded delivering the news to Lil. Before making that call, I phoned Dorie and asked her to be on standby to help Lil with the baby. Then I dialed Lillian Two Moons.

When she heard Holly had been shot, she shrieked and burst into tears.

"The ambulance is on the way to the hospital, Lil." But that was not the kind of calming information she was looking for.

Finally, she asked if he was unconscious.

"He was alert and he asked me to tell you that he loves you and Hank very much."

"That means he's frightened, Maggie."

I struggled for a response. I could have told her that he'd even made a little joke about getting blood on my sergeant stripes, but the less said about blood, the better. Besides, I knew she was right. Hollis was plenty frightened.

"I know this is hard."

"I'm not sure I could go on without him."

"He's very strong, Lil." Though I wasn't sure I could go on without him either.

Sam Damon arrived with his hearse to retrieve the body of John Vickers. "What's happening in our county, Sergeant Blackthorne? All these violent deaths."

I was in a shitty mood by then. "Too much brutality in the world?"

"Can't say as I disagree with that," he said.

Once Sam left, Bach, Taylor, and I met in Larkin's achingly stark and impersonal living room. One of the bright white walls was now tarnished by blood residue and a bullet hole. Al was oddly silent, relying on me to suggest our next move. I thought about what he had said when we were upstairs attending to Hollis, that he'd made a huge mistake and there'd be a price to pay. I had no idea what had prompted his pessimism.

Remembering the scene from less than an hour ago—John Vickers holding the Glock to Taylor's temple—I turned my attention to Mark. "How are you holding up?"

"All right, I guess. I'm worried about Hollis. He didn't look good. And it's my doing."

"This was not your fault, Mark. One of us probably should have been guarding those men with you."

Taylor leaned across the space between us and gave me a tiny, awkward hug.

I cleared my throat. "Detective Bach and I are going to question Larkin in his office. I'd like you to stay with Wayne Smith in the dining room if you're up to it."

He glanced at his watch. "Let me give Ellie a quick call, let her know I'll be late getting home."

While he stepped outside to phone his wife, I checked my phone for messages, but there was no word yet from Lil or the EMTs about Hollis.

Al had wandered into the kitchen and returned with a pitcher of water and a stack of glasses. He placed the pitcher and glasses on Larkin's *Jetsons*-like coffee table along with his duty belt, Taser, and service revolver.

"Maggie, these were officer-involved shootings. Which means I'm to be placed on administrative leave. And you need to put in a call to regional dispatch and report the shootings. They'll send a detective out to interview everyone and begin an investigation of both."

Bach appeared curiously relieved to be citing OSP protocols. "I can't participate in the interviews either."

"Al, I need your help with this."

"No, you don't. You're a natural. You occasionally talk too much, but you'll figure all that out with more experience."

"I don't particularly want more experience with homicide investigations."

He began filling the glasses with water. "We'll talk about that later."

I sipped some water. "What did you mean when you said you'd made a huge mistake?"

"I didn't warn Ruben Vickers before firing my weapon."

I shrugged. "Heat of the moment."

"No. That's why we're trained and why we have directives in place. Many of which I developed, by the way. This is not the Wild West, and we're a professional law enforcement organization. We live and die by our rules."

I thought he was being a tad dramatic, but I kept my commentary in check. "It was really just a flesh wound."

His glare burned through me. "That's not how we have to look at it. That stunt contributed to Hollis being shot. And John Vickers might have killed Mark."

"That last was a distinct possibility from the moment he nabbed Taylor's gun."

"Just call regional dispatch and report the shootings, all right?"

After I spoke to regional, the three of us gathered back around the living room coffee table.

"A couple of detectives are being dispatched from Ontario," I said.

Bach nodded. "Makes sense."

I picked up my glass of water. "First thing tomorrow."

Taylor turned to Al. "What's going on?"

"I'm technically on administrative leave."

"Oh, right. Officer-involved shootings."

"And Maggie's officially in charge of our murder investigations."

Which meant I didn't need Bach's permission to interview Ruben Vickers tonight in his hospital room. Something I planned to do right after I checked in on Hollis, no matter what the damn medical director or anyone else had in mind.

"Instead of Larkin, I'm starting the interviews with Smith. What's left to search upstairs, Al?"

"Hollis and I hit up the bedrooms and bathrooms, but there's a small storage room still to go."

"I know you're technically on administrative leave, but I can't have you standing watch without even your Taser while I take turns interviewing Smith and Larkin. It makes more sense for Mark to do that. Would there be some breach of protocol if you finished our search of the house?"

Bach wrestled with that for about half a minute. "Since this is Larkin's residence and we've already gone through the double-wides the Vickers men occupied, I think I can find a rationale for that and document it to everyone's satisfaction."

God, I thought, this dude must be a pain in the ass to live with.

23

We hastily searched Asa Larkin's small office and then proceeded to the dining room. The scene there was surreal. A bruised and anxious Larkin waited quietly at the table alongside Wayne Smith, who gave the impression of a contrite and possibly hungry guy caught up in someone else's shit. Neither of them were innocents, though—of that I was sure.

Taylor removed Larkin's handcuffs and sat across from him, stun gun at the ready. I checked for word on Holly, and finding none, I slipped my cuffs from Smith and clipped them back on my duty belt. Then Al and I escorted him to Asa's office.

I set up and clicked on the Tascam voice recorder, then stated my name and rank, along with his name and today's date. "Out of curiosity, why didn't you hightail it out of here when you saw our police vehicles parked down the road?

"Well, ma'am, y'all have been out here to visit with Mr. Larkin several times, so I didn't really think much about it." Smith spoke with a true Southern accent, not the countrified affect spoken by a lot of eastern Oregonians. "Besides, I wouldn't just drive off and leave my things in the double-wide."

"Like your gun and this?" I pointed to his file box now sitting atop a bookshelf.

"Asa bought the Beretta, so I wouldn't call it mine. There's nothing but personal papers in the file box. I can show you, if it's okay to get the key out of my pocket."

I nodded, then rose, retrieved the file box, and placed it on the desk. In the meantime, Detective Bach stepped out to search the storage room upstairs.

Smith handed me the small key, and I inserted it into the lock. Inside I found more photos of the two young women in the picture he kept on his refrigerator. Along with some old letters, bills, his birth certificate and passport, and several personal documents having nothing remotely to do with our murder cases.

"About Mr. Larkin. How is it he hired you?"

"I met him at our church in Lake Oswego, right before I got excommunicated."

"For?"

"They accused me of stealing from the children's charity. I tried to tell them it wasn't me, but they threatened to call the police if I didn't leave the church premises immediately." In the stuffy, overheated room, Smith had begun to sweat profusely. "But I suspicioned who the thief really was. Turned out I was right."

"The thief was your current employer, correct?"

"Soon to be my former employer."

"Why do you say that?"

"Well, ma'am, he spent last night in jail, and you're back out here today. Seems like something serious is going on. Serious enough to put him at odds with John and Ruben this past week."

"Over what?"

"I couldn't figure that out."

Smith's alert that his boss was a thief wasn't exactly news, but I was curious about Larkin's row with the Vickers men. Just this morning, Brady had also mentioned some friction between them.

I moved on. "What do you know about Dan and Joseph Nodine?"

"They were supposed to steal market-ready steers and hand them off to John and Ruben. The Nodines said they could do it on a regular basis, but then they didn't come through even once. That pissed them off."

"Pissed off the Vickers men, is that what you mean?"

"Yes, ma'am."

"How do you know all of this? Were you part of this arrangement with the Nodines?"

"Only after I overheard John and Ruben talking about it. We were supposed to split the money three ways. After paying off the twins."

"Why didn't the Nodines come through?"

"Don't know. I was plenty relieved, though. I dreaded getting messed up in cattle theft."

"Why did you, then?"

"You gotta believe me. The Vickers brothers are dangerous men, or were, in John's case. When I told them I knew what they were up to, they threatened me."

"So you're telling me you were coerced into joining the Vickers' gang?"

"Well, yeah."

This idiot could justify anything, and he was starting to irritate me. "Why on earth should I believe a single word you say?"

"John and Ruben were as angry as I'd ever seen them, John

especially. They were going after the Nodines, planned to mess them up pretty good."

"Why didn't you call the police?"

He shrugged. "Afraid I'd get fingered along with the Vickers boys, I guess. But at least I let Dan and Joe know."

"Go on."

"I'd figured out where they parked their camper. So, the morning of the day they were killed, I drove to the campground to warn them. Met up with them just as they were about to leave in their jeep, told 'em John and Ruben were mad as hell and out for blood."

In the phone call that sent me out to the wigwam burner, Joseph had said they'd been warned.

"Out for blood and armed. How's that not a recipe for murder? Or at least worth a call to the authorities?"

"I thought if the Nodines got word ahead of time, they'd hightail it, and everything would blow over."

"And no one would learn you were in on their cattle-rustling scheme, right?"

"Yeah. That too."

"Did you know where they stowed your boss's Ram 3500?"

The man was momentarily speechless. "Is that what happened to that hog? I thought Asa took it back to the dealership or something."

"So you had no idea the Nodines were in possession of it?"

"No, ma'am. But I guess that's how they were going to steal cattle, right? So they must've stole Asa's livestock trailer, too."

"Mr. Smith, did the Vickers brothers kill the Nodines?"

"I sure think so, but in all honesty, I don't know. But I do know for a fact they killed that Mr. Trudeau."

"How do you know that?"

"Because I was there. I saw it happen. That's how I knew they might kill me too."

"Start from the beginning."

"John and Ruben figured out that Asa had somehow got ahold of a painting by some famous artist, one of those old-fashioned Western painters. Anyway, they thought the painting was worth a lot of money and knew it was stored upstairs." He pointed awkwardly toward the ceiling.

He continued. "When Asa didn't go through with buying Mr. Trudeau's steers, they come up with the bright idea of trading the painting for the beef cattle. They called the old guy and set up a meeting somewhere south of Seneca, gave him the painting, and he told them where they could find his steers."

Driving out here last Saturday, I'd passed Guy Trudeau whipsawing his Gran Torino all over the highway heading north toward the turnoff to Big T. That was the day before Holly and I found his body.

"How were they going to haul all those animals?" I asked.

He shrugged and smiled. "Don't know, but before they had a chance to work all of that out, John figured out the painting could be worth millions. So then he was itching to get it back."

"Again, how did you know all of this?"

"I didn't know anything about trading the painting for cattle until I drove them to Mr. Trudeau's house last Sunday. That's when they told me."

No doubt Smith was expecting a cut of the proceeds, but that was a road I could travel down later.

"Tell me about Mr. Trudeau's murder."

"We took my Pathfinder into John Day for groceries. They noticed Trudeau's clunker at that hamburger joint by the high school. John had me park there and wait. Then we followed him out to his place."

"And then what?"

Smith swallowed. "I sat in the car for a while. Finally I

decided to take a walk. But I heard the old coot screaming, went to the kitchen window, and saw they had him strung up."

He breathed deeply. "Honestly, I don't think they went out there to kill him. But they did and without coming away with any painting."

I stood and moved to the other side of the desk. "Wayne Smith. You're under arrest for withholding evidence in three homicide cases. Accessory to murder, with possible murder and theft charges pending. Stand up."

"I'm really sorry, ma'am," he said as I pulled his arms behind him and handcuffed his wrists.

I reached across and turned off the recorder. "You've got that right. You're about as sorry an individual as I ever met."

Al was waiting for me in Larkin's living room.

I checked the time. "Five thirty. Still no word on Hollis."

"Waiting's always the hardest part. For now, though, I think you'll want to see what I found upstairs."

I followed him to the storage room. Against one wall stood a row of tall file cabinets. Bach opened one of the drawers and drew out a thick legal file. "Mostly old documents from Larkin's law practice in Lake Oswego. But open the bottom drawer of that far cabinet."

I crouched down, pulled the drawer open, and lifted out a heavy cardboard box. A mailing label affixed to the box read "Mr. Frank Sylvester, Little Juniper Road, Wagontire, OR 97758."

"What's inside?"

"A Frederic Remington sculpture. I googled it on my laptop, and it's worth about five grand."

"Have you got an extra pair of gloves?"

He reached in a pocket of his outer carrier and pulled out

two latex gloves. I put them on, opened the box, and brought out the sculpture affixed in bubble wrap. I spotted Remington's signature and the notation indicating it was number two of one hundred bronze castings.

"If you lift up the bubble wrap gently, it comes right off," Al said.

I removed the wrap and placed the sculpture on top of the file cabinet: a cowpoke on the ground wrestling for control of a bucking horse. It was nearly two feet tall, and as I turned it slowly around, each new angle presented a new way to see the piece.

"Do you know the title of the sculpture, Al?"

"*The Wicked Pony*."

"It's time for a conversation with Larkin. Are you sure you don't want to sit in?"

He shook his head.

"Would you like to know what I learned from Wayne Smith?"

He said nothing, so I spelled it out.

"His story's especially compelling because Trudeau's cause of death hasn't been announced to the public. Smith knew he'd been strangled." I carefully wrapped the sculpture back in its bubble cocoon and placed it in its box.

Al couldn't hold in a question any longer. "Any thoughts about whether or not Smith participated in the killing?"

"He comes off as devious, scheming. But prone to murder? I'm not sure."

Bach nodded. "I'll collect Asa Larkin for you."

"That's another thing, Larkin was pretty nervous when I returned Smith to the dining room already in handcuffs."

"Good."

"There's one other thing I want to let you know about Asa

Larkin before you fetch him from the dining room. You don't have to say anything, just hear me out."

"All right," Bach said and lifted the box holding the Remington sculpture.

"Ariel Pritchett tells me the Nodines acquired the Ram 3500 through some kind of transaction with Larkin. Payment for doing something in return. I don't know what, but I plan to press him on it."

Al couldn't mask his desire to join the questioning of Larkin. "Do you have a theory about what they were supposed to do in return for the truck?"

"I'll just say this, Asa Larkin has a keen interest in getting ahold of Frank Sylvester's wealth."

"He does indeed. Shall we head downstairs now? We wouldn't want to cause Mr. Larkin any more anxiety."

I nodded toward the package he held. "I'll take that. I plan on beginning with his Remington fascination."

"While you question Mr. Larkin, I'm going to finish what's left of our first-floor search."

Larkin was shepherded to the office, where I waited, the boxed sculpture on the desk in front of me. Spying it, his face reddened.

I switched on the recorder and stated the purpose of the interview.

He plopped himself in the chair across from me. "I want my attorney."

"Sure. Have him meet us at the county jail."

"He hasn't answered any of my calls since yesterday, nor has he answered the ones your officer made."

"And I understand he checked out of his hotel."

"That's right."

"We've got lots of time. What's the number? I'll try calling again."

"I've already left several voicemails."

"So would you like us to contact a local attorney?"

"No. But I might refuse to answer your questions."

"So noted. First let's talk about Frederic Remington. Mr. Sylvester is a collector. So are you, it seems. A collector of Sylvester's Remington artwork. For example, this sculpture and the painting in your dining room."

I expected to get no reply to that. Instead he nodded.

I indicated the recorder. "A verbal response, please."

"Yes, the sculpture and the painting in the dining room belong to Frank Sylvester, at least until his demise. As I told you before, in his state, what use are his earthly possessions?"

Larkin's justifications were always rich. And imbued with some tinge of the biblical.

"Remington's *The Blanket Signal* is upstairs where you found the sculpture. You couldn't have missed it," he added.

"It now resides in the Oregon State Police evidence room in John Day. It was found in Guy Trudeau's storage locker after he was killed."

"What?" He was stunned. "How's that possible? It was wrapped and leaning against the far wall of the storeroom the last I knew."

"When was that?"

Larkin quietly considered the question. "Well, not more than a week ago."

"Think about it. Guy Trudeau and you had a heated discussion about the cattle he hoped to sell you on Thursday last. Eight days ago. He was killed three days later."

His self-confidence had begun to wane. "I don't understand what you're saying."

"Between that Thursday and the following Sunday when

he was murdered, at least two of your men traded the painting to Trudeau for his cattle."

He took that in. "Had to be John and Ruben. Those steers were worthless, really. Puny and sick."

"Seems a couple of your ranch hands didn't recognize the difference between good or poor beef stock."

He sat silently for a moment. "But John would've figured out the Remington was potentially valuable."

"Possibly up to four or five million, right?"

He closed his eyes. "Yes."

"Vickers did figure that out, but too late. It had already been turned over to Mr. Trudeau."

"Did they kill that old man over the painting?"

Smith nearly convinced me they had, but Trudeau's murder was not the direction I wanted to take the interview at the moment. "What I'm wondering is this. Did they have something to do with the deaths of Dan and Joseph Nodine?"

"Why would you think that?"

After what had happened earlier this afternoon, it seemed an obvious question. "Apparently the Nodines reneged on a deal they had with the Vickers men."

"What kind of deal?"

"Stolen steers for cash."

He almost smiled. "Six months working my ranch, and they'd begun to fancy themselves as cattlemen, I guess. Explains those ridiculous cowboy hats."

"I know how you met Wayne Smith, but how did you meet John and Ruben Vickers?"

Larkin hesitated, but only briefly. "They were working an embezzlement scheme on one of my clients. I intervened, offered them something better. Life out in the country and no prison time."

"Ah, I get it. It's always wiser to employ thieves if you're a thief yourself."

He sipped from the glass of water he'd brought with him from the dining room.

"Back to the Vickers men and the Nodines. I'll be interviewing the surviving brother later tonight. What might his answer be?"

"He'll deny it, of course."

"Here's another question I've been wondering about. Did you kill Dan and Joseph Nodine over that one-ton pickup?"

Larkin slowly raked a hand through his dyed hair. "As I've said before, possessing it was pure vanity. God judged me a hypocrite and rendered His reckoning."

I couldn't handle much more of his Sunday school dogma. "You were willing to let them get away with stealing your expensive diesel truck, the one you had coveted?"

"To save my soul, the Lord exacted a fitting punishment. And I had come to terms with that."

"Really? You followed them to Logan Valley and watched them shoot a mule deer. Then you called the poacher tip line and reported them."

He was mildly surprised I'd put it all together. "Wasting that animal for sport was disgusting and evil."

I bit my tongue, judgment being up to God and all that. "It was against state law, Mr. Larkin, but they killed the doe to eat."

"Being against state law should have been enough for you, Sergeant."

"Oh, I planned to arrest them for it, but someone murdered them before I had the chance."

Larkin's bloodless lips trembled. "Could I please have some more water?"

I stood, opened the door, and called for Bach. He emerged from a closet in the hallway.

"Mr. Larkin needs more water." I handed Larkin's empty glass to Al and took my chair. "I have another theory to pass by you."

"What's the theory?"

"What if the Nodines didn't steal your beautiful Ram truck?"

Al knocked, placed a full pitcher on the desk, and closed the office door behind him.

Larkin filled his glass with water, swallowed some, and sighed heavily. "I don't understand."

"What if it was payment for agreeing to provide a service, let's say?"

"I'm still confused."

"Oh, I get that. Fifty grand is a heck of a down payment, especially since you really wanted to keep the truck, I suppose. Plus there'd been all that rigmarole getting ahold of Frank Sylvester's money to buy it in the first place. I mean by rights, that diesel one-ton should be yours."

"Except it's not."

"Yes, I know. It belongs to Mr. Sylvester. Problem is, he's not dying fast enough for your purposes. So you hired the Nodine twins to kill him in exchange for that ostentatious piece of equipment."

"And your evidence?"

"Joseph Nodine had a fiancée. She came forward and told us everything." An exaggeration, but she'd revealed enough to inspire me to coax Larkin to disclose the details of the deal between the twins and him.

"Did she tell you they would have gotten another fifty grand when the deed was done? It wouldn't really have been that hard to arrange, but they kept putting it off."

I wondered why he kept digging himself a deeper hole. Guilt, maybe? "Go on."

"Then I learned they talked Brady into getting his pal to pilfer cattle prods and other supplies from his uncle's store. My son traded it all to the Nodines for marijuana."

Brady Wakefield, the boy who didn't lie. Since I had never asked him about the theft from Duncan's store, he hadn't expressly fibbed to me. But plainly, he was dishonest and disingenuous. What else was he hiding, and what did all of this say about Rain?

"Was that the last straw?"

"Last straw?"

"The Nodines. Had they crossed some line even God wouldn't forgive?"

"I don't speak for God."

Like hell.

"Did you kill the Nodine brothers, Mr. Larkin?"

"It was John and Ruben Vickers who were angry enough to kill those men."

"Start from the beginning."

"They were anxious to have it out with the Nodines, probably over that cattle deal you talked about. They had gone looking for them earlier that day, to no avail."

He gulped down more water. "I had once followed the Nodines and found out where they kept the red Ram truck. So we took my Bronco to the abandoned mill."

"Were the Vickers men armed?"

"Yes."

"And you knew they had served time for multiple felonies, that it was illegal for them to carry weapons?"

"I follow God's law, not the government's. Besides, I bought the Beretta 9s for all three of my men."

I could've countered that the law refers to possession, not

ownership, but I needed to stay out of my own way. "So you follow God's law? Such as 'thou shall not steal'?"

Larkin had no answer, perhaps in part because he clearly didn't consider the absconding of Frank Sylvester's money and artwork to be theft.

I tried another one of God's laws. "How about 'thou shalt not kill'?"

"I only accompanied John and Ruben to make sure things didn't get out of hand when they met with the Nodines."

"So it was an accident that you ended up shooting them to death?"

The man wasn't biting, so I kept pushing. "The Nodines weren't killed with a Beretta. Your Kel-Tec 9 was the murder weapon. But you already knew that."

"That proves nothing."

"You forget. Ruben Vickers is still alive. My guess is he'll be eager to name the shooter."

"My word against his."

Then it came to me how I might compel this fraudster's confession. "Did you know Brady was inside the wigwam burner when the Nodines were shot? He was there hiding on the floorboard in the backseat of the Ram 3500."

The color left his face.

I leaned closer to Larkin. "He heard them scream, heard them beg for their lives. Heard the shots. Two for each man."

His breathing intensified. "You're lying."

"No, Mr. Larkin, I am not."

He shut his eyes tightly. "What have I done?"

"You tell me."

His eyes remained clenched.

"Did you shoot and kill Daniel and Joseph Nodine?"

His eyes snapped open. "It's unfortunate your detective

only wounded Ruben Vickers. He and John were blackmailing me, you see."

"For the murders they witnessed you commit?"

"A momentary lapse. But I've made my peace with it." He extended his arms dramatically, waited for me to ratchet up and clamp down the cuffs. "I wiped the Nodine brothers from the face of the Earth."

Stepping out to the hall, I called for Bach. He was busy in the living room rummaging through cabinets, but I needed his set of handcuffs. Mine were still locked around Wayne Smith's wrists.

Back inside the office, I found Larkin holding a tiny Derringer .22 against the thin flesh of his temple. Yesterday, Brady had inadvertently passed along the combination to his father's safe, and we'd opened it during our search. No baby gun was stashed inside.

"You fools missed the small compartment in the under-belly of my desk."

Underbelly. The word brought to mind a snake. I drew my Glock. "Put the weapon down."

"No, Sergeant. I don't think I'll do that."

Al moved in beside me. "Mr. Larkin. Think carefully, now. Consider your son."

"Detective. Welcome back. Did you know what I put my son through just to rid the world of that bit of scourge?"

Bach searched my face for an explanation.

I nodded, hoping to convey news of Asa Larkin's confession.

Al edged slightly forward and extended an open palm. "*For the Lord is a God of justice: blessed are all they that wait for him.* Hand over the pistol."

"So you can bring me to man's justice?"

Bach nodded. "Yes."

Larkin smirked. "*Vengeance is mine; I will repay, saith the Lord.*"

I nudged closer to the desk. "I don't have any cherry-picked Bible verses, Larkin, but 'that bit of scourge' you murdered had loved ones who deserve to see justice done."

"You're not very good at this, are you. Sergeant? You're supposed to say something uplifting and call out the mental health unit."

"How about this for uplifting? You're under arrest for the murder of Daniel and Joseph Nodine." In speaking those words, I lifted a heavy load of sorrow from my heart.

He jabbed the gun barrel deeper into his temple. "I'd rather be dead than go to prison."

"At least you have that choice. The Nodine brothers didn't. Do you want to know how they died? The bullets ricocheted through their bodies, but that's not what killed them. They bled to death."

The man smiled. "You don't really care if I shoot myself, do you?"

I shrugged. "Go ahead. Spread your brains all over your office and leave the mess for someone else to deal with. That won't traumatize Brady much."

"Leave my son out of this."

"Why? You're using him as an excuse for offing yourself."

"What do you know about it, Sergeant?"

"My mother killed herself when I was fifteen. It's not a thing you ever get over."

He shut his eyes tightly and stood with them closed. "My own father gave me away and never looked back."

I inched my hand slowly toward Larkin's revolver. "That's not a thing you ever get over either."

I slapped his weapon and sent it skidding across the desk and onto the floor. Larkin opened his eyes, screamed, and dove for the Derringer, but Al and I managed to restrain him and force him to stand.

"Detective Bach, I need to borrow your set of handcuffs," I said.

"Anytime, Sergeant Blackthorne."

We delivered Wayne Smith and Asa Larkin to the Grant County jail. After making sure the night deputies had set up a suicide watch for Larkin, we drove straight to Blue Mountain Hospital, where Hollis was still in surgery. We found Lil and baby Hank in the waiting room seated next to Dorie.

I hadn't remembered the multistory bank of windows from the times I'd hung out here waiting for Tate to get patched up after his many inebriated falls. Outside, the sky had faded to dark, allowing the crescent moon to shine emblematically: A sign of hope?

I sat in the seat on the other side of Lil and put my arm around her. "How are you holding up?"

She smelled of clean sweat and lavender soap. "I'll let you know after I talk to the surgeon."

"I think it's a good sign they didn't fly him to Bend."

"At first I thought they might. I would've had to drive. Three hours in the car with a crying baby, trying not to freak out the whole time wondering whether or not Hollis was still alive."

"What did the doctors say?"

"The same thing you told me. He's very strong."

Dorie stood. "Let's take up the offering, and I'll go get us some pizza."

We pooled our cash, and Dorie traipsed off to the Cave Inn, satisfied in having a task that involved delivering sustenance.

Beside me, Lil nursed the baby and held my hand. "Thanks for Dorie. She's kept me sane."

"She's a real sweetheart."

The surgeon, Dr. Zahn, appeared. "Mrs. Jones? Can we step into the hall?"

"I'd like the sergeant to come along. She's our best friend."

I shook the doctor's hand. "Maggie Blackthorne."

"Of course, then." She led us to the hallway outside Holly's room.

The doctor's tone was all business, her manner direct, and she was exquisitely beautiful. "Your husband was very lucky, Ms. Jones."

"Thank God." Lil breathed deeply as tears formed. I placed my arm around her. "Please, call me Lillian, Dr. Zahn. And my last name is Two Moons."

"Sorry to assume. The bullet missed the large intestine and the bladder and grazed a hipbone, slipping out through the right buttock. I did the initial repairs, but we'll want to watch for complications. Plus he may need follow-up reconstructive surgery."

"When can I see him?"

"He's back in his room, but a bit groggy. Only one visitor at a time for now. And it's best, for tonight at least, that he be isolated from the baby." Dr. Zahn shook hands with Lil. "I'll talk to you tomorrow, Lillian."

I held out my arms for Hank, who was sound asleep. "Go check on your husband."

Lil kissed both her baby and me on the cheek and hurried off.

Back inside the waiting area, I shared Dr. Zahn's good news and rocked Hank in the visitors' rocker while Team Hollis ate cheesy cheese pizza and drank flat cherry cola. The gathering had been almost festive, but we were all ready to put this day behind us.

After our supper, Al sought me out for a side conversation. "You did a great job out there today."

"I feel better about how things turned out knowing Hollis is on the mend."

"Amen to that. So explain to me how you managed to get a confession from Larkin."

"It helped that his attorney left him hanging. And despite Ruben Vickers not being the best witness around, Larkin probably recognized Vickers's testimony would be a problem."

"Seems Mr. Vickers has his own worries."

"Which I plan on exploring tonight, Al. Just to let you know."

He nodded in agreement.

I continued. "Then there's his Kel-Tec 9. Hard to get around it being the murder weapon. But learning Brady had been at the scene is the piece of news that finally led Larkin to confess."

"Turns out he was less beholden to his literal reading of scriptures than he let on."

"What's that mean, Al?"

"His anger over the theft of his truck turned to homicidal rage."

"Nah, I don't think that's why he did it. The deal the Nodines had with Larkin? The Ram 3500 in exchange for the expedited death of Frank Sylvester. Larkin got tired of waiting for Sylvester's assisted demise and had 'a momentary lapse,' as he put it."

"Wow. How do those religious views of his square with murder?"

"He'll have a long stretch in prison to figure that out."

"Let's hope so." He glanced down at Hank. "Now that's a gorgeous baby."

"I'll say." I held little Hank closer. "We didn't finish our search today, the other vehicles and the outbuildings."

"The warrant gives us the leeway to do that as time and manpower dictate."

About the last thing I wanted to ever do again was head back out to Bear Valley Cattle Company.

"Mark and I are going to the office to get the paperwork started," he said. "But I wanted to mention something to you before I take off."

"What's that?"

"I'd like you to consider going through detective academy and joining the homicide unit."

"You're not serious? And by the way, I should remind you that my personnel file's been flagged. No promotions, no transfers."

"I'm very serious, Maggie. I'll take care of the flagged file. Anyway, you don't need to make up your mind tonight, but tell me you'll think about it."

I should have been flattered, I guess. But all Bach's encouragement did was make my life more complicated than I wanted it to be right now. "All right. I'll think about it."

He nodded. "I'll see you in the morning."

"Don't lose too much sleep over the officer-involved shooting interviews, Al."

"I shot the first man, who I knew was unarmed, and I didn't give him any warning. Except for my own inner misgivings, I have no qualms about the tactical soundness of the second shooting."

Detective Alan Bach, a cop who saw but two hues on the spectrum of police decision-making: black and white.

I rewrapped Hank's swaddling and cradled him in my lap. "Thank you so much for taking care of Lil and the baby tonight," I said to Dorie, now sitting across from me.

"I'm glad to get to know Lil better. She's a good woman and an awesome mom. Told me her own mother doesn't want to have anything to do with her or little Hank."

"I'm afraid so."

"Not even an auntie somewhere?"

"I'm not sure." I hadn't asked Hollis about Lil's people. Hell, I knew next to nothing about his people. What kind of a best friend doesn't pry, even just a bit?

"Well, I'm here if they need a hand. It wouldn't be the first time I was some child's stand-in auntie."

God, I loved Dorie. Her sweet voice, her even sweeter nature.

"You look good rocking a baby, Maggie."

"Well, I think I'm past all that at this point."

She yawned. "Could be, but who knows?"

I was pretty sure I knew. "You should go home. And would you mind feeding Louie?"

"Happy to," she said, grabbing her purse and coat and kissing me on the forehead. "Get some sleep. You were out late last night."

. . .

Hollis was awake, waiting for my visit. He looked awful, like a man who'd been shot in the gut and undergone hours of surgery. His oxygen tube made it difficult to talk, so he'd been given a pad of sticky notes and a pen.

"And then what happened?" he scrawled.

I smiled. "Bach imposed administrative leave on himself and put me in charge of the investigation."

"Congratulations?"

I rolled my eyes. "Long story, but I ended up interviewing Smith and Larkin by myself. Smith claims John and Ruben Vickers murdered Trudeau over the Remington painting. Says he saw the whole thing."

"Holy shit!"

I nodded. "And Asa Larkin confessed to murdering the Nodines."

Hollis held up his "Holy shit!" note again.

"And without asking for an attorney."

"???"

"Yeah. The lawyer skipped town."

"But, a confession?" he wrote.

"That needed some prodding, so I painted the picture of Brady, scared shitless and hiding out in the Ram 3500 during the murders."

Dr. Zahn entered the hospital room dressed in a black silk pants suit and cream silk blouse. She wore a diamond bracelet and matching earrings. How had she ended up being assigned to our Podunk hospital?

"Visiting hours are over, Sergeant. Mr. Jones needs his rest."

I winked at Holly. "See you tomorrow, dude."

. . .

I found Ruben Vickers sitting on the edge of his bed in a cotton gown tied at the back of his neck. He faced the window opposite the door, leaving his hairy backside exposed to whoever entered the room. So much for being grief-stricken and hysterical; he was involved in a game of two-player pinochle with the so-called security guard.

"Excuse me," I said.

The guard reluctantly shifted his gaze from his hand of cards to me. "Can I help you?"

"I'm here to interview Mr. Vickers."

"The doctor give the okay?" the guard asked.

"I don't answer to the doctor. Besides, Mr. Vickers looks to be in good enough shape to play cards. I'd say he's fit enough to answer my questions. Now if you'll excuse us."

The guard stood, tucked his hand of pinochle in his shirt pocket, and walked from the room. I didn't bother telling him the card game was over.

In an effort to appear pained and pathetic, Vickers lay back on his stack of pillows and pulled the blankets over his legs and torso. I adjusted his motorized bed to the fully upright position, which forced him to grasp the blankets tightly and tuck them under his chin.

I pulled up a chair, switched on the recorder, ran through my for-the-record spiel, and made myself comfortable. "Sorry for your loss."

He lay silent and mopey for half a minute. "John had a temper. It was a problem. But he was my brother, and I loved him."

I let that sit. He hadn't asked for an attorney, and it was highly doubtful he had one on retainer.

I cleared my throat. "Tell me about last Sunday, the day Wayne Smith drove you and your brother to Mr. Trudeau's home."

The man's ruddy face peeking over the white hospital bedding turned several shades paler, giving him the pained appearance he'd been aiming for when he crawled back under his covers. As far as looking pathetic, I had the sense Ruben Vickers always held that countenance.

He let the sheet and blanket fall onto his lap, exposing his hands and arms. "I think I need a lawyer."

"I can turn off the recorder right now and call one."

He sighed. "All we wanted was for the old guy to give us back the painting."

I needed to word my next question very carefully. "We?"

"Me and John and Wayne Smith. But he croaked before telling us where to find it. We hoped the cops would think suicide. That part was Wayne's idea."

Smith hadn't mentioned that, but I was sure there was a great deal he hadn't mentioned.

Without further prompting, Vickers swallowed, coughed, and proceeded to describe Guy Trudeau's killing.

That old man had become an angry recluse at the end of his life. Little wonder given that he was estranged from two of his children and robbed blind by the other. Even so, he was a bastard through and through. But no one deserved the lonely, humiliating, protracted death by strangulation that Ruben Vickers laid out in horrifying detail.

I had the urge to handcuff the cretin and haul his ass to the most uncomfortable jail cell the county had to offer. But there were other homicides to discuss.

"What can you tell me about the night you confronted Dan and Joseph Nodine? The night they were murdered."

That caught Vickers off guard. He stared at his large hands. "I'm afraid John's temper got the better of him again. He knocked them both around some. We wanted to get those steers they'd promised. They kept saying the cattle were too sick, that we wouldn't get a nickel for them."

"Because they'd stolen several of Trudeau's unhealthy steers. Realized too late how bad off the animals were."

He paused. "Wish they'd told us that before John got all bent out of shape."

"And they used Mr. Larkin's diesel truck and livestock trailer to transport the cattle."

Ruben Vickers was finally connecting some dots. "Yeah, I never could understand why Larkin let that go. Them stealing that expensive vehicle."

"Did he let it go?"

"Did he say something?"

"Any deal you and your brother cooked up with Larkin is no longer in play."

"All right, but it was Larkin who killed the Nodines, not me and John. And preaching nut bag that he is, he enjoyed it."

"And afterwards, you drove Dan and Joseph's jeep and parked it next to their camper?"

"Yeah. John picked me up in the Bronco after he hauled Larkin back to the ranch and nabbed the extra key to the red pickup."

"Why move the jeep?"

"John was afraid it would attract attention before we could come back for the truck. He'd already figured out who might buy it from us. Didn't matter, though. You got there first."

I unclipped my handcuffs from my duty belt, clasped one cuff around the bedrail and the other around his right wrist. "Ruben Vickers, you're under arrest for the murder of Guy Trudeau and for being an accessory to murder in the deaths of Dan and Joseph Nodine."

He huffed a long breath and stared at the hospital ceiling. "I probably should've had you get that lawyer for me."

I pulled up my phone and called the county jail. "Evening. This is Maggie Blackthorne again. I'd appreciate you sending one of your night deputies over to the hospital. Room 218. I've just arrested a patient for murder, and we need a sworn officer guarding him instead of the rent-a-cop sitting out in the hall."

On my way out of the hospital, I spotted Duncan in the waiting room. The lone occupant, he'd tucked himself into the rocking chair and fallen asleep. Seeing him, I was reminded of last night. Tired as I was, a charge raced through me.

I tiptoed into the room and stood next to the rocker. A thick strand of hair had fallen across his forehead and over one eye. He woke as my fingertips touched his brow.

"Didn't mean to wake you," I whispered and kissed his cheek.

He sat up and massaged his temples. "Maggie. Are you okay?"

I moved a chair closer to his and sat facing him. "I'm exhausted in every way possible."

Duncan regarded me soberly. "I heard about Hollis."

"Dorie?"

He nodded. "I was pretty worried."

"Holly came through emergency surgery in pretty good shape." I leaned into the space between us. "But I could sure use a kiss."

He bent forward and kissed me lightly on the lips. "You're the one I was worried about."

I laid a hand on his knee. "You shouldn't be so somber. We caught the bad guys."

"Not before Hollis was shot." He closed his intensely green eyes. "It could've been you, Maggie."

So true, but now was not the time to go into detail.

"But it *wasn't* me. I'm here. I'm alive."

Duncan sighed deeply. "There's something else. Rain admitted stealing the cattle prods and the rest of it. Apparently Brady passed it all on to the Nodines."

I placed a finger on his lips. "Yes, I know. But I don't want to think about any of that right now. Just hold me close for a while."

He pulled me onto his lap. "We'll have to talk about it sometime. We'll have to talk about everything, including that nasty scar of yours, okay?"

I rested my head on his broad shoulder. "We will. I promise." But I was dubious about that last matter, largely because it involved a protracted discussion of my short and sordid marriage to Jeremy T. Lake.

Duncan stroked my hair. "I'm sorry you had such a shitty day."

"I'm sorry you were worried about me."

"I guess I might have to get used to that."

"Can you get used to that?"

"I hope so."

I raised my head from his shoulder, and we kissed.

"I want a woman to love and to love me back, and I believe with all my heart that could be you," he said. "And I still want kids."

"I might be too old to bear children."

"But you wouldn't count kids out entirely?"

I pressed my hand over his beating heart. "Can I get back to you on that?"

He smiled. "Sure, beautiful."

The lights in the waiting room had been dimmed some time earlier, and as we rocked slowly in the rocker, I felt myself drifting to sleep. Duncan might have been carried there himself, for he suddenly sat up straighter in the chair.

"You should call it a night, go home to Louie, and rest."

"We both should call it a night. Brady's still at your house, right?"

He yawned. "I was damn pissed when Rain and Brady came clean about stealing from my store. So mad, I sent Rain home. But I wasn't about to kick Brady out with nowhere to go. Last time I saw him, he was studying for some test."

I grasped one of his immense hands and kissed the palm. "You've had a pretty shitty day too."

We both stood to leave, and he wrapped an arm around my shoulders.

"When can I see you tomorrow?" he asked.

My phone buzzed before I could answer. I eyed the screen. "I have to take this."

I listened to Al Bach's tense voice, then said, "I'll meet you at the courthouse after I talk to the boy."

I clicked off.

"Something else happened, didn't it?"

"Tonight we arrested Brady's father for the murder of Dan and Joseph. Half an hour ago he hung himself inside his jail cell. He's dead."

"God. Brady."

"I'll follow you to your house and explain it all to him."

I said this as if all I had to do was pull out some tool from my duty belt, one that steeled me for delivering news of a father's suicide. Calmly, professionally, without sentiment. Exactly the way I'd been trained.

Fact was, my fortitude had been knocked off plumb over the last ten days, and I suspected this last senseless death had depleted all my reserves. Could I summon the strength to put aside the old ghosts and the losses and heartaches? Could I speak the terrible truth to Asa Larkin's nineteen-year-old son? Could I do all of that and meet Bach at the courthouse, process the incident, and oversee the transport of another body to Sam Damon's mortuary?

I could.

I could because Sergeant Maggie Blackthorne—tough gal, smartass, tenacious, and profane—was a damn good cop and a strong fucking woman.

I could because I had to.

MURDERERS CREEK
A Maggie Blackthorne Novel

Sergeant Maggie Blackthorne's latest case gets personal as she risks everything to prove her innocence and bring a killer to justice.

After an unexpected and unpleasant visit from her ex-husband, Oregon State Police Sergeant Maggie Blackthorne is called to a grisly crime scene. Her ex has been found dead—the victim of a vicious attack.

Her earlier confrontation with the deceased places Maggie squarely on the list of suspects, and she is soon the subject of an internal investigation. Desperate to clear her name and uncover the truth, Maggie and her partner, Trooper Hollis Jones, have no time to waste.

With a couple of townspeople acting suspiciously, reports of missing or stolen property, and evidence of drug deals gone bad, the case is proving to be a difficult one to crack. And just when Maggie and Hollis think they've finally caught a break, the lone eyewitness turns up dead.

As the personal and professional pressure mounts, Maggie struggles to catch a remorseless killer who has nothing to lose. And one wrong move could cost Maggie her career... or her life.

**Get your copy today at
www.SevernRiverPublishing.com/LaVonne**

JOIN THE READER LIST

YOU MIGHT ALSO ENJOY...

Maggie Blackthorne Novels

Dead Point

Murderers Creek

Never miss a new release! Sign up to receive exclusive updates from author LaVonne Griffin-Valade.

SevernRiverPublishing.com/LaVonne

ACKNOWLEDGMENTS

Pat Dannen, my high school English teacher, often praised my writing. More than a decade after we lost contact, she reached out to encourage me to keep writing. Thank you, Pat. I'll always remember that.

Others who have been particularly wise and instructive are the writers Emily Chenoweth, Martha Gies, Debbie Guyol, Karen Karbo, Nam Le, Angela M. Sanders, and Leni Zumas. The folks in both of my current writing groups have been tolerant, insightful, encouraging, and occasionally a pain, but I'm indebted to all of you: Debbie Guyol, Charlotte Rains Dixon, Jenni Gainsborough, Angela M. Sanders, Ann Littlewood, Doug Levin, and Dave Lewis. I'd also like to thank the writers Dan Bern, Alan Rose, Deb Stone, Colleen Strohm, and Laura Wood for their thoughtful comments and encouragement.

Many, many thanks to friends and colleagues who agreed to beta read a draft of the full novel: Mary-Beth Baptista, Charlotte Rains Dixon, Jenni Gainsborough, Debbie Guyol, Sarah Landis, Angela M. Sanders, and Mark Wiggington. Your comments and encouragement were exactly what I needed.

Special thanks to Angela M. Sanders, whose wisdom and practical advice has been amazing, and always a plus—she's got good taste and a damn good sense of humor, too. Also special thanks to Rachel Crocker for whipping me into shape.

I want to thank my agent, Gail Fortune, along with the team at Severn River Publishing—Andrew Watts, Amber Hudock, Cate Streissguth, Mo Metlen, and my fabulous editor, Kate Schomaker.

Finally, Tom Griffin-Valade is my rock, but our children and their partners—Shawn and Erin; Amy and Tony; Alexis and Ahmed; Kai and Hannah—have been abundantly supportive, along with my grandchildren, Lauren, Logan, Piper, and Zio.

ABOUT THE AUTHOR

LaVonne Griffin-Valade was born and raised in the high desert country along the John Day River of eastern Oregon—a place that stoked her imagination and inspired her to become a lifetime writer of short stories, essays, poetry, and novels. She has worn many professional hats: elementary school teacher, mentor, education equity advocate, and Auditor of the City of Portland. Griffin-Valade has published essays and pieces of fiction in multiple publications including the *Oregon Humanities Magazine* and the *Clackamas Literary Review*. After receiving her MFA from Portland State University in 2017 she moved to fiction writing. LaVonne lives in Portland, Oregon and works as a full time writer. *Dead Point*, the first book in the Maggie Blackthorne series, is her debut novel.